THE HEART STONE

THE HEART STONE

Judith Barrow

HONNO MODERN FICTION

For David

First published in Great Britain in 2021 by Honno Press 'Ailsa Craig', Heol y
Cawl, Dinas Powys, Vale of Glamorgan,
Wales, CF64 4AH

1 2 3 4 5 6 7 8 9 10 Copyright: Judith Barrow © 2021

A catalogue record for this book is available from the British Library. Published
with the financial support of the Books Council of Wales.

ISBN 978-1-912905-27-0 (paperback) ISBN 978-1-912905-28-7 (ebook)

Cover artwork by Gordon Crabb
Cover design by Isabel Ashford

Text design: Elaine Sharples
Printed in Great Britain by CPI Group UK

PROLOGUE

The grinding judder of the train wakes Jessie and when she leans forward to glance out of the carriage window, the only thing she sees is her own reflection. They've stopped at a station. Dencross Bridge, still two stops to go before home. But there's something wrong; the crowd of men in the corridor are walking back and forth, talking loudly. Others run outside, past her compartment, laughing and cheering. Stanley, her friend's husband, is already on his feet, opening the door.

'What is it? What's happened?' Jessie looks across at Clara.

'I don't know.'

They stand to peer out at the platform. A man is there, his back to the ticket office, wearing an advertising A-board. She can't read it; she can't grasp why he is there so late at night. 'What's happening?' she calls to Arthur, who turns to look at her. She doesn't understand his expression: disbelief mingled with enthusiasm.

He moves to one side and she sees a boy in a flat cap, holding a large canvas bag to his chest. He pulls a newspaper from the bag and slams it to the train window. Jessie reads the words.

'BRITAIN AT WAR.'

She says the words aloud, clinging to the luggage rack above her. She's paralysed. The women around her are silent, frozen, just like her.

A cheer starts somewhere in the train. Grows louder and louder until all the men on the platform are cheering as well, including Arthur. His mouth wide, he turns to look at her again; on his face, in the strange, yellow glow of gaslights, there's elation.

Jessie's legs give way. She sinks down on the bench and looks around. The feeling in her chest is expressed on the faces of all the women around her. Fear.

This isn't the way the day was supposed to end.

PART ONE

Chapter 1

August 1914

'Why?' Arthur Dawson kicked at a stone; it skittered along the road. 'Why can't you go? This'll be my first proper day off since Wakes Week in June. First proper works' outing. You said you'd come. Stanley and Clara are going. You said you'd talked to Clara about it.'

Her friend had been in the shop earlier, trying to persuade her. At nineteen, Clara was three years older than Jessie but, despite their different backgrounds, they'd been friends from the first day they'd met. Jessie didn't know how to explain it to Arthur. She wanted to go with them yet still needed to say, 'I can't leave Mam on her own because—'

'Stanley said it was all sorted between you and Clara?' Arthur frowned. 'I've saved up in the works' club,' he said, lifting another stone with the toe of his boot and kicking it up into the air. 'We're going on the train. I've been looking forward to it.'

'I know – and I'm sorry.' Jessie was. Before her father died six months ago, she'd looked forward to going on her first Kindle Mill summer trip with Arthur. Living on the same street, he had, over the years, become the brother she never had. Being the youngest children on Castle Street, they'd been inseparable. 'How was work today?' She wanted to change the subject.

'Okay. I like the spinning shed. Better than being a bobbin carrier in the weaving shed. I hated that.'

'I know.'

'And better money,' he added. 'My treat...' He opened his eyes wide in mock pleading. 'Aw, come on, Jessie,' he said. 'It's the seaside. We're sixteen and we've neither of us been to the seaside. Unless you've been without me knowing?'

'I haven't, you know I haven't.'

'It'll be an adventure then. The men told me what the sea is like—'

'Wet, I should imagine.' Jessie knew she was being sarcastic, but in her disappointment she couldn't help it.

Arthur ignored her. 'And the beach. The men said there's a pier. And a fairground. You enjoyed the Switchback ride when the fairground came to town.'

'I know.' Though the Venetian Gondola roundabout had been her favourite; she'd insisted they went on it twice.

'Say yes, then.'

'I can't.'

'Why? Give me a reason.' He crossed his arms.

'It's Mam. Dad's only been dead three months, you know that. I don't think I should leave her on her own.'

'She's not, she's got Bob. If you asked him, he'd take your place in the shop for the day.'

Clara had said the same, Jessie remembered. Had she told Arthur that?

'He'd do anything for you—'

'What do you mean by that? Anything for me?'

'You know what I mean. He likes you.' Arthur scowled.

'Don't talk daft.' Jessie returned his frown. 'Why can't you go with the Hampson twins? Tommy and Teddy would probably be glad; it'd stop them fighting one another.'

'Because I don't want to go with them. I want you to come with me. With me and Stanley and Clara. I promised Stanley you'd keep her company. You know how the other women are with her; them thinking she's posh.'

Jessie sighed; they were going round and round in circles.

'I would love to go, Arthur. I'm very fond of Clara, we've been friends since her and Stanley came to Nether Brook and you and him got on so well. But I can't go – I can't go ... because of Amos Morgan,' she admitted after a long pause.

'What do you mean? What's he got to do with anything?'

'Since Dad died he's never away; he's always at the shop, pretending he wants something or other. But I've seen him watching Mam all the time. It's not decent, the way he looks at her, Arthur.'

'How do you mean?'

Jessie hunched her shoulders. 'I don't know. I just know it's not right. And he's seen me watching him doing it and he glares at me. I think he's going to start calling on her. What if he finds out I'm away for the day and he calls on her when she's alone?'

'Your mam wouldn't have anything to do with him, you must know that. And she won't be on her own, Bob will be there, so what could happen?'

'I don't know...'

'It will be a great day out, you, me, Stanley and Clara. Stop worrying about something that won't happen, Jessie, and say yes. Please...' He pulled down his mouth in a pitiful expression.

Jessie laughed. 'Oh, all right.' She held up her arms. 'I give in. I'll ask.'

'Great.'

'And, if I can come, I'll go on the pier and the beach and the fairground with you. But if there's one of those swing things, that Steam Yachts affair, I'm going nowhere near it.' She shuddered. 'All that rocking about in it when that fair came to Manchester – made me feel sick.'

Arthur gave a shout of laughter. He picked her up and twirled her around.

'Get off, you daft thing. Put me down.' She stood, unsteady on her feet, a strange fluttering in her stomach at the feel of his hands on her waist. 'And I still have to ask Mam and Bob. So don't take it for granted.'

Chapter 2

Jessie hung on to the back of Arthur's jacket when they walked onto the station platform. Even at six o'clock in the morning the place was packed with families. The laughter and raised voices throbbed with the excitement she'd felt since her mother had given her permission for the Blackpool trip. But now all the noise echoing and rebounding from the roof over the platform raised a sense of panic in her.

'Arthur, can we go in the waiting room?' Looking down on the metal rail track from the platform made her light-headed. 'It's very crowded. I can't see Clara and Stanley anywhere'

Arthur moved to put himself between her and the edge.

'Good, though?' he grinned, looking around. 'They'll be here somewhere.'

'Hey up, Arthur. Got your girl with you then?' Tommy and Teddy Hampson ran past, laughing, pushing and shoving at one another.

Jessie felt the heat of mortification. She hoped Arthur wasn't embarrassed; she'd hate things to be awkward between them. She saw the wives of the other men glancing at them. What if they thought the same thing? It was daft; they'd been friends forever. Still – she looked at him – he would be a good catch for some girl one day.

'Arthur, look, there's Clara and Stanley.' She gave him a slight push.

Stanley clapped Arthur on the back. 'Change to see you out of your overalls, mate.' He performed a mock bow. 'Nearly didn't recognise you.'

'Bit of a toff yourself,' Arthur said.

They rocked back on their heels, grinning, self-conscious.

Jessie thought Arthur looked smarter than Stanley in his dark suit and tweed cloth cap.

'Jessie.' Clara held out her hands.

'Clara.' Jessie brushed a kiss on her friend's face, breathing in the faint scent of lavender.

'I wasn't sure what to wear. Stanley thinks my hat will be blown away. He says it will be quite breezy in Blackpool.' She touched the shallow brim decorated with a cream ribbon. 'So I've fastened it with the longest hatpin I have.'

She still had hold of Jessie's hands and leaned back to study her.

'Burgundy does suit you. I'm afraid I'm not tall enough to wear a long jacket. And,' she leant forward and whispered in Jessie's ear, 'that skirt would make my hips look enormous.'

'Nonsense!' Jessie couldn't help feeling pleased as she looked down at her pleated A-line skirt. Seeing Clara had made her feel that her own outfit was, perhaps, not as grand as she'd thought. 'And I love your hat.'

They moved aside as a porter bustled past them, a frown of importance on his face.

'Let's get out of the way or we'll all finish up on the tracks.' Stanley pointed to a wooden bench where a row of women sat, their husbands standing nearby.

There was the distant hollow sound of a whistle. The hubbub of anticipation rose all around her and Jessie felt the vibration of the approaching train under her feet. Clara moved closer; Jessie could feel her friend's quickened breathing against her cheek.

'Exciting!' Clara squeezed Jessie's arm.

Chapter 3

The train squealed its way into Blackpool Central Station.

'We're here,' said Stanley, moving two small boys away from the window. Their mother licked her handkerchief and rubbed at the specks of soot which covered their faces.

'Soon as we get out of the station, look for the Tower, it's only a stone's throw from here.' Stanley herded Clara and Jessie into the corridor where Arthur was standing shoulder to shoulder with other men waiting for the train to stop.

It was a stifling crush getting off the platforms and away from the station. Once outside, the salty breeze cooled Jessie's face. The brim on Clara's hat flipped back, the ribbons flapping.

'Perhaps not such a good idea to wear my best hat after all,' she murmured with a smile. 'Not that I'll admit it to Stanley.'

Jessie was glad that she had decided to wear only her second best straw boater.

'Where first? The Tower? They say it's the same shape as the Eiffel Tower in Paris, in France.' Stanley shielded his eyes from the sun with his hand, looking towards the large construction looming into the sky. 'They've got a zoo in there, someone told me, with lions and bears, apparently. And an aquarium with all sorts of fishes from all over the world.'

Jessie watched the Hampson twins pushing their way past the people in front of them. Tommy knocked one man's bowler hat off. She could hear them laughing as they ran towards the Tower.

'Just look at those two,' she said, seeing Clara's look of distaste and hastening to distance herself and Arthur from the twins.

'About time they grew up.' Arthur grimaced.

'It'll take a lot for them two to grow up; they're a right pest in work with their messing about.' Stanley put his arm around his wife. 'So? The Tower, the fairground, or what, Clara?'

'The pier first, please,' Clara said, reading some of the posters on a noticeboard. 'Look, there's a music hall with minstrels and pierrots.' She pointed to one poster. 'And an Oompah band.'

'There's a children's Punch and Judy show at ten o'clock on the beach, it says here.' Arthur peered at a notice stuck on a lamp post. 'One for you, Jessie.' He grinned.

She tossed her head but spoiled the effect by laughing.

'Actually, I love Punch and Judy,' Clara confided, linking arms again with Jessie. 'I often went to Brighten with my mother and

father when I was a child. Saw Punch and Judy shows there. So...'
She put on a stern face and looked at Stanley and Arthur. 'We'll all
go to watch it.'

'Come on then.' Arthur linked Jessie's arm, guiding her through
the rest of the mill group.

At first she couldn't take her eyes off the sea. It was nothing like
she'd imagined; there seemed to be so many shades of dark blue and
grey following strange swirls and lines before it rose and fell in
splashing waves far out on the pale sand. And it was a long, long
way before it met the sky in the distance.

'Tide's out,' Stanley stated, watching her. 'The sea'll be closer this
afternoon. We can go down on the beach later, if you fancy a
paddle?'

Jessie wasn't sure. Would the water suck her in, she wondered,
but said nothing in case the others laughed at her. She grasped
Arthur's arm tighter.

'Let's see everything else first.' She felt him pull her hand to his
side. She liked the feeling it gave her and smiled at him.

They sauntered along the promenade, weaving through the
crowds, the horse and carriages, the occasional noisy, slow-moving,
shiny black cars. There were so many stalls. Jessie breathed in the
sugary smell of the pink candyfloss, striped rock and toffee apples,
but hurried past the tables with the small pots of smelly, grey
cockles. She stopped with Clara to pick up and admire the engraved
spoons and badges, miniature brooches of the Towers: souvenirs of
Blackpool.

'There's so much to see.' She felt slightly overwhelmed by the
noise: people talking, laughing, shouting, a man playing an
accordion. Jessie took in a deep breath and closed her eyes.

'Are you all right?' Clara sounded anxious.

'Yes, fine.' Jessie smiled, opening her eyes and looking around.
'Just so much to see,' she said again. 'Oh, look.' She pointed to a red
and white hut on large thin wheels far out on the beach. A plump
woman stood on steps at the side of it. 'What's she got on?'

'A bathing costume,' Clara said. 'I've seen them in a magazine.'

'Goodness me.' Jessie squinted to get a better look at the navy tunic and pantaloons that the woman wore. 'Extraordinary!'

But she was soon distracted. 'Oh, look, is that the Punch and Judy show?' She stood to get a better look. Children were sitting in a semi-circle in front of the booth. They could hear them laughing, the high-pitched tones of the Punch and Judy man.

'It is.' Clara clapped her hands.

'Come on then.' Arthur grabbed Jessie's fingers and the four of them ran down the steps from the promenade onto the beach.

'Let's go on the pier now. It's only thruppence to get on and I've been told there's loads to do.'

Jessie hadn't enjoyed the Punch and Judy show after all. The inflections in the puppeteer's high-pitched voice for Punch sounded grotesquely like Amos Morgan's; at least that was what she'd imagined. And the violent way it had battered the Judy puppet with the baton had made her cringe. She felt it was wrong that everyone was laughing, though she hoped the others hadn't noticed how upset she was; she didn't want them to make fun of her.

'You okay?' Arthur murmured.

'Fine.'

'Bit odd, that Punch and Judy show.'

'Yes.' It was all he said, but she was glad he seemed to think the same way as she did.

'Pier next?' Stanley suggested, his arm around Clara.

They hadn't walked twenty steps on the pier before Jessie noticed the sea swirling underneath them. Her stomach lurched. It looked dark and menacing; nothing like it had from the promenade. As though it could suck her in. The salty smell floated up on the spray. It made her slightly nauseous.

'I can feel the pier swaying. It's a bit high up.' She clung to Arthur, surprised that she liked the unexpected tautness of his muscles under her hand; liked the feeling of his protection.

'*Oh, I do like to be beside the seaside,*' he sang, obvious in his efforts to distract her. He grinned at two girls who passed them.

Jessie tugged at his arm, an unfamiliar sensation of jealousy disturbing her. 'I'm sorry, Arthur, I don't like this.' She pointed at the wooden boarded pier floor.

'But the show's about to start. I can hear the National Anthem.'

'I'm sorry, I don't feel safe. You stay if you like but I need to leave.'

'I'll come with you.' Clara linked her arm. 'I'm not that bothered about a show anyway.'

Jessie saw Stanley glance at Arthur, one eyebrow raised.

'The Tower then? Or the fairground?'

'The Tower,' Clara said. 'Please.'

Jessie would have preferred the fairground, but she felt she'd already spoiled things a little by refusing to go any further on the pier. 'Yes, the Tower,' she said, 'Let's go there.'

Stanley clapped his hands together. 'And afterwards fish and chips in a cone?'

'Should we?' Clara looked doubtful. 'Outside? Not sitting down at a table with a knife and fork. Isn't it a little common?'

'Aye, but who's to see?' he answered, giving her a squeeze.

Jessie was looking forward to everything. But perhaps she wouldn't tell her mother if they did have fish and chips in the street.

Chapter 4

Squashed between two large women, swaying with the rhythm of the train, Jessie couldn't get the image of the panther in the Tower menagerie out of her mind. She'd been surprised to find it made her angry. Its eyes looked sad as it paced backwards and forwards in front of them. She'd asked Arthur if he thought it was unhappy, but he'd said that the people in charge must know what they were doing. Jessie wasn't so sure; that animal was trapped where it wasn't supposed to be. It must be awful to be trapped in a life you hated.

I wouldn't be able to bear it, she thought, glancing across to the opposite bench where Clara was already asleep, resting against her husband, her face shadowed in the low gaslight above her head. Jessie often wondered how Clara felt, living in that tiny terraced cottage she and Stanley rented on Station Road. When she'd talked about her life before she met him, it was evidently a far cry from her married life; the large house she'd grown up in, surrounded by fields. And yet they were so clearly in love. Even as Jessie watched, she saw Stanley reach for Clara's hand, hold it gently between his.

The compartment was quiet. It seemed everyone was as tired as she was. Arthur had given up his seat to a mother with a sleeping baby and was leaning against the wall of the corridor. She was relieved the sliding door was closed; she could see the fug of cigarette smoke above the heads of the men alongside him.

And she was also relieved he wasn't sitting next to her anymore. If she wasn't careful, she could easily give away how her feelings towards him had changed over the last few hours. It puzzled her. The easy relationship, the companionship she'd felt for as long as she could recall, was sliding into something else, at least for her. This new feeling, was it love? She didn't know. It wasn't something she'd felt before for anyone, this yearning need to touch Arthur, to hold his hand. Let him hold hers. She wanted to tell him, and yet she wouldn't. Couldn't. It would change things forever between them. There'd be no going back to what they'd had.

Jessie shifted in the seat, easing away from the woman's elbow. It had been a strange day altogether. Although they hadn't left enough time to go to the fairground, she'd enjoyed most of it. Seeing the sea for the first was a thrill – the fear she'd felt on the pier had faded a little. And it had been lovely to spend proper time with Clara.

She would have chosen to go to the fairground rather than the aquarium in the Tower. Dark, like a cave, with each tank of fish set into grey rock and divided by low misshapen archways, she'd felt trapped, unable to get enough air. The only sounds had been the subdued murmurs of other people and the rustling of clothes. She hadn't wanted to make a fuss but had been relieved when the others were ready to leave.

Outside Arthur told her that the walls of the aquarium were made of rock from a place called Matlock, where his father was born. The matter-of-fact way he'd then said that he was killed in a railway accident near Manchester shocked her. She hadn't known what to say. It was the first time she'd heard him mention his dad in all the time they'd known one another. They were both quiet on their way back to the railway station. Jessie wondered if telling her had made him as sad as she felt.

Lulled by the gentle snores of the women beside her, she closed her eyes.

Chapter 5

Britain at war. This wasn't the way the day was supposed to end.

Jessie was last out of the compartment and by the time she stepped onto the platform the crowds had thinned to a few stragglers. Arthur was waiting for her by the dimly lit stationmaster's office, his hands thrust into his trouser pockets, his cap perched on the back of his head.

'Britain at war,' she said to Arthur, pointing at the newspaper stand at the far end of the platform. The fear had not subsided.

He nodded, his face serious; the earlier excitement faded. Or hidden, Jessie thought.

'Stanley and Clara said to say goodnight,' he said. 'Clara was a bit upset.' He swung around as she joined him and they walked side by side out onto the road.

'Yes, I saw her. I hope she'll be all right.' Jessie had a cold sickly sensation in her stomach. 'What will it mean? Britain being at war?' She'd asked the question but didn't want the answer.

'I don't know. We'll have to wait and see, I suppose.'

Almost the same words he'd used earlier at the menagerie, that awful place with those poor animals. They hadn't a clue what was happening to them, she thought, just like we don't know now. She tried to imagine what war would mean, but failed. All she was sure of was that she was scared. And that it was a feeling she would have to live with for however long the war went on.

Jessie stopped to look up into the night sky; the moon was a pale disc, the stars white pinpricks in the darkness.

'Thank you, Arthur. I'm glad you persuaded me to go...'

Her voice sounded shrill, brittle. The trip and the new secret feeling she felt for him were tainted now by what was to come – a war. Still, it was what he expected her to say, she knew that.

'I'm glad too.'

'I need to get home to Mam.' She would have to talk to him about his father another time.

'Yes.'

She expected that, at eleven o'clock at night, except for the others leaving the station, the streets would be deserted. But women were standing on the doorsteps of their terraced houses. Crying. Groups of men were huddled in the pools of light under the gas lamps, their faces an odd mix of excitement and terror.

Arthur stopped by an older man standing on his own. His eyes were bleak when he faced Arthur.

'Heard anything else other than we're at war with Germany, mate?'

'Ain't that enough? The man stared at Arthur. 'Things ain't going to be the same ever again.'

Chapter 6

'Mam? Why are you sitting in the dark? Are you all right?'

Jessie closed the back door and went through the bakery to the kitchen. The room was only dimly lit with one gas mantle turned low. Crossing to the hall, she hung her suit jacket on the stand and then went to the sideboard to get a box of matches and a taper.

'Have you heard?' Her mother's voice was hoarse.

'Yes.' Jessie struck a match and held it to a thin taper. Pulling at the chain to turn on the gas, she carefully held it towards the mantle. 'Yes, I have.' She tried to keep her voice steady; she needed to stay calm if only for her mother's sake. 'Let's not talk about it tonight, we'll feel better when we know more tomorrow.'

'I'm frightened, Jessie.'

'Don't be.' A soft popping sound accompanied the glow of light. 'I've told her not to be.'

The voice made Jessie jump. Hot wax from the taper fell onto her hand.

'What are you doing here?'

Amos Morgan had his hand on the back of her mother's chair. As though he belonged; as though he had a right to be standing in their kitchen. So close to her mam.

'What are you doing here?' she said again, her tone sharper, seeing his complacent expression as the light from the mantle grew brighter.

'Jessie, where are your manners?' Dorothy's eyes were bloodshot, her face puffy. 'Mr Morgan thought I might need some company with you not being here.'

The implied accusation hovered.

'How did he know I wasn't here?'

Neither of them answered. Jessie saw the man's fingers lift, as if to touch her mother's shoulder.

'Well, I'm here now, so you may go, Mr Morgan. I'll see to Mother.'

She shifted to let him go past her, his usual limping walk seeming exaggerated somehow. His mouth lifted in a sardonic smile. He tapped the brim of his bowler hat at her.

Horrid man, Jessie thought, looking straight into his eyes. She didn't miss the flicker of dislike in his answering glance.

The windows rattled when he slammed the back door.

'You shouldn't be like that with him, Jessie. He was only being kind.' Dorothy blew her nose. 'He knew I'd be frightened.' She stood. 'I'm going to bed, now you're home – *at last.*'

Jessie flinched and she resented the instant guilt. 'You knew I'd be late. And that man wasn't being kind, Mam, he's after something, I know he is. I've seen how he is with you in the shop. And now he's here in our kitchen? He's after something. You mark my words.'

She flopped onto the chair her mother had been sitting on. 'Mark my words,' she muttered, gazing into the barely lit shifting coals.

Chapter 7

6 August

'I went through both newspapers on my way 'ere.' Bob perched on the high stool in the corner of the bakery by the window, his leg jiggling rapidly in excitement. He took a gulp of tea. 'By that's good; I was spittin' feathers coming up Union Street this morning. That's some 'ill, Missus.' He took another slurp. Shook the paper, whistling, a long tuneless sound. 'It's a rum do, that's for sure. See 'ere...' He shook the pages of the *Nether Brook Chronicle*. 'They're quoting from the *Manchester Courier*. Listen to this. "*Englishmen do your duty,*" Bob paused to look up at them. 'Listen to what they say next. "*And keep your country out of a wicked and stupid war.*"' He raised his eyebrows.

Jessie stopped scrubbing the wooden table, waiting while he folded the paper with deliberation.

'But the *County News* 'ere...' He picked up the second newspaper. 'It's printed the speech that the Prime Minister's made to Parliament. He says there are two reasons we're going to war—'

'I need something from the shop,' Dorothy interrupted.

'What is it?' Jessie looked up from the table. 'I'll get it—'

'No, I'll go.' Her mother almost ran to the door.

Jessie stared after her. 'She's frightened,' she said quietly. 'Amos

Morgan's told her we could be invaded by the Germans, that they are a monstrous nation.'

'It says...' It was as if Bob hadn't noticed or heard. He slowly read the words. 'Mr Asquith says if he's asked what we are fighting for, 'e can say in two sentences.' Bob shook the paper and peered closer to the print. "*First, to fulfil a solemn international obligation.*" He stumbled over the words and looked challengingly at Jessie before continuing. "*An obligation which, if it had been entered into between private persons, would have been regarded as an obligation, not only of law but of honour, which no self-respecting man could possibly have—*" 'Bob stopped before dragging out the last word, syllable by syllable; "*repudiated...*"

'I'm not sure what that means.' Jessie rested the heels of her hands on the edge of the table.

'I think 'e's saying we got to go to war or be ashamed.' Bob's lips moved silently as he read the next bit. 'Oh, he says we have to fight, we 'ave to protect small countries from being crushed...' He read silently again, his forehead furrowed before adding, 'He says we 'ave to go to war to stop powerful countries such as Germany just doing what they want.'

'At this rate we won't be ready to open up.' Dorothy reappeared, rolling her overall sleeves higher. Jessie noticed her mother's hands, empty of whatever she'd gone into the shop for, were shaking. She gave Bob a warning glance.

He jumped off the stool and put his empty mug into the sink. 'First lot of loaves'll be ready by now.' Slipping his hands into the thick cotton gloves, he went towards the oven. 'Don't worry Mrs Jenkins; they say it'll all be over in months, if not weeks. We'll put that lot in their place and then we can get on as though nothing happened.'

'What d'you think your mother will do?' Bob rested his hands on top of the long sweeping brush and balanced his chin on them.

'What about?' Jessie leaned against the back door frame,

watching him sweep the last of the soapsuds into the grid in the middle of the yard. She straightened up, taking off her cap and untying her overall.

'The bakery, of course, dopey. All this talk of the war. It has to affect it somehow. You don't know what...'

Jessie frowned, waiting for him to finish what he was saying, but he stopped. Banging the wet brush against the house wall to knock off the worst of the water, he followed her into the bakery.

'It's nothing to do with us.'

'Course it is. You heard what I read out this morning.'

'Seems to me from what you read that the government can't properly decide, even though they've said we're at war,' Jessie shrugged.

'The papers said there's trouble in Ireland as well; like civil war, 'cause of our government and this Home Rule thing. Summat to do with a general strike. And we all know Ireland in't too fond of the British at the moment. Bit close to home that. What if they take sides with any bugger that don't like Britain either?'

'You're just trying to frighten me, Bob Clegg.' She gave an uncertain laugh. He didn't answer. 'And, anyway,' she added, 'people will still want bread, won't they?'

She hung her overall on one of the hooks by the door. She couldn't worry about it; at least she'd try not to. Amos Morgan, and his mithering of her mother, was enough to be fretting about.

Bob draped his overall next to hers and added his cap over it. 'You're right, of course. We'll still 'ave customers.' He grinned at her. 'Right! If you and your mam can manage, I'm off. I'll see you tomorrow. He dithered in the doorway. 'We're a good team, the three of us, aren't we?'

'We are.' Jessie smiled.

'See you...'

'Okay. See you tomorrow then.'

He laughed when she gave him a quick hug.

'Crikeybobs,' he said. 'Soft ha'porth.'

But she saw him blush and she giggled; he was always so easy to tease.

He closed the gate behind him, whistling his usual long monotonous one-note whistle.

Chapter 8

August

Over the next week, things changed in the shop. There was either a stunned silence between the customers as they waited to be served, or an almost uncontrollable buzz of excitement.

'I went down to Manchester. There were Union Jacks everywhere and in all the pubs chaps were singing around the pianos.' A red-faced man rocked on his heels and spoke through the stem of the pipe clenched between his teeth. 'It were grand.'

One of the woman nodded, the green feather in her hat flicking to and fro. 'And they say that when the Royals appeared on the balcony of Buckingham Palace in London, there was great cheering.'

'And have you seen the trams? All decorated,' someone else said. 'And with music playing in them—'

'*Rule Britannia*, I heard.'

There was a general murmur of amusement and pleasure.

'Quite right.' This from Mrs Underwood, wife of the local councillor, Jessie noted. 'My husband organised that in celebration of our standing up for what is right.'

'That'll be tuppence ha'penny, Mrs Underwood.' Jessie handed the tissue-wrapped bread over the counter. 'Next, please.' She looked over the shoulder of the woman, who showed no sign of moving.

'And he's organised the Nether Brook brass band to march with the first lot of volunteers.' The woman looked at Dorothy and Jessie. 'Will that lad of yours be signing up, Mrs Jenkins? That Bob?'

'We wouldn't know.' Jessie spoke briskly. 'Now, next please?'

But there was no stopping Mrs Underwood. 'If all the able-bodied young men go, my husband says it will be over in no time.'

'Should do it quickly before it's over,' her friend next to her agreed. 'They say they're going to put on special trains to take the volunteers off to war. I'd be proud if my Charlie went to fight for king and country.'

Jessie looked across at the small *woman*. 'But he's only fourteen, Mrs Herbert.'

She shrugged. 'He knows his duty. Fighting to make England a better place.'

'Quite right. And, according to them in Parliament, we will be much better off after the fighting.' The red-faced man pointed his pipe at anyone who would look at him. 'And they must know.'

'Well, I don't know...' This time it was the old woman that Jessie's mother was now serving. 'They say there are guns that can kill more men faster than ever before—'

'Oh, shame on you, Mrs Ebsworth.'

'Be quiet, woman.'

The queue subsided into a low muttering. They shifted, making a passageway for the old woman to walk through to leave the shop. At the door she turned, clutching her basket to her, and lifting her chin, said, 'Mark my words, we'll be sorry we got taken in by them in charge. We will.'

'I do wish everybody would stop talking about it,' Dorothy whispered, looking out of the corner of her eyes at Jessie. 'I don't know what to think. It all just scares me to death.'

'I know, Mam.' Jessie forced a smile to serve the next customer.

When the man with the pipe stood at the counter, he blew a cloud of smoke towards them. Jessie wafted her hand in front of her face, biting her lip to stop herself from telling him just what she thought of his manners.

'Mr Horrocks?'

'I'll have two scones and a muffin,' he said. 'Glad to see you've got young Jessie here doing something useful, Missus.' He pointed the pipe at Jessie. She fought back the urge to snatch it from him. 'Keeping her busy will stop her joining in with that there stuff those silly Suffragette women are doing all over the place. Mrs Horrocks were accosted by a group of 'em last week outside the market hall. Scared her out of her wits, they did—'

'Mrs Horrocks?' Dorothy handed change over to the young mother who was juggling a shopping bag with a wailing baby.

'Wanted her to join them. She told me she said she had enough to do looking after me and the house. And quite right.' He looked around to address the fresh audience of customers standing behind him. 'Upsetting decent women with their dangerous ideas. I told Mrs Horrocks, there'll be no more of her going out on her own for the foreseeable future, not with the Germans and all the shenanigans those women have brought to our doorstep.'

'And what shenanigans would that be, sir?'

Jessie looked up in surprise. Clara Duckworth stood with her hand on the shop door handle, a calm, quizzical expression on her face. She nodded a greeting to Jessie before saying, 'Ah, you mean us trying to get the vote for women – the same rights that you men have? Those shenanigans?'

The veins in his cheeks and nose flushed even more, his jaw set, teeth clamped. A line of spittle linked his lips to the pipe when he half-turned and took it from his mouth. But he wouldn't face Clara when he spoke, looking up to the ceiling.

'Violence, burning houses, letterboxes, breaking windows. Need I go on?'

'You obviously are not in possession of the facts, sir. Not all women have resorted to those actions. There are Suffragettes and Suffragists, of which I am one of the latter. We believe in peaceful protest—'

'And if I was old enough I would have joined the Suffrage movement as well,' Jessie blurted out. 'Sorry, Mam,' she said, seeing Dorothy's agitation. 'But I would.' She had never thought about it before, but she was determined to side with her friend.

Clara flashed her a grateful smile and continued. 'Nevertheless, sir, you may like to know that Mrs Pankhurst has called for all of us to put our *just cause* on hold because we are at war. She has asked for women to help with the war effort. I myself will be working on a local farm, on the land to help our country. What will you be doing, Mr ... er?'

'Humph!!'

Jessie stifled a giggle, passed his order over to him and watched as he counted out the exact amount of coins. Without making eye contact with anyone, he marched out of the shop.

Jessie grinned at Clara. 'Time for a cuppa? That all right, Mam? Will you manage for a bit?'

'Of course.' Dorothy nodded. 'First time I've seen anyone shut that man up,' she said, smiling, relief in her voice.

A burst of laughter lightened the mood.

Until they were all halted by a loud voice.

'I don't know about *working on the land*'. There was sneer in his tone. 'But *I'd* certainly volunteer to go and fight if I could...'

Amos Morgan elbowed his way through the group of women. He jostled Clara Duckworth on purpose as he limped past her.

'But as you all know, it's impossible for me.' He stopped at the counter. 'I'll have my usual loaf, Mrs Jenkins.'

'These ladies are before you—' Jessie set her mouth. Ignorant man!

'I'll serve Mr Morgan,' Dorothy said quickly, ignoring the murmurs of annoyance from the queue.

Amos Morgan smirked.

Chapter 9

'Thanks for this, Jessie. I was a bit shaken up by that horrid man.'

'Well, I wouldn't have known it; you were so calm. Mr Horrocks is such an opinionated man he needed taking down a peg or two. And it's no problem. Mother said she could manage and I'm glad of the break now the morning rush is over.' Jessie spooned tea leaves carefully into the warmed pot. She really wanted to tell Clara about Amos Morgan and her mother, how worried she was, but found herself saying, 'Now, I want to hear all your news. We haven't seen one another since Blackpool.'

'I've been meaning to call round but things have been hectic.'

'It sounds to have been. But why a farm, Clara?' It wasn't something Jessie could imagine: Clara was far too elegant.

'It was Lady Constance's idea. You know, from the Manor?'

'I know of her, but she never comes into the shop.' Jessie waved the spoon around, thinking. 'Well, she won't do her own shopping, will she?'

'No, I suppose not. Thanks.' Clara took the cup and saucer from Jessie. 'Anyway, she called the first meeting. She's in charge of this area, of our group of Suffragists. After Mrs Pankhurst gave us the order to stop activities for the duration of the war, Lady Constance gathered us together to discuss what we should do. Although Mr Asquith is the bête noire of the Suffragettes, we must put that to one side, Jessie. Don't you think so?'

'I suppose.' Jessie, feeling the slight panic she always felt when Clara started talking about politics, busied herself by cutting a slice of seed cake and sliding it onto one of their best china plates. 'I mean, yes, yes, of course. Although he is a – er – problem to – the movement...'

Her friend nodded in agreement. Jessie took in a breath of relief that she'd understood what Clara meant.

'The Suffrage of women – of us – is so important.' Jessie handed the plate to Clara, uncomfortably aware she hadn't really given any thought to such matters.

'Thanks, that looks lovely.' Clara smiled. 'Of course, Mr Lloyd George, you know, the Chancellor of the Exchequer...?' Jessie nodded. 'He has such wonderful ideas for reforms for the welfare of the country, including his belief in our cause. He would be quite perfect as the Prime Minister, don't you agree, Jessie?'

'Yes, I read something about that the other day...' As soon as she'd spoken, Jessie worried that Clara would ask her something about the non-existing newspaper article. She glanced up at her friend, saw the spark of humour in her eyes and grinned. 'I didn't really. I know so little about what goes on outside this place, Clara. But I love listening to you.'

Clara laughed, a kind, gentle laugh. 'And I like telling you about our movement. Another year or two and you'll be able to join us.'

'I will. I'd love to.' Heat rose in Jessie's face. 'I believe we are equal to men...'

'Better in some ways. Well, than some men.' Clara pulled a face, but laughed again.

'Such as that horrid Mr Horrocks – and Amos Morgan,' Jessie added, grimacing. She wanted to get back on safer ground. 'So, tell me, Clara, why a farm, it doesn't sound like your kind of thing.'

'Some of the single women said they would work in the munitions factory in Manchester. Apparently, the government will be recruiting for more workers. But I don't think I could stand being cooped up in a factory all day. Stanley agrees. I've said I'd rather work on a farm. Lady Constance asked around local farms to see if any help was needed and she found Tibbet's.' She waved vaguely towards the window. 'That big old place on the moor above the mill.'

'I know it.' Jessie took a sip of her tea. 'Mrs Tibbet comes into the shop every now and then.' She poured the tea into cups. 'Bit grumpy?'

'Yes, he is rather,' Clara said. 'Lady Constance went with me to talk to the farmer.' She frowned. 'I had the feeling he thought I wouldn't be useful, would you believe? But his wife was lovely and, of course, I wouldn't see much of him; I'll be helping Mrs Tibbet. She told us that she can show me how to make cheese, look after the poultry. She said the two labourers they had working for them have already volunteered, which was rather foolish of them because they could have stayed, with farming being so necessary for the country.' She took a breath and glanced across at Jessie. 'And Mrs Tibbet wears breeches, would you believe?'

'No!' Jessie held her slice of cake half in and half out of her mouth.

'Yes.' Clara nodded. 'She says they are far more practical. And...' She giggled. 'She said she would lend me some of hers. Though I doubt they would fit; she's only tiny – and rather round. So, I might buy some of my own.'

'Would you dare?' The thought of any woman wearing men's breeches sounded scandalous to Jessie. 'I read once in a newspaper about two women appearing in public in men's clothes and being arrested for not being natural.'

'Mrs Tibbet looked perfectly natural, Jessie. She took me out to the barn and some of the hens had laid their eggs in the loft, so she went up the ladder to get them. I'm sure if she'd worn a skirt it wouldn't have been as easy for her.'

'Hmm, I suppose.'

'She says I might have to do the same. Climb the ladder, I mean.' Clara raised her eyebrows in alarm. Jessie couldn't help laughing. Clara giggled again. 'Apparently the hens are always going up there.'

'My goodness!'

'I'd only wear the breeches on the farm, of course,' Clara added hastily. 'Stanley said he wouldn't mind. Mrs Tibbet said they'd pay me ten shillings a week, which is rather good, I thought. I've never earned a wage before.'

Nor me, Jessie thought; she earned what her mother called spending money. She felt a tinge of jealousy that instantly made her feel guilty. 'How will you get there?'

'Bicycle. And Stanley says he'll walk me there when he can.'

'Won't he miss you?'

Clara paused. 'Knowing Stanley, he'll volunteer if they need more men to join the army. He says they will.'

She nodded, for a few seconds lost in her own thoughts, before straightening in her chair and smiling brightly.

'You know him; he's a man who always believes in doing the right thing. He won't shirk his duty – what he thinks is his duty. Which is why he thinks I should do mine now, since Lady Constance has made such an effort to find me this place at Tibbet's'.

'Until the government asks for volunteers, we'll have Saturday afternoons together and Sundays. I won't be on the farm at all on Sundays.' She took another bite of the cake. 'This really is delicious.'

'It's not our very good seedcake; it's the one we make from the leftover dough and dripping. Though I do tend to put more brown sugar and caraway seeds in it than in our best.'

'Well, it's lovely.'

'Thanks. Anyway, they say this war will be over by Christmas, so perhaps you won't have to do it for long... Up at the farm.'

'Oh, I'm looking forward to doing my bit. However long it takes.'

'You get time off on Sundays. We will still be able to get together sometimes, then? Meet up for a walk somewhere? If Stanley does go?'

'Oh, yes.' Clara frowned. 'But I don't really want to think about that.'

'Of course not.' What a thing to say. What on earth was she thinking? 'Sorry.'

'Never mind...' Clara paused, her eyes widened. 'I've got an idea. Why don't you and I go to a cinematograph show in Manchester? I read in the newspaper that there's a new one on, with that actor Charlie Chaplin, at the Trocadero Picture Palace. Stanley won't mind, he only asked the other day if I'd seen you since Blackpool. What do you think?'

'Really?'

'Yes, why not?'

'I've never been there. I know Arthur went, when it first opened, with some friends. But I haven't been, of course.'

Clara laughed and clapped her hands. 'Oh, do say yes, Jessie, it'll be fun. Just the two of us. How daring will that be? Of course it will have to be the afternoon performance; it wouldn't be seemly to be out on our own at night. And I'm sure Stanley will escort us there and back.'

It took only a second for Jessie to answer. It would be an escape from all the talk of war. 'Why not?' She echoed her friend's words. 'Why not?'

Chapter 10

'Oh, I did enjoy that. I loved the orchestra playing to all the fast bits and I don't think I've laughed as much since this horrid war was declared.'

'I loved that bit when he was outside on that balcony and it started to rain and the policemen thought he was a burglar.'

'And me. Oh, look, there's Stanley.' Clara waved. 'Like I said, he insisted on waiting for us till the film finished. He didn't think it right we would be on our own.'

'Enjoy that, ladies?' Her husband touched the neb of his cap.

'That Chaplin fellow, he's so funny.' Clara stretched up to give him a quick kiss. 'And, during the interval we ordered tea and biscuits and they brought it to our seats.'

'Thank you for treating us, Stanley. I should pay you, you know.'

'Nonsense. You are very welcome. What's eight pennies when they're spent on my lovely wife and her friend? Good seats?'

'Wonderful.'

'Though I was glad I only wore this.' Jessie touched the low crown of her blue hat. 'Did you hear the man behind us complaining about the hat of the lady sitting next to me?'

'Oh, piffle.' Clara laughed. 'He could have moved. A lady can't go out without a hat.' She ran her hand over the long green feather fastened to the band on her own hat. 'Silly man.'

She moved in between Jessie and Stanley and linked arms with both of them. 'There were a few different little films; something for everyone, I thought, didn't you, Jessie?' Clara didn't wait for an

29

answer. 'And an interesting piece on Suffragettes in the news, Stanley. I'll tell you about it later.'

'I'm, sure you will, dearest.' Stanley peered at her under her hat, smiling.

'They showed a little of what it is like at the front and they collected for an ambulance to go there. I don't think they let the cameramen see much, but I should think lots of the audience have brothers or fathers or husbands that have already volunteered, so it's good they did that.'

Jessie's shoulders tightened. She'd hated seeing those images. She was glad Arthur was too young to go.

Travelling home on the tram, she let the conversation between Clara and Stanley drift over her head. Trying to make sense of the new feelings she had for Arthur was difficult. Even thinking about it brought heat to her cheeks; she hoped her friend didn't notice. The tram rattled to a stop and Clara turned from her husband to tug at her arm.

With Stanley a little way in front of them, they walked slowly, savouring their time together until they stopped outside the shop.

'I'll see you again before I go to Tibbet's.' Clara hugged Jessie. 'We'll sort something out so we can do something like this again?'

'Yes. Yes of course.' All at once, Jessie felt very low. This war was going to make everything change.

'We can. I promise. I'll be in touch.'

Jessie managed a smile, but it was difficult not to feel miserable. If she was older, even two years older, like Clara, she would have more control over her life.

'You know,' Clara said, 'don't you, that you are already helping.' She waved her hand at the shop window. 'You're already doing a service to the country.'

Not like you, Jessie thought. Not like you.

But she had troubles closer to home.

Chapter 11

'He gives me the creeps.' Jessie stood alongside Bob, kneading the bread dough, her arms aching. She brushed a lock of her hair away from her face with her forearm.

'Who?' Still mixing the yeast into a large container of warm water, Bob stopped his usual, droning, low whistle and looked across the table at her.

'You haven't listened to a word I've said.'

Jessie rested the fists of her hands on the dough and gazed through the bakery window. The sun had risen enough to be slanting diagonally across the yard, emphasising the dark corner by the outside lavatory. Jessie remembered when she was small, how frightened she'd been to go there first thing in the morning; how her father had waited by the back door of the bakery, talking to her all the while, until she emerged from the small dark building. She blinked, looked down at the table.

'Amos Morgan. I can't stand him, he gives me the creeps.'

'Don't stop, barmpot.' Bob waved his free hand at her, still stirring the yeast mixture. 'Don't stop, we can't have 'oles in the bread.'

Jessie lifted the large lump of smooth dough and slapped it down onto the table. After giving it a few more thumps, she picked up a large knife and began cutting it into smaller pieces. 'You don't understand…' She stabbed her knife through the dough. 'That man – he's never away.' She squeezed her eyelids tight, forcing back the tears. 'It's only six months since Dad died.'

Bob came around the table and put his arm over her shoulder. 'I know, kid. It must be 'ard for you.' He gave her a quick squeeze. 'You and your dad were close, weren't you?'

She nodded. It was good of him to offer sympathy; he'd always been kind to her. Since her father had died, he'd been especially good and had taken on a lot of her work in the bakery. Sometimes he even helped in the shop when he should have gone home.

'I need to get this lot in tins.' She smiled at him. 'Thanks.'

'It's okay. We're mates you and me, aren't we? Yer can talk to me anytime.'

He patted her shoulder and went back to the container, ladling flour and sugar into the yeast mixture. 'I know what yer mean, though. He's a queer bloke, for sure.' He sprinkled in salt. 'What d'you think 'e wants with your mother? Surely it's too soon for 'er to be thinking...' He didn't finish his sentence.

'I don't know.' Jessie shrugged. 'I don't understand Mam either.' She formed balls of the dough and pressed them into each of the tins lined up in front of her.

''Ere, I'll put that lot in. Last lot should be ready by now.'

Bob opened the oven door and a rush of steam filled the bakery. He tipped the hot tins onto the slatted wooden worktop.

'Think that'll be enough for today.'

It was a statement not a question; Bob was experienced enough for Jessie to accept what he said.

She nodded, her face shiny with moisture. 'I'll start cleaning up.'

They worked in silence, easy in one another's company, Jessie scrubbing the table and Bob cleaning the used tins.

Outside, sparrows fluttered and bickered around the pile of breadcrumbs she'd swept off the baking trays onto the steps in the yard.

Before long, she heard her mother unbolt the shop door. Heard the subdued greetings of early customers. Not once did she hear her mother laugh and that made her sad. She sighed.

Bob glanced at her. 'You okay, kid?'

'Everything's changing so fast,' she said. 'What's next, Bob? What else can happen?'

She remembered her words later that day; it hadn't taken long to find out.

Chapter 12

'No, Mam. Dad's only been dead a few months...'

'Your father's gone. I need to do this.'

'Please say no.'

The back door was open, letting in fresh air to counterbalance the heat from the oven. Jessie lined up the loaf tins due to be washed on the table.

'Hush now. I've made up my mind. Mr Morgan will put money into the shop and he's worked in a bakery before. Bread-making is a skill you don't forget and I need him.' She wouldn't meet Jessie's eyes. 'I can't manage on my own.' There was an odd wheedling pitch in her voice. Her throat was flushed and mottled.

'You've got me—'

'Jessie—'

'And Bob. Dad taught Bob all he knew; he's a good baker.' Jessie persisted. The thought of that man taking her father's place sickened her. 'If we need more help in the kitchen I could ask if Bob's brother, Eddie, can come in sometimes. And I'm good in the shop.'

'I've made up my mind.' Her tone was sharper now. 'You're too young to understand.' Her mother pulled a floral pinafore over her head and wrapped the ties around her, fastening them at the front.

'I'm sixteen, I understand more than you think.' Jessie felt the panic tightening her chest, hindering her breathing. 'My Dad's only been dead—'

'Over six months.' Her mother lifted the copper kettle off the range and poured the steaming water into the large sink. 'He's been gone more than six months.'

She used a cloth to lift the lid off the kettle and began to fill it again with cold water. Steam hissed from the open top and the spout.

'I can't manage,' she said again. 'Try to understand, love.'

She was struggling to hold onto the kettle while turning off the tap. Jessie took it from her and used both hands to stand it back on the range.

'I work in the bakery with Bob and, like I said, I can ask about Bob's brother. And I'll help more in the shop as well.' She took her own pinafore from the hook and put it on. 'Let me wash the tins.'

She saw Dorothy's shoulders rise and fall with a sigh. 'A man around the place will make me feel safer.'

'Safer from what?' Jessie pushed for an answer.

'From all this war business. It's bad.' Her mother took the tins from Jessie without looking at her and made a great clattering show of scrubbing them with the dishcloth. 'We don't know what will happen—'

'This is about Amos Morgan saying the Germans will invade us, isn't it? You do know he only said that to scare you, don't you, Mam? To get his feet under the table?'

'Why do you think you know better, our Jessie?' The words were harsh, but the tone was coaxing.

'Why does he?'

Her mother sighed again. 'Bob may leave us to join up. He's nineteen, plenty old enough. We'll need Mr Morgan if that happens, surely you realise that?'

'No, I don't. Why him?' Jessie knew she was being stubborn.

Her mother's next words made her drop the tin she was holding, crash onto the stone floor. 'What did you say, Mam?'

'I said we're going to be married on Saturday, after we close up here.'

That night her mother's words came back to her, frightening her so much she sat up in bed. Bob was old enough to volunteer for the army. What if Arthur was daft enough to do the same? But he was only sixteen. Surely he wouldn't be accepted? She settled back on the pillow. Once they knew his age they'd say he was too young. But wars sometimes lasted for years. Arthur might have to fight.

The fear tightened her throat and she swallowed, squeezing her eyes shut against the quick tears.

Everything had changed for her on that day in Blackpool. Whether he would ever know, or even care, she knew she loved him – was in love with him. And she couldn't lose him.

Chapter 13

End of August

The marriage caused quite a lot of raised eyebrows and whispered gossip amongst the neighbours. The fact that it took place in the registry office on the Saturday afternoon and the married couple were behind the shop counter first thing on the Monday was even more cause for disapproval. But it didn't stop the customers coming in. Jessie cringed with embarrassment when she saw the prying, sideways glances at Amos and her mother. They made an odd couple, her mother large-bosomed, at least a foot taller than her new husband; Amos slight and thin with his heavy, built-up boot. That didn't bother her, but his habit of slapping Dorothy on the backside each time he passed her behind the counter certainly did.

'Got my money's worth when I wed this one,' he'd say, grinning, if there were any men in the shop.

'He's truly awful, Clara.' Jessie held onto her hat as she ducked under a low sycamore branch at the side of the river.

They passed an old couple. The man's eyes were kind. He'd linked the woman's arm through his. They reminded her of how her mother and father had treated each other.

'Amos Morgan is an obnoxious man. Coarse. Crude. I think he embarrasses Mam on purpose.'

'Does she think so?' Clara stopped walking and faced Jessie.

Jessie shrugged. 'I don't know; she doesn't stop him.' Her friend wasn't as sympathetic as she'd hoped. 'You don't know him, Clara.'

'I have seen him, obviously. And he was awful that afternoon in the shop, I remember that. But you're right, I don't know him as you do.'

Jessie's mood contrasted with the hazy early autumn evening. It was warm for September and the cloudless sky still held onto a pale lemon light. Even the five local mallard ducks rippling the water alongside them didn't amuse her as they usually would. Ahead, a group of small children threw bread into the slow-moving river. Jessie watched. There seemed to be so many contented people around, despite there being a war on. Or was she just imagining that?

They walked on.

'Does she seem happy?'

'I can't tell.'

'Well, I'm sorry, Jessie, I don't think there's anything you can do about it.' Clara linked arms with her. 'Now, come on, it's a beautiful evening and this has been a lovely treat. Let's not spoil our walk with any more talk about Amos Morgan. We don't know when we'll be able to do this again. I'll be starting work at Tibbet's farm next week.'

Jessie allowed herself to be led. Slowly. The last thing she wanted was for the walk to be over and to have to return home.

Chapter 14

'I hate him.' It was the first thing she said to Arthur. She'd kept her anger to herself for the last two weeks, but she thought she'd burst if she didn't tell him what kept happening in the shop.

'What?' He looked up at her. She was sitting on top of the stone wall outside the mill. Men, pouring out from the huge green doors, jostled past him.

The embarrassment curdled in Jessie's stomach, but she let the words burst out of her.

'I hate him.' She jumped down, her mouth twisted. 'Amos Morgan. He's a pig.'

'Well, we knew that.' Arthur took his flat cap off his head and brushed cotton dust from his hair. 'What's he done now?'

'It's bad enough that he mauls Mam. But today he touched me. Again.'

Arthur's eyes narrowed. 'How do you mean – touched?' Conscious of stares from the passing weavers, he gave a flick of his head to show her they should move away. 'Come on, let's get gone from here. Then you can tell me properly what he's done.'

Grateful for the understanding in his voice, Jessie swung round to walk alongside him; she knew he'd be on her side. Not that he'd be able to do anything about it. But it helped, knowing she could tell him.

They followed some of the other mill workers down the stone steps to the canal path. Jessie noticed there were even fewer young men among them than the week before.

'Mam says he doesn't do it on purpose. She says I'm fussing over nothing, that we're all on top of one another behind the counter.'

Jessie stopped to let two women pass them. One of them was crying. Jessie stared at the water in the canal. Streams of blue, green and red mingled together in the sluggish flow, the residue of the cotton dyes flowing from the pipes in the mill wall into the canal. In places, different hues were caught on the clumps of thick grass along the edges.

'It happens whenever he's near me.' Jessie patted her buttocks. 'Here – and...' She hesitated before touching her chest. 'Here. And he always grins.' She glanced at Arthur. 'I hate it. He makes sure Mam doesn't see.'

'I'll kill him,' Arthur muttered. His hand shook as he lit a cigarette. He coughed. He'd only just taken up smoking and she thought it made him look like the actors they'd seen at the pictures. But his eyes were watering and she couldn't tell if it was the smoke or if he was upset. Jessie had known him long enough to know he could sometimes almost cry in his anger.

'No, I don't want you to get into trouble. He'd bring the bobbies round, no danger. You could get sacked from the mill.' She caught hold of his arm. 'I can look after myself, Arthur, it's enough that I can talk to you. It'll be okay. Honest.' She thought he was going to argue when he faced her, blinking. But he only nodded.

'I don't doubt you can, sweetheart, but just be careful.'

The affectionate term took her by surprise; it wasn't a word he'd used before. *Sweetheart.* Jessie turned the word over in her mind and bit down hard on her lip to stop her smile.

Did he feel the same way she did then? Had he fallen in love with her in Blackpool, just as she had fallen in love with him?

She waited for him to speak again but he didn't, and she saw his ears were red; a sure sign he was embarrassed. Was she wrong, thinking their friendship had changed, grown into the kind of love Clara and Stanley had? She couldn't bear it. She wanted him to touch her, to take away the loathing she felt whenever Amos Morgan touched her.

Arthur walked to the edge of the path to throw the tab end of his cigarette into the canal. It gave a short hiss when it landed on the surface. She studied the small circles that rippled from it. Still he didn't speak.

Jessie ordered herself to stop yearning to feel his skin, for him to hold her hand. With an inward shrug, and to break the silence between them, Jessie plucked a broad piece of grass from the side of the path and, holding it flattened and tight between her thumbs, blew on it. The screech was piercing, and Arthur laughed, holding his hands over his ears. In the distance a dog barked, and then another.

'Your turn,' Jessie challenged.

Arthur chose a different long blade and, arranging it as she had done, made the same shrieking noise.

Grinning at one another, they each chose more grasses and competed to get the loudest sound before walking on towards the bridge and the steps that led up to their street.

Jessie thought back to the countless times they'd dawdled home like this, reluctant to get there too quickly in case they were found jobs to do. Not wanting to let go of the day, of each other's company. Being with him meant much more now, even if he didn't know it.

'Everything's different.' Jessie threw the last piece of split grass into the canal and blew her lips out in a huge sigh. Despite their laughter, she felt the unease between them. 'I hate everything,' she said, trying to cover over the awkwardness. 'The only thing anyone talks about is this war. And I heard him...' She wouldn't even use his name. 'I heard him tell Bob that he doesn't need to go into the army; working in the bakery is apparently called a reserved occupation. I don't understand. Mam said she needed to marry him because Bob might join up to go to fight.'

Arthur didn't speak. And he wouldn't look at her.

They'd reached the bridge.

Jessie pressed her lips together. *Sweetheart*. Why, oh why, had he said it? He never called her anything but her name. What did he mean by calling her sweetheart? She was stupid for hoping. Stupid, she berated herself, stuffing her fists into her cardigan pockets to stop the trembling.

'I'd better get home,' she said, one foot on the first stone step. 'Else he'll be raising the roof; I said I'd only be half an hour.'

'Wait.' Arthur leant against the wall by the bridge. 'I've something to tell you, Jessie.'

She closed her eyes, not daring to let him see the hope in them.

'I need to tell you...'

He took hold of her arms, pulled her hands out of the pockets. Held them. The shivering, the heat came from somewhere deep inside her. But she waited. She saw the knot of his Adam's apple move up and down his throat. He had to say it, she had to let him say he felt the same way she did. Decent girls didn't say anything; they waited. She lowered her eyes.

'Look at me, Jessie.' Arthur squeezed her hands. Her fingers felt small, fragile, between his.

She couldn't look at him. She glanced up at the stones under the arch of the bridge, glistening with damp, dark-green moss, then at the surface of the canal where the earlier bright colours now merged into a sludge brown. Slimy weeds trailed just under the surface of the slow-moving water. The path was rutted and uncomfortable under the thin soles of her boots. Arthur moved so close to her that she could feel the warmth of him, even through the layers of her clothes. She lost her nerve.

'I must go. They'll be wondering where I am.'

'No, please. Wait.'

She felt the hard skin, the callouses on the pads of his fingers. A long time ago they'd held hands as children. This was different. This new quivering inside her brought heat to her cheeks.

'Jessie?' His hand moved to her shoulder; she felt the slight tug as he wrapped a strand of her hair around his finger.

'Arthur...' It was a plea. She looked at him at last, knowing every feature of his face. And yet, it was as though she saw him for the first time. Why had she never noticed the darker flecks mingled in the light blue of his eyes, the lashes, so thick and long, the straight eyebrows, the way a lock of his hair fell, wayward, across his broad forehead? It was the face of a man.

She watched his lips move and, shamed by the sudden flare of warmth between her thighs, took her gaze from his mouth.

It was wrong; what she was feeling, thinking, was wrong.

And yet he'd called her sweetheart.

'Jessie.'

Even his voice was different: deeper and softer.

Three crows landed nearby in a flurry of feathers and squawks, fighting over some quarry one of them held in its beak. The noise startled her, drowned out his next words. She saw his glare of irritation towards the birds. He started to speak again.

Jessie laughed and, in a rush, said, 'I know, Arthur, I know. I love you too.'

She was talking over him but caught his last sentence.

'...So I've joined up and I'm going to fight the Hun.'

Chapter 15

Jessie turned and walked away from him. He called after her, and she ran faster, his words so loud in her head that by the time she burst through the back door of the bakery, she was saying them out loud, '...joined up.'

Too loud. Too bitter.

'What's up with you?' Amos Morgan stood in front of her, fists on his hips.

'Nothing.' She pushed past him, avoiding his grasp. 'Get off!'

'Don't speak to me with that tone, missy.'

'Then keep your hands to yourself.' Jessie ran through the kitchen, pulled open the door to the stairs. 'Or I'll tell Mam,' she shouted.

His sharp, sarcastic laugh followed her to her room. She could still hear him when she slammed her bedroom door and threw herself onto her bed.

'Joined up.' This time the words were choked with tears.

She was still in her room at nine o'clock, despite the many calls from her mother. When Dorothy finally gave a tentative knock on the door, Jessie didn't turn away from the window. The sun was sinking fast over the hills in the distance, the sky a peachy-orange, broken by long trails of purple-tinged cloud.

'Jessie?'

'I'm not hungry, Mam.'

Her Mother peeped in. 'I've brought you some toast and a mug of tea, love.'

'Just leave it on the shelf, will you, Mam?' She was reluctant to take her eyes from the sky. Subtly changing second by second, there were now streaks of ruby red against the contrasting black of the ground. Even though she knew it was superstitious nonsense, she made herself believe that if she saw the last of the colour disappear, Arthur would change his mind.

But could he? Would he be allowed to?

'You all right, love?'

'I'm fine, Mam. Just want to be on my own.'

'It's not your stepfa ... Amos, is it? He's not done anything?'

'Only the usual.'

'I have told him—'

'To keep his hands off me, you mean, Mam?'

'He doesn't mean any harm...'

Jessie sighed. Glancing at her mother she saw the crease of worry around her eyes. Looking back to the window the streaks of red were gone. The steel-grey sky had only a hint of pink above the hills now.

'Thanks for the toast.'

'Try to eat it. Busy day tomorrow; we've a lot of orders to get out.'

'I know.' Jessie half-turned to stretch out her hand to touch Dorothy's.

'What is it, love?'

'Arthur...' Jessie wavered. Should she say? Had he told his mother?

'You've had a fall-out.' Dorothy smiled; the relief seemed to lighten her eyes. 'Well, I'm sure you'll sort it. Not the first time you two have had a spat. You've always been like brother and sister bickering. Too strong willed, the both of you.' She pressed Jessie's fingers, gave a low chuckle. 'Eat the toast, drink your tea before it goes cold. Then bed.'

Jessie stared at the closed door for a while before reaching up to tug the curtains along the wire. She glanced down on the street.

Arthur was on the pavement in front of the shop window. He waved, mouthing words: 'Come down. Please.'

Jessie shook her head, the earlier anger and wretchedness flooding back inside her.

'Please.' He was shouting the word now.

She pressed her head close to the windowpane, peering along the street both ways. If he didn't stop, someone would hear him. Worse still, Amos Morgan would see him. She held her finger to her lips, raised her hand.

'Shush. Wait,' she mouthed.

At the foot of the stairs, she was thankful to see the door to the kitchen closed, the murmur of voices told her both her mother and Amos were in there. Grabbing her mother's grey shawl she tiptoed through the shop, holding on to the bell above the door before stepping outside.

'I'm sorry, Jessie.' Arthur held out his arms. 'I should have told you sooner—'

'Not here!' She gripped his hand. Even through the misery she still felt the unfamiliar quiver inside her at the touch of his skin on hers. 'We can't talk here.'

She led him along Castle Street to the lane by the side of the small C of E church. 'In here.' The shadows in the graveyard didn't scare Jessie; it was somewhere she'd often gone to get away from the house, away from Amos Morgan. To think about her father. 'We can sit here.' She stopped at a bench under an oak tree by the path.

And waited. She wasn't going to make it easy for him to explain the stupidity of what he'd done.

He still had hold of her hand. She heard him swallow.

'Earlier,' he said, 'earlier, you said you loved me.'

He'd heard her then? The heat rose from Jessie's throat to her face. She sat down onto the bench

'Well, I need to tell you, sweetheart—'

That word again. Jessie tensed.

'I love you too. I have for as long as I can remember—'

'Then why go...?'

'I have to. Haven't you seen all the posters, all the recruitment drives in the Square?'

'So? They're not for you, Arthur, you're too young.'

'I told them I am eighteen.'

'You lied?'

43

'My mates are going, Jessie. The Hampson twins. They're my age. We've been promised we can train together, fight together—'

'Don't!' Jessie winced, put her fingers over her ears.

Arthur leant towards her, kissed her cheek. 'You'll wait for me?'

When she lowered her hands and looked at him, she saw his eyes glitter with excitement. 'You won't go,' she said, her voice firm. 'Your mam won't let you.' She flicked her hair away from her face with the back of her hand and glared at him. 'You're too young,' she repeated.

He moved away from her. 'I'm going.' His voice low, sulky. 'No one will stop me.'

'Well, if that's the case, Arthur Dawson, no, I will not wait for you. I'll not be your – sweetheart. I'll not.'

The hurt in Jessie was unbearable. She stood, ready to pull away from him, but he moved quickly, standing, and grasping hold of her around the waist, his forehead against hers.

'Don't go, Jessie. I have to do this, all my pals are going. Please...'

He leaned back, watching her. In the light from the gas lamp on the lane nearby, she saw his face. Pleading. 'I can't let them think I'm a coward.'

'I wouldn't think you're a coward, Arthur.'

Chapter 16

Was it the bad dream or the clatter of her mother and Amos Morgan in the bakery that woke her? Jessie rolled over onto her back and listened to the familiar movements downstairs. Lately, her mam had allowed her to stay in bed until seven o'clock, as long as she was ready for the shop opening at eight, and she luxuriated in those few minutes between waking and having to push back the covers for a quick wash and to dress.

She flung out her arms, stretching, knocking the alarm clock on the bedside table. She squinted at its green illuminated face.

Four o'clock; too soon to be awake. She yawned. No wonder she was so tired.

And then she remembered. The tears that she'd been unable to stop when she crawled into bed the night before came easily again and she sat up, resting her head on her knees. Why did men, boys, have to be so stupid? What had Arthur said about him and his mates from the mill? A Pals' something or other? They'd been promised they could train together, fight together, as though it was a game. 'Fight together.' What did that mean? How? It was as though they were all back in the schoolyard. Jessie wiped her face on the eiderdown.

Train together, fight together – she swallowed against the hard lump that almost closed up her throat – get killed together. The thought chilled her. She whimpered, rocking back and forth, her fear for Arthur unbearable. Fear mixed with anger. 'Stupid. Stupid.'

A rattle against the glass startled her. A second made her jump from her bed.

'Jessie!'

'Arthur?' Jessie struggled to push up the sash window. She leant out, glancing up and down the street. 'What are you doing? D'you know what time it is?'

'Never mind that. I need to speak to you.' He was screwing his cap in his hands, moving from one foot to the other. 'Please, Jessie, come down.'

'Have you changed your mind?'

'No, I can't, It's all done. I've signed the papers now. Please, Jessie...'

'What's the point, Arthur?' Determined not to let him see her cry, she pushed herself away from the window ledge into the room and swiped her knuckles across her eyes.

'Jessie?'

She ignored him.

'Jessie. I won't go from here until you come down to talk to me.'

She heard the oven doors being slammed, the slap of metal on the racks as Amos Morgan emptied out the bread from the tins.

There were only a few minutes before her mother started carrying the trays into the shop.

She knew Arthur meant what he said. Mam would want to know what he wanted if she saw him outside the shop window so early. Then Amos Morgan would shove his oar in; interfere, cause bother. She'd have to go down. It wouldn't matter if she wasn't dressed, she could put her coat on. Before she could talk herself out of it, she ran down the stairs and into the shop, carrying her boots and coat.

The bolt on the door squealed as she pulled it back. Jessie stiffened, looking over her shoulder, sure her mother, or worse, Amos Morgan, had heard. Her stepfather's voice was raised in anger, not at her but at Bob. He must have been late and was now suffering for it. Relieved, Jessie held onto the bell, opened the door and was out on the pavement in a second.

Arthur's face was taut, his eyes as red as though he'd been crying too.

'Come on.' He jammed his cap on his head, looking around.

'Wait.' She leaned against the wall, pushing her feet into her boots, struggling with the buttons. 'I can't go anywhere like this. I'm not dressed.'

'It doesn't matter. No one will see us if we go now.'

He grasped her hand.

Against all her instincts, she tried to shake him off, but he held firm.

'You said you just wanted to talk.' Even though she was determined to be calm, she heard her voice tremble.

'Please?'

She told herself he was too strong but still she didn't resist and allowed herself to be pulled along the street.

'Where are we going?'

'I worked something out in the night. I tried it before I came to see you this morning. I want to show you.'

He still held Jessie's hand as they passed the chapel and went up the narrow steps at the end of the lane. Arthur climbed over the wooden stile that led to the fields.

'Come on, I'll show you.'

Jessie looked up at the fields rising above them and divided by meandering stone walls. A blend of wispy orange clouds and pale sky, reluctantly giving way to the rising sun, darkened the branches of the sycamores dotted around Wharmton Hill. Her curiosity was irresistible.

'Well, okay. But look away,' Jessie said, before hoisting her nightdress and coat up to her knees and following.

'I've seen your knees before, silly.' But Arthur still turned, hands on his hips, and looked with great exaggeration up at the sky.

'Okay,' he said when she stood by him, brushing down her clothes. 'I've worked out that it's a hundred and twenty days between today and Christmas Day. That's how long everybody says this war will last. So I want us to count our steps up the fields and see where we are. And then on Christmas Day I want you to come up here to meet me. See?' He grinned. 'One hundred and twenty days. That's all. I'll be home in no time. You won't even miss me.'

I will, Jessie thought but said nothing, allowing herself to be taken by the hand again and be led through the long grass, following the stone wall.

The sun shimmered on the horizon as they climbed, Jessie silently echoing Arthur's counting.

A hundred and twelve, thirteen...' He was little breathless now, the field steeper than when they started.

Jessie's coat and nightgown, wet around the hem from the morning dew, clung to her ankles with each step. But the sun was warm on her face and she barely noticed.

'A hundred and eighteen, nineteen...' Arthur took one huge stride and stopped. 'A hundred and twenty.' He laughed, swinging Jessie around in a half-circle until he held her in his arms. 'See?'

'See what?' Jessie looked around.

'This stone on the wall?'

Wedged between two tall thinner stones was a smaller one.

'This one.' Arthur patted it. 'What does it look like?'

47

'It's heart-shaped.'

'It is.' Arthur laughed, triumphant. 'I found it and I put it here. And right here – right by where *our* heart stone is – is where we'll meet in a hundred and twenty days.'

When she realised what his words meant she was bewildered. 'What do you mean? You're not going today, are you?'

Jessie pushed him away; he'd never held her like that before and she'd been only too aware of the way her body had reacted to the feel of his.

'Today?' she said again. 'You're going today?' She swallowed, the action making a dry clicking noise at the back of her throat. The anger quickly followed.

She pushed her hands against his chest again, pummelled him. 'You can't.' She was shouting and crying at the same time.

He stood still, his arms by his side, tears trickled across his cheeks. 'I'm sorry, Jessie. I should have told you sooner.' He tried to hold her up as she sunk to the ground, but couldn't and fell to his knees beside her.

She collapsed on to him and they fell sideways, the long curtain of grass around them.

Jessie wept, great gulping sobs that wracked her body, heedless of Arthur's arms holding her to him, of his mouth close to her cheek, his whispered words of comfort that would have offered no comfort even if she heard them.

Finally, too exhausted to cry anymore, she lay still.

'Jessie?'

She moved her head. Moaned.

'Jessie, I'm sorry. I wouldn't hurt you for the world. I love you.' He was stroking her throat. 'But this is something I need to do.'

'No.' Her voice muffled.

'Yes.' His voice firm. 'I'll be back before you—'

'Stop.' She held her fingers over his mouth. 'Don't say it.'

She felt his lips move under her hand in a soft kiss and closed her eyes. Lay still.

'Jessie?'

She moved her head. 'Yes.' Though really not knowing what she was agreeing to, only answering the need in her. She felt him unbuttoning her coat, sliding it from her shoulders, lowering her onto it, still warm from the heat of her body. She waited, not sure of what would happen next; not sure of what she should do.

'I love you, sweetheart,' he whispered, his breath hot on her ear. And then he wasn't holding her.

Jessie murmured in protest, held up her arms. When she looked up at him, he was taking off his jacket, then his shirt. She could only see the outline of him at first but when he lay alongside her she was struck by the paleness of his skin. Her hand hovered inches from his chest, hesitant to touch.

He drew her to him. Through the thin cotton of her nightdress, she felt the rapid rhythm of his heart.

'Just hold me,' she said.

'That's all I want, love. Just to hold you, feel you near me, so I can remember when—'

'Don't say it.' If he said it, she would make him stop. 'I don't want to think about it.' They'd come too far. She knew what they were doing; just lying together, even if it ended now, was wrong. But it was too late. 'Say you love me, Arthur.'

'I love you, Jessie. I've always loved you. I always will.'

Somehow the ties of her nightdress were loosened and his fingers were inside the material, stroking her throat, her shoulders. Then it was his mouth on her skin.

'Arthur – I don't...' She raised his face to hers, kissed him, a shy touch of her lips. 'I don't know what happens...'

'I know, sweetheart.'

'It's the first time...'

'I know. And for me. But you must know that. There's never been anyone else but you.' He rolled away from her. 'I'm sorry – I shouldn't...'

'No. I didn't mean...' Jessie wanted him to kiss her, to love her.

She pushed aside any idea that they needed to stop. She didn't want that; she wanted to learn what love was, meant, with him – with the boy she'd always loved, even when she hadn't understood how she felt about him. 'I didn't mean that, Arthur.' She edged closer, wrapped her arms around him. 'I meant I don't know what to do.'

'It's okay, Jessie.' He stayed still in her arms. 'This is new to me as well. We'll learn together.'

For a few minutes they stayed as they were, content just to be close. The only sounds were the whisper of the grass, the early morning calls of the skylarks rising, in the distance the cows lowing, ready for milking.

Arthur's hand moved lower, covered Jessie's small breast. Her nipple stiffened in response. Her body took her by surprise with its instant pleasure and she ran her hand over his smooth chest.

He was moving more urgently now and she became aware that he was unbuckling his trousers with his other hand.

'Wait.' Suddenly frightened, she stopped him. 'You do love me, Arthur?'

He groaned. 'I've always loved you, Jessie. If you'll have me, I'll love you till I die.'

The chill ran through her. 'Don't say that.' He was tempting fate. 'Just say for always. Please.'

'For always, then.' His hand moved down along her stomach, rested on the soft hair between her thighs. 'Jessie?'

She looked into his eyes. 'Yes,' she said, 'yes.'

The pain was unexpected and she cried out.

Arthur lay still, swelling inside her.

The urge to move, to lift herself towards him, came without warning and she wrapped her legs around his waist.

'I have to go, Jessie.' Arthur held her face between his palms. 'It's the last thing I want, but I have to.' He kissed her, his lips brushing her breasts, her throat, her mouth.

'Not yet.'

She realised he was leaving her. Not just leaving the place where they'd made love, but leaving the life they'd shared for so long. It terrified her. What would she do without him? What if what they'd just done had made her so different her mother would know?

'What happens to me now, Arthur?'

For the first time in her life he wasn't going to be there for her whenever she needed him. And she needed him more than ever.

'I'm sorry, Jessie. I shouldn't have...'

She stroked his face, felt the soft stubble on his jawline. She was a woman now; it was her place to smile, to see her man leave to do what he thought he needed to. And she would wait for him.

'Hush. It's done now. I'm yours forever, Arthur. And I'll be here, on this very spot, waiting for you on Christmas Day.'

She let him lower her nightdress over her head, help her to stand, wrap her coat around her. She wouldn't think of anything else; he would come back to her in a few short months. She had to believe that.

'I want to show you something else, Jessie.' Arthur moved to the wall and lifted the heart stone to reveal a folded piece of paper. 'Read it.'

Jessie saw him swallow, his mouth lifted in a self-conscious smile. He was blushing. She unfolded the note. On it were written in block letters the words: I LOVE YOU.

'I've put it there so whenever you come up here you can read it. Or just know it's there,' he added in haste. 'Always and forever, Jessie.'

'Oh, Arthur.' There was a hot feeling in her throat; all the tears she wanted to cry but couldn't were trapped there. 'I love you too.'

Gently he took the paper, folded it again, placed it in the wall and covered it with the stone.

'It will stay there 'til Christmas, 'til I get back home.' He held out his hand. 'Come on. Time to go.'

The sun was higher in the sky when they walked back to the village, arms around one another. Jessie couldn't believe how quiet it still was; that there was no one around when she looked along Castle Street. After all, it was a lifetime since she'd left the shop.

'How will you get back in?'

They'd stopped by the gate to the chapel, sheltered by the archway for a last kiss. Arthur buttoned her coat around her neck and rested his hands on her shoulders, his forehead creased in anxiety. 'What will you say?'

'Nothing.' Jessie produced a key from her pocket. 'I brought this with me. Shop door. It's not opening time yet and they won't be in there, with a bit of luck. If they are, I'll just say I wanted a walk on such a lovely morning.'

Arthur gave a low laugh. 'Well, well. What a minx I have for my sweetheart.'

His words smarted; she wasn't sure why. 'Don't say that.'

'I'm sorry. I just meant—'

'I know.' Jessie kissed him, stopped his words. 'I know.'

They held onto one another for a while.

'I have to go, sweetheart.' Arthur pulled away from her. 'Best I go first, eh?'

Jessie nodded, not trusting herself to speak. She didn't watch him walk away.

Chapter 17

20 September 1914

She didn't go to watch him leave the town with the other two hundred men and boys either. Through her opened bedroom window, she listened to the uneven thud of their undisciplined marching between the changing tunes of the brass band and the singing. How she resented the singing. And the cheering.

Sitting on her bed, her handkerchief sodden between her fingers, she tried to shut down the images she'd conjured up in her mind of what Arthur might face. She had no idea, but she'd read in the newspapers about the atrocities the German were committing in

Belgium; killing randomly, deliberate cruelty. What kind of men were they? And raping women – this last made her shudder; the thought of strangers doing to women unbidden what Arthur had done with her in love was unbearable to imagine. She was certain she'd kill herself if that happened to her.

Despite Amos Morgan's constant calls to go down to serve in the shop, she ignored him. She wouldn't face the excitement, the proud chatter of the customer. She didn't, wouldn't, couldn't share it.

Eventually the crowds moved away from in front of the shop. She heard the noise from below quieten to a low murmur and thought bitterly that Amos Morgan would be worried about making less money now so many men had gone. Gone to a foreign land to be killed in a war that her own country shouldn't have become involved in. It didn't make sense to her.

'Are you coming down to help or do I have to drag you down here, missy? Your mother and me have been run off our feet. Lazy little...' Amos' voice trailed away. Jessie heard the shop bell. He wouldn't let customers hear how he spoke to her, she knew that.

She knew what to do. Wrapping her shawl around her shoulders she ran down the stairs, through the kitchen and bakery and out into the yard.

Bob was cleaning the red spokes on the wheels of the delivery cart. His mouth was set in a straight line. His face had a strange pallor.

'What's wrong, Bob?'

'Nowt. I'm sound as a pound.'

'There is. You're not whistling. You always whistle.'

He straightened up, wringing the cloth between his fingers so hard his knuckles whitened. 'When I was out front, seeing the lads off, like...?'

Jessie dipped her head. 'Yes?'

'A woman came and stood in front of me and gave me a bloody white feather.'

'What?'

'Gave me a white feather; called me a sodding coward.' He sniffed, ran his palm up over his nose. 'Asked me why I bloody wasn't going with that bloody lot?'

Jessie glanced back at the house to make sure her mother wasn't around; Dorothy hated what she called 'bad language', even though she never said anything when Amos Morgan used it. 'Didn't you tell her you had a reserved occupation? That you worked here?'

'Didn't have a chance. But your mother tackled 'er.' His smirk was a poor imitation of his usual grin. 'She fair went for the woman and told 'er I worked for 'er in the bakery. As you said, reserved occupation.' His mouth twisted in a grimace. 'Still, s'pose I'll 'ave to get used to it. There'll be others that think the same.' He shrugged. Sniffed again.

For the hundredth time, Jessie wished her mother had known about reserved occupations earlier, before all the enlisting. Bob leaving was the reason she'd insisted on Amos Morgan coming into their lives.

Or was it? Was it just that her mother needed a man around to lean on, to tell her what she should do, in the shop, in her life? Why was she so weak? Needing a man was no reason to marry, love was. But even then, there was no way Jessie would let a man tell her what to do. Even Arthur. Though she doubted he would try. She swore to herself she would be different to her mother, whatever happened once this awful war was over.

She moved to pass Bob. 'Don't fret about it. It might not be that bad. Local people know you're working here.' She opened the gate. 'I have to go before...' She looked back towards the bakery.

'Where're you goin' then?' He began working on the cart again, rubbing a cloth over the spokes, drying them. 'Aren't you needed in the shop?'

Jessie shrugged.

'Where're you goin' then?' he repeated, moving on to polishing the metal rim of the wheel nearest her, watching her over his shoulder.

'Arthur's. Arthur's mam's.' Jessie tied her shawl into a loose knot over her chest.

'Ah, one of the local 'eroes.' His tone was resentful.

'Don't. Don't be like that, Bob.' She lifted her chin. 'He's my – friend…'

'Aye, summat like that.'

Jessie couldn't stop the heat rising up her throat. 'I don't know what you mean.'

'Ah, ignore me.' But his smile seemed more like a sneer to her.

'I will.' Jessie lifted the latch on the gate. She hesitated, wondering how else to let him know he shouldn't speak to her in that way, but knew she wouldn't say anything. 'I'd be grateful if you didn't tell him,' she tipped her head towards the bakery, 'I've gone?'

He nodded, not looking at her now. 'Nowt to do with me.'

'Mrs Dawson?' Jessie tapped on the back door. She'd always just walked in, but now Arthur had left, and after what had happened between them the day before, she wasn't sure how to act; everything felt different. 'Mrs Dawson?' She pushed gently at the door and peered around the gap.

Edna Dawson was sitting in her kitchen, her face swollen and red-blotched.

'May I come in?'

'This is what set 'im off.' Without even greeting Jessie, Arthur's mother jabbed a finger at a folded newspaper. 'The damn *Nether Brook Chronicle*. A letter from the Mayor. Apparently there was no one from round 'ere, from the mill, who'd volunteered.' She threw it across the table towards Jessie. 'I couldn't stop 'im. He said he'd never speak to me again if I did.' She covered her eyes. 'I wish 'is dad was still alive.'

Jessie unfolded the paper. 'This piece here? This piece that starts, *Message from the Mayor*?' She read slowly:

> '*Young men at Kindle Mill, what are you waiting for? This is a time of trial for your country. I tell you now what is the plain truth.*

You are wasting good time. Let older men take your jobs. Think what you should be doing. No more wasting your lives; no more dithering; no more lounging around discussing tactics of a warfare in which you are not playing your part. Go, fight for the honour of your country. As your Mayor, I am appealing to you. Captain Howard Shire-Martin.'

'See? Who the 'ell does he think he is?' Edna narrowed her eyes, her voice bitter. 'Read the next bit.'

'And now for a message from my dear wife, your Mayoress, Lady Sophia Shire-Martin.'

'What right, Jessie, what right does she have to stick 'er oar in?' Jessie read the words aloud, slowly:

'Young men of Nether Brook, you have heard what your Mayor has said. England needs you – yet still you wait. Watching others go to fight – yet still you loiter. Be men, make up your mind. The day has come for you. Will you fight for your King and Country, or will you hide in the shadows? Will you be cowards? Every man in Germany, in France; all save the frail, the old, have answered their country's call, have proved their manhood. Will you hide behind your women?

And now I speak to those women, those wives, those mothers. Wives, send your husbands. Mothers give up your sons. It is time for you to rise, bid them go. Or you must hang your heads in shame before the courageous women of other countries. Do not let those women ask where is the manhood of England. Awake! Awake! England needs her sons. Do not let us be ashamed of our Englishmen. Do not let your men hide at home, safe and secure, while the manhood of Europe is shedding its blood on the battlefield. Awake! England needs you men to save her liberty, to protect her shores. Oh, if I were a man I would go but alas, I am not. And nor are you. So tell your men to go forth and fight to keep you and your children safe. Sophia Shire-Martin.'

Jessie's voice faltered. Tears dripped onto the paper, blurring the words. When she looked up, she saw that Arthur's mother's face was also wet, but there was fury in her eyes.

'Has 'e gone? This Mayor? No! If anyone is hiding at home it's 'im. Him and his blathering wife.' She stood, paced the kitchen. 'Between them they've sent my boy to his death. Them and those bloody recruitment officers. Do you know what they do it for?' She flung out her arms. 'Two shillings and sixpence. Two shillings and sixpence for each new recruit. That's what my Arthur's worth to them: two shillings and bloody sixpence.

'King and Country needing him, they said. What about me? I need him. What right 'ave they to get lads to join up, eh? What right 'ave they to take 'im away from me to be killed?' Her voice rose into a wail.

'No!' Jessie cried out. 'No, Mrs Dawson, don't say that. Please don't...' The worry that gnawed at the back of her brain took over. 'I can't stand it.' Only the day before she'd lain with Arthur. The thought of him lying dead, alone, somewhere in a foreign country was unbearable.

Edna Dawson turned and stared at her. After a moment she said, 'You love my Arthur? Is that it, Jessie? You're in love with 'im, aren't you?' She shook her head. 'You're not just friends anymore. You love 'im.' She moved swiftly, gathered Jessie in her arms.

'You don't mind?'

'Why should I?' Arthur's mother held her at arm's length, lips pursed in puzzlement.

'My not being a Catholic? With me being chapel?'

'Oh, that.' She tipped her head back. Breathed out a small, low laugh. 'No, my dear, no. You don't know 'ow I've longed for this day. How I've always hoped you would see my son for the wonderful boy – man – that 'e is.'

'Thank you.'

'I have loved you like a daughter ever since I could remember,' Edna said. 'Does Arthur know how you feel?'

Jessie nodded.

'Then I am glad, glad that he knows that we'll both be waiting for 'im. He'll make sure he keeps safe knowing that we are both 'ere, waiting for 'is return.'

Chapter 18

The days dragged on. Jessie had yet to receive a letter from Arthur. Keeping her worry from Amos Morgan was no problem. Apart from a sly stroke of her buttocks when he passed by behind the counter, he ignored her. But her mother was different. And persistent with her questions.

'You're very quiet these days, Jessie.'

'I'm fine, Mam.'

'Why don't you go to see Clara?'

'She's on that farm these days, remember. I don't think I can just go there.'

'I thought you'd had a note from her? I thought you were arranging to get together?'

'No, they keep her too busy.' It had been a hurriedly written letter full of what her friend had been doing on the farm. It sounded as though she was thoroughly enjoying herself: mucking out the hens, collecting the eggs, learning to bake with Mrs Tibbet. Jessie was envious.

'Doesn't seem fair that. Should have some days off...'

Jessie didn't answer. With both Clara and Arthur gone, there seemed to be nowhere for her to go to escape the house, except to see Mrs Dawson. And she couldn't stand seeing the look of expectation in her eyes, the hope that Jessie had heard from her son.

'You are well, aren't you?'

'I'm fine, Mam,' Jessie said again.

'So, besides missing Clara, what is it?'

For a second Jessie was tempted to confide in her mother about her love for Arthur. But Amos Morgan came into the shop.

'What are you mithering about, woman? She's playing up so you'll give her a day out of the shop.'

'I'm not!' Jessie fixed her best glare on him.

'And watch your mouth, young lady.' He nodded a warning at her.

Dorothy waited until he'd gone through to the bakery. 'Don't wind him up, love.'

'I hate him. I hate living here since you married him, Mam.'

'Don't, love.' It was all she said, but Jessie saw the wariness in her mother's eyes when she glanced at the open door to the kitchen.

'Tell him to leave,' Jessie pleaded. 'This is our home, not his. He didn't put any money into the bakery like he said he would, did he?' She knew the answer without even asking; the man was a skinflint.

'Not yet, no. But he says he will.'

'When?'

'When the shop needs it. If business gets bad.'

'So the shop's okay? Business isn't bad?'

'No.'

'So, tell him to go. We don't need him.'

'I can't.'

'Why not?'

'He's my husband. You don't understand. Respectable women don't get divorced.' Dorothy drew in a long breath and levelled her shoulders. 'Now, if you're feeling okay, let's open up.'

The shop was quiet for a Friday when, in the middle of the afternoon, Jessie saw Edna Dawson peering through the window. She opened the door.

'You on your own, Jessie?'

Jessie backed up and closed the door between the shop and the hall to the kitchen, without taking her eyes off the older woman, the fear icy in her stomach. Surely there was nothing wrong; Edna didn't look upset. But she still had her pinny on under her coat. Jessie had never seen her outside her house with her pinny on.

'What is it? What's happened?'

'Don't fret, it's good news.' Edna fumbled in her coat pocket. 'A letter from Arthur. To you.' She held out an envelope. 'He sent me one an' all. Said to give you this when you were on your own.' She gazed past Jessie. 'Out back, is 'e?'

Jessie nodded. The envelope was crumpled and grimy but she held it carefully, stroking her name written in Arthur's large, scrawling handwriting.

'Will you open it?'

She could see Edna's barely concealed impatience.

'Later.' She stuffed the envelope into her overall pocket. 'Later. I'll come round tonight and tell you what he says.' Or almost all, she thought, the quiver of excitement, of hope, making her fingers tremble.

'Right then.' Edna stepped back, obviously disappointed, her mouth moving into a strained smile. 'Tonight, then. I'd better go to church, I reckon I owe a confession or two to 'im upstairs.' She rolled her eyes. 'Father Thomas will 'ave me jumping through hoops.' She squeezed Jessie's hand. 'Tonight then...'

As soon as Jessie saw her pass the shop window, she called to her mother.

'Sorry Mam, do you mind taking over for a bit? I've a shocking headache, think I might have a lie down.'

She heard the loud snort of derision from Amos and when Dorothy came through, a worried frown lining her forehead, she felt remorseful.

'I'll be all right, Mam. Just had a bad night. I've not been sleeping too well.'

'You'll be missing Arthur, I expect.' Dorothy gave her a quick hug. 'Understandable. He's your friend.' But then she added, 'Silly lad shouldn't have joined up at his age. I don't know what Edna was thinking, letting him go.' She put her head on one side to study Jessie. "Spect that what it is, right? You missing him?'

'A little, maybe.'

'Go on, then. Just an hour, mind. You promised to help with getting tomorrow's pastry orders ready.'

In her room Jessie perched on the windowsill, looking across the street to Arthur's house. She wondered if his mother was reading her letter over and over, just as she knew she would her own.

And yet she was reluctant to open the envelope. What if it didn't hold words of love? What if Arthur had realised he'd made a mistake, telling her he loved her? What if he regretted what they'd done and he'd decided he wanted to be just friends again? She ripped open the envelope, steeling herself for his words.

Her eyes skimmed over the short note. At first she was dissatisfied; there was so little written. Slowly, to savour each word, she read aloud:

My Dearest Jessie,

I think of you all the time, especially about our last day together. I was so sorry to leave you but I know it's my duty to be here. It is a great cause and I came out willingly to serve my King and Country. My greatest concern is that I have the courage and determination necessary to face what's in front of us. I hope to get a weekend leave before we go but, if not, remember I'll always be thinking of you.

Remember our heart stone, sweetheart.

I love you. Your Arthur xx

Kissing the sheet of paper Jessie stared up at the sky. A trail of smoke from a chimney, somewhere out of sight, veiled the sun and muffled its brilliance. Might Arthur, even now, be looking up, seeing the sun, thinking of her? She closed her eyes and whispered,' I love you, too, Arthur.' And then thought the phrase over and over again, willing the words to fly to him.

61

She held a breath inside her, knowing if she let it go the tears would come. It was all too cruel; for him to be taken from her just as their friendship had grown into love. Pressing the paper to her lips again she rose and crossed the room to lie on the bed.

'Jessie? Jessie!'

She'd fallen asleep.

'Arthur?' Levering herself up onto one elbow, she listened until the shout came again.

'Jessie, your mother needs help down here.'

Amos Morgan. She pulled her mouth into a scowl.

'Coming.'

She hoped her mother wouldn't leave her on her own with him and that he wouldn't keep them both working too late. She was determined to keep her promise to Mrs Dawson.

Chapter 19

Jessie heard the loud piano playing even as she turned the corner at the end of the terrace. She didn't recognise the tune. It sounded as though Edna was hitting the keys as hard as she could. But it wasn't so loud that the older woman didn't hear her knocking on the back door; she opened it before Jessie could raise her knuckles to rap again.

'This is his letter to me.' Edna handed the paper to Jessie as soon as she entered the kitchen. 'He doesn't say much but at least I know he's safe.' Her eyes screwed against quick tears. 'For now.'

Jessie gave Arthur's mother her letter, hoping she wouldn't ask about the part where he'd written of their last day together.

Dear Ma,

Just a line to let you know I am getting on all right. I hope you are the same. I am sorry I did not write before. We are so busy with

62

the training that I haven't had time. And then we were confined to barracks so I could not get a stamp. I'm in the same hut as Tommy and Teddy Hampson which is good. We talk about home lots of times. Tommy fell out with his mother before we left Nether Brook so he gets a bit upset. I try to cheer him up. If you see Mrs Hampson can you tell her about how Tommy feels, Ma, please? This is all at present.

Your loving son,
Arthur.

PS. Please give the envelope inside to Jessie but not when her stepfather is around.

They sat, each staring at the open door of the fire range. Jessie leant forward, her hands to the low flames. She was always cold these days.

'I don't suppose he's allowed to tell us much, Mrs Dawson.'

'Aye, you're probably right.' Edna folded her arms and sat back in the kitchen chair. 'So, that bit 'e says in your letter? That bit about your last day together? Was that when 'e told you he loved you, was it? At last.'

'What do you mean – at last?' Jessie glanced over her shoulder at her.

'He's been sweet on you for a long time.' Edna grinned. 'I told 'im to tell you but he said you were too young to know how you felt about 'im. He didn't want you to turn 'im down.'

'I'm sixteen, same as him, plenty old enough.' She couldn't stop the heat in her face and turned back to stare at the fire. The coals shifted and flared again. 'And I wouldn't. I didn't – turn him down.' She closed her eyes. 'I love Arthur and I'll be waiting for him to come home. Two months isn't that long. With a bit of luck he won't have been sent anywhere by the time this war is over.'

Chapter 20

November 1914

My Sweet Jessie,

Well, we're still here but not for much longer. I have to say we're dying to get a crack at the Hun. Tommy's got knuckle-dusters with him but I've told him we won't need them, we won't get that close, so don't worry, dear. Bit bored and tired now with all the training and marching for miles but one good thing, since one of the old blokes told us about putting candle grease in our socks, my feet don't get as blistered. Took a while to get used to these boots. Next time you hear from me, we'll be in the thick of it I hope. The top brass are still saying it'll be over by Christmas. I just hope we don't miss out. Still, will write often. I can't tell you how much I miss you.

Remember our heart stone, sweetheart.

Your loving Arthur xx

'Thank you, Jessie, love.' Edna passed the letter back to her. 'Looks as though he'll be going, whatever we thought.' She blew her nose. 'I'll put the kettle on. We both need a brew.'

Edna's answer to everything. It was the third cup since Jessie had arrived at the house an hour ago and the thought of yet another milky mug of tea made her feel queasy.

'He seems quite jolly from your letter though, Mrs Dawson?' She fingered the note his mother had shown her earlier. 'I didn't know you were sending him cigarettes. He didn't ask me.'

'He says he doesn't smoke much, but 'e can exchange fags for other stuff, so I sent some,' Edna said, her voice choked. 'I can't stand the thought of 'im needing anything. He says 'e's going to the front on the tenth? Just over a month of training and he's already going…'

She walked back to the table and slumped down on her chair. 'I was in the butcher's yesterday. He was telling the woman before me that our lot have had heavy casualties from some battle in France, that a load of the poor buggers are already on their way home wi' some awful injuries.' She moved her head from side to side, sucking in her cheeks. 'Dreadful.'

'Where did Mr Butland hear all this?'

Edna shrugged. 'I dunno. He said it was because there are more soldiers in the German army than we 'ave and that them in charge aren't letting us know how bad it is because they need even more of our lads to enlist. That's why we keep seeing that Kitchener chap in the papers, on them posters. Well, they've already got our Arthur. He's all I have left, Jessie.' She flipped a finger towards the letter Arthur had sent to her. 'And all he cares about is that I'll get three shillings from 'im as some sort of wages and the same from the War Office. Six shillings! Is that what he thinks I'm bothered about? Is that all 'e's worth to this awful war?' She swiped her hand over her face, over her eyes.

'He just wants to make sure you're being looked after, Mrs Dawson.' Jessie stretched her hand across the table.

'I know.' Edna took in a long breath and patted Jessie's fingers. 'And I told you, love, call me Edna.' She stretched her lips into a small smile. 'You're a lovely girl. Arthur chose well – even if it did take a war for him to tell you.'

It was something she'd said a lot over the last few weeks but Jessie didn't tire of hearing it. Each night she relived that last time they'd had together. And sharing her days with his mother at least got her away from the bakery. From Amos Morgan.

'I won't have another tea if you don't mind, Edna. I should get back to the shop.' Jessie stood, wrapping her shawl around her head. 'Thanks for giving me Arthur's letter.' She tucked it into her skirt pocket. It would go in her jewellery box, along with the others, locked away from Amos Morgan's snooping.

She knew she'd get a row from staying away from the bakery for the last hour. 'I told Mam I was coming here, not him. But I bet he'll have something to say when I get back.'

'He's a bully,' was all Edna said. She kissed Jessie on the cheek. 'See you tomorrow?'

They shared a low chuckle.

'Of course. He'll not stop me.'

But when Jessie crossed the cobbles on the road, she could see him peering out of the shop window, his face contorted with anger.

Deliberately she passed the shop without making eye contact and turned into the passageway at the end of the terrace. At the back gate she paused, her hand on the latch, and breathed in a long draw of air.

'It's okay, shop's busy. I just heard the bell go.' Bob pulled the gate open from the other side. 'He's been looking for you though.'

'Mam?'

'Upstairs 'aving a lie down. I finished wiping down the last of the trays for 'er after I'd cleared out the oven ashes.' He tilted his head, struggling at the same time to put his arms into the sleeves of his overcoat. 'Been to see the 'ero's mother 'ave you?'

'Don't call him that.' Jessie's momentary gratitude for his help dissolved into irritation. She glanced up to her mother's bedroom window. The curtains were drawn, shutting out the late afternoon light. 'Was she not feeling well?'

'I don't know.' Bob's tone was petulant. He refused to look at her when he stood to one side to let her pass. 'I thought you'd be at least grateful I did the trays. I could 'ave left them for you.' His arms drooped by his side.

'I am.' Jessie touched his hand. It twitched as though Bob was going to catch hold of her and she quickly moved away. 'I'll go and check on Mam.'

Bob didn't answer. As she opened the bakery door she heard him bang the gate shut. She sighed. She liked Bob but his resentment of Arthur made her uneasy. He'd chosen not to enlist. It was his decision to stay on at the bakery. Her next thought came unbidden: perhaps his bitterness was a disguise for relief because he had a reserved occupation.

Stop it, she told herself; he didn't deserve her scepticism. It was just fretting for Arthur that was making her think like that. She wouldn't be right until she heard from him again.

She refused to even imagine what being 'in the thick of it' meant.

Chapter 21

November

'Jessie?'

'Clara!' She hadn't heard the back gate open. It was only when the cold air swept into the bakery that she realised her friend was standing, breathless, in the doorway. 'Come in, come in.'

Dropping the brown paper she was using to grease the cake tins into one of them, she wiped her hands on her apron, took a quick look at the clock on the wall and then at the darkness outside. 'It's five o'clock in the morning, what are you doing here?' She closed the door. 'Come through to the kitchen. It's warmer in there.'

Clara followed her, watching while Jessie shifted the smouldering coals around, releasing warmth.

'I couldn't wait to tell you my news. I'm – we're – Stanley and me – we're going to have a baby.'

'No!' Jessie straightened up to hug her. 'How wonderful!' She leant back to look at Clara. 'It is wonderful, isn't it? You look pleased, I must say, but what about your farm work? Does Stanley know? Have you written to tell him? He'll be over the moon. Will he be able to get leave? Oh, I hope so, for your sake.'

Clara giggled. 'Stop, you're making my head spin. But yes, I've written to Stanley. He should get the letter next week, I think.'

'Sit down.' Jessie pushed the armchair nearer to the hearth. 'Cup of tea?'

'One thing at a time.' Clara took a breath, unbuttoned her coat and sat. 'I won't have a tea, if you don't mind. I'm going to my parents' in Greenbridge and I'm not sure I'd last before needing the lavatory. It's a good two hours on the train.'

'Oh, okay. I never thought of that.'

'Trips to the lavatory? One of the drawbacks...' She smiled. 'A very small price to pay, of course.'

'When will the baby arrive?'

'The doctor says the baby will be born in May.' She smiled again. 'Shall I tell you something?' She put her hand to her mouth as though considering, before giving a slight nod. 'Please don't be shocked. When Stanley told me he was going to fight, I was very angry with him...' She stopped.

'He signed up at the same time as Arthur, didn't he?' Jessie said.. 'The same day as Tommy and Teddy Hampson, as well.' She remembered Mrs Hampson, coming into the shop, declaring how proud she was that her twins were part of the Nether Brook Pals alongside the young men from Kindle Mill.

'He did. I was so upset with him. But that night I made a decision. I wanted him to love me.' Her face coloured a vivid pink. 'You know...'

Jessie shifted in her chair, embarrassed.

'He didn't want to. He said it wouldn't be fair to me if I – if I was on my own and – you know – if I had a child.' She looked away, towards the kitchen door and lowered her voice. 'I wouldn't take no for an answer ... I love him. I wanted a baby. I wanted a baby, a child, his child, just in case he didn't come back to me.'

'Don't think like that, Clara. Of course he will. And so will Arthur. You'll see, they'll be back with us in no time.'

'Yes, well, I couldn't chance that. And so...' She waved her hand over her stomach. 'Here I am.'

'And you're well?'

'Oh, yes. I do miss Stanley such a lot though. And you must miss Arthur? I wasn't surprised when I received your note to say you were walking out with him. I could tell he was sweet on you that day in Blackpool.'

'Could you?'

'Of course. And you him.'

'We wasted so much time. We didn't get much chance to be walking out. And only his mam knows we were – are – will be, when he gets back. I haven't even told Mam yet. I had a letter last week from him. But the post seems to take ages either way.'

'I know. It's a fortnight since Stanley's last letter. Hopefully I'll hear from him soon. I told him to write to my parents' address in Greenbridge. I'm going to stay with them until the baby comes. But I couldn't leave without coming to see you first.'

'I'm so glad you did.'

Clara glanced at the mantelpiece clock. 'I'll need to go shortly.'

Jessie heard the creaks of the floorboards upstairs.

'He'll be down in a minute,' she said, the skin around her mouth tightening.

'Things still as bad?'

'Yes.' Worse than you know, Jessie thought, and wondered whether to confide in her friend.

'Anything I can help with?'

'No. It will be all right, I'm sure.' Are you, she asked herself? The man was a menace, him and his revolting wandering hands. But what could Clara do?

'If you're sure?'

Jessie nodded, flapped her fingers. 'It'll be fine.'

'I'll get off to the railway station, then.'

'I'll walk with you.' Jessie wiped her greasy hands on her white apron, untied it, and went through the kitchen to unhook her coat from the hall. She followed Clara to the back door. Rain slanted over the doorstep and glistened in the grey-flagged floor.

She heard Amos Morgan shuffling down the stairs.

'Come on,' she said, opening Clara's large umbrella for her. If only she was leaving here as well.

They huddled underneath the umbrella and splashed towards the back gate.

Chapter 22

December 1914

It was almost three weeks since Arthur's last letters. However many times Jessie reassured Edna that it wasn't the same as when he was in the camp at Preston, that they couldn't expect to hear from him every week, still the fear lay cold in her stomach all the time.

A fear that consumed so much of her mind, she couldn't bring herself to answer Clara's almost daily letters full of details about her life in Greenbridge. Short cheerful notes which, somehow, stopped Jessie putting pen to paper, unwilling to let Clara know how unhappy she felt, even though her friend asked time and time again about how she was. She was ashamed to admit she had had twinges of envy at Clara's contented tone.

And her mother had been ill with a chest infection for a whole week.

Jessie battled every day with Amos Morgan to get help for Dorothy.

'Arthur's mother will know what Mam needs.'

'I'm not having that old witch in this house.'

Jessie clenched her teeth, biting back her anger. 'Then the doctor—'

'I'm not made of money.' He slammed shut the drawer of the cash register. 'Cost a fortune, a bloody fortune, do doctors.'

'It wouldn't be your money. It would be our money, Mam's and mine. I wouldn't ask you for money.' I wouldn't ask you for anything, Jessie added in her mind. 'I would have thought you'd want my mother to get better, if only so she could be back in the shop.'

'We do all right between the two of us, don't we?' He gave her a lascivious grin that sickened Jessie.

'You really are disgusting.' She pushed his hand off her waist. 'If Mam knew what you ware really like—'

'She'd do nowt.' He laughed. 'She's weak, your mother, she won't say boo to a goose. And before you ask again, like I said, I'm not having no doctor in this house.'

'Then I will go and get Mrs Dawson.' Jessie glared, before pushing past him to go up the stairs. 'And you won't stop me.'

'Keep her out of my way and mind you make sure she knows she'll get nowt if she does come,' he called after her.

She ignored him.

Her mother appeared to be sleeping. Jessie looked down at her; her face was flushed and each breath crackled in her throat.

She jumped when her mother whispered, 'What time is it?' Dorothy squeezed her eyelids tight before opening them. 'I can smell the bread.'

'Nine o'clock.' Jessie perched on the edge of her mother's bed. 'How are you feeling today?'

'I'm fine. You shouldn't have let me sleep in again.' Dorothy pulled at her pillow behind her and shuffled up against the iron headrail. 'The orders...'

'Are all done. I got up the same time as him, and Bob was already here, firing up the oven as usual. We did them together.'

She didn't mention her stepfather's wandering hands. It was cramped enough in the bakery with only two working there. Worse with the three of them, almost unbearable when Eddie came to help out with the clearing up. She didn't tell her mother how she cringed, hearing with dread the scrape of his boots on the flag floor each time he came near her. How she hated his rapid breath on the side of her neck. Or how she failed to stop him brushing her breasts with the back of his hand each time he reached past her to pick up something, anything, on the shelves by the counter where she was rolling the pastry for the meat pies.

But it was as though her mother could read her mind. While she wouldn't acknowledge her husband's obsession with her daughter, Jessie was sure Dorothy knew. Just as she knew there was little she could do about it. His temper had appeared after their marriage and she was only too aware that her mother was afraid of him.

71

So when Dorothy asked, 'No problems?' Jessie smiled and answered, 'Just tired.'

She stood when she heard the coke in the oven being rattled, the clatter of the pie trays. 'It sounds as if Bob's started on the clearing up again. He's been so good while you've not been well. You have another day here and I'm going to get Arthur's mother to call over and see what she suggests for you.'

'Good gracious, no.' Her mother tried to push back the bedclothes. 'It's just a bit of a cold.'

'That's kept you in bed for over the last week.' Jessie covered her over again. 'Another day or so won't hurt,' she insisted. 'Now stay there while I go and get Mrs Dawson.'

'I've made this mustard poultice to put on your chest, Mrs Jen — Morgan. Can I...?' Edna Dawson waited until Jessie's mother nodded before opening the front of her nightdress and putting the muslin in place. 'Normally I'd spread it on, but it'll be just as effective in this.' She refastened the ties of Dorothy's nightie. 'An' I've made up this expectorant from the juice of thyme. Take it at least three times a day. We'll soon have you as right as rain.' Edna straightened, folding her hands on her stomach in satisfaction.

'Thanks, Edna.' Jessie smiled at her.

'Thank you, Mrs Dawson.'

'Well now, it seems daft for your daughter to be calling me by my first name and not you, Dorothy. So how about we skip the formalities? After all, now I've seen you in your night attire...' She gave a soft chuckle.

'Edna, then.'

There was a loud yell from the shop. 'You thinking of doing some work today, girl?'

Jessie pulled a face. 'I'd better go.'

'Aye, and me. Leave you in peace to get some sleep, Dorothy. Don't forget where I am. I can come across anytime.'

'Have you heard from your Arthur lately?'

'No, not lately.' The woman's tone was bleak.

Jessie stood still at the door, her fingers on the handle. She didn't turn around. Out on the landing she pressed her hands against the walls, gulping against her misery.

Chapter 23

It took another week before Dorothy was fit enough to leave her bed. On the following Sunday, Amos demanded they attend chapel. Afterwards they sat in silence around the small table in the kitchen eating the slices of bullock's heart, turnip, cabbage and boiled potatoes that Jessie had prepared earlier. There was no conversation between them; mealtimes were for eating not talking, according to Amos. The only sound was the dull crack of his jaw with each chew.

Dorothy ate little. Head down and never making eye contact with Jessie, she constantly stifled a cough.

'Are you all right, Mam?'

Her mother gave her a slight smile and nodded. She put her fork down and took a sip of water. Her hand trembled.

'She'd be better if you helped more,' Amos said, through a mouthful of meat. He still wore his best chapel suit, shirt and tie and had tucked a large white handkerchief into his collar to protect it from the gravy.

'Jessie's doing a lot in the bakery, Amos.' Dorothy fingered the cuff of her white linen blouse where the water had dripped on it.

Amos frowned. 'Don't make a mess of your blouse, Dotty. Cost me a pretty penny, that did. You'll have to starch it again.'

'Sorry, dear.'

'Aye, and she can carry on working in there until you're proper rested. She's doing nowt else.'

He was gloating; he knew she would say nothing to her mother. And even if she did, there was nothing Dorothy could do about the furtive touches that she endured. She often wondered if Bob saw. But what could he do anyway?

'I'm not really hungry, Mam. May I leave the table?' Jessie moved the turnips and cabbage to cover the meat and put down her knife and fork.

'Stay where you are.' Amos picked at his teeth with his thumbnail. 'This meat's a bit tough, Dotty.' Gravy dripped down his chin and he wiped it away with the back of his hand. 'I thought I told you I didn't care for bullock's heart?'

Jessie caught her top lip between her teeth. How she hated everything about him.

'Jessie said it was cheaper at the butcher's, dear. I thought you'd be pleased. And I know she soaked it for two hours.' Dorothy's tone was apologetic. 'And she used the best forcemeat, though only with one egg. I am trying to keep the eggs for the cakes.'

'That'll be it then. Or she hasn't basted it enough.' A potato fell off his fork onto the flowered oilcloth covering the table. 'No need for us to skimp, though,' he added, picking up the potato with his fingers and stuffing it into his mouth. 'I can always get plenty of eggs.'

'Yes – no, Amos.' Dorothy took another sip of water, forcing back another cough. 'Sorry…'

Amos sat sideways to the table, his foot crossed over his other leg. It jerked, just missing Jessie's knee. She saw the half-hidden leer.

'Mam?' She had to leave the table; she couldn't stand being near the man any longer.

'Amos?' Dorothy was almost pleading.

'Oh, get away, then.' He licked his knife and waved it in her direction, dismissing her.

The relief mixed with anger. She pushed her chair back and stood. Crossing the kitchen, she placed her plate by the sink. 'I'll wash up afterwards, Mam. When I've changed out of these clothes.'

'Should think so too.' Amos didn't look up. 'What's for pudding, Dotty?'

Jessie perched on the windowsill in her bedroom, nibbling at the skin at the side of her thumbnail, relieved it was evening and she was free to stay in her room. She missed Clara so much. The last short note from her was full of joy. She was enjoying being fussed over by her parents in Greenbridge and she'd written to Stanley, who was thrilled about the baby and was hoping to be home by the time it was born. Jessie wondered if he knew something about the war that was not being reported in the papers. Might it end soon? How she prayed for that to be true. And not just for herself, but for her friends as well.

The street gaslights were already flickering, spreading a wavering, pale glow onto the wet pavement. There were faint lights behind the curtains of some of the houses opposite, but not Edna's.

Keeping positive for the two of them was hard, but Jessie knew Arthur would want her to.

It was only at night that she let her anguish spill over.

Chapter 24

December

Jessie held her breath when she saw the postman stop his tricycle outside Edna's house. She watched him fumble through the sacks in the basket fastened to the handlebars and take out a bundle of envelopes and parcels. When he walked past Edna's door without halting, she closed her eyes; the agonising disappointment expelled in a sigh.

'You serving or what?' Below the counter, Amos gave her thigh a vicious pinch.

Jessie scowled at him. 'Sorry, Mrs Wetherall,' she said to the large woman, who was waiting with her hand out to take the loaf that Jessie had wrapped in tissue paper. 'That'll be tuppence ha'penny please.'

'Head in the clouds,' the woman said, but smiled. She turned as the shop doorbell rang. 'Like your new tricycle, Wilfred,' she said to the postman. 'Should think it's easier than carrying your bag around over your shoulder.'

'Oh, it is, Missus. First in the district an' all. Bit awkward to ride at first, 'aving three wheels, like, but getting' the 'ang of it now.'

The postman! Jessie peered round the woman. Grinning, he waved an envelope in his hand. 'Letter for you, Jessie. From Army Postal Service no less. You got a sweetheart?' He reached around Mrs Wetherall to give it to her.

Before she could take it, Amos Morgan tried to snatch it from the postman's fingers. 'I'll have that.'

Wilfred held it higher. 'You won't. That's His Majesty's official post and it's not addressed to you.'

Jessie pushed past her stepfather to grasp the envelope, the blood pulsing loud in her ears. 'Thank you, Wilfred.' Ignoring her stepfather's annoyed shout, she pulled open the door and ran from the shop and across the street, ripping open the envelope and taking out the two pieces of paper.

'Mrs Dawson! Mrs Dawson. Edna.' She hammered on the door.

It was flung open. Arthur's mother clutched her hands to her throat. 'What? What is it?' Her voice wavered, shrill and high.

'A letter, a letter from Arthur. Look, it's his handwriting.'

'Oh dear Lord.' Edna fell back against the door. 'Come in. Come in.' She grabbed Jessie's arm and pulled her into the hallway. They hugged. Jessie could feel the older woman's body quivering.

'Let's sit down.' She led Edna into the kitchen. 'Here.' Jessie pulled out two chairs from the table. 'I'll put the kettle on...'

'No. Read it. Read it, first. Please.'

The relief suddenly hit Jessie, her legs gave way and she bumped down onto the chair. Fingers shaking, she opened the envelope and took out two pieces of paper. Unfolding the first, she saw the heading.

'This one's for you.' She handed it to Edna.

'I wonder why he didn't send it here? Why address it to you?'

'I don't know. But at least he's let us know he's safe.' Jessie was already reading her letter:

My Sweet Jessie,

Well, here I am, though I know I can't tell you where, dearest. I am missing you so much and think of you all the time and I keep your letters in my pocket over my heart which makes me feel safe. Which is good because we were only here a few hours before we went into the trenches. We were there for eight days and then came on to what is called a Rest Camp. I suppose it is called that to distinguish it from the trenches because the men are at work all day, trench making. But we are still under both rifle and artillery fire. We got here at 7 o'clock yesterday morning and were shelled at 9 o'clock. In the trenches it is fairly bad, they are so narrow and smell something awful and we are being potted at and shelled all the time. A turn of eight days was really quite long enough because it is hard work and even when you do turn in for a rest you have to be ready to turn out at once on an alarm. The dirt falls on your face when you are trying to sleep and when it rains you're up to your knees in mud in no time, and that always seems to be at night.

And that's when the memory of when we were together gets me through the long hours. That and the lovely scarf and socks you sent. They came with the other parcels last week. I didn't even know you could knit, my love. Tommy Hampson, yes, he's here with me, is very jealous. He says his mam can't knit for toffee. We had rum served out tonight and do you know, Jessie, I can't bear the stuff.

I wanted to tell you a bit of what it's like out here but not Mother. You know how she worries. I don't want her opening the envelope first and reading this. So I'm chancing sending it to you in the hopes he doesn't get hold of it. Promise you won't let her read this. And promise to write soon, dear. I wait every day for your letters as I

hope you wait for mine. We are lucky here, the post chaps from the
Royal Engineers come round every day to collect our letters for home
so expect to hear from me often, even if it's only a few lines. And we
also have something called a field postcard which I will send when
I don't have time to write. Do not worry if bits of my letters are
blacked out, it will be because I have said something which might
be of use to the enemy but I will try hard not to do that.
<u>*Remember our heart stone, sweetheart.*</u>
Always yours, Your loving Arthur xx

Jessie put the paper to her lips. Arthur was making almost
nothing of what he was going through, but she was perfectly capable
of reading between the lines. And she read the newspapers: the
reports of the cold, wet weather, and accounts of what it was like
for the men, living in the trenches and being shelled and fired on.
She'd seen the list of casualties, the obituaries.

She waited, those thoughts running through her head as she
watched Edna laboriously reading, mouthing the words.

When his mother finally raised her head, Jessie nodded. 'It doesn't
seem to be too bad where he is, does it?' She folded her letter and
slipped it into her overall pocket, ignoring the other woman's frown.

'You can read mine if you like.' The hint was obvious.

'No, you're fine, Edna. As long as we know he's safe...'

'Hmm – well. 'E sounds it. He says it's cold. but they've been
given nice thick underclothes and waterproofs and top boots. And
he says the food is as good as anyone could want. I suppose I 'ave to
be satisfied with that. Does he say the same in your letter?'

'Much the same.'

'Daft bat that I am. Course you don't want me to read 'is letter!'
Edna shook her head, gave a low laugh. 'He's probably said stuff he
wouldn't want 'is mam to read, eh?'

Jessie couldn't stop the heat rising to her cheeks. But all she said
was, 'He's safe. That's all we need to know.'

Back in the shop, Amos ignored her for the rest of the day.

Chapter 25

Jessie knew there was something wrong, almost as if she'd been waiting for it. She'd sensed she was being watched more than usual.

She lay still, forcing herself to breath evenly and listened. Every nerve in her body screamed at her to leap from the bed. And then the smell of sweat and the unsteady scuff on the linoleum told her what had woken her: Amos Morgan was standing within inches of her bed.

'What do you want?' She spoke into the darkness.

There was no reply. Her skin crawled, cold with fear. For a moment she thought to yell out to her mother, but then she felt his hot breath on her ear and his hand over her mouth.

'Don't even think about it.'

The bedclothes moved and she tried to twist away. Too late: his other hand cupped between her thighs as he kneeled on the mattress. Throwing the covers to one side, he lay on top of her, his fingers probing. 'Be nice now, missy—'

'No!' She grabbed his hair and yanked his head back. She heaved her body upwards, throwing him off balance, away from her. She heard the thump as he fell to the floor and she scrambled to the other side of the bed, clasping the eiderdown in front of her. The darkness in the room was dense, the fear thick in her throat.

'Get out.' She pushed the words through gasps of breath, shifting her head from side to side in an effort to catch any movement from him. 'Get out.'

She heard him grunt, a rustle that told her he was holding onto the edge of the bed, trying to stand. Moving quickly, she crossed to the door and wrenched it open. 'Out!' she yelled.

'Jessie?' Pale wavering candlelight surrounded the figure of her mother in the doorway. 'Amos? What's happening?'

'Ask him. Ask him, Mother.' Jessie put as much contempt in her voice as she could, a mixture of distress and relief.

She watched the man shuffle past in his nightshirt. He shoved Dorothy back into their bedroom and slammed the door closed.

'Ask him,' Jessie whispered, turning into the darkness of her own room.

Her legs gave way and she almost fell onto the end of her bed. Reaching for the stub of the candle on her bedside table, she lit it. Shadows flickered on the landing wall. She leaned over and pushed the door shut, and then scrambled backwards until she was pressed against the iron bedrail. Dragging the covers up to her shoulders, Jessie drew her knees to her chest and wrapped her arms around them, wondering when she'd ever feel safe again.

She didn't sleep. It was hours before she heard Bob rattling the dead cinders from the oven, his loud tuneless whistle grating on her.

Chapter 26

'What am I to do, Edna,?' The hatred in her for Amos Morgan made Jessie's hands shake 'Every night I think he'll get into my room. I can't bear to be near him.' The thought of his hard fingers brushing against her breast or buttocks was repugnant.

'Well, yer can't go on like this, that's for certain. You're living in a bloody nightmare. And with my Arthur not around to protect you we 'ave to think of summat. Especially now we've seen this.'

Edna poked at the newspaper on the table. 'After everything we were told about this blasted war. I can't believe it.' Jessie looked down at it; they'd brooded over the words when she'd first brought it into Edna's kitchen an hour earlier. The heading on the front page burned in her brain.

The False Belief of the Duration of the War
10th December 1914
Ever since the outbreak of war, speculation has been widespread as to its duration. The belief that it would be a three-month campaign to be followed by a collapse of Germany's economy has proved

altogether misleading. The confident assertions that it would be 'all over by Christmas' have grown fewer and fewer. Germany's resistance is great. Now Lord Kitchener forecasts that we are to be at war for another three years at least.

'Arthur could be away from us for years,' Edna said, bitterly.

Jessie nodded. All at once the room seemed to be closing in on her. 'I'm sorry I need to get out.'

'Not back there?' The alarm flushed Edna's face. 'Not while your Mam's in bed?'

'No.' Her mother had taken to having afternoon naps while Bob and Eddie helped in the shop. 'No, not there.' Jessie didn't even call it her home anymore. 'I need some fresh air, Edna, I'll see you later. And I'll be fine,' she whispered, hugging her.

'Yer will.' There was a hard edge to her voice. 'I'll make sure you'll be all right. Leave it with me.'

'What?' Jessie frowned. 'What do you mean, Edna?'

'You'll see. Leave it with me.'

The cold burned into Jessie's lungs with each gasped breath. The sky seemed to press down, heavy with the snow that brooded in the clouds above Nether Brook. The wind made her eyes water. It was only when she had counted a hundred and twenty steps and stopped to put her hand on the heart stone, mouthing the words on Arthur's love note, that Edna's words came back to her. Then it wasn't the wind that made the tears stream down her face...

Chapter 27

'I don't understand.' Jessie stared at the two leaves nestled in Edna's palm.

'It's foxglove. Put it in the stew tonight. Be careful neither you nor yer Mam eat it once you've done that.' Edna took hold of Jessie's

81

hand and curled her fingers around the leaf. 'Make sure you get yours, then put it in just before you dish his up.'

Jessie shook her head slightly, just the once.

'Yes,' Edna insisted.

'What will happen to him?' Jessie was fearful of the answer.

'He won't die. But the sickness will be enough to keep him in bed.' Edna nodded her head towards the little building in her backyard. 'Or in the privy.' She gave a short scornful noise, almost a laugh. 'The right place for him.'

'I don't know...'

'Yer want him to keep away from you, don't yer?'

'Yes. Oh, yes.'

'This will give you a few days of peace.'

If only, Jessie thought. 'Okay. What must I do?'

'Crumble it into his stew, after you've taken yours and yer Mam's, and stir it well in. If you can leave it a minute or two, so much the better. Afterwards, the old sod will be too busy nursing his painful belly, having the runs and being sick to be mithering you.'

'A few days?'

Edna moved her head in agreement. 'Or, if you're lucky a week or so. They say it can raise the dead and it can kill the living. But this small amount won't kill 'im, it'll just make 'im feel as though it will.' Her face was grim. 'And no more than he deserves. The owd bastard. Now I'm off to confession.' Unexpectedly, before she left, she winked at Jessie.

It worked. Jessie, with trembling fingers, crushed the tiny piece of leaf into Amos' stew in the evening, and that night she lay awake listening to him vomiting into the chamber pot he kept under his side of the bed and thundering down the stairs and out through the back door.

Jessie crept into her mother's bedroom. It stank, a vile sour smell. 'You all right, Mam?'

'Yes, love. I think he's eaten something that doesn't agree with him.' Dorothy rose up on one elbow and reached over to light the candle. When she turned back to face Jessie, the lines around her mouth were deep. 'No doubt I'll be blamed for it.'

A stab of guilt vied with the sense of satisfaction inside Jessie.

'He'll probably be fine in the morning.' Hopefully not. 'If you're all right...'

'Yes, you go back to bed, love. No point in us all being awake. And I'll need to move that.' Dorothy thrust her arms in her pink dressing gown and pointing to the chamber pot.

'Do you want me to empty it?' Dreading the answer, Jessie stepped back, letting her mother pass her, the throne held at arm's length.

'Good gracious, no. It's not your job to clean up after your stepfa – after him.'

But it is my fault, Jessie thought, when she blew out her candle and slipped under the bedclothes. Strangely, she felt no guilt about that.

The following days were a mix of peace and trepidation. Except for the fleeting moments as he stumbled past them to get to the lavvy, Amos Morgan had disappeared from her life. Whenever they heard him retching, Bob and Eddie grimaced at one another and talked more loudly or clattered the tin trays. The three of them were managing both the baking and the shop. Dorothy wasn't much use. As Bob dared to say once or twice, she was constantly, at her husband's beck and call, even though she still looked fragile herself. Jessie soothed her remorse about the extra work she'd given to her mother by telling herself that the man was too weak to bully Dorothy now. Even while cleaning up the vomit or sitting alongside her husband cooling his forehead with cold cloths, Dorothy appeared to be more content than she had for a while.

Even so, Jessie still pushed the chair under the handle of her door; the terror still swept through her in the dark, lonely hours of the night.

As the days passed, the fear that she could have killed Amos Morgan lessened. Edna was right: the fragment of foxglove leaf was only capable of keeping him in his sickbed. Yet the worry lingered that he would suspect his illness was her fault. Occasionally, returning from the lavvy, he would catch her glancing at him and scowl. Then she would meet his gaze calmly, hoping he was still too weak to be any danger.

However, as Edna often said, all good things come to an end.

Even so, she gave Jessie another foxglove leaf when she came to visit on Christmas Eve.

'Oh, I couldn't,' Jessie said. 'It's too soon. Someone would realise.'

Edna nodded. 'Something to keep for when it all gets too much. He's still stopping in bed most of the time anyway, you say?'

'Yes.'

'So I don't suppose he's up for eating much at the moment?'

'I don't suppose he is.'

Edna got up and bustled about, peering into a large steaming cooking pot on the range and occasionally stirring a spoon in a saucepan next to it.

'I was wondering if you and your mam would come 'ere for a bite to eat tomorrow?' She hurried on, holding up her hand to stop Jessie answering. 'I doubt yer Mam will feel like cooking; she must be exhausted after this last week or so.'

She crossed her arms and faced Jessie. 'And I'm not saying that because I feel bad about what we did and you mustn't either. That man got everything he deserves. But it'll do the both of yer good to get out of that 'ouse for a couple of hours. I've some celery stewing in milk here and I'll make a white sauce to pour over it with a bit of cheese and some breadcrumbs. We can have it lovely and hot with some of the potatoes and turnips Mrs Whittle off Golders Terrace gave me after I gave her the poultice for her husband's chest. And...'

There was triumph in her voice when she gestured to the cooking pot where the steam was rhythmically lifting the lid.

'I've made a Christmas pudding. There's no eggs in it, o' course, but carrot is just as good to keep it nice and moist and help make it a bit sweet – with it not having much sugar. The longer I let it boil, the richer it will be.'

All this said in such a rush that Jessie had no chance to get a word in.

'It's very kind of you, Edna, but I doubt Mam will come. She'll not want to leave him.' And he wouldn't let her, she added to herself. 'And I can't leave her...'

She faltered, watching the light of excitement in the older woman's eyes turn bleak. 'Let me ask her anyhow. It would be a lovely change for her. And,' she added, 'it all smells so tasty.'

Edna sat at the table, her hands flat on the surface. 'I'd be glad not to be on my own, Jessie, love. 'Appen it'll stop me mithering 'bout where Arthur is and what he's doing.'

'I know.' Jessie covered Edna's hands with her own. 'I feel the same. I worry all the time about why we haven't heard from him. But,' she stood up, 'no news is good news, is what I tell myself. I'll go over to ask Mam right away, Edna.' She deliberated for a moment. 'Oh, what the heck, one way or another, we'll both be over here tomorrow.' Whatever the old bugger says, she thought, inwardly smiling at her swear word.

To her surprise, it didn't take much to persuade Dorothy to cross Castle Street for a few hours on Christmas Day. Jessie didn't ask what she'd said to her husband. All she knew was that, for the first time in ages, she heard her mother laugh. And watched her eat her food with enjoyment.

After dinner, while the two older women snoozed by the fire, Jessie slipped her arms into Arthur's old overcoat and made her way up the fields on Wharmton Hill. The crisp air burned into her lungs and she was gasping by the time she stopped.

'A hundred and twenty,' she whispered, lifting the heart stone off the wall to pick up the note. The paper was softened now, thin at the folds, the words slightly blurred by damp.

'I love you,' Jessie read aloud. 'I love you.' For once, the phrase brought little comfort.

She straightened and turned to look back at Nether Brook. The low sun was a flash of steel through thin layers of clouds. The lines of the buildings in the village were sharp, the edges of the roofs hard and, here and there, windows, glinted.

'Well, I'm here, Arthur. Where are you?'

His words echoed in her thoughts. 'A hundred and twenty days between today and Christmas Day. That's how long everybody says this war will last … on Christmas Day I want you to come up here to our heart stone to meet me … I'll be home in no time. You won't even miss me.'

'Oh, I do, I have, my love. And you promised you'd be here now.' She tilted her head back and shouted to the heavens, 'You promised!'

Though she hadn't known it at the time, Jessie looked back on that day as the last peace she was to have for some time.

Chapter 28

January 1915

How had she not realised? Jessie sank onto the bedroom floor and lowered her face to her knees. She rocked, her arms over her head, her mouth dry with fear. A sudden line of light underneath the door and the sound of Amos Morgan stumbling down the stairs, made her straighten up. The thought of how it would be, how he would react, tightened her scalp.

It hadn't been the knocker-up woman rattling the hard peas against the bedroom windows, as she made her way down the street, which woke Jessie earlier. Nor the muffled horse hooves and wheels of the Nightman's cart carrying the waste pails past on the snow-covered cobbles. What had woken Jessie was the strange fluttering in her stomach, a rippling under her palm when she placed her hand on her belly.

She should have known: the feelings, the changes to her body that Clara described in her letters, that she had refused to acknowledge in her own body.

She started whimpering and it frightened her. It was a sound she couldn't stop, it escaped even with both her hands pressed tight over her mouth. And then she was gagging, choking, coughing up the bile, as she had been doing for weeks. She'd thought it was worry for Arthur or fear of her stepfather. Not for a moment had she thought there was a baby inside her.

She dragged the chamber pot from under the bed and hung over it, cold sweat on the back of her neck.

'Jessie?'

The soft scrape of nails on the door was the signal her mother had devised so that Jessie would know it was her and not Amos. Dorothy tried, in her own way, to protect her daughter.

It wasn't enough to stop him. The low creak of the handle turning, the slight shift of the chair legs on the linoleum, his crackling heavy breath on the other side of the door, happened most nights. Sometimes she wondered if he kept doing it out of some sort of sadistic pleasure, as if he knew he wouldn't actually get into her room; his actions were only to terrify her. And, although she didn't let him see her distress, he always succeeded.

The next soft scrape was accompanied by a slight jiggle on the handle.

'Jessie?'

Jessie tucked sweaty, damp strands of her hair behind her ears and crawled to the door to move the chair, still silently heaving.

Dorothy slipped through the gap and closed it with care. 'What is it, love? Are you ill?' The light of the candle, held at waist height, emphasised the tense lines around her mouth and between her eyes.

There was no avoiding it. Jessie would have to tell her mother. And tell her now. But what would happen then? If only her father was alive. He would have enfolded her in his arms, told her it would be all right. He would have protected her from the outrage and gossip that would inevitably follow as soon it was known she was having a child and not married.

Jessie clenched her teeth with bitterness. She hoisted herself onto the bed and pulled the covers over her, fingers tight on the cotton sheet.

'Jessie?' Her mother held the candle higher. 'Talk to me.'

Though all she wanted was to be held by her mother, Jessie turned her head away, angry that her mother had brought Amos Morgan into their house, fear into their lives.

And then the baby moved again. Shame overtook any other emotion. She sat up, her hands on her stomach.

'What is it?' Dorothy took a step towards her, followed Jessie's gaze. 'Oh, no,' she whispered, eyes wide with shock. 'You're not ... How?'

Jessie was engulfed in resentment at her mother's next words.

'What will Amos say? What will he do?'

Chapter 29

'Spoiled goods, that's what you are. Who'd have you now?' Amos Morgan sneered. His thin lips worked over his teeth. Not a tall man, he looked wizened after his illness and even more stooped, but still his words still frightened Jessie. She knew he was right: if Arthur didn't write, didn't tell her that they would be married, that he would make her respectable, she was ruined.

Her mother's arms were around her waist, but that meant nothing. The man who stood in front of her, who she despised more than anyone in the world, held her future in his hands.

'Pack your bags and get out.'

'Amos, no,' Dorothy protested. 'It's bitter cold out there. Sleeting. Please...' She'd paced the kitchen all day, fretful and restless, waiting until the shop was closed to tell him. The constant, fearful tears blurring her features. Now, even though Jessie saw her mother's face crumpled with apprehension, she still battled to protect her daughter in her own feeble way.

Jessie kept her head bowed. She wasn't ready for what happened next. Amos swung the back of his hand across her face. She wasn't braced for the blow and she fell backwards, dragging her mother with her to the floor.

He didn't even glance at them as he stamped back into the bakery. It was too early to open the shop but Bob and Eddie were already at work. Jessie listened to him shouting at them and her cheeks burned with shame. They would have heard everything,

'Don't go.' Dorothy face was pale.

'I have to. You heard him, Mam. I'll be all right. I'll go to Edna's; she'll take me in.' Jessie put her hand over her stomach, protecting the life that was growing unbidden within her. 'She'll look after us.'

Amos Morgan was waiting for Jessie at the foot of the stairs when she left her bedroom with her valise crammed with everything she owned.

'Don't think you'll ever set foot in this place again.'

He stood in her way, forcing her to stop on the step above him. She willed herself to feel contempt for him, but the venom in his face terrified her and she instinctively held the case in front of her like a shield.

'Let me pass.'

'I'll let you pass when I'm good and ready. When I've said what I want to. You're a slut, that's what you are, and I'll make sure I don't let her,' he jerked his head upwards towards Dorothy standing on the landing, 'see you either.'

Gripping hold of her arm, he shoved her off the stair tread and manhandled her through the bakery.

'I need my coat. My hat.'

'You'll go in what you stand up in.'

Bob and Eddie swung around to watch, open-mouthed, their hands dripping water from the wet loaf tins onto the floor. Jessie saw Bob take a step forward, his eyes narrowed, saw Eddie hold him back. She shook her head, relieved that Amos hadn't noticed.

He flung open the door. A flurry of snow swept in on a rush of cold air. 'Sluts leave the back way.' He gave Jessie a final brutal push. He was going to follow, but he stumbled over Bob's outstretched foot.

She landed on the flagstones on her knees, her hand on her stomach. The heat of pain juddered through her, vying with the icy, wet snow already soaking through the back of her blouse. Impeded by her long skirt, she scrambled to her knees. The flakes were thickening; in the light from the bakery window a slow thin line of sleet and water glistened as it trickled towards the grid in the middle of the yard. Jessie knew the ground would soon be thick with ice. Shivers goose-pimpled her skin. Gathering her skirt in her hands, she pushed herself to her feet. Amos was yelling in the bakery. Bob would suffer for helping her. Another reason to feel shame.

There was tapping on the window above her.

Her mother was silhouetted against a flickering candlelight; both hands pressing up the window frame. It opened just enough for Dorothy to push a shawl through the gap. Jessie caught hold of it before it landed on the wet ground. She wrapped it around her shoulders, looking upwards.

'I'm fine,' she mouthed, hoping the light from the kitchen lit up her face enough for her mother to see. 'Don't worry. I'm going to Edna's.'

She waited until she saw her mother nod and move one hand in understanding. Jessie flapped her own fingers in a shooing motion and breathed a sigh of relief when Dorothy disappeared from the window.

Picking up the valise she moved towards the steps.

'Go. Bugger off.'

She half-turned at a sound behind her, the clank of the handle of a metal bucket.

Cold water drenched her. She staggered back and fell heavily onto the step. The edges of the stone caused a line of pain across her back. She heard Amos snigger, the squeak of the bucket swaying in his hand. Beyond him she saw the outline of the two lads watching from the bakery window.

Winded, she swung her head from side to side, swiping the water from her face, trying to drag air into her lungs.

She knew he was studying her, enjoying himself. Without speaking she pushed away her helplessness and made herself stand tall, going back up the steps. Ignoring the agony in her spine, she towered over him and stared down at him. His face was shadowed so she couldn't make out his expression, but that didn't matter. She heard his sniggers falter, tail off, heard the shallow breaths as he waited.

She let a few moments pass while the silence stretched between them. Ignoring the cold weight of the woollen shawl, the chill that was seeping through the whole of her body, she kept her gaze on him.

He cleared his throat. 'Sod off, whore.'

She reached out and picked up her valise where it had fallen.

He gestured towards the gate. 'Get out of my yard.' His face moved out of the shadows, his scowl visible.

'My father's yard. His business.'

Jessie tossed a glance towards the bakery door. Bob and Eddie were watching from there. She raised her voice loud enough for them to hear. 'And now my mother's business.'

Despite her teeth chattering, she smiled at the unease that crossed his face.

'A business that will never be yours, whatever you think.'

Not giving him a chance to say another word, she hitched the wet valise over her arm, turned and carefully picked her way down the steps. Crossing the slippery flags, she left the home she'd lived in all her life.

Chapter 30

'My god, you're wet through. What the 'ell 'as 'e done now?'

Jessie stumbled through the front door, shivering, wracked by silent sobs that had begun the moment she'd closed the back gate. She didn't remember walking across the road and banging on the door.

Edna ushered her through to the kitchen.

'Come in, come in, you're soaked through. You'll get your death o' cold.'

Jessie sank onto one of the chairs by the table.

'I wondered when something like this would happen.' Edna pulled Jessie's shawl from her shoulders and shook the worst of the wet off before hanging it over the pulley rails. 'Here, let's get these soaking things off you. Stand up.' Even as she said it Edna was unbuttoning Jessie's blouse, unfastening her woollen skirt and easing them of her. 'Take your underthings off and wrap that blanket round you while I get the brandy.' Her voice was gruff. She kept her eyes averted, giving Jessie some semblance of privacy until her nakedness was covered and she was sitting in the chair.

'Here, drink this.' She held out the glass. 'You look frozen.'

Jessie took it, her fingers numb with cold. She gasped against the sharpness of the alcohol. It stung her mouth, burned as she swallowed.

'Better now?' Edna drank her own brandy with a sigh of appreciation. She knelt down at the fireplace, her knees cracking and creaking. 'I'll have this blazing in no time, don't fret.' Placing sticks of wood and small precious pieces of coal on top of the embers, she took the blower and balanced it on the hearth before holding a large sheet of newspaper against it. Neither woman spoke, watching the edges of the paper turn orange, dull at first and then bright. In a well-practised movement Edna scrunched up the charring paper, whipped away the blower and shoved the paper up the chimney. 'There,' she said. 'That's better.'

She twisted around and unbuttoned Jessie's boots, drawing off her stockings which had fallen around her ankles.

'You're still shaking. It's the shock as well as the cold. 'E's a right nasty old sod. Brandy'll sort that.'

She reached up, gently holding Jessie's cheek and studying the bruised lump by her eye. Using the leg of the chair to help herself to stand, she patted Jessie's shoulder. 'It'll all work itself out. You'll see.' Pouring some of the brandy on a cloth, she pressed it into Jessie's hands. 'Dab this on yer face, love.'

She filled their glasses again and, her hands wrapped around her own drink, sat across the table to Jessie and waited. Only the low splutter of flames and shifting of the coal in the fireplace broke the silence. Gradually the room grew shadowed in the winter evening. Only then did Edna speak. 'Feeling better?'

'A little.' Jessie gave the woman a tremulous smile. 'You knew?'

'I was waiting for you to tell me.'

'It is Arthur's.'

'I know.' Edna tilted her head. 'Surely you didn't doubt I would know that. I know you, Jessie. I've known you all your life. I never doubted your loyalty to my son. Your love for 'im.'

'Thank you. I thought you'd disapprove – your beliefs...'

Edna shrugged. 'God will understand in these strange times. Father Thomas can get on his bike if 'e tries to say owt.'

'Thank you.' Arthur was right. He'd always said what a lovely woman his mother was. Jessie swallowed grateful tears.

'So what now?' Edna said. 'What's happened across the road?'

'I told Mam this morning about the baby. She told him tonight.'

'He kicked you out?'

'Called me a slut and a whore. He threw me through the back door. Into the yard. Did this.' Jessie touched her face and winced. She waved her hand upwards to the pulley where her clothes were now beginning to steam in the warmth of the kitchen. 'Threw water over me.'

The other woman pressed her lips into a narrow, white line. 'And your mother let 'im?'

'She wasn't there. It was in the yard. She was upstairs. But, anyway, she had no choice. She's scared of him and she's not well, Edna. I've told her she must do what's best for her to keep the peace. She knows I'm here.'

'And here you'll stay.' Edna thumped the table, rattling the cutlery in the drawer underneath. 'I'd like to give that little runt a taste of 'is own medicine. You should 'ave talked to me, love.'

'I didn't know. I didn't know why I was feeling so ... so odd. And with Mam being ill...' Jessie watched as Edna stood to light the two gas mantles over the range, anxious to see the woman's face, wanting reassurance. 'I hadn't long been having the monthlies before – before what happened. Before Arthur and me...' She stopped, embarrassed. 'We only did it the once, just before he left.'

'It's okay, lass. I understand.' The words were oddly abrupt and fragmented as though the discomfort was shared but then Edna swung round and bent to hug Jessie. 'My grandchild,' she murmured. 'Arthur's child.'

'I was frightened.' Fear had roiled around in Jessie's stomach all day but now it soothed her to hear Edna's acceptance. 'So scared.' She didn't say the rest aloud: that she'd sat for hours in the outside lavvy, straining as she peed, hoping to squeeze the baby from her. 'I'm frightened, Edna.'

'No need to be, love. You're safe now.' Edna studied her. 'You must be around five months by now?'

Jessie hesitated. It occurred to her how little she knew about her own body. 'I...'

'The baby will be due in May. We must write to tell Arthur.' Edna stood abruptly. 'It will be something for him to look forward to. To...'

...Live for, Jessie thought, the words she knew Edna didn't dare say. It was now over two months since they'd heard from him.

Chapter 31

February

It was the following Sunday before her mother crossed the road to Edna Dawson's.

'Amos has gone to chapel,' she said, almost pushing past Jessie in her rush to get into the house. 'I told him I had a headache. He wasn't best pleased, but I stayed in bed until I knew he'd left. He's been in a foul mood all week.'

'Edna's at church as well. We have the house to ourselves. Come into the kitchen there's a fire in there and I can make a brew.' Jessie made to walk down the hall towards the kitchen.

'No. No, thank you, love. It's better in here.' She pushed her way into the parlour and stood by Edna's piano, softly running her fingers over the keys. 'Your dad and me; we used to love coming over some evenings to have a bit of a singsong with Edna when you were little. You probably don't remember?'

'I do.'

There was a pause. The memory of Jessie's father and the spectre of Amos Morgan stood between them. Dorothy cleared her throat and adjusted her shawl over her head before going to sit on the settee by the window. 'Sit here with me.' She frowned. 'What has Edna said? Does she mind—?'

'My being here?' Jessie sat at the far end of the settee. A bubble of anger burst to the surface. 'Mam, I'm carrying her son's child, she wouldn't have dreamt of turning me away. Where else would I go? I told you I'd come here.'

'I'm sorry. You didn't tell me about you and Arthur. About... Why?'

Jessie shook her head. She didn't know why she hadn't confided in her mother.

Dorothy lowered her head. When she raised it again, Jessie saw the anguish. 'Please believe me, Jessie, I am sorry. About everything. I should have listened to you. Your father...'

Contrition overcame Jessie's anger immediately. Her mother was a weak woman, she'd always known that. Her father had cosseted and cared for her as far back as she could remember. Just as he had Jessie herself until the day he died.

'Hush, Mam, it's too late now. We can't go back.' Much as she wished they could, this was how it was now.

Dorothy pulled in her lips and sighed. 'I've missed you this week.'

'I've brought shame on you.'

'And it's Arthur's—?'

'Of course. But Mam, we only did it the once.'

'I believe you, love. You're a good girl. Really.' Her mother nodded.

Really? Why did she need to add that word?

'I should have protected you from Amos. I'm sorry.'

'There's nothing you could have done.' Jessie saw her mother's frequent glances through the parlour window towards the shop. How frail she was. And still that cough, that small, edgy clearing of her throat. Her mother leaned forward to look out of the window again. The shawl fell away. Jessie saw a yellowing bruise on her jawline. She gasped. 'He doesn't hit you, does he, Mam?'

'No, don't be daft, love.'

'Well, he hit me. So—'

'No!' But it was said too quickly. Jessie's hatred of Amos Morgan doubled. But what could she do? It was clear Dorothy wouldn't – couldn't – do anything about the situation she was in. Jessie watched her mother, convinced it was fear of her husband that was making her restless.

The grandfather clock in the comer of the room chimed. Automatically Jessie counted the rich sonorous low rings, accepting that there was nothing she could do for her mother. For now, anyway.

'That's twelve, Mam. He'll be coming out of chapel now.'

'I'm sorry, Jessie, truly I am.' Her mother half-rose then sat again. 'There's something I need to tell you first...'

'Mam, you go. I don't want you getting into trouble.' She forced a smile. 'I'll sort out a way for us to see one another again.'

'I'd like that, Jessie. But listen, I've got some money put by. *He*...' she tipped her head towards the window. 'He knows nothing about. I've been taking the odd shilling or two from the till for a while.' She smiled. A weak smile but nevertheless triumphant. 'I'm not sure why; it was just something I started to do.' She pulled a small biscuit tin from under her shawl and handed it to Jessie. 'It's not much but it should help.'

'Oh, no, I couldn't take your money...'

'You can. I want you to have it. Please.'

'If you're sure?' Jessie still hesitated.

'I'm sure. And there are other things: some small pieces of jewellery that belonged to your grandmother. I hid them under the floor of the wardrobe so he wouldn't sell them. You only have to prise the panel up and you'll see a bag there. It's yours.'

'Well – thank you, Mam.' Jessie took the tin and caught hold of her mother's hand.

'There's one more thing. I want you to know. If – when – something happens to me, the shop – the business will be yours.'

'What? What about him?'

'He won't be able to do anything about it.'

'I don't understand.'

Dorothy looked anxiously at the grandfather clock as it chimed just the once. 'I'll have to go—'

'Mam!' What did her mam mean, the shop will be hers?

'I'll explain another time. That's quarter past. I'll be lucky to get in before him.'

'Okay, then. Go straight across the road and through the shop door, it'll be quicker than going round to the alleyway. I love you.'

'I love you, too.' Dorothy squeezed her hand. 'And I'm sorry I let you down, I'm sorry I've been so...'

'It's not your fault.' Her mother had been no match for Amos Morgan. 'I'll check if the coast's clear.'

'Yes.'

Jessie poked her head out of the front door. 'All right, you can go, Mam.'

Dorothy paused on the step. 'Have you heard anything from Arthur yet?'

Jessie shook her head.

'Perhaps soon, eh, love?'

'Hopefully, Mam. Now go.'

'We'll talk sometime about the shop. I'll explain ...'

'Yes, yes.' However much she wanted to know what her mother meant, Jessie was more worried about her being seen by Amos Morgan. 'Just go, Mam, please.' Jessie waited until her mother had gone into the shop and closed the door. Glancing along the street she saw him turning the corner in a group of other men.

Chapter 32

February

Jessie carefully placed the small plaited ring of grass back in the box and pushed it into her cardigan pocket. It was quite withered now. Arthur had taken so much trouble to make it, that last time they were together. She'd watched him fumble with the narrow blades, his face screwed up in concentration. In the end she'd taken it and finished it for him.

She crouched over the fire trying to keep hold of the memory of his fingers that day. She loved his hands, the strong feel of them in her own. Sometimes she was torn apart by her need for him. Before the war there hadn't been a day when she'd not seen Arthur. Now she often wondered what he would be like, after six months fighting a war through a bitterly cold winter of rain, snow and floods in France. Forced to live in rat-infested trenches, in mud and slime, unable to stand up for fear of snipers, according to the accounts in newspapers. She'd seen the photographs of horrendously injured soldiers in hospitals up and down the country and had nightmares where each one was Arthur.

And there were the rumours of German boats being seen off the coast. She must make sure Edna didn't get to hear about that; it didn't take much to make her panic.

Some days Jessie drifted through the hours, reliving their times together, the hours they spent by the canal, watching for dragonflies, floating sticks on the surface from one side of the bridge to the other or swinging on the rope they'd knotted around the largest branch of the oak tree by the river.

Staring into the fire now, she remembered the shock of him going to work in Kindle Mill at twelve while she stayed on at school until she was fourteen – to make sure she knew all her figures so she could help with the shop bookkeeping. Every day she'd waited for him outside the mill and, once a week, after he'd tipped his wages up to his mother and got his spends, he bought a sherbet and a liquorice stick to share with her, while she taught him what she'd learned in school. When he was older and making more money, he'd treated them once or twice to a trip to Manchester or to a fair.

But the best memory she kept for when she was really low: the day she'd gone with him to Blackpool. Her distress for the animals in the Tower, her fear of the sea under the pier, even the bewilderment that a war had started, faded into the background – it was the day she'd realised she was in love with a friend she'd known all her life. A lifetime ago. And yet with her every day.

The smell of the bread Edna had made earlier and left on the shelves to cool filled the kitchen and gave her a lurch of homesickness in her heart. Not homesickness, she corrected herself, a yearning to go back to when she was a child watching her father in the bakery. But there was no going back. And there was no safety in the future. She held her hands over her eyes, pressed back the tears, lost in her thoughts.

Edna burst through the back door and thumped her basket onto the table. Jessie jumped.

'They're going to starve us into giving in to 'em.' The panic in the older woman's voice was also in her wide-open eyes.

'Who?'

'Them buggers. Them Germans. Mrs Whittle was in the butchers...' She flapped her hand, impatient with Jessie. 'Mrs Whittle off Golders Terrace? She was spouting off about how we'd all be paying over the odds for stewing steak if the Germans went ahead with what they're threatening in the papers...' She held her hand to her throat, completely out of breath.

'Sit down, Edna.' Jessie led her to the armchair. 'Calm down and start again.' She perched on the arm of the chair, resting the bulk of her stomach in the palms of her hands and shifting to a slightly more comfortable position. The child inside her moved as if sensing her uneasiness.

'She said that Germany 'as declared the sea as part of the war. I don't understand – but she says every ship bringing in food from...' Edna flailed her hand around again. 'Somewhere – some country – to here, to England, will be sunk.' Her eyes widened. 'The shop was packed, everybody in a flap.'

'What did Mr Butland say?' Jessie thought the butcher, always a cheerful man, would have managed to pacify the other customers.

'He said it was something to do with our government misusing what they call neutral flags – you know, not our country's flag?'

Jessie nodded.

The words poured out of Edna. 'Having them on some ships that they shouldn't 'ave, pretending to be merchant ships bringing food here or something – or pretending to be passenger ships, when they were actually what he called "hostile" ships.' She looked up at Jessie. 'He said Betty Whittle is right, things are going to get worse. There won't be enough food for everybody.' She lifted her hand, let it hover over Jessie's stomach. 'For all of us.' It dropped back into her lap. 'What will we do, Jessie?'

There was no answer except, 'I'm sure it won't be as bad as that, Edna.'

Jessie sighed, not really believing her own words; things were already worse than they'd been led to believe. They'd been told the war would be over by Christmas. Arthur had joined up believing that. Thinking he needed to go with all his mates from the mill before it ended. But, lately, on the few occasions she'd been in any of the shops, she'd heard the rumours. Germany had prepared for a long war; those in charge had made sure their army had plenty of guns, rifles, ammunition and explosives, whereas Britain had barely bothered. The government had been convinced the war wouldn't last this long. Didn't even believe it would happen.

'We'll be fine.' She rested her cheek on top of Edna's head. 'We'll be fine.' She felt a headache begin, tightening her forehead. 'I'll be back in a minute. Just need the lavvy.'

In the yard she gazed upwards. Clouds, grey-laden with snow, hung, heavy in the sky. It had been a long dreary winter.

'Where are you, Arthur?' She couldn't remember the last time they'd heard from him and, although Edna refused to admit how worried she was, she couldn't hide the fear.

Hot tears smarted at the back of Jessie's eyes again and she pressed her lips together to smother the wail that constantly threatened to escape. Lately, more than ever before, her courage had thinned, dissolved.

Now this. How much more were they expected to bear? Jessie wrapped her arms around herself, tucked her hands under her armpits. Shivered.

Chapter 33

Jessie leaned against the back of the settee holding the curtain to one side, waiting for the postman. She wasn't sure if she'd missed him. She saw her mother slip out of the shop and stand by the door, and moved closer to the window so Dorothy would see the question on her face. Seeing the slight movement of her shoulders, Jessie drew in a sharp breath, the anticipation plummeting into dejection. No post. No hope.

'No? Nothing from the postie?' Edna sat in the armchair by the range, her legs spread to catch the jumble of the multi-coloured scarf she was knitting and the two balls of wool in the dip of her skirt. She lay the long needles down with a sigh when Jessie shook her head.

'Perhaps tomorrow. I saw Martha Hampson from Cranbrook Street in the greengrocer's yesterday. She hasn't heard from either of her boys She said it was a comfort to 'er to know that at least Tommy was with our Arthur. She said he'd keep him on the straight and narrow. My lad has a steady head on his shoulders.'

Knowing how wild the twins were, it was no comfort to Jessie to know one of them was in the same place as Arthur, but she said nothing.

'I don't think I'm ever going to get the 'ang of this,' Edna grumbled.

Jessie sat next to her and examined the knitting. A hole was slowly unravelling a few inches below the needles, where Edna had dropped a stitch and not noticed. Clumsy knots tying together the different colour wools gave the scarf a curiously lumpy appearance.

'Hmm.' Jessie caught the inside of her cheek to stop her smile. 'Would you like me to sort it?'

'Aye. Okay. I just wanted to do the same as you. I saw the scarf and sock you sent out to Arthur. And I've seen the scarfs and such Mrs Jones down the street 'as given in to that place on Beech Road where they collect stuff for our lads out there. I just wanted to do my bit.' She snorted a short laugh, holding up her hands. 'You'd think I'd know better with these fat fingers, wouldn't you? Good for nothing.'

'You shouldn't say that, Edna. You play your piano lovely.'

'Played, pet. I 'aven't been on it for ages – just don't 'ave the heart.'

It was true. Jessie realised it had been a while since she'd heard Edna playing in the parlour. 'Well, you're doing your bit looking after me and your son's baby, Edna.' Jessie hugged her. 'And never forget that.'

She forced the stitches off the needles with difficulty. In her enthusiasm Edna had battled with the knitting so much they were hardly moving on the needles. 'Now, how about you make a brew while I do this?' She didn't look up from unravelling the wool as she said, 'How about we cheer ourselves up? We could go to one of those new shows, a revue? Mrs Giles said her niece went and there were acrobats and a ventriloquist as well as a singer. And they had a singalong at the end. Mrs Giles said she wouldn't mind going. We could ask her as well?'

Edna stopped drying the cup in her hand. 'I don't know, pet. It feels wrong to be going out enjoying ourselves when...'

Jessie didn't answer. But she knew they wouldn't go. It was as if Edna had decided she would put her life on hold until her son returned to her. And that made Jessie feel guilty, even though she knew it wasn't what Arthur wanted for either of them.

She began to thread the stitches back onto one of the needles. What did she know? How could she say what he might want? What if this war changed him so much that when he came home he wasn't the boy she grew up with, the young man she loved?

Chapter 34

Some mornings Jessie couldn't wait at the house for the postman and, despite her increasing reluctance to be seen outside, she'd borrow the old overcoat that Arthur had left hung on the back of the cellar door. Wrapped in its comfort, she'd wait on the bench at the bottom of the Wharmton Hill for the first sign of the postie's tricycle.

It was a particularly bitterly cold day. Jessie's breath wisped in white, short bursts from her lips. She tucked her chin down to her chest and pulled together the ends of the collar of the overcoat to keep warm. When the postman passed her, shaking his head, she hauled herself off the seat, stamping some semblance of sensation back into her feet.

Three women walked towards her, heads turned away, mouths tight in moral indignation and judgement. Resentment blotted out the shame Jessie had carried for months. She knew that the husbands of two of them had scuttled off to work on farms to avoid enlistment.

'Ladies.'

They ignored her but her small rebellion made her feel better. She straightened her shoulders like Edna had told her to do. 'There's few around here, what can afford to cast stones,' she often said to her. 'It's my lad's babby you're carrying. He's out there fighting for 'is king and country, so be proud.'

Still, not wanting to catch them up, Jessie trudged as slow as she could behind the women, the thin hard layer of grimy snow crunching under her feet.

When she turned the corner onto Castle Street, she saw Edna on the footpath outside number fifty-five, hopping from one foot to the other. The large figure of Mrs Whittle, off Golders Terrace was waddling away from Edna's house in the opposite direction.

'Jessie!'

'What is it?' Holding her arm under her stomach and hampered by the heavy overcoat, Jessie did her best to stumble into a run. 'Edna? Is it Arthur?'

'No, no. Mrs Whittle's been to the shop. She says yer mam's really ill.'

Chapter 35

Jessie veered off, crossing the street, skidding over the frozen cobbles, oblivious to Edna calling after her. It had been over three weeks since her mam had come over to Edna's. She should have found a way to see her again when Amos Morgan wasn't around. But he kept a tight rein on Dorothy, and it had been impossible. Now the remorse swamped her. 'Edna, I should have—'

'Stop it. It's not your fault. I'll get my coat and follow. Make sure you get no flak from yon mon.'

Jessie burst into the shop, the door rebounding on the wall behind her. Bob and Amos were behind the counter. Bob froze, his eyes wide.

Jessie thrust her way past the women waiting to be served.

'What the hell...?' Amos barred her way, his hand flat on the wall. To her shock, Bob knocked his arm down. 'Let her get through.'

She threw a grateful look at him as she passed.

Upstairs, only dim light filtered through the closed curtains. The room was sour. Jessie knelt by the side of the bed, stroked her mother's damp hair. Dorothy's face was thin, haggard with lines of pain. Her illness had stripped the flesh from her large frame. Each breath she took crackled in her chest.

'What's wrong, Mam?'

'It's nothing, love. Bit of pain.' The words were halting. 'Can't breathe.'

'There's no air in here. I'll open the window.' Jessie leant on the frame of the bed, pushed her herself to her feet and went across the landing into her old bedroom to grab the eiderdown from the bed.

'What does the doctor say?' She spread it over her mother, tucking in the covers as best she could.

Her mother closed her eyes.

'He has been? Doctor Tregorran?'

'Amos...' Dorothy shook her head.

'Wouldn't send for him.' Jessie finished the sentence. The enormous anger building inside her helped to force open the stiff sash window. She stood, breathing in the fresh cold that rushed into the room, clearing the stale air.

'You've got a bloody cheek, missy.' Amos Morgan appeared in the doorway, glowering.

'Why hasn't the doctor been? Why haven't you sent for him?'

'We'll have no money-grabbing bloody doctor in this house, any more than we'll have dirty whores.' He staggered over, lifted a clenched fist and shook it in her face. 'I told you not to set foot in this house again.'

'And I'm telling you, you'll have to drag me out.' Jessie stood her ground and raised her eyebrows. She looked over his shoulder. 'And her.'

Edna stood close behind him. 'Touch her and I'll knock the living daylights out of you.'

Jessie knew the woman would as well. Seeing the uncertainty on Amos Morgan's face, she could tell he felt the same. He shoved past Edna.

'Get out the road.'

She didn't move making him squeeze past her to the stairs.

He had gone.

'I'll get the lads to carry up the armchair from the kitchen, shall I, lass?'

'Please, Edna. And can I borrow some covers from your place? I don't think Mam's bedclothes have been changed in weeks.'

'No need to ask.'

'I'm sorry,' her mother whispered. She turned her head on the pillow, wiping away quick tears from her cheek. 'I'm so ashamed.'

'No need to be, Mam. If he,' Jessie pointed at the floor, 'was the Christian he pretends to be he'd have sent for me – better still the doctor.' She crossed to the window and pulled the sash down so it was only open an inch. 'When Edna brings the change of bedding over, we can wrap you up and put clean covers on. Then, perhaps, a little wash? I'll ask her to bring a bowl of her vegetable soup over, shall I?'

'I'm ... not really... hungry...' The effort to speak ended in a choking cough.

'See how you feel when it's in front of you, eh? Then I'll go to the surgery, make sure the doctor comes. And I'll stay with you.'

'I'd like that, love.'

'Good. Because I'm going nowhere until you're better.' Determined, Jessie shook her head. 'Nowhere,' she said.

The fear of the dark nights welled up in her again.

You're doing this for Mam, she told herself. And there's nothing Amos Morgan can do to stop you.

Chapter 36

The first thing was to get her mother warm. Jessie stood by the bedroom door, listening. Bob and Eddie were still in the bakery. With them there, it was safe to go downstairs. She glanced at her mother, now sleeping, worn out by the constant coughing. Picking up the coal bucket, Jessie crept down the stairs. Conscious of the resentful stare from Amos Morgan and the brothers' curiosity, she kept her head lowered until she was out in the yard.

By the time she'd filled the bucket she was panting and, stretching her arms out, she took a moment to stop outside the lean-to roof and look around. The grey day reflected how she felt; somewhere a dog howled, and then another and another. Beyond the wide gate of the yard she heard the scrape of clogs, the deep voices of men, a faint whiff of pipe tobacco as they passed. Miners, she thought, on the way to their shift.

The bucket handle dug into her hands. Too heavy to get up the stairs. She'd need to empty some of the coal out. She'd tried to take as much as she could – the fewer times she had to go through the bakery and face Amos Morgan, the better. But there was nothing for it. She reached for the shovel.

'Here, let me 'elp.' Bob pushed her hand away, his voice gruff. He picked up the bucket.

'Thank you.'

'I don't pay you to waste your time—'

'It's me break time. I can do what I like.' Bob brushed past Jessie's stepfather.

'You'll be paying for that, missy. I'm not flogging my guts in the shop to keep you warm.'

Jessie tightened her stomach muscles against her rising anxiety, only saying, 'The doctor will be coming tomorrow.'

'And you'll be paying him.'

She gave him what she hoped was a withering look. 'His fee will come out of the shop takings.'

'Over my dead body.'

'One can only hope,' Jessie said, allowing herself a small grin. She followed Bob, rather pleased with herself for her courage.

Her smile disappeared when she entered her mother's room. She stopped in the doorway, blocking Bob's view.

'Thank you,' she said again, waiting until he'd gone back down the stairs before closing the door.

Dorothy hawked, coughing up phlegm into the chamber pot, holding her side.

'Sorry.'

'Don't fret about it, Mam.'

'Where's...'

'Downstairs.'

'Is he—?'

'Hush.

Jessie replaced the warm cloth on her mother's forehead with a cold one. 'The doctor will be here in the morning. He'll soon have you as right as rain.'

But that first night was long. Her mother was suffering and agitated. The dark hours passed slowly with Dorothy constantly twisting the sheets, sweat-wet, tight around her body, despite Jessie's efforts. She couldn't bear the fact that her mother had been in pain for at least the last week and she'd known nothing about it.

It wasn't yet dawn when Jessie went to stand by the window, the glass stippled with icy patterns. Breathing closely on the pane, she made a clear space to look out onto the yard. It would be hours before the doctor came. She hated Amos Morgan.

Chapter 37

March

'I'm afraid it's pneumonia. It's a good thing you are here to look after her.' The doctor stared at Amos, snoring by the fire. The flames flapped and popped in the wind blowing down the chimney. 'She'll need you.' He tilted his head towards the ceiling. 'And she'll need to keep warm. Jessie.'

'What else can I do?'

'If you can get some fluid down her...' Doctor Tregorran picked up his bag. 'But I'm afraid your mother is very poorly. I should have been sent for over a week ago, to be honest.' He coughed, a discreet, almost apologetic clearing of his throat. 'And how are you keeping?' Without waiting for her reply, he hurried on. 'Come and see me at the surgery. Let's make sure you and...' He smiled gently. 'You're both all right. Yes?'

Jessie avoided his gaze. 'I will. When I have time, I will.' The young doctor, new to the town, was direct if nothing else. And yet the relief that he didn't appear to judge was overwhelming. 'Thank you.'

He nodded. 'I'll be back tomorrow.'

'Oh, I don't know if I'll be able to get the money...' Jessie picked at the hem of her handkerchief.

'I'll be back tomorrow.' His voice firm.

'Thank you,' she said again, this time meeting his eyes. Kind eyes, she thought. I can trust him.

'Please Mam, fight this. Don't give up.' Jessie squeezed her mother's hand, feeling helpless, wanting Dorothy to take strength from her touch.

'Tired, love.' Dorothy's voice was faint, husky.

'I know, but please try to eat this.' Jessie held the bowl of thin vegetable soup near her mother's nose.

'Can't. Take ... it away, please, Jessie.'

It was a rare moment of lucidity. Moments that became more spaced out as the day wore on.

In the night Jessie sat beside the bed wrapped in blankets, moving only to bank up the fire or replace the bedclothes her mother continually threw off in her distress. Her skin was pallid, gleaming with sweat. There was little chance of sleep; Dorothy's breathing, noisy and erratic, filled the room. Jessie waited for dawn, the chink in the curtains slowly changing from pitch black to grey. It must have been warmer outside; there was no ice on the panes. Instead, slow heavy drops of rain on the windowsill rapidly increased into a noisy gushing downpour

The young doctor arrived shaking the water from his hat.

'What kind of night?' he asked, unbuttoning his full-length raincoat. The rubber material was making a puddle on the linoleum.

Jessie had lifted her mother higher on the pillows and was coaxing her to try some milky porridge, holding the spoon to her lips.

'Not too good.' Jessie leaned back in the chair, the bowl on her lap. 'And I can't get her to eat any of this.'

'Let me try.'

He took the chair and porridge. Jessie watched for a few moments, admiring his patience.

'I need to go...' She faltered, embarrassed.

'Of course. It does you no good being cooped up here.' He spoke without turning his head. 'Come on now, Dorothy, try to eat some of this.' He was met with a tightening of her lips, a murmur of protest. 'Go, Jessie. We'll talk when you get back.'

Jessie slipped through the bakery without making eye contact with either Bob or Eddie. She could hear voices through the closed shop door, a sharp shout of laughter from Amos Morgan.

Holding up her skirt with one hand and clutching her shawl under her chin with the other, she splashed through the water in the yard and up the steps to the lavvy. Rain seeped under the closed door and hammered on the tin roof.

For the first time since she had been back to the bakery, she allowed herself to cry, accepting the doctor's unspoken diagnosis: her mother was going to die.

'Oh, Arthur, what am I going to do? I need her. I need you.'

'She won't eat and there is no point in trying to make her. I believe in the theory that each patient knows what their body needs and wants. Try her later with thin soups and water but nothing else. I've given her brandy and she's settled for now. I've left the bottle in her room.' Doctor Tregorran rested his hand on Jessie's shoulder. They stood in the hall at the bottom of the stairs. 'The only thing we can do is make her as comfortable as possible.'

'I must pay you.'

'Let's worry about that another time. I'll be back tomorrow morning.'

The rumble of men's voices came from the shop. Jessie heard her stepfather chuckling.

'I'll be having a word with Mr Morgan before I leave.' He shook Jessie's hand. 'Try to get some rest yourself; you'll need to stay well – for you and...' He stopped. Smiled. 'As I said yesterday, make that appointment at the surgery. Let's make sure all is well...'

'Yes, I will.' The heat rose in Jessie's cheeks.

'So, I'll see you tomorrow, then.' He looked past her to the bakery. Bob was hovering in the doorway. The men nodded a greeting.

'How's your mother?' Bob asked when the doctor had left.

'Not good. I must get back up there.'

'I could bring you a cup of tea?'

Jessie stopped, one foot on the first tread. 'Thank you, Bob. That would be lovely.' She heard a raised voice from the shop: Amos Morgan's, followed by the low, measured tones of the young doctor.

'Sounds as if he's getting it in the neck,' Bob chuckled, then made a gulping noise at the back of his throat. 'Sorry.'

'Don't worry about it.' Jessie knew her smile was strained even though she appreciated his remark. Amos Morgan would keep out of her way if he knew what was good for him. 'I'll go up.'

'See you in a minute.'

Her mother was sleeping peacefully for the first time. The brandy had clearly worked. Jessie dropped into the chair. By the time Bob arrived with the tea, she too was asleep.

Chapter 38

'I ... I saw ... Harold ... this morning.' The words were the first Dorothy had spoken in the last two days. Her voice, though faltering, was strong. She sat up, pointed to the end of her bed.

'Dad?' Shock ripped through Jessie. She stopped wringing out the cloth she was using to wash her mother's face and stared at her. 'Mam?' She dropped the cloth into the bowl on the tallboy. 'What do you mean?'

'Did.' Dorothy collapsed back against the pillows, sweat glistening on her face. 'Did...' She closed her eyes.

She didn't speak again. Sometimes she tossed around, throwing back the covers. Mostly she lay still, the breath rattling in her chest, her eyelids fluttering.

Chapter 39

The doctor held her mother's hands, studied them. Jessie saw the blue discolouration in her fingers.

'What is it?'

'She isn't getting enough oxygen – air,' He pressed his lips into a thin line. 'The infection has damaged her lungs. See? Her mouth is quite blue as well?'

'Yes. I see.'

'I am sorry but I do think you should prepare yourself for the worst.'

Jessie held herself still, shook her head quickly.

Doctor Tregorran put one hand on her shoulder. They stood like that for a few moments.

Jessie saw the hollowed cheeks, the sunken eyes, the loosened muscles of her mother's face and knew he was right.

'How long?'

He raised his shoulders slightly, let them fall. 'I don't know. Soon.'

'She's not in pain?'

'No, she's unconscious. I doubt she'll wake up again.' He let his hand drop. 'When did you last sleep?' His voice was soft.

'I don't know. I can't remember.'

'Then you need to go to bed now. Your mother won't know whether you're here or not. Is there anyone else who can take over and sit with her?'

'Edna. Mrs Dawson. Across the road. She's my – sweetheart's mother. That's where I live now.' Jessie put her hand on her stomach, her need for Arthur cutting through her.

His brow furrowed. Was he judging her?

But then he closed his eyes. Nodded. 'I understand. And you're not the only one, Jessie. This dreadful war has changed all our lives in so many ways.'

His kindness seemed to release something inside her. A weakness rushed through her, made her stumble. The doctor caught hold of her.

'Steady! Right,' he said, 'Bed, right now. What number does Mrs Dawson live at?'

'Number fifty-five. But *he* won't let her in.'

'He will.' There was no doubt in his voice. 'Now go, get over there and get into bed and sleep.'

She wouldn't sleep. She was sure she wouldn't.

Chapter 40

'Jessie.'

Jessie moaned, unwilling to wake. She was dreaming of walking along the canal path with Arthur; it was summer, the warm sun high above them, hot on her arms as she linked his. She burrowed further down in the bed. She was being shaken. Arthur looked at her, a smile creasing the corners of his eyes. 'Jessie,' he said. But his face faded away...

'Jessie, love, wake up. It's your mam.'

'Edna?' Jessie thrust back the sheets and stood, almost knocking the older woman over. 'Mam?'

'Yes, Jessie.' Edna folded her in her arms.

And then Jessie knew. It was how Edna had said her name. Her legs gave way. She tried to gulp in air but it hurt and a strange choking sound filled her head. Edna had hold of her, was helping her to sit on the side of the bed.

'She's gone, pet.' Edna crossed herself. 'She's at peace now.'

'I should have been with her.' The words were a wail.

'She wouldn't know. But she knew you were with her all the time before.'

'I need to see her.' Jessie stood again. Her legs shook as she stumbled down the stairs and out of the house with Edna following. The shop door was open but there were no customers inside. Jessie heard voices in the bakery but ignored them as she went up the stairs to her mother's room.

'I opened the window, let her soul go. She's safe now.' Edna pulled at the frame; it closed with a quiet thump. 'And I've asked young Eddie to go for the doc.' She hovered behind Jessie, her hand on the small of her back. A comforting touch.

Jessie dropped to her knees at the side of her mother's bed. Dorothy's face was white, waxy. Her hands were folded across her chest and Jessie placed her own over them. They were lukewarm. But they didn't feel like her mam's hands; they were bony under her fingers. 'Oh Mam.' Jessie rested her head on the covers.

'I'll go downstairs – tell *him*.'

'No! I don't want him in here.' Jessie twisted her head upwards to look at Edna. Her voice rasped in her throat. 'I don't want him anywhere near her. He hasn't been in once since I've been with her. Why should he come now?'

'Because she was my missus.' Amos Morgan stood by the bedroom door, one hand raised on the frame. Jessie didn't understand his expression. Sneering? Satisfaction? Triumph? She didn't understand.

Until she heard his next words. 'An' I go where I want. This is my place. My shop. My house.'

'I need to go.' Giving in to the urge to escape, she pushed past him, down the stairs, through the shop and out into the cold air. She ran.

She ran until she got to the stile and climbed over. Looking towards the top of Wharmton Hill, she kept her eyes on the stone wall as she dragged herself up, holding on to the grass. Counting every step. Eighty, ninety, one hundred. Now she could see the heart stone standing out on top of the wall, wedged in by the two tall ones. She kept her eyes on it as she climbed, her chest filling, emptying with rapid breaths, one arm under her stomach, taking the weight of it.

She reached out for the heart stone as she took the last few steps. It was strangely warm under her palm. Strangely smooth. Comforting. She raised the front edge of it, touched the note.

'Arthur.' Jessie closed her eyes. She saw him walking towards her, smiling. Unwilling to open her eyes, she leant against the wall, picturing him, holding on to the memory of the day he had shown her the heart stone. Shown her the paper with his vow written on it. 'Forever,' he'd said. 'I'll love you forever.'

The first of the icy raindrops shocked her. She forced herself upright, suddenly conscious that she had left the shop without a shawl or coat. She shuddered, opening her eyes.

The sky was slate grey, the moors above misted, promising more rain. Jessie turned to look down on the dark buildings of the town.

'Mam!'

She'd left her mother alone with that man. No, Edna was there. She would have stayed. Wouldn't she?

Slipping and sliding on the now wet grass, Jessie lurched back down the hill.

Chapter 41

April 1915

'I'll leave the certificate here on the set of drawers, Jessie. You'll need to show it to the undertaker.' Doctor Tregorran closed his case looking from Edna to Jessie. 'Make sure you come and see me soon, all right?'

Jessie nodded, not trusting herself to speak.

'I'm sorry for your loss.' He touched her hand which was rested on her stomach. 'Look after yourself. And anything I can help with...'

'Nice young chap,' Edna said as they listened to him going down the stairs.

'He is. He's been very kind.'

'Good.' Edna looked drawn, exhausted. It occurred to Jessie that her mam and Arthur's mother had been friends for a long time. Her mother's death was a loss almost as much for Edna as herself.

'You don't have to do the laying out, you know, pet. Mrs Waters said she'll come over for her usual two shillings.'

'I'm all right.' Even though she was dreading it, it was something Jessie needed to do. 'I want it to be me and you, Edna...'

'Well, I'm honoured to do this for Dorothy – and you, Jessie.'

She left the bedroom to go downstairs. When she came back, she was carrying a metal bowl. 'I did both my mam and my dad,' she said. 'I helped my mother with my grandmother – I think I was your age.' She looked around before putting the bowl on the bedside table and reaching out to hold Jessie's hands. 'You'll be fine, pet.'

116

'Just tell me what to do, Edna. Let's get this over and done with – but done right for Mam.' It had to be right. 'Tell me what to do,' she repeated.

'We need to get her undressed and washed as soon as we can, before it gets too difficult to move her. The undertaker said he'll bring a coffin that'll tide us over until the proper one comes to the house later.'

Jessie slipped her mother's nightgown off, keeping her eyes on her mother's face.

'Let's just put a couple of these pillows under her head and shoulders. It'll make it easier for us to manage and afterwards for us to settle her arms over her chest.'

Jessie lifted her mother up off the bed while Edna manoeuvred the pillows. It was like picking up a child. But she could feel every knobble of her mother's spine under the paper-thin skin. Jessie couldn't help comparing the feel of holding Dorothy now with the woman she used to be. Before Amos Morgan took over their lives. She pushed the bitterness away; she wouldn't allow anything else to be in her head but love while she did this last thing for Mam.

'There, that's better. Here.' Edna handed the tin bowl of warm water to Jessie. 'Put it on the bedside table on your side. You see to your mother's hair and face and neck, I'll do the rest. If you can, try to move your mam's head from side to side a little, Jessie, and then settle her head on the pillow so she's face upwards, she'll look more tidy, like.'

'Right.' Jessie kept her eyes averted as Edna plugged parts of her mother's emaciated body with soft cotton material. If Edna noticed she said nothing. They worked quietly; only the splash of water, the gentle wiping of cloth on skin, and the sound of the brush broke the silence.

Eventually Edna spoke, her voice softer than usual. 'When you've finished her hair, we'll get her dressed. Did you choose her clothes?'

'Yes.' Jessie gestured towards the wardrobe. 'She has a grey dress, her favourite. And a grey scarf she liked. It'll match her shoes.'

'Good.'

They carefully put the clothes on Dorothy, only speaking when necessary to help one another.

The shop doorbell rang as they finished.

'That'll be the Mr Davey now with the coffin, Jessie. Let's finish off and then he can take over. Just arrange her arms over her chest – crossed over, like – that's right – now I'll fasten these ribbons around her elbows, her wrists and ankles. Make her lie straight and tidy.'

Jessie stood back; it was something she couldn't bring herself to do.

'She'll be ready for him.' Without saying anything else, Edna tied another ribbon under Dorothy's chin, 'There,' she said at last. 'Pretty as a picture.' She put an arm around Jessie's waist as heavy footsteps sounded on the stairs. 'You've done your best for your mam, pet. Let's leave them to it now.'

'Where will they put her, Edna?'

'They put your dad in the kitchen, didn't they?'

'Yes. Yes, you're right.'

'Well, then.'

But as Amos Morgan led the undertaker and his assistant into the bedroom, he said, 'You can leave the missus up here. It's best she's in here.'

'You can't.' Edna looked outraged.

'People will want to come and pay their respects.' Jessie did her best to keep her voice calm.

'Oh, we'll have none of that nonsense. Your mother was a quiet woman, she wouldn't want that kind of fuss.'

'She has – had – friends who will want to see her.' Jessie itched to slap the man.

The undertaker stood, shifting from one foot to the other. 'It's really not usual, Mr Morgan...'

'Well, that's what will happen, Mr Davey.'

'Here, pet, help me.' Edna took the sheet off the bed and covered the glass on the wardrobe. 'There...'

She glared at Amos Morgan. Holding onto Jessie's arm, she

guided her towards the door. 'Thank you, Mr Davey. We'll leave things with you now.' She lowered her voice. 'Keep moving, Jessie. You've done your bit for your mam,' she said again. 'She wouldn't want you upset any more than you need to be.'

Neither of them acknowledged Amos Morgan when they left.

Chapter 42

April

'Ready?' Edna pulled on her black gloves.

'Ready.' Jessie nodded.

From the parlour window they watched Dorothy's coffin being carried from the shop doorway on a bier and slid into the waiting hearse. Jessie stared through the glass sides of the carriage. Compared with the elegantly decorated black hearse, the coffin was unadorned: no flowers, no carvings, no brass handles. Amos Morgan wasn't wasting any more of his – of any of her mother's money on her than he could get away with.

'Look, Edna,' Jessie whispered.

'I know, pet.' Edna grimaced. 'Tight-arse. And he's only had an 'orse and carriage because he couldn't get away with anything less.'

The hearse moved off with the undertaker at the front and his men following at a dignified pace, their top hats tucked into the crook of their arms. A small group of men walked behind.

'I don't care what he says, I will be at my own mother's funeral, Edna.'

'And quite right, an' all.'

'Thank you for coming with me, Edna.'

'As long as Father Thomas doesn't cotton on.' She nudged Jessie. 'He'd explode if he found out. I'll 'ave to hide behind you if 'e's lurking around anywhere.'

As upset as she was, Jessie couldn't stop the smile that curved her lips; the size of her, there was no way Edna would be able to hide behind her.

They waited until they couldn't hear the horse's hooves any longer and stepped out onto the pavement.

'Edna!' Jessie's mouth slackened. Outside every house on the street women stood in their doorsteps, some even in black.

'They wanted to show their respects to your mam. Show 'ow much they liked her.' Edna smiled, looking around. 'And see, all the curtains are closed. Amos Morgan can't have it all 'is own way.'

Whether she was supposed to or not, Jessie couldn't let the gesture go.

'Thank you!' she called out. 'Thank you. I'm grateful for your respect for Mam.'

Every one of the women acknowledged her by raising a hand or with a movement of her head.

When she and Edna reached the end of the street, Jessie turned to look back. No one had moved. Strengthened by their support, she pulled her shoulders back and lifted her head.

'Right,' she said.

'Best foot forward,' Edna answered.

'Best foot forward,' Arthur murmured in Jessie's head.

They made their way through the narrow, terraced streets of Nether Brook towards the Methodist chapel.

Chapter 43

The afternoon sun shone through the windows of the chapel, bouncing off the brass candles, the polished pews and lectern and hurting Jessie's eyes, already sore from all the tears shed over the last ten days.

The place was full of men, only men. Amos Morgan had got his own way with that, except for her and Edna: the two women he had least wanted there.

120

They'd waited, ignored by all, until Mam's coffin was carried in. Then they slipped into a back pew.

As on the coffin, there were no flowers in the chapel. The wheezy notes of the organ, playing some dirge Jessie didn't recognise, stopped as soon as everyone took their places and the minister raised a commanding hand. There was a moment of complete silence. Then, just as the shuffling and clearing of throats started, just as Jessie thought she wouldn't be able to swallow the gulping sob that threatened to rise from her throat, the minister spoke. 'We are all on a journey through life...'

At the end of the short service, the bearers shouldered Dorothy's coffin and filed down the short aisle towards Jessie and Edna. In turn the men rose to follow Amos Morgan. Only he glowered at them, the rest of them determinedly kept their eyes averted.

'If looks could kill,' Edna muttered, clutching Jessie's hand. 'You'll need to watch that bastard in future, pet.'

Jessie couldn't stop the smile that quivered on her lips.

'Sorry – and I don't know 'ow I'm going to explain in confession – swearing *and* being in a chapel,' Edna muttered, glaring back at Amos Morgan, holding his gaze until he turned away, his lips thinned. 'Like a gathering of black crows,' Edna added for good measure, making sure the last of the stragglers heard her.

One or two did look then and Jessie noticed a shamefaced half nod, a closing of eyes to acknowledge them.

They waited a while before leaving the chapel.

The internment was short. As they came to the doorway, they heard the minister speaking. 'From ashes to ashes, dust to dust.'

They watched him take a handful of earth and sprinkle it on the coffin.

And then the men were already placing their hats back on their heads and moving towards the path, through to the archway and out onto the road.

'Can't wait to get away for their tea and biscuits.' Edna's lip curled.

Jessie had heard that Amos Morgan had already made it plain there would be none of the usual ham and trimmings or a long wake for her mother.

'The man's a monster, Edna. He has no respect for anything or anyone but himself.'

'You're right. But he'll get his comeuppance one day, pound to a pinch of salt he will. Never mind him, let's go and pay *our* respects to your mam.'

Jessie stood looking down on the coffin. Since her mother's death, grief had overwhelmed her, but now she also felt fear for the future.

The two gravediggers, waiting to put the earth back over Mam, backed away from them. One touched the neb of his cap. It was a courteous gesture that brought instant tears and she leant against Edna, giving way to her grief for the first time that day.

'Come on, Jessie, you've been strong so far and shown that lot we don't all descend into hysterics. Now do what you came for, say your own goodbye to your mother.'

Jessie stepped forward and threw the posy of early bluebells on top of the lowered coffin. They were wilted after being clutched in her hand over the last hour, but she knew her mam wouldn't mind; they were her favourites.

'Bye, Mam. I love you.' Jessie turned away. 'Thank you,' she said to the two men.

'Miss.'

Edna linked her arm. 'Come on. Home.'

Chapter 44

Jessie watched from behind her bedroom curtain, waiting until she saw the last man leave the bakery. Amos Morgan stood in the doorway, looking over towards Edna's house. She saw the mocking grin on his face, the way he rubbed his hands together. Then, instead of going back into the shop, he stepped out, closed the door behind him and clumped off along the road.

She ran downstairs.

'I'm going over, Edna. I need to get those things of Mam's.'

'I'll come with you.'

'No, it's okay. I won't be long. I still have the door key Mam gave to me. I'll be in and out as quick as I can.'

Outside, Jessie glanced around. The street was deserted and at the end of the row, the trees in the fields above the town were black, jagged shapes against the pink and gold sunset. Starlings were gathering in long ribbons and coils. Over the roof of the bakery, Jessie could see the pale disc of a full moon.

It had been a long day. She'd be glad when it was over.

She crossed to the shop, let herself in, and locked the door behind her. Slipping up the stairs, she took a deep breath before going into what had been her mother's room. The bed had been stripped. On the mattress was the imprint of the coffin, where Amos Morgan had insisted her mother lay for the days before the funeral. There had been no flowers or candles to disguise any odours so the room held a pungent, sickeningly-sweet smell that made Jessie gag. Holding her breath, she opened the wardrobe and prised up the wooden base. It lifted easily and she took out the canvas bag her mother had told her about. Not bothering to look into it, she closed the wardrobe and went downstairs.

Her heart thumping in her chest, she halted in the hall, listening for any sounds. She heard a catfight, a man shouting, a child crying. But nothing from inside the shop.

She paused, the urge to say goodbye to the place that had been her home too strong to ignore. Going into the kitchen, she looked around. Already there were changes, furniture she didn't recognise: a new red-and-green-striped moquette armchair, a new grey rug over the old linoleum, brass ornaments on the mantelpiece. Jessie's lips twisted. Amos Morgan had wasted no time in making the place his own.

There was nothing for her here now. She decided to leave by the back door; she didn't want to chance seeing Amos Morgan on the street.

The bakery was in dark shadow. The loaf tins on the shelves glinted, reflecting the moonlight that lit up the yard walls. Jessie remembered how, when she was little, it frightened her to come into the bakery at this time of night, how her father had consoled her and convinced her there was nothing to be scared of.

She sighed. She really should leave; she'd told Edna she wouldn't be long, she'd be worrying. But there was something else she wanted of her mother's. She dropped the canvas bag on the floor and opened the long table drawer. It only took a minute to find the wooden stamp her father had made. The design was an intertwined D and H.

'Dorothy and Harold,' Jessie murmured, running the tip of her forefinger over the initials. Her father had taken the idea from the grocer's butter stamp. For as long as she could remember all the pastry tops for the pies had been decorated with the motif. Until Amos Morgan.

All at once something oppressive puckered her skin with fear.

A voice said, 'Fancy you being here.'

Chapter 45

Amos Morgan pressed against her, his breath hot, wet, on the back of her neck.

'Get away.' Jessie twisted her shoulders, trying to shrug him off. But, despite the bulk of her womb, she was slight. Over the last two months the weight had dropped from her under her misery and she was no match for Amos Morgan. For the strength in his arms.

He pushed her forward and she sprawled across the table, her stomach pressed against the edge. Her only thought was for the child inside her. She curled her arm around her stomach, doing her best to protect it from the hard wood.

'No! Please, no. My baby...'

124

He didn't speak. Spreading himself against her, he struggled to push up her skirt. In her terror she barely noticed the elastic digging into her when he pulled her bloomers over her buttocks and down her legs. She flapped her other hand, trying to push him away, but he caught her wrist in a vice-like grip and twisted her arm up her back, laying against it to hold her down.

At first she resisted him, squeezing herself tight, but somehow he was forcing her legs further apart and pushing himself into her. She stiffened, gasped in agony, while he heaved and panted, the rhythmic pounding matched by his breathless wheezing. His hand moved to the back of her head, holding her down, rubbing her face against the wooden table with each violent thrust.

And then it stopped.

And he was gone.

For a few moments Jessie didn't move. A gulping sob, a long loud cry when she straightened, bearing the weight of her stomach with her hands. The room spun. She closed her eyelids tightly together, forced herself to take in a long mouthful of air.

The baby moved under her fingers as she dragged her bloomers up over her stomach. Oh God, was it all right? Her fear spewed out in a great rush of bile, covering the surface of the table.

For a second the need to escape seemed to paralyse her, but then panic drove her to the back door.

Arthur, I'm sorry. I couldn't stop him. I couldn't...

Pain shot down her thighs with each step, but then, even as her hand reached towards the key, she stopped.

The bag. She wasn't going to leave the bag. Holding on the side of the oven and the edge of the table, she knelt to retrieve it. In her struggles she'd kicked it under the table. The floor was gritty under her hand. Splatters of vomit darkened the beige material. An image of her mother's face spurred her on. Clutching the bag, she hauled herself upright and staggered to the door.

The yard was dim in the moonlight, the steps blocks of light and shadow, the line of wall of the lavvy and nearer the coal shed lost in

125

the dark. She dragged the yard gate open and stumbled along the alleyway. She wasn't frightened of the dark. She would never be scared of it again. She would never be able to erase this memory. Nothing worse could happen to her now.

Chapter 46

'Oh my Lord, what's happened? What's he done to you?' Edna gathered Jessie into her arms and led her to the kitchen. 'You're shaking like a leaf. And look at the state of you.' She peered at Jessie in the wavering light of the fire. 'You're as white as a sheet. Sit. Sit. I'll get a drop of brandy.'

'No.' Jessie waved her hand in dismissal, lowering herself onto the chair. Winced. 'I couldn't. I'll be sick again.'

'Again? What's happened?' Edna put her hand to her chest. 'Oh dear Lord. Jessie?

'He attacked me.' The shuddering came from deep inside Jessie. 'He – he – violated me, Edna.' Even though she didn't believe her legs would take her weight, she stood, tearing at her clothes. 'I need to get out of these.'

'I'll help.'

But before Edna could move, Jessie pushed, frantic, at the sleeves of her jacket, threw it on the floor.

'Let me help.'

Through the pulsing in Jessie's ears, Edna's voice sounded faint. She felt as if she was alone in the kitchen. Taking hold of the neck of her dress with both hands she yanked at the material. Buttons flew in all directions. She ripped and tore at her clothes until she was completely naked. Tipping her head back, she screamed.

'Oh, dear Lord. Oh, dear Lord.' Edna jerked a bedsheet from the overhead clothes pulley and draped it around Jessie. 'Hush now. Hush now, Jessie.'

She held her close, rocked her, until the screaming stopped and subsided into sobs. 'Sit there.' She lowered Jessie back into the chair and stroked her hair. 'Give me a minute.'

Jessie wrapped her arms around the bulge of her stomach, watching Edna bustle about as though from a distance. The sobbing stopped but the tears still flowed unheeded. She felt numb inside.

At the range Edna put sticks of wood and small pieces of coal on the fire. 'I've got some water on the go already,' she said. 'I'll get the bathtub in.'

It wasn't long before she was helping Jessie into the tin bath in front of the fire. The kitchen was warm and steamy. Yet Jessie couldn't stop trembling.

Edna washed her without either of them speaking. In silence she helped Jessie out of the bath and dried her with a large piece of towelling.

'There, better now?' She looked anxiously at Jessie.

'A little.'

'You've a bit more colour in your face, anyway. Put your nightdress on and sit in front of the fire. I'll get that brandy now. No arguing,' she said, when Jessie opened her moth to protest. 'It'll do neither you nor the bairn any harm to have a sip of the stuff. And, to be honest, I need a good drop of it myself.'

The fire had settled into a shifting of coal glowing red and a good inch of brandy had dropped in the bottle before Edna spoke again.

'I'm sorry, Jessie, I thought I'd kept a good look out but I didn't see him come back.'

Jessie's voice sounded strange even to herself. 'I don't think he really left. He must have gone around the back and sneaked in that way. I think he was there all the time.' The realisation made her shudder. 'He must have been creeping about downstairs while I was getting the...' She swung her head from side to side, looking down at the floor. 'The bag. What happened to the bag? I brought it—'

'It's in the hall. You dropped it when you came in. Wait there, I'll get it.' Her knees cracked when she pressed her hands on the table to help herself stand. 'That brandy's gone right to my head.'

She puffed out her cheeks, wobbling a little. 'Don't move. I'll get it.'

Jessie listened to the shuffle of her Edna's slippered feet, the slight groan when she was picking up the bag.

'It's in a bit of a mess,' she called.

'I was sick on it.' Jessie spoke in a dull voice. 'Can you open it, please, Edna.'

'You don't mind?'

'No, it's just some bits and pieces Mam wanted me to have of hers. He can't have seen ... he would have taken it from me...'

Edna struggled with the buttons and opened the top of the bag. She stared into it and then turned to look at Jessie, her mouth gaping.

'What is it? What's wrong?'

Edna tipped the bag on its side. 'Look.'

It was packed tight with crumpled pound notes.

Chapter 47

The bedroom was still in darkness when Jessie finally gave up all hope of sleep. Each time she closed her eyes the same nightmarish scene played through her mind. Amos Morgan had made sure that there would always be that dark place that she would never escape from. She knew it would always be there, waiting for her weakest moments.

She threw back the bedclothes and put on her dressing gown. Every movement brought fresh hurt. When she walked down the stairs she ached all over.

The tin bath was still there, waiting to be emptied into the yard, the water opaque. But the clothes she had worn the previous evening, the clothes she had ripped off, were nowhere to be seen. With luck Edna would have thrown them away.

Jessie rubbed her hands over her face, felt the soreness on the side of her chin. She looked at herself in the small mirror on the hook of the back door. A bruise had appeared overnight on her jawline from when her head had slammed against the table. She lowered herself onto one of the chairs, pushed her sleeves up. Her arms were covered in bruises, including a set of fingermarks. When she lifted her nightdress there were red wheals on her thighs.

'We could report 'im.'

Jessie jumped.

'Sorry, pet, I didn't mean to startle you.' Edna stood in front of Jessie. 'You look shockin', we should report 'im,' she repeated.

'No. I don't want anyone to know, Edna. Nobody! Ever!'

'But Arthur?'

Arthur. What would she tell Arthur? The tears started easily again.

'Oh, I'm sorry, Jessie. What a fool I am. We'll cross that bridge when we come to it. And don't worry, I'll be right by your side when you do tell him.'

So there would be no getting out of it. However Edna would support her, she still would make sure Arthur knew what had happened. But when? Jessie was shocked to realise the days were going by so quickly. While she'd looked after her mother, she'd managed to write only two letters. But had had no reply.

'We haven't heard from him yet, have we?'

'We 'aven't. It's been over two months since 'is last letter.' Edna's voice quivered.

'What should we do, Edna? I can't bear this not knowing where he is.'

'We keep writing.'

'You won't tell him – about what's happened, will you? I feel so ashamed...'

'There is no need for shame, Jessie.' Edna spoke with a fierceness that momentarily reassured Jessie. 'The shame is on that man's shoulders and 'is alone.'

'So you'll say nothing to Arthur? I need to see his face when I tell him.'

'Course not. I wouldn't do that. It can wait until 'e comes home.' Edna began to drag the bath to the back door.

'Let me help...' Jessie couldn't help the gasp of pain when she stood too quickly.

'Don't be daft, pet. In your condition. You need to keep that babby safe.'

Was there something in her voice? Something harsh? Still Jessie needed reassurance. 'You don't blame me, do you, Edna? For what happened? For what *he* did?'

'There's only one bugger I blame for what 'appened to you, Jessie. And sooner or later I'll make sure he's sorry.'

'What will you do?' Jessie immediately thought of the poisonous plant Edna had given her before.

From the way she heaved the tin bath and its contents into the yard and the glance Edna gave over her shoulder, there was no mistaking the hatred she had for Amos Morgan. 'He'll wish 'e'd never been born, lass.'

'What will you do, Edna?'

'Oh, I know what you're thinking, love, and I won't be doing that.' Her mouth softened. 'So don't you fret. I've got you and the bairn to look after. No, I'll just make sure Arthur understands exactly who's to blame.' She lifted the bath onto the hook on the outside wall of the house. 'And then we'll leave it to him.' She came into the kitchen and slammed the back door. 'Amos Morgan will get his comeuppance, there's no doubt about that.'

Chapter 48

'Do you think we should do something about that?' Edna jerked her thumb towards the canvas bag that had lain on one side of the table where she'd dropped it the evening before.

'I suppose we should hide it somewhere?' Although it was evening again, Jessie hadn't been dressed all day. 'I can't think about it yet, Edna.'

'Don't you want to know how much there is?'

'I suppose.' Jessie was aware that Edna had never asked her for a penny towards the rent money and the other bills. 'Would you tip it out?'

Edna didn't need telling twice. The screwed-up pound notes tumbled onto the table.

'Dear Lord, there's more money there than I ever imagined. And it was all yer mam's?'

'Yes.' Jessie stared at the pile of paper notes and then at Edna. 'Mam told me she was hiding some of the shop's takings from him – but I thought she meant what was in the tin she gave me. I never guessed it would be this much.'

'Can I?' Edna's hand hovered over the money.

'Yes. Yes, do.'

Edna handed one to Jessie before picking up another and smoothing it out between her fingers.

'Aren't they small? I've not held one of these before. A ten bob one, yes. But never a pound note.' She glanced at Jessie who looked stunned. 'You know what Old Powell calls these?'

'The landlord? No?'

'Bradburys. Because of some chap in the government who writes on them.' She pointed to a slanting signature under the picture of George the Fifth.

'But they're legal?'

'Oh yes, they most certainly are, pet. Your mam knew what she was doing, hiding these from that old bastard.' She stopped, poking her fingers into the money. 'There's something else 'ere. A box.' She handed the little brown cardboard carton to Jessie.

It opened easily. Two gold wedding bands and a silver locket dropped into Jessie's lap. She picked them up, held them in her palm and looked up at Edna. 'This one is Mam's wedding band from Dad.' She stroked it with the tip of her finger. 'This one was Granny's, I never knew her but I remember Mam showing me once.' She put the rings back into the box and let the chain slide through her fingers. She prised the locket open. 'Oh! This has photos of Mam and Dad. See...' She held it out to Edna.

131

'They were a handsome pair.' Edna peered at the images. 'You should treasure this.'

'Oh, I will.' Jessie sighed. It was lovely to see her mam and dad looking so happy, yet it was sad at the same time.

'Right!' The older woman sat down at the table. Resolute. 'Let's count what yer poor mam saved for you, shall we?'

It took almost an hour to unwrap and smooth out the money. The only sounds in the kitchen were the ticking sideboard clock, the creaking of Edna's corset each time she reached forward to retrieve another note, her heavy breathing and Jessie's exclamations as the pile of money grew.

'There!' Edna sat back in her chair. 'One hundred and fourteen pounds.' The metal curlers in her hair rattled as she shook her head, her eyebrows raised in amazement.

Jessie held her fingers over her mouth. 'Where can we hide so much?'

'There are a couple of loose floorboards in your room. Arthur made a space under there. He had a box to hide. Edna smiled. 'He was only small, but 'e said he had special things 'e needed to keep in it. Turned out it was a collection of birds' eggs, but he didn't know to blow them out. Made his bedroom smell something awful. I don't think he used 'is secret place ever again. Well, I know he didn't. I cleaned it out and I put my insurance papers and wotnot in there.' She began packing the bag again. 'You could put this in there?'

'Keep some out, Edna. I owe you.'

'Like thump you do. This'll give you and Arthur a good start to married life.'

'No, I insist. I need to pay my way. Arthur would want me to.'

'All Arthur wants is for you to be safe. I failed on that, Jessie—'

'Don't. You didn't.'

'Well, let me look after you and your babby from now on. And no more talk of owing.' Edna rose and placed the money back in the bag. 'Would you like me to show you where this lot will be safe?'

'Please.'

'And remember, Jessie, you owe me nothing. You're giving me the

132

most precious thing I could ever wish for—' She stopped. 'Except for my son coming 'ome to us. You're giving me a grandchild.'

Chapter 49

One night, a week after her mother's funeral, a line of twenty women walked up to the chapel to pay their respects to Dorothy.

Every house on the street had given three pennies to the collection organised by Edna for the wax flowers in the glass dome, carried by Jessie. It had taken all her strength to step out of the house but surrounded by the neighbours and with Edna's arm around her waist, she found the courage.

At the cemetery she knelt by the grave and placed the dome on top of the soil.

One of the women began a prayer: *'Eternal rest grant unto Dorothy, Oh Lord, and let perpetual light shine upon her.'*

The others joined in: *'Through the mercy of God, rest in peace. Amen.'*

'Amen,' Jessie repeated. 'Do you think there'll be a headstone?' She looked up at Edna.

'With that skinflint? I doubt it.'

'Then I'll pay for it with the money.'

Edna glanced around, anxious. 'Hush now. We'll talk about it later.' She raised her voice. 'Tea and cake at our house, ladies? Or a drop of brandy? A toast to Dorothy?'

There was a muttering of approval. Everyone moved towards the path, except for Jessie.

'I'm going now, Mam,' she said. 'I'll be back next week. And when your grandchild arrives I'll bring him or her to introduce you. I'm just sorry you won't really see...' She pushed herself upright, the weight of her stomach almost tipping her forward. 'And I'll make sure you'll have a headstone, as well.'

She followed the others along the path.

Chapter 50

'Always could hold 'er ale, Mrs Giles.' They watched the stout woman support two of her neighbours as they tottered alongside her down the street. 'Mind you, with an 'usband like hers, I'd want to be drunk every day.'

'And it was good of Mrs Hampson to come, Edna. Especially as it's only last week that she heard her Tommy had been killed. I didn't like the twins much but I wouldn't wish either of them dead.'

Jessie could have bitten her tongue off when Edna answered, 'She's a good woman and at least she's got another son to give 'er comfort.' She patted Jessie's shoulder ushering her back into the house, speaking in a more determinedly cheerful voice. 'Well, I think that was a good send off for your mam, eh?'

'It was. And thank you, Edna.' She knew Arthur's mother had hurriedly steered her through the front door as Amos Morgan came to the door of the shop to stare at them. Anger and distress merged inside her – she thought she would always feel them, every time she saw him. The anger she would nurture; it would make her strong. She wouldn't let him ruin her life, her future with Arthur.

'I think I'll play a few tunes – would that be all right? Not disrespectful? It always soothes me.'

'No, Mam would like that, I'm sure. She always loved to hear you play. Something cheerful, eh, Edna?' Jessie was glad Edna had started playing her piano again; in the first months of hearing nothing from Arthur it was as though she'd lost the heart to touch it.

In the kitchen Jessie stoked up the fire and settled in her chair, listening to Edna, smoothly changing from one tune to another. She always marvelled that Arthur's mum had such a talent– her fingers were not suited for delicacy until she touched those keys.

She pulled the note from Clara out of her skirt pocket. It was only a few words but they had been a comfort to her since her mam's passing. She straightened the paper and read it. The last couple of sentences caused her tears to flow again.

...It will be a great comfort to you when your neighbours, your mother's friends, go with you to pay their respects at the graveside. That's the day you must remember, not the day of the funeral that that awful man arranged. Put that day out of your mind forever. I love the thought that you will be placing the dome of flowers on your mother's grave, with her friends and neighbours around you.

And remember, your mother knew how much you loved her. Her last thoughts must have held that knowledge and given her great comfort before she passed on. Thinking of you as always, dear,

Your loving friend,
Clara x

If only it were possible to put that day out of her mind forever. Jessie doubted she would ever tell her friend what had happened to her, however close they were. The misery and shame were hers to carry in secret.

And if only she was able to tell Clara about the baby. Jessie rubbed at her forehead. Each time she'd sat down to write and tell her, she persuaded herself to wait. Arthur could come home, they could be married before she next saw her friend. They could be young married women who met to walk the babies in their perambulators in the park. Just like other mothers.

Ten minutes later, Jessie heard the creak of the parlour door. Lifting the hem of her skirt, she quickly rubbed at her face, folded Clara's note and put it back into her pocket.

Edna bustled into the kitchen. 'That's better!' She sat in the armchair next to Jessie.

'That was lovely.'

There were things unspoken between them. Edna put her hand on Jessie's knee. 'You'll be fine,' she said. 'When Arthur comes home, you'll be fine... And me.' She gave a gusty sigh. 'If we could only hear how he is...'

Words that went round and round in Jessie's head every night.

135

'We will, Edna. Soon.' Despite her own despair, she tried to brighten the mood. 'It was so thoughtful of them all today.'

'They are good neighbours.' Edna nodded. She shifted in the chair, stretched. 'Mind if I go and take these corsets off?'

'No, you get comfy. I'll make a brew.'

A few minutes later Edna appeared in her dressing gown, scratching at her waist. 'That's better.' She put a few pieces of coal on the fire, refilled the kettle and put it on the range hob. 'For later,' she said. 'We'll both need a bit of a wash, later.'

They sat in comfortable silence drinking their tea before Edna said abruptly, 'I just want to say something, Jessie. And then I won't mention it again. But if ever you need to talk about what happened over the road, the day of your mam's funeral, I'm here to listen...' She took a slurp of her tea.

Jessie didn't speak for a while. 'Thank you, Edna. I won't if you don't mind.'

Edna trailed a finger around the rim of her cup. 'Just wanted you to know, pet. Sometimes, things can haunt us for years if we don't have anyone to talk to about them.' She looked pensive. 'I was lucky when we moved here, I had your mam. She was a great listener.'

'Was she?'

'Aye.'

Jessie waited a while before saying, 'I hope you don't mind my asking, Edna, but did something happen to you, once? Before you came to the street? And you had no one to talk to? To help you?' She couldn't believe that the popular, gregarious woman hadn't always had friends to share her troubles with. Or relatives. Though Jessie had never heard her talk of family, other than Arthur.

Edna gazed at her, holding her lower lip between her teeth. She took in a long breath.

'There was a time. Before we moved here. We lived in Manchester where we knew no one. We'd gone there with, Jim's, Mr Dawson's job. He was a fire stoker on the railways. I'd been married to Jim for five years. We'd tried for ages to have a family, so we were over the moon when Arthur was born because we were beginning to think I was getting too old to catch, you know?'

Jessie nodded, but said nothing. She didn't want to interrupt with trivial questions.

'And then, when Arthur was only one, I found out I was expecting another babby. I was a bit worried, you know, about the money side of things but Jim was chuffed to bits.

'Anyway, when I was seven months gone there was an accident on the line. Not the one he usually worked on, but he was covering for some chap who was sick. The accident was something to do with the signals being wrong. It happened just outside Manchester.' A shadow passed over her face. 'There were several injuries. But Jim was the only one killed.'

'Oh, Edna...' Jessie remembered Arthur talking about his father's death, recalled the sadness in his eyes.

'I lost the babby.' Edna blinked back sudden tears. 'Course I got a bit of compensation but not much. And the railway paid for his funeral, such as it was. But I knew no one around there. Me and Jim kept ourselves to ourselves...'

She pushed herself out of the chair and bent over the fire, rattling the poker around in the coal. A few burned bits of coke dropped into the ash can below the grate. When she straightened and put the poker back onto the hearth, she looked at Jessie. 'I were that lonely the day I brought Arthur back to the house after the funeral. I think the neighbours thought me stand-offish, so no one came near.'

She gave a small shake of her shoulders. 'But *you've* got me, pet. And always will have. So, like I said, anything you want to talk about. Anything at all, I mean – I'm here, Right?'

Chapter 51

Jessie rested for a moment against the wall on Bury Road, looking up at the horizon on Wharmton Hill. There had been no word from Arthur for months. It was four months since Christmas, when he'd said he'd be home, that the war would be finished. The baby moved restlessly inside her as if acknowledging her distress, her overwhelming anxiety.

'Hush,' she murmured, spreading her fingers across her stomach, feeling the rippling as her child turned again.

'Jessie!'

She spun around.

'Clara? What...? Her friend was hurrying towards her.

There was something about the frantic waving, arm high in the air, that brought the familiar fear to Jessie. So she too, began to run, a clumsy shambling pregnant gait, uncertain on the uneven footpath. As she ran faster, Arthur's coat fell open. She saw her friend slow, stop. Clara's hand lowered to cover her mouth.

Jessie braced herself. Standing in front of Clara, bending forward and holding her side to ease a stabbing stitch, she waited for the question. It came immediately.

'Jessie?' Clara gripped to her elbows, pulling her upright. 'You're ... It's Arthur's?'

The hint of a question made Jessie move her head. 'Yes. Yes, of course!' Why ask? Who else's would it be? Her resentment burned.

'Oh my God! Why didn't you tell me? Write to tell me? None of your letters even hinted...'

'I couldn't.' Jessie twisted to look at Clara, feeling the ache in her side ease.

'But I told you about our baby.'

'You're married.' No more explanation was needed as far as Jessie was concerned.

'You think that would matter to me?' Clara's voice was husky. 'You should have told me. I'm your friend.'

She saw despair flicker in Clara's eyes and Jessie was afraid. 'What's happened, Clara? It's Arthur isn't it? You've heard something about Arthur...' Her legs threatened to give way under her.

'No. No, it's Stanley.'

'He's not...?' Why else would her friend look so stricken, so drawn? So old. 'He's not...?' she repeated, gentler this time.

'Oh, no. But he's been injured, Jessie. He's in a convalescent home just outside Manchester.' She crumpled, her hands over her face.

Jessie pulled Clara close. Despite her pregnancy she was skinny, almost to the point of being gaunt. 'So why are you here? What about your parents?'

'I haven't told them.'

'What!'

'I left a note. Saying I was coming to visit you. I caught the train— '

'They will be out of their minds with worry, Clara. They'll know something is wrong.' Jessie couldn't help the sharpness in her words. Clara had gone to them when she'd discovered she was pregnant, now she'd obviously just left without letting them know why.

'Please don't shout at me, Jessie. Stanley said I was to bring you with me. As my friend,' Clara said. 'Please, Jessie.'

'I didn't mean to shout, love. Sorry. Come on, let's get out of the cold.' A thin strand of guilt wound around the relief of knowing it wasn't Arthur who'd been injured. But was that so much worse than not knowing where he was?

She led Clara along Castle Street, stopping her from crossing the road towards the bakery. 'No. I'm living at Arthur's mam's house now.' She offered no more explanation, just put the key in the lock and pushed at the brown-varnished door.

Stanley, Clara's lovely Stanley, injured. She hated this war.

Chapter 52

'I'm scared to go on my own. He hasn't said how he was injured, what – what it's done to him. Please say you will?'

'Of course I'll come with you, Clara.'

139

'I'm not sure you should,' Edna interrupted. She poured water from the iron kettle into the washtub and pushed down the sheets with the posser. She shook her head towards Clara. 'I'm not sure she should.'

Jessie had seen Edna watching Clara with suspicion. She didn't know why, other than that Arthur's mother had become even more protective of her as her pregnancy progressed. 'You don't know this, I'm sure, but Jessie 'asn't had an easy time of it over these last few months.' She glanced out of the window at the grey morning. 'The weather is going to get worse and it'll be a long day getting to and from Manchester.' She gave the wash an extra prod. 'Why not your parents? I remember Jessie sayin' you'd gone back to live with them? Can't they go with you? Especially in your condition.'

Clara stared down at her stomach. 'Mother and father love me. And they are good parents; they've looked after me so well these last few months. And they are thrilled about the baby. But they never really took to Stanley. They didn't want me to marry out.'

'What?' The lines between Edna's eyebrows deepened. 'What do you mean, "out"?'

'Edna—'

'It's all right, Jessie. I don't mind.' Clara gazed steadily at the woman. 'We – my family – are Jewish, Mrs Dawson. My parents would have preferred me to marry a Jewish young man. Stanley wasn't who they'd planned for me to marry.'

Edna bent over the washtub, her face flushed. 'Oh. Oh, sorry.'

Jessie knew that Edna, being a Roman Catholic, would understand, however much she herself flouted Father Thomas' governing. She covered the awkward pause. 'Will you be all right doing the washing on your own?' she asked Edna.

'Yes. Yes, of course. I'll be fine, no worries about that, pet. It's just that I worry...'

'I know.' Jessie smiled, reassuring her. 'I'll be okay. Honest. I'll be careful.'

'Well, mind you are.' Edna leaned lower over the tub and, with a small knife, grated flakes off a large green bar of carbolic soap. 'I'll walk you both to the station. No arguing.' She stopped Jessie's protest with another shake of her head, swishing her hand around in the warm water. 'I need to leave this lot to soak anyway and it's the least I can do. And you, Clara, can stay here for the night, if it's dark when you get back.'

'Thanks, Edna.' Jessie knew that was a big concession. She could see that Arthur's mother was wary of Clara; she was what the woman would call 'posh'.

Chapter 53

The two women stood by the tall black wrought iron gates at the end of the drive, looking towards Doveton Manor. Jessie felt Clara fumbling for her hand. She'd been quiet on the train, now, when she spoke, her voice was low and shaky

'I can't do this. I am so scared, Jessie.'

'I'm sure it won't be as bad as you think, Clara. Stanley would have warned you if he was seriously hurt.' Her words sounded hollow even to her. She fingered her locket to give her courage, took in a long breath. 'Come on, let's go in.'

They walked along the gravel drive, still holding hands. The lawns on either side were pristine. Faint light shone from almost every window on all three levels of the grey stone mansion. Jessie could see silhouettes. It seemed to her that they were watching their progress. Clara's anxiety was catching; she began to wonder what they would see inside this building.

A nurse wearing a grey serge uniform appeared at the top of the steps, tugging at her white cuffs, and waited by one of the wide oak double doors.

'Hello. I'm Sister O'Neil.' The smile was slightly strained; she had dark circles around her eyes and lines angled down from her mouth. 'I was warned you were on your way by some of the men in there.'

She gave a small roll of her head towards the front rooms leading off the hall behind her. 'They are much excited to see two ladies walking up the drive. We don't get many visitors, especially female ones.'

She paused, taking in for the first time their obviously pregnant figures, and sighed. Still her smile didn't waver. 'And,' she added briskly, 'I'm sure they will take heart that the world outside is – if not normal, well, at least some things that are perfectly normal carry on.' She directed this remark pointedly at their stomachs. 'This way, ladies. Follow me to the office and we can get the formalities over with.'

The strong smell of disinfectant didn't quite override other odours that Jessie couldn't place. She swallowed and breathed through her mouth. Glancing at Clara, she saw she was doing the same. There was a rattle of metal on hard floors, voices behind closed doors, shouts. The harsh sound of a telephone bell.

They followed the Sister across the hall, their heels sharp clatters on the brown tiles.

A man was lying alone on a stretcher in the hall by the broad, sweeping staircase. His face was deathly pale, wet with sweat, and he moved his head frantically as though trying to get away from his pain. Or perhaps, Jessie thought, from the memories of what he'd seen where he'd fought. The muscles in his jaw bulged with effort and he groaned. Under his red blanket his feet jerked constantly.

Jessie hesitated before passing him. It felt wrong just to carry on as though he wasn't there, as though he wasn't a human being. A stench hit her immediately, a foul gassy smell like nothing she'd ever known before. She held her breath. For a second the man's red-rimmed eyes focused on her. He lurched over to one side, throwing off the blanket and revealing both his feet They were engorged and dark red, the blisters on his swollen toes leaked a noxious bloody fluid.

Behind her, Clara coughed, gagged. Jessie heard her stumble, then push past her, her hands covering her mouth.

'Please don't do that.' The nurse's tone was sharp.

'Why is he alone?' It filled Jessie with a bitter sadness. This could be Arthur, somewhere, lying on a floor, waiting to die. Because that, surely, was what this poor man was doing. 'He shouldn't be alone.'

'He won't be.' Sister O'Neil nodded towards an open door.

A man appeared, dressed in a flannel blue uniform and leaning heavily on crutches. Ignoring them, he painstakingly made his way across the hall to the stretcher, one empty trouser leg, folded up and pinned, swinging in rhythm to his ungainly movement. Every time he stopped to regain his balance, he touched the four medals that were fastened to the left side of his jacket, almost as though they gave him courage. Eventually he lowered himself to sit in on the stairs beside the wounded man, speaking low reassuring words even as he struggled to steady himself. He glanced up at the nurse and nodded, exchanged a smile.

It was as though they weren't there, Jessie thought, uncomfortable. She felt as though they had intruded on a private moment.

'This way, please.' The Sister's black shoes squeaked on the red-tiled floor of the hall. Jessie and Clara followed her into a small office only big enough for a desk and chair, two wooden cabinets. 'Do sit, ladies.' She pointed to two grey canvas and metal chairs squashed into a corner.

Clara sank onto the nearest one; Jessie sat on the edge of the other and looked around. On the beige-painted wall facing the curtain-less window was a large imposing portrait of George the Fifth. More interesting to her, above and below the painting, were rows of photographs of men in the hospital blue uniform with red ties over white shirts. Most wore regimental caps and medals; all had messages of thanks, good wishes and signatures scrawled across them.

'Clostridial myonecrosis,' Sister O'Neil said without preamble, clasping her hands on the desktop. 'Gangrene.' She raised a finger towards the door. 'That poor man out there shouldn't have been transferred here this morning. He's going back to the Red Cross Hospital in Cheadle Cross. We're waiting for the ambulance.'

She stared directly at Clara. 'We are a convalescent home here but still, I'm afraid, you will see some upsetting sights. I must ask you to control how you react to the men here.'

Clara dipped her head. 'I'm sorry.'

'They've more than enough to deal with without feeling judged for their injuries.'

'Will he be all right?' Though she guessed the answer, Jessie had to ask.

'No, I'm afraid not. Now ladies...' She opened a file. 'Who is it you're here to visit?'

'Stanley Duckworth.' Clara spoke in subdued voice. 'Captain Duckworth. He's my husband.'

'Oh!' The nurse's cap swayed as she raised her head from the file to look at her. 'He wrote to you. I remember.' She closed the file, placed her pen in a blue velvet case. 'Then you'd better come with me. He will be pleased to see you looking so well and with...' She waggled a finger in the direction of Clara's stomach. 'His child?'

Clara's cheeks reddened. 'Of course, his child.' She set her mouth in indignation but the nurse didn't notice.

Before opening the door, she fixed a stern gaze on them. 'And remember what I said. Please control yourselves.'

Chapter 54

A man in a wheelchair had joined the other two in the hall. He rocked his wheelchair to and fro with one hand, his jacket hanging loose to show a white lining, his sleeve pinned. A mask painted the colour of skin covered half his face and was held in place by wire-rimmed glasses. He returned Jessie's tentative smile with a defiant glare. She felt heat colour her cheeks.

'This way.' The nurse led them across the hall to a door to the left of the stairs, before leaving them with another warning. 'I would ask you not to go in any of the others rooms on this floor and certainly not go upstairs. Unfortunately, one of the men was unwittingly admitted with Spotted Fever, er, meningitis. Despite isolating him, others have followed. I suspect it was the overcrowding on the transport ships with poor ventilation.' She flattened the front of her white collar with her palm. 'As though we and,' she pushed the door wider, 'the men don't have enough to contend with. Let's just hope it doesn't become an epidemic as it has in other parts of the country where we have returning soldiers.'

Clara exchanged glances with Jessie, clearly shaken. Jessie held a hand to her waist.

The sister nodded, satisfied she had given enough warning.

'Remember, ladies...' She took in a long breath that flared her nostrils. 'Self-control.' Checking the fob watch pinned to her apron, her voice softened. 'Please let me know if I can help in any way. I'll probably see you before you leave. Now, I have things I must do.' She spun on her heels and walked away, towards the three men.

They looked at one another.

'Listen. Jessie.' Clara raised her eyebrows, smiled. Someone was playing a piano music and they heard the low bass of men singing. 'They sound cheerful. Perhaps it won't be so bad after all.'

The voices trailed off when the two of them entered the room. It was stifling hot. In the large ornamental marble fireplace, flames rose high in the chimney breast. Compared to the bright hall, the room was in half-light. Jessie felt as if everyone was looking at them, as they stood in the doorway.

They moved forward, scanning the room. There was an overpowering smell of sweat and disinfectant, boiled cabbage and the metallic taint of blood. The central candelabra had half its bulbs missing. In one corner there was a group of men huddled together. At first she could only see their figures. As her gaze moved to their faces, the horror hit her.

Some of them were so disfigured their features were indistinguishable. Many had noses missing, lips hanging, jawlines and chins gone. Faces pulped, torn, mutilated. Despite loathing herself for it, Jessie held her breath, afraid she'd be sick. She willed herself only to look into the eyes of the young men. But the images would be locked forever in her mind. So young, she kept thinking as her eyes slid from one to another.

The soldier at the piano began playing again, a slow classical piece. Otherwise there were no sounds in the large room other than the snap of the fire and, from somewhere above them, a man crying. All watched the two women as they haltingly walked forward.

The silence was unnerving. Jessie took off her broad-brimmed hat and nudged Clara to do the same. Despite the smothering heat she pulled her black woollen coat over her stomach as best she could.

Clara copied her.

One of the men, dressed like all the others in a blue uniform, with his cap pushed to the back of his head, gave a slow, hoarse whistle. He waved and grinned at them. Not knowing what else to do, they gave him vague half-smiles.

'I can't see Stanley,' Clara whispered, her breath ragged in Jessie's ear.

'He has to be here. She said he was in here.'

And then Jessie saw Stanley at last.

'Oh, God. Oh, God.' Clara's outburst told Jessie they'd seen him at the same time.

Captain Stanley Duckworth was sitting in the middle of a group of men, looking at them, a nurse by his shoulder. He was in a wheelchair. A blanket was over his legs, but the cover hung strangely flat. Even across the room Jessie could see his white knuckles as he gripped the sides of the wheelchair. As though he was holding on. As though he would fall if he didn't.

He has no legs. The realisation sucked the air from her lungs. A pulse throbbed in her neck and, for a moment, she thought she would faint. When she turned to Clara, she saw complete shock in her friend's face.

'We need to get a hold of ourselves,' she murmured. 'We can't let him see what we are feeling. You have to be strong.'

'He's lost his legs.' Clara's voice was faint.

'I know.' Jessie gripped her hand. 'Be strong,' she said, fierce in her desperation to make her friend move forward. 'Clara! Breathe!'

The girl drew in a sharp intake of air. Jessie thought she would cry out but she didn't. She lowered her head and when she looked up she'd fixed a wide smile to her lips.

'I'm fine,' she whispered. 'Give me a moment.'

'We don't have a moment.'

The nurse alongside Stanley had her hand on his shoulder. It seemed as if she was balancing him, though her touch looked light. Her mouth was curved into a smile but her eyes were wary, watching them weaving their way through the wheelchairs towards him. Her expression warned them not to say or do anything that would destroy even more this man who had been in her care for the last two weeks.

'Sweetheart.' Even his voice sounded different, frailer. Jessie wondered if Clara thought the same. She pressed her hand again on her friend's back. Felt her shudder.

'Stanley.' It was all Clara said.

Someone pushed a chair behind her and she dropped onto it. Jessie was grateful when a chair was pressed against her knees as well. Her legs folded under her and she sat in one sudden movement, glad that now they all three were equal in height. For a short time.

The nurse stepped back. 'I'll bring some tea, Stan.' She went, her uniform rustling, leaving behind a faint perfume of lavender.

Stan, Jessie thought, wondering if Clara had noticed. The shortened name made him seem even more different.

She watched the nurse, admiring the calm smile, the laughter shared with some of the men as she moved from one disfigured, limbless soldier to another, even bending down to put her arms around one or two, before she left the room.

Turning back, Jessie noticed the way Clara was sitting in the

147

chair: rigid, her hands, fingers wound tight together, clasped on her lap. She didn't speak.

The noise level around them grew, but they were left in a pool of silence only broken by Stanley giving a slight cough.

'Jessie.' He ran his fingers through his hair. The action made him sway in the wheelchair.

Clara gave another sudden gasp but still said nothing.

To disguise her friend's reaction, and relieved he'd spoken directly to her, Jessie smiled at him. 'It's good to see you home safe, Stanley,' she said quickly. 'How are you?' Stupid thing to say, she told herself. She was babbling to cover over Clara's silence.

She told herself not to ask him if he'd heard anything about Arthur. This was their moment – his and Clara's – their time to find one another again, to deal with what this awful war had done to him – to them.

'As you see.' He waved his hand over the blanket. 'But well enough, thank you, Jessie. And thank you for coming with Clara. I didn't want her travelling alone in her condition.' He stopped, his eyes travelling down from Jessie's face to the open front of her coat. She smiled, self-conscious.

'Yes, it's Arthur's.'

'Good.' His nod was emphatic. Too emphatic. But he didn't meet her eyes.

She couldn't help herself. 'Have you heard anything from him?'

His forehead creased. He rubbed the pad of his thumb along the frown as though to smooth it away. When he raised his eyes to hers, he couldn't disguise the anguish in them. She understood.

'When?'

He held onto one arm of the wheelchair and grappled with the button on the breast pocket of his jacket. He reached in with two fingers. The envelope he drew out was soft, crumpled, smeared with stains. Mud and splatters of something else. Somewhere, somehow, it registered with her that it was blood but, just as quickly, she shut out that knowledge.

'I need to give you this.'

Stanley handed it to her. The edges were crinkled as though it had once been wet. Perhaps by rain, she thought...

Clara turned her head from one to the other. Uncomprehending. Lost in her own distress.

Jessie opened the envelope and tipped its contents into her palm. A small photo slid out. Even before she flipped it over, she knew it would be her image. Just as she knew the small scrap of folded paper would be the note she'd given to Arthur the day before he marched out of Nether Brook. And the withered and dried out bits of grass were the remains of the makeshift ring of grass, once the same as the one she had in the box in her drawer at Edna's.

'He was writing to you,' Stanley said softly, pointing to another crumpled piece of paper.

'You've read it?' Jessie resented that. She should have been the first to see Arthur's words.

'I'm sorry.' Stanley offered no explanation.

'Oh, no.' At last Clara spoke. She stroked Jessie's arm, leant against her, at last understanding. 'Oh, no.'

Jessie straightened out the letter. Some of the words were obliterated, spread out into inky smudged stars. She read to herself what she could, touching the words.

Darling Jessie ... so we may move somewhere else ... don't be alarmed if ... before you hear from me. For... having a rest for a day or two ... way from the line. There is a farmyard near ... fowls laying ... I sell the eggs I ... not stealing ... round here we ... and people make us pay such a lot for things so ... There is a chap writing in the next bed from ... had a letter from home ... why his cousin hasn't wrote to his mother ... been killed ... God help his mother ... only son ... Sweetheart ... I...

The letter ended abruptly, as though Arthur was meaning to finish it later.

'There's no date on it,' was all Jessie could say, not trusting herself to ask if Stanley knew what had happened. Not trusting how her body would react.

'No.' Stanley's mouth is set in a hard line. 'The soldier who gave it to me wrote on the envelope.'

She turned it over.

The writing was in large childish capitals. She read it aloud. Slowly. Mouthing each word with deliberation.

'Sir, I am trusting you with this envelope found in a wood here in the battlefields outside Neuve-Chapelle. It was among these other things I am passing to you. I am very sorry to say I could not find the owner. I cannot say if he has been wounded or killed but there were many bodies. Too many for us to bury. For that I am also sorry.'

'Who?'

'A soldier. Just one I came across in the train on the way to the Casualty Clearing Station. Huts where we were all assessed, a few miles behind the lines,' he said, his tone expressionless. 'Where they – where I had the operation. I was the only officer in that carriage, so he gave what he'd found to me. He was sent back to his unit. He only had shrapnel in his left shoulder and left hand. As he was right-handed they reckoned they'd patched him up enough to go back.'

Jessie took care to put the contents back into the envelope and held it in her hand.

She had a vivid image of Arthur lying face down, in mud. Wondered how long he'd suffered. Had he suffered? She hoped not, how she hoped not. Had he even known those were his last moments? Had he thought of home? Of her?

Gazing above the heads of the broken men to the large window, Jessie saw the snow-covered moors in the distance. They'd taken on the hues of the setting sun, straggling through darkening splintered clouds, changing shape with each moment. How many thousands of feet had trampled over those moors, the heather, the bracken, in

150

search of work? How many thousands are still trudging, still fighting over similar places in foreign countries, land no longer fertile, only mud and slime? And bodies. Men who didn't know her Arthur had gone? Not caring probably, intent only on staying alive.

She had an indefinable feeling of vulnerability, of being truly alone. She had to leave.

She saw Clara lean over Stanley, put her head into his shoulder, put her lips to his throat. It felt like an intimate moment she should be no part of.

She turned her head, caught the eye of one of the men propped between cushions in a large chair. He had no arms or legs. She kept her gaze steadily on his face. And smiled. He grinned back at her.

She heard her friend murmuring.

'I love the feel of your skin on mine,' Clara said to her husband. 'Always have, my love. Always will.'

Chapter 55

Jessie was glad to be alone on the return journey to Nether Brook. Glad that Clara had chosen to stay at the convalescent home. The Sister had organised a room for her next to Stanley's. Her friend had a difficult time in front of her, but she'd seen determination in Clara's face so perhaps there was hope for her and Stanley.

As it turned eight o'clock, the sky was already getting darker. She was thankful for that, no one to see her, no questioning glances. Across the street the shop was closed with only a dim light from the kitchen visible through the edges of the shop window.

Jessie hunched her shoulders against the cold and, turning to Edna's front door, pushed the key into the lock.

Going through to the kitchen, she saw Edna was still washing. Clothes were dangling from the pulley above and steaming around the fire on the clothes horse. She must be worn out, Jessie thought, standing still and watching.

She pinched the bridge of her nose. In a few seconds she would be destroying this kind woman's life, ending all hope. For her. For her son. Everything was so mundane, so normal. But nothing, for either of them, would be normal ever again.

Edna pulled a blouse from the tub and wrung it between her hands, grimacing with the effort before throwing it into the sink and prodding it with the wooden tongs. She straightened up over the washtub and pressed her hands to the small of her back. Turned to see Jessie.

'Good grief, pet, you gave me a scare, standing there so quiet-like.' She looked behind Jessie. 'You on your own then?' Grimaced, bending her neck towards one shoulder and then the other. 'My rheumatism's playing up something shockin' today. I've dosed myself up to the eyeballs with Kutnow's Powder...

'And Mrs Giles came over today waving her newspaper and telling me about some blasted new stuff – some poisonous gas stuff – them bloody Germans are using on our lads in France. Somewhere called Whypress it said on the headline. I just hope to God our Arthur's nowhere near where they're using it...' She faltered, her eyes on Jessie's mouth.

Jessie's lips felt stiff, unable to form the words she knew she had to say.

'Edna...'

'Don't say it!' Edna shouted, her cheeks flushed, quivering. She dropped the tongs into the soapy water, banged the ridged washboard against the side of the metal tub. 'Don't. Say. It.'

Holding on to the tub she fell to her knees, dragging it with her. The water streamed over her and across the kitchen floor. She splayed her arms across the round side of the tub and rested her head on it. 'No. No.'

Lifted out of her own grief, Jessie moved to heave Edna up and onto the nearest chair. She felt the drag in her stomach and a twinge of pain.

'We'll get through this, Edna,' she said. 'I promise.' She knelt in front of Arthur's mother, cradled her hands in her own.

Chapter 56

May 1915

She had no pain at first, just the sort of discomfort she used to feel during the week before her monthlies were due.

The days after she'd returned from the convalescent home had passed in a haze of grief and sleeplessness. That first night she'd lain alongside Edna, holding her, rubbing her arms to warm her, to stop the shivering. To cry with her. Since then, each night, curled into a foetal position in her bed, she listened to the low keening through the wall, willing herself not to go to her, knowing Edna wanted to be alone in her misery now.

They were the same in the daytime. Alone and hugging their grief to themselves. Barely speaking. Jessie felt as if there was a distance between them neither could cross. They were both grieving for the same man, yet it was different: one for a lover, one for a son. And the feelings were so diverse, no words could help them find a common ground.

So Jessie ignored what her body was telling her.

Edna sat at the kitchen table staring through the window. Near her elbows, a puddle of tea had stained the faded flowery oilcloth and spread under the plate of half-eaten bread and dripping that Jessie had given her earlier. The tap was dripping unheeded, a monotonous regular splash into the stone sink. The room was chilly and grey ash shifted in the grate when Jessie came downstairs.

Edna spoke in a flat voice. 'My son's not dead. You do know that? You do know you're wrong about that, don't you, Jessie?'

Chapter 57

'I don't know what the world is coming to.' Mrs Giles lowered herself onto the kitchen chair, which disappeared under her bulk. 'I brought the paper over for Edna. Where is she?'

'In bed.' Jessie said in resignation. Edna had refused to get up all day except to go out to the lavvy. She wouldn't eat, she wouldn't talk. When she'd said Arthur was not dead, that was the last time she'd spoken to Jessie. 'She's in bed, Mrs Giles, she's not very well.'

'Taken it bad, has she?'

Jessie nodded.

'And you?'

'I'm okay.'

'Well, you don't look it, if I might say so.' Mrs Giles tilted her head. 'You look proper peaky.'

'I'm fine.'

'Hmm.' Mrs Giles shuffled around in the chair. The legs creaked. 'Well, if you say so.' She touched the newspaper. 'So, what d'you think? It might take her out of herself if I go up for a natter. Tell her what's goin' on and that?'

Jessie sighed. Good-hearted as she was, the woman had a thick skin.

She didn't even read the headlines of the paper Mrs Giles had slapped down on the table in front of her. She didn't want to know what horrors were going on outside the house, the country. They'd left the radio switched off since Arthur was gone. She pressed her hand on the tightly-stretched bowl of her stomach, fought against the ready tears.

'Shall I go up?' Mrs Giles rested her arms on top of the table to take her weight, ready to heave herself off the chair, her large bosom spreading out.

'No, don't, Mrs Giles. It's kind of you but I don't think she's up to it today.'

Jessie motioned towards the paper, reluctantly reading the bold print:

'Lusitania' is sunk by a German submarine.

'Over twelve hundred lives! Fancy that. Twelve hundred! Mostly from America.' Mrs Giles jabbed her finger at one of the columns of writing and peered at the words. 'And still the President – er – this – er – Woodrow Wilson says, "the United States is too proud to fight". Can you believe that?'

Jessie shook her head. Please go away, she thought, just go away and leave us in peace.

'What does he mean anyway? Our lads are fighting. Does he mean they're not proud?'

'Oh, Mrs Giles ... Please...'

'Well, I tell you, I'm proud of our lads out there defending us. Dying for us...' Her voice trailed off, self-realisation and shock showing through her open mouth and raised eyebrows. 'Oh, I am so sorry, lass. I never thought. Me and my big gob.'

The chair squealed on the lino when she finally managed, after a couple of attempts, to push herself upright. 'I'll be off then. Give Edna my love. Tell her if she wants owt she knows where I am. And I'm sorry for your loss as well, Jessie. Especially,' she nodded towards the mound of Jessie's stomach, 'with Arthur's bairn in your belly.' She waddled to the back door. 'Don't get up. I'll see myself out.'

But she left the back door open behind her. Jessie crossed the kitchen and closed it. She stared at herself in the small pitted mirror hung on the back door. Her eyes looked enormous in her pale face, dark shadows colouring the hollows beneath them.

'What's to become of us, little one?' she muttered, spreading her fingers over her aching stomach.

Chapter 58

Jessie woke up sweating. She rolled onto her side, letting her eyes adjust to the darkness. The shapes around her were strange to her, different from the familiar bulk of the wardrobe, the tallboy in her room at ... She stopped her thoughts. She'd almost said *home*, although the bakery hadn't been home to her for months.

Something had woken her. She waited, listening.

The sash window rattled in the wind; the harsh sound made her start. She lay still listening to the tiles shaking on the roof, a dustbin lid crashing along the alleyway. Somewhere someone shouted.

Her stomach clenched, the pain taking her by surprise. She felt a tightening inside her, a strange feeling. A warmth spread between her thighs. Frightened, she put her hands on her legs, touched something sticky, smelt blood.

'Edna!' The cry came out like a strangled gasp. Jessie took a deep breath. 'Edna!' She listened, heard nothing. Took another breath. 'Edna!'

The bedroom door was flung open.

'What is it?' Edna, holding a small oil lamp above her head, shuffled across to Jessie. 'What's wrong?' She placed the lamp on the table and bent over to stare at her. 'Oh my God, girl, it's not what I think it is?'

'I think so.' Her voice rose in a wail. 'But it's too soon!'

'Aye, it is.' Edna sounded grim. She fastened the cord around her dressing gown in one decisive movement. 'It is.'

'Something's happened. Down there.' Jessie's fingers shook as she held them out. 'Look.'

Edna peered close. 'It's a show, means you're on your way whether we like it or not. Are you having pains?'

'Just the one. Well, the one proper one.'

'What d'you mean?'

'I've felt funny – achy – for the last week or so. Since...' Jessie felt sweat trickling down her neck and back. 'Since I came home.'

'Why didn't you say?'

'You've had enough to deal with. I thought it would go away.'

Edna tutted. 'How do you feel now?'

'I don't know.'

'You all right if I go and put the kettle on to boil?' She stroked Jessie's cheek with the back of her hand.

'Please don't be long.' Jessie used the top sheet to wipe her neck and face, lifted the blanket and eiderdown and wafted them to let cold air into the bed.

'I'll leave you with the light, then.'

As soon as Jessie heard her going down the stairs, the fear of being alone came back. The glowing wick in the small lamp gave only a pool of light. The rest of the room and the open doorway seemed darker. She concentrated on the sounds Edna was making downstairs: the squeak of the tap being turned on, the rush of water into the kettle, the loud bang as it was placed on the range, the rattle of the iron poker as Edna riddled the fires. All comforting and familiar to Jessie. She relaxed.

The pain came again: slow at first, another dull ache. But then it strengthened, held her in its grip. Jessie closed her eyes, clenched her teeth and slid down in the bed.

It had subsided by the time Edna came back upstairs.

'Okay?' Her tone was light but there was no hiding the concern in her eyes. 'I've filled the hot water bottle.' She lifted the bedclothes and placed the stone jar next to Jessie's stomach.

'I'm already too hot,' she complained.

'It'll help the pain.'

'I wish Arthur was here.'

'And me, love.' A flash of anguish crossed Edna's face but when she spoke she sounded determined. 'But he's not. So all we can do is make sure his child is born safely.'

Nothing happened for hours. No pains; they just stopped. There was only a vague ache between Jessie's legs.

Dawn arrived bringing with it a steady downpour of rain.

Twice Jessie, refusing to pee in the chamber pot, supported by Edna, waddled downstairs, out to the outside lavvy. The second time she sat so long, unable in the end to pass water, she thought a pain was building and was terrified she'd have the baby there and then down into the can.

Later in the morning, when the pains came again, there was no rhythm to them. Some came and went in seconds, short overwhelming contractions that tore through her, hot burning torture. Others were long and rippled through her whole body, tightening her stomach. When Edna lifted Jessie's nightdress, they saw her skin had thinned, taken on a transparent, blue-veined appearance.

Jessie wasn't aware that the deep gasping breaths came from her. Nor was she conscious of throwing the bedclothes onto the floor, wanting nothing to touch her body.

The pains strengthened, became unbearable.

'I need to move.' Jessie heaved herself onto her knees, flattened her hands on the sodden sheet and let her head drop. Her hair, stringy with sweat, hung over her face.

'I can't do this anymore. Edna, I can't stand it.'

'Yes, you can. This is Arthur's child you're bringing into this world.' Edna stroked Jessie's back, moved to the end of the bed. 'Oh my god, Jessie, push.' Her voice rose. 'Push. I can see the head.'

Jessie moaned. She gripped the rail, her mouth wide in a long soundless scream.

Then a release from the pain.

The baby was tiny.

'It's a boy. Arthur's boy.' Edna scooped him into her arms.

Wrapped in the towel, the child lay limp, his eyes closed.

'He's not moving. Why isn't he moving?' Jessie knelt up, fear bringing a different pain.

Edna put her face near to the baby's and blew gently. A few seconds passed. She lifted her head and closed her eyes.

'No!'

Neither of them heard the thin cry at first, but Jessie saw the slight jerk of the baby's hand, the splay of fingers.

'He's alive. He's alive!' Jessie held out her arms to take hold of her baby.

Edna wiped away the dampness from her face with the hem of the towel. Jessie couldn't tell if it was tears or sweat.

Chapter 59

June

'I thought you would call him Arthur?' Edna said stubbornly.

'No, I said. He's called Harold after Dad. Harry for short.' Jessie struggled to hold on to the baby, who wriggled and squirmed while she tried to wash him in the kitchen sink. His name had been an ongoing wrangle between them since he was born.

Edna stuck out her lower lip and shrugged. 'Your choice, I suppose.' She sliced the tripe into cubes and threw the pieces into the large pan on the table.

Yes, it is my choice, Jessie thought, sick to death of the argument that had been going on over the last two weeks. She looked with distaste at the offal. 'I hate that, Edna, I know it's what you like, but we've had it twice already this week.'

'It's good for you and it's cheap.'

'We have enough money for good meat, Edna.'

'I still have a bit of my savings left from that what Arthur arranged to be sent from his pay. Not a lot, but enough for the time being, now the rent's been paid for the next month. There's been a bit of a mix up this last month but once his money starts again, we'll be okay.'

'Mam's—'

'No.' Edna held up her hand to stop Jessie speaking. Her lips pressed tight before she said, 'We're not using your mother's money. That's for you and Arthur when he's back home.'

Jessie gave an inward sigh. 'There's no point in hoarding it, Edna—'

'Don't.' Edna pointed the large knife towards Jessie. 'Don't say it. All right?' She slammed the knife onto the table. 'I'm going to the lav.'

The baby jumped, his arms and legs stiff when the back door banged. 'Shush.' Jessie wrapped him in the coarse cloth of the towel and held him to her, looking through the window at Edna shuffling across the yard.

Arthur's mother had been both withdrawn and yet over-protective of her and the child since the news of Arthur's death. It was understandable that she would change from being the strong woman she'd been before; her son was her only child. If Jessie thought that something might harm Harry, it made her feel sick. But Edna seemed even more afraid than her. At first Jessie had appreciated her care, but she was beginning to feel smothered by it. They needed to talk.

There was a loud knocking on the front door. Jessie glanced back at the yard: no sign of Edna. She went into the parlour and peeped through the window at the priest, standing on the step. He noticed her, she could tell, but didn't acknowledge her. Well, he could blummin' wait there until Edna let him in. Jessie went back into the kitchen and, folding the terry-towelling nappy into a triangle with one hand, laid Harry onto it.

The priest hammered on the door again just as Edna came in from the yard.

'What the 'ell?'

'Priest,' Jessie said, pinning the nappy on Harry. 'I'll go upstairs.' She knew what he wanted; he'd been twice before. An elderly man, he bitterly disapproved of Jessie even being in Edna's house.

'No, stop there, I'll get rid of 'im.'

Jessie had no chance of escape. The man stomped past Edna into the kitchen.

'I've had a word with the nuns at St. Catherine's,' he announced. 'They've agreed to take in the child. There are many good Catholic families waiting to adopt.' The lyrical Irish lilt was offset by the harsh disapproval in his voice.

'He has a good Catholic home here, Father,' Edna insisted, though there was a conciliatory tone in her voice.

The spark of temper rose instantly in Jessie. 'No.' She spoke at the same time as Edna but louder, more strident. Glaring at him, she hitched Harry further up in her arms, deliberately turning him to face the priest. 'My child is going nowhere.' She glanced at Edna. 'I'll be upstairs.'

In her room she could hear the rumble of the man's voice but little from Arthur's mother. She lay Harry on the bed and carefully pulled the long cotton nightdress over his head, tugging his arms gently through the sleeves. Leaning him against her, she slumped against the pillow.

It was a long time before she heard the door crash to. Swinging her legs over the side of the bed, she went to stand by the window. The priest had crossed the street and was outside the bakery. Red in the face and shaking his head, he was standing close to Amos Morgan. She watched as he pointed towards Edna's house. She saw her stepfather follow the priest's hand and stare up at her window. Jessie stepped back. So he was in on it, as well.

'What am I going to do, Harry?' Not trusting her legs to carry her downstairs she collapsed onto the bed, patting the back of the small form snuggled into her neck. No one was going to take away her child. No one.

Chapter 60

When the door knocker was given three sharp taps, Jessie went straight away to look through the parlour window. If it was the priest again she would not answer and, with Edna at the shops, he could stand there as long as he wished.

But it wasn't the priest. It was a grim-faced young girl in an ill-fitting Post Office uniform. She had her hand in the leather pouch of her belt over her jacket.

She wouldn't open the door. Jessie clutched hold of the curtain, willing her legs to hold her upright. Stan had given her Arthur's letter and she knew in her heart he was gone. But a telegram – a telegram made it official.

The Telegram Girl had noticed her and had shifted around to face Jessie. She lifted the envelope, pulled in the corners of her mouth in an expression of contrition.

Jessie let go of the curtain, forced herself to walk into the hall. She stopped, listened. If Harry was crying she would go upstairs to him and not answer the door. But there was no reprieve. She fumbled with the catch, opened the door slightly and peered around.

'Telegram for Mrs Dawson.' The girl's voice was shrill, anxious. She thrust it at Jessie.

'I'm not ... She's not...' Even so, she found the envelope in her hand.

'Any answer?' Now the girl was keen to escape. 'Sorry, I'm new to this. I mean, will you be replying?'

Jessie stared from the envelope to the badge on the girl's jacket, read the number, seven, four, six. The numbers repeated in her head, over and over, seven, four, six, seven, four, six. She couldn't open the envelope.

'I don't know, it's not for me.'

'This address.' The girl checked the number on the door. 'Yeah, number fifty-five. You not Mrs Dawson?'

'No.'

'But she lives here?'

'Yes.'

'So can you take it for her?'

Jessie heard Harry cry out. 'I need to go...' She closed the door, pushed the envelope into her apron pocket and ran upstairs.

Holding Harry, she rocked back and forth. There was no doubt in her mind that the telegram was to tell Edna that Arthur was officially declared dead. It was the end of any glimmer of hope for both of them.

She wouldn't wait for Edna to return from the shops. She laid Harry in the wooden cradle and, taking the envelope out of her pocket, ripped it open. She read it twice.

Something wasn't right. There was no place name by the line that said where he'd died. No date to say when. The only thing that she really understood was the line: "...notifying the death of..."

NO 12074
ARMY FORM B 104-2
MANCHESTER............................RECORD OFFICE
29th June 1915

It is my painful duty to inform you that a report has been received

for the War Office notifying the death of...

(No)19319 ....

(RANK)...................... PRIVATE ....

(NAME) .... ARTHUR DAWSON ....

REGIMENT .... Lancashire Fusiliers ....

Which occurred ....

On the .... NOT KNOWN ....

The report is to the effect that he was killed in action ....

By His Majesty's Command, I am to forward the message of sympathy from their Gracious Majesties, the King and Queen. I aim at the same time to express the regret of the Army Council at the soldier's death at the Country's service.

I am to add that any information that may be received as to the soldier's burial will be communicated to you in due course. A separate leaflet dealing more fully with this subject is enclosed.

I am

J D Arbuthnot
Your obedient servant
Officer in charge of Records
PTO

'A separate leaflet dealing more fully with this subject is enclosed...'
Edna read the telegram slowly. She turned the paper over, examined
the back. 'So, where is it, this separate leaflet? See...' She thrust the
page at Jessie. 'It says PTO at the bottom. That means "please turn
over", doesn't it? But there's nothing on the back. So where's the rest
of it?' Her voice rose. 'This leaflet which should tell us where my
lad is?' Her chin wobbled.

'That's all there was,' Jessie said. 'That's all the girl gave me.'

'Girl?'

'It was a telegram girl. With the shortage of young lads, the Post
Office is using girls.'

Why was Edna asking about that? Didn't she understand what
this meant? Arthur is dead. The word echoed in Jessie's head.

'Oh, a girl ... Well, it's not right. This not telling us is not right.
I'm 'is mam. I should be told.' She unbuttoned her coat and took
off her scarf. 'It's because they don't really know themselves. He'll
be missing, so they're just saying that...' She flicked her fingers at
the telegram, dismissing it.

She doesn't believe it. Jessie watched Edna's mouth tighten. Of
course she doesn't want to believe it. I don't want to believe it.

'Perhaps they don't know where...' Jessie stopped.

'Well, they should – they should know. If they do really know.'
Edna stared at Jessie when she picked Harry up and turned away.
'Where are you going?'

'I thought I'd take him out for a bit of fresh air. I need a walk.'

'I'll come with you.' She began to refasten her coat.

'No. Honestly, Edna, I'll be fine.' She wrapped her shawl around
herself and Harry, firmly fastening him to her. I need to be alone,
she thought. I need to get out of here. It was something she'd been
yearning for over the last hour. She had to go up to the heart stone,
to touch it, to feel the place where Arthur had rested his hand on
it. To read the three words he'd written. Left for her: *I LOVE YOU.*
Months ago. So many months ago.

'It's not safe out there. Not with him across the road—'

'I'll be fine.'

She's grasping at straws. She doesn't want to be on her own. Not after this, not now. But I do. I need to be alone.

Jessie finished tying the knot of the shawl. 'He'll not do anything in broad daylight, Edna. This time of year it's light until around eight. I'll be back before then.'

'No. I'll get my coat and scarf. I'll...'

The tap on the back door interrupted her.

'Who'll that be?'

'I'll go.'

Bob was standing turned away from the door watching the sparrows crowded together on top of the yard wall. He was whistling, his usual one note low whistle, his hands clasped behind his back, but when Jessie opened the door he swung around.

'Evening, Jessie.' He looked uncertain. 'I saw the...'

'Who is it?' Edna's voice was querulous.

'It's only Bob from the shop'. She poked her head around the door. 'He's brought back our bucket from this morning.'

'Hello, Mrs Dawson,' he called. 'Just to say Mother says thank you for the loan. 'Er old one 'ad a great hole in it and she wanted to clean the windows. I've bought 'er another now.'

'I'm sorry, Bob, I can't stop, I'm just taking Harry out for a bit.'

'Oh, okay,' he said, turning to go to the gate.

'Just a minute.' Jessie heard Edna shuffling across the kitchen. 'Wait on, Bob...'

'He's gone.' Jessie put her arm under Harry; he snuggled lower in the shawl. 'Honestly, Edna, you put the kettle on. We'll have a brew when I get back. I'll be quarter of an hour at the most.' She closed the back door, moved swiftly across the yard and out through the gate.

'Jessie!' The latch on the door rattled as Edna struggled with it. 'Jessie?'

'Won't be long,' she called.

Bob was standing on the corner of the last house before Bury Road. 'Need company?' he asked.

'No, I'm fine thanks.' Not you as well, she thought.

'I saw the telegram lass.'

'Yes.' Proof of the truth that she'd dreaded, half-disbelieved, so wanted not to believe.

She noticed Bob looked up and down the road before he put his arm across her shoulder. 'Need a friendly ear?'

Strangely, even though he'd been her friend for as long as she could remember, it made her uncomfortable.

'No. Honestly, Bob, I'm not good company today.'

'Don't matter.'

'Anyway, you'll get yourself talked about, being with me.'

'Don't matter,' he said again.

'Please, Bob, I just want to be on my own.'

He lifted his shoulders with an exaggerated sigh. 'Okay, please yerself. See yer.' He spun on his heel and walked away. She heard his one note, tuneless whistle after he'd turned the corner of the street.

Jessie glanced upwards at the field. Then, peeping inside her shawl at her sleeping son, she hitched her skirt above her ankles and began to climb towards the heart stone.

Chapter 61

July 1915

'A letter came this morning from the CO of his regiment. I thought we would only get the telegram that came last week. I suppose it's what they do for all the families. But it's made it worse for Edna, she's very bitter.'

'So it's definite then?' Bob screwed up his mouth in sympathy.

'Yes. Well, that's what they're saying.' Jessie shifted the basket from one arm to the other. The weight of the unwieldy handle was digging into her skin. Going all the way to Kinders Street for bread was hard work but she would never set foot in Amos Morgan's shop ever again. 'I don't understand, Bob. How can they say Arthur's dead? Why has no one ever found out where he died?'

'I don't know, Jessie.' He stopped her walking by putting a hand on the basket. 'But I do know it's daft for yer to be trailing to Vince Smith's bakery for your bread when I can get it for you.' He took the basket from her. 'Let me walk back with you. I've told Eddie to tell Mam to keep my dinner warm in th'oven.'

'I shouldn't be keeping you from your dinner and your bed, Bob. You'll need your sleep, surely. Don't forget, I know you've been in the bakery since four this morning.'

'Oh, begger that. But I must admit Morgan's got us running around like blue-arsed flies these days.' He yawned.

'There you are then. You must be so tired. Honestly, I'll be fine. It's not far now.' Jessie didn't want Edna seeing her with Bob; especially not with the letter coming from Arthur's CO in the post earlier. She'd already started objecting to the number of times Bob called at the house on one pretext or another. 'And I don't want Edna to get upset.'

'Why would she be upset?'

Jessie felt stupid; she was reading too much into Bob's actions. After all, they were just friends. It was something she'd been saying to herself a lot over the past weeks. But she still felt she should say something.

'It's not been that long since she – we found out about Arthur, Bob.' She stopped walking, looked straight at him. 'I loved Arthur, I still do.' The tears came easily. 'Edna thinks you want to be more than friends with me.' Her cheeks were burning. 'I'm sorry, I shouldn't embarrass you.' She shrugged. 'It's just what she thinks.'

He didn't give his usual snort of derision when dismissing something. Instead he met her gaze. 'Would that be so bad, Jessie?'

'Yes, Bob. Yes, it would. Because that's not how I think of you. Of us.'

'You need to move on, Jessie. You and 'is mam.' He frowned. 'I'm 'ere, Dawson's not.'

'I don't know how you could imagine I'd forget Arthur so soon, if ever I could.' Her whole being recoiled at the thought of being with Bob in that way. 'And aren't you forgetting Harry?'

'I'm thinking of the lad. 'Ow he's going to be treated—?'

'What?'

'Well, he's a—'

'Don't you say another word. How dare you, Bob Clegg!' Jessie didn't give him a chance to say anything else. 'I can't believe...' She pulled the basket from him. 'I'll take that. I can manage, thank you.'

'I'm just sayin' 'ow it is.'

'Shut up.'

Walking away as fast as she could, she berated herself. 'Stupid. Stupid.'

How could she have been so stupid? How could she have not seen what Bob was doing? The shame took over. It was because she had Harry. Bob thought she must be desperate as a single mother. Or he saw her now with different eyes, a girl with loose morals. Yes, that was it.

But was it? He'd known her for so long, he couldn't believe that of her, surely?

When she turned the corner to the alleyway of the houses she stopped and leaned against the wall. A thought jolted through her whole body: what if Amos Morgan had told Bob what he's done to her? What if that hateful man had made out she was willing? Turning to lean over the gutter she retched: dry, painful spasms that brought tears to her eyes.

Edna was still sitting in the kitchen on the chair in almost the same position she's been in an hour earlier, a piece of paper in her hand.

Jessie put the basket on the sideboard and took out the tissue-wrapped loaves. 'Would you like this with some of Mrs Whittles' home-made jam?'

'No.' Edna dismissed the suggestion. 'That's it, then.' She put the letter on the surface of the table and smoothed it out with the palm of her hand. 'They've given up. They won't tell us where he is, just that he's...' When she looked up at Jessie her eyes were dark with hostility. 'Just that he's dead.'

Jessie sank into the chair opposite her. 'Oh, Edna.' She turned the letter towards her and read the words again.

...I regret very much to inform you that your son Pte Arthur Dawson of this Company was killed in action. I and all the Company deeply sympathise with you in your loss. The Company was taking part in an attack which was successful, and all guns reached and established new positions. Your son always did his duty and now has given his life for his country. We all honour him, and I trust you will feel some consolation in remembering this. Lord Kitchener expresses his sympathy. In true sympathy...

Jessie couldn't read the signature.

'I don't want him honoured, Jessie. I want him back home with me, with us.'

'I know, Edna, I know.'

They clutched hands.

'I know,' Jessie said again

Chapter 62

August 2015

In the weeks that followed, the time drifted by with both women trapped in their own thoughts. Jessie's grief, mixed with the fear that Amos Morgan had lied to Bob, could lie to anyone else, haunted her, robbed her of sleep and appetite. Edna grieved for her son and lost hopes, sometimes refusing to get dressed, sometimes only getting out of bed to go to the lavatory.

169

One morning it was all too much for Jessie. 'We can't carry on like this, Edna. It's not good for Harry.' She caught hold of the older woman's hand as she tried to shuffle past from the back door to the stairs. 'Look at the place, it's a mess. And we can't keep relying on Mrs Giles to do our shopping.'

Edna tried to shake her off. 'I can't help it.'

'We're both grieving, love.' She hadn't told Edna what Bob had said. Nor had she shared her worries about Amos Morgan. But they were sharing the same grief. 'I need you.' She held out the baby. 'And Arthur's son needs you.'

It took Edna a few moments to take him in her arms. She rocked him in silence. But it wasn't long before the silence was broken by a low moan that rose from inside her and erupted into a wail. Frightened, Harry squirmed, his own screams adding to the noise.

Jessie gently took hold of him and pulled Edna to her at the same time. She swayed from side to side. 'Shush, shush. It'll be okay. We have one another. Shush, shush.'

She didn't know how long it was before the calmness settled. When she finally glanced down at Harry, he was asleep.

'Sit down, love.' She helped Edna into the nearest chair. 'I'll put him in his cradle and make us a brew.'

Stepping through the curtain at the bottom of the stairs, into the kitchen, Edna met her gaze. 'I'm sorry, pet.'

'We'll be fine. It will all be fine,' Jessie repeated. 'We have one another.'

The knock on the back door startled both of them.

'That'll be Mrs Giles, I bet. She's early with the shopping.'

But when she opened the door, it was Bob.

'What do you want?' She kept her voice low before turning back to say to Edna, 'It's Bob. I won't be a minute.' She stepped out onto the yard flags, pulling the door behind her. 'What do you want?'

'Just ter say I'm sorry. I dunno why I said what I did.'

'Really? I think you knew exactly what you were saying to me.'

'No. 'Onest. An' I'm that sorry.'

170

She studied him.

He moved from foot to foot in discomfort. 'Can wi be friends again, Jessie?'

She shrugged. 'I don't see how.' She caught a movement out of the corner of her eye. The net curtains at the kitchen window twitched. She saw Bob glancing at it and was ashamed how grubby the curtains looked. 'I have to go.'

'Will yer meet me?'

'And be spoken to in that way again?' She raised her eyebrows.

'No, I promise. I were wrong, I know that.'

There were movements behind the door, the latch rattled. 'Just go, will you?'

'Will yer meet me? Please. Just so I can put things right between us. I miss us being friends.'

Jessie sighed, looked over her shoulder. Edna was tugging at the door. 'Look you have to go. I will meet you...' She glared at him as he grinned. 'But I'm giving no promises about us being friends again.'

'Where?' He was walking backwards across the yard.

'I'll be taking Harry out for some fresh air later. Along Bury Road. Probably about six o'clock.'

'Great. See you then.' After he'd closed the gate, she heard his familiar monotonous whistle.

'What did 'e want?' Edna stood in the doorway holding the teapot. 'You were long enough nattering to 'im. I was waiting to throw the tea leaves down. What did 'e want?'

'I'll do it.' Jessie took the teapot, gave it a shake and emptied the leaves over the grid under the kitchen window. 'We can run the tap a bit now, swill them down.'

'You didn't say what 'e wanted?' Edna frowned.

'Only to ask if we needed anything. And to ask if we were all right.'

'Well, I hope you told him we were. We're all right, the three of us. We'll allus be all right ... just the three of us.'

Chapter 63

'But what does he want this time? Why did 'e come round? 'E's never away.'

'He's going into Manchester and wanted to know if we needed anything.'

'That's twice today.' Edna scowled.

'He's just being a friend. He's trying to help us.' Jessie lifted Harry from her breast and pulled her blouse around her. She held the baby to her shoulder and he burped; a low blowing with the sweet smell of her milk. 'Good lad,' she whispered, standing and putting him into his cradle.

Edna softened. 'He's coming on grand, 'n't 'e? Looks the spit of Arthur at his age.' She leaned over him, tucking the cotton sheet around him. 'You could put 'im in his pram in the yard for a bit of fresh air? Then you could have a nap? I'll watch 'im.' Her animosity towards Bob, voiced for the day, satisfied.

'Thanks. I will.' Jessie rubbed at her face. A headache tightened the back of her neck. 'I am a bit tired.'

She knew that both of them were well aware of what day it was, even if it hadn't been mentioned. She pushed away the memory of the brass band playing, the sound of marching feet, image of the cheering, singing crowds and flags waving as they hung from bedroom windows.

It was wrong to be even thinking about the problem of Bob today, it felt like disloyalty to Arthur, but it had been tormenting her for weeks.

Bob hadn't made any more advances towards her but he was a constant presence and she didn't know what to do. It wasn't that she could see him in any other way than as a friend and he seemed content with that after her sharp words. But his insistence on calling at the house was causing friction between her and Edna. And

Arthur was never far from the conversation between the two of them. It was as though Edna was deliberately keeping him alive and in Jessie's thoughts. Just in case...

She watched Edna manoeuvre the perambulator into the yard, wondered if the relationship between them would have been different without all that had happened over the last year. It probably would have been completely different if Arthur had lived, if the war hadn't rent them all apart. She probably wouldn't have had Harry, at least not so soon. Edna wouldn't have had to worry about the future, about Bob. Wouldn't need to be so possessive. Life made people change so much. Suddenly she needed to get away.

'Actually Edna, would you mind if I went out for a walk? I need to think.'

'Aye, I thought you might, pet, I thought you might.' Edna pushed the brake down on the pram and crossed the kitchen to enfold Jessie in her arms. 'I know what day it is an' all.' Her voice was choked. 'You go for one of your wanderings in them fields, Jessie. I don't know what comfort you get from that but you always come back with more colour in your cheeks. So wrap up and off you go.'

She held Jessie at arm's length. 'You're a good lass. You would have made my Arthur a good wife. And I think of you as a daughter-in-law anyway.' She sniffed, swiped her forefinger under her nose. 'Me and the babby are fine here.'

The brisk breeze tugged at the fringed edges of Jessie's woollen shawl causing her to pull it tighter over her head and fold her arms across her chest. Orange and yellow leaves quivered on the branches of the few small stunted trees. The long grass, now washed-out blades, moved in rhythmic swathes, halted only by the stone walls that dissected the fields.

Mostly she kept her gaze on the steep ground in front of her, counting her steps but now and again she stopped to catch her breath and look around. She loved the view of Nether Brook from so high up; she could see right across the town. It looked so quiet, so peaceful, some of the windows of the houses and the mill intermittently flashing the reflection of the late afternoon sun, drifts of smoke trailing upwards from the chimneys.

Each time she turned and started the counting again. As usual she spoke aloud for the last ten steps until... 'One hundred and eighteen, nineteen, one hundred and twenty.' She rested her hand on the heart stone, tipped it. It was cold under her palm as she took and unfolded the tattered note. Most of the words were illegible, but she could read his name.

'Here I am, Arthur,' She murmured.

She looked upwards to the silvery swirls of the clouds against the pale translucent background of the sky, not even realising she was crying until the tears cooled on her face. 'Arthur?' His name was carried away on the whine of the wind. She couldn't even try to picture where he was anymore.

And yet there was some comfort even in that. Shocked, she recognised that for the first time she could take comfort in the fact that Arthur could no longer suffer. Her sadness was tempered by a strange release of the grief she'd been holding inside her. She could almost feel the freedom in that knowledge, in that lack of hope.

The light of the day was draining away when she finally headed back, clutching the note in her hand. Her faint shadow lengthened in front of her. Like the rest of her life.

PART TWO

Chapter 64

The days, the weeks, the months moved on. Harry grew into a sturdy toddler, giving joy to Jessie in her darkest hours. She filled her days as much as she could with household chores and games with him so she could tire herself enough to sleep at night.

Her grief for Arthur may have been tempered by memories of the years they'd shared through childhood and growing up, but she couldn't escape the anguish imagining what he may have endured before his death. The pain hurt the worst when she woke from dreams where she and Arthur strolled hand in hand along the canal path. Nor could she stop nightmares of Arthur hideously wounded and writhing in the mud of the trenches, fed by the graphic stories in the newspapers. Those mornings she avoided both Bob and Edna, taking Harry and fleeing to hide in the tiny chapel on the hill, close to her mam.

Or she'd climb Wharmton Hill, when it was warm enough to take her son. She would lift him over the stile to make her way alongside the stone wall, counting all the one hundred and twenty steps aloud to Harry until they reached the heart stone. Sometimes she would let him pat it with his chubby hands. If the grass was dry, she would settle him onto the ground so that she could touch the stone herself. Always she would send a prayer and her love up to the heavens.

It was her secret place: hers and Harry's. And Arthur's.

Yet she knew she couldn't carry on living as she was. Bob's stubborn insistence at calling at the house made the atmosphere there increasingly fraught with tension. It worried Jessie that it was affecting her son; he was a timid child who cried when voices were raised and those times increased.

There was only one person she could confide in…

Dear Clara,

I am in such a desperate tangle I cannot think straight, and you are the only person I can trust to help and advise me.

Life has changed so much since we lost Arthur. I know I will never love another man as I loved him. But I am wondering if I am expecting too much. I do wish you were here, Clara. Then we could have a proper talk and I'd know what to do. Because what I do will not only affect me but little Harry as well. And for Arthur's sake, I must do the best for our child.

Do you remember Bob Clegg? He worked for Mam and Dad in the bakery. In fact I've known him since I was four and he would have been thirteen or so. I've always seen him as a friend, and he has been good to Edna and me over the last few months. But she resents him, and we quarrel because she thinks he's trying to take Arthur's place in my affections. She says people are gossiping about us. But I swear to you, Clara, that nothing has happened between us. The thought makes me feel quite sick. As a married woman you will understand how precious that time with Arthur was; I cannot imagine such a time with any other man…

Jessie knew she couldn't tell her friend the whole truth. She would never tell anyone what Amos Morgan did to her. Only one other person besides that revolting man knew what happened and she wouldn't tell. For a moment, Jessie hesitated: would Edna tell? If only to keep her little family together, the three of them? Jessie berated herself for letting the thought even cross her mind.

She reread the next words she'd written:

…To me Bob is a friend, nothing more. At least on my part. But lately I feel that things have changed for him and I've noticed he has become more attentive, acting a little differently towards me.

How could she describe it? He was being the perfect gentleman. He was courting her, she admitted to herself. The quarrel, the coldness she felt towards him for all those weeks, was not only because of the way he spoke to her, as though she would fall at his feet for him to save her from being an unmarried mother – a social outcast – but also the way he spoke about Arthur. Something else she hasn't told Clara. There was nothing like that now.

...I fear he is going to ask me to marry him, Clara, and I am at a loss what to do or say to stop him. I only want us to carry on as we are. Friends. But is that possible in this day and age? Would that be something society would accept? And Harry? He has his whole life in front of him. I must also think what is best for him.

Would just being friends, being seen as only friends, be something Bob would accept? In her heart of hearts, she doubted it. More importantly, as Harry grew older, would he?

I don't know what to do, Clara. Please, my dearest friend, please help me to decide the path I must follow.
Yours Jessie xx

Jessie knew there wasn't much more of the situation at home she could take. Edna, bitterly resentful of the man, would do anything to stop Jessie leaving the house with Bob, even feigning illness. One day it all came to a head.

'I don't know how you can go out of this house, leaving me in such pain when there's all this washing to do. Most of it yours and the babby's, Jessie.' She bent over in the chair, clutching her stomach. 'I've done so much for you and Arthur's child. You've grown a heart of stone.'

'I haven't, Edna. And I've said enough times I'll do the washing, you don't have to be a martyr. You're not really ill. I know that as soon as that back gate is closed, you'll be up and about.'

The older woman stopped groaning enough to glare up at Jessie, her face beetroot red.

'Please don't do this, Edna. I'll be back in a couple of hours. I just need to take Harry out for a run around—'

'And *he's* going with you...' Edna turned away from her and scowled through the window towards the yard where Bob was waiting.

'Yes. Yes, he is. He's a friend, no more.' She spoke to the back of Edna's head. 'I know what's worrying you, love – and that will never happen.' She knelt by her side, trying to look into her face while still holding on to Harry. 'Bob will never, ever, take Arthur's place, not in my heart, not in our son's heart if I have anything to do with it—'

'And that's it, isn't it?' Edna sat up so suddenly that Jessie fell back in her haunches. Harry whimpered. She made shushing sounds in his ear. 'It won't be up to you. If you get properly with 'im he'll take you over. I know his sort, I know 'im. I watched him grow up the same way I watched Arthur and you grow up. There's summat about 'im. Summat missing.'

'I don't know what you mean, Edna. He's a friend. And I need a friend.' She held Edna's hand. 'You know I don't get to see Clara anymore. She sends lovely letters, but I can tell, between having her little girl and helping Stanley to come to terms with what's happened to him, she isn't free to visit here. And I can't visit her, it's her parents' home she's living in.' Even if, as an unmarried mother, they would welcome her.

Edna raised her head, a light of comprehension in her eyes.

'The neighbours are kind to us, Edna, but they are really just being kind to you. They don't want their daughters being friends with me.'

They both turned to look down to Harry.

'They don't want their daughters tarred with the same brush. Please, love. I only have you and Bob for company these days.'

'And Harry.' Edna almost smiled watching her grandson roll the ball and then totter to his feet to go to pick it up. 'You have Harry.'

'Arthur's son.' Jessie nodded. 'You and I will always have Arthur's son.'

The words were followed by a few quiet moments before Edna slapped her hands on her thighs and sat up. 'Well, then, I suppose I'd better shape myself and stop whinging. There's washing to be done.'

'Let me do it when I get back.'

'No. I'm all right.' She gave Jessie a sheepish grin. 'I am, pet. Don't fret.' She gave a low chuckle. 'This young man finds dirt where there is none these days. Just like 'is dad did.' Despite her humour, the dark sadness didn't fade completely from her eyes, but still she insisted, 'You get off, pet.'

'Thank you, Edna. And I'll be back in no time to help hang it out.' Jessie glanced through the window. 'It'll be a good drying day.'

Bob must have heard the altercation but said nothing when she joined him. And he waited until they were out in the alleyway before he took the weight of Harry from her.

Jessie smiled at him. They walked in silence to the small park, sat side by side on one of the benches in companionship, watching Harry play on the grass, saw him unsteadily approach other children, mostly older than him. Watched them kneel down to him, passing his string ball back and forth with him.

'He needs company,' Bob said all at once. He hesitated. 'He could do with a brother or sister—' He broke off, his cheeks scarlet. 'I mean ... I meant.'

'I know what you meant, Bob.' Jessie felt the heat on her throat rise to her face. Please don't start that again, she thought. She stood, made a great show of looking up at the sky towards the sun. 'Gracious me, we've been here so long. I really must get back. I promised Edna I'd be back at the house by the time she'd finished the washing. She can't manage all that hanging out on her own...'

They didn't speak at all on the way back. Jessie carried Harry all the way. The space between her and Bob wasn't only physical, they were miles away in thought. When she glanced towards him his face was set in hard lines.

Chapter 65

Jessie could ignore the gossip about herself, but she knew she needed to do something to protect Harry; to give him a secure and peaceful home to grow up in. A safe future. Time after time she caught sight of the judgmental sideways glances when she was out of the house with him. She was aware she was meant to hear the snide, purposefully loud whispers when women passed her. And, from Mrs Giles' well-meant indignation, she knew that some of the spite was driven by Amos Morgan's remarks in the bakery. Did Bob ever say anything in her defence? After all, he knew what the man was like.

She was too proud to ask him. She wished Clara would reply to her letter.

'I've been patient, Jessie. I've asked nothing from you, taken nowt for granted.' Bob scowled. 'But you're mekin' me look a fool. People are laughing at me—'

'By people I suppose you mean Amos Morgan and his cronies.' Jessie rounded on him, irritated.

'Yes. Him and others.' He was defensive. 'But 'im mostly. Every day.'

'So say something. Tell him to shut up.'

'I do ... sometimes.'

'Well?'

'But 'e goes on all the time. I'm sick of 'is jibes. Sick of him sneering at me for being weak, for not mekin' you—'

'Making me what, Bob? Making me what?' The memory of the night Amos Morgan forced himself on her an instant image that turned her stomach. She almost blurted out to Bob what the man had done but some instinct made her hold back. She swallowed, straightened her back, lifted her chin in the way she forced herself to do so often over the years. 'Well?'

A small, stiff silence rose between them.

'Don't you want to be respectable?' he said eventually, his voice sulky.

Thunder rolled in the dark dense clouds above.

'I beg your pardon?'

'Don't you want to be respectable?' he repeated. 'If not for your own sake, then for Harry's.'

'How dare you!'

'I meant—'

'I know just what you mean. But I am respectable, Bob Clegg.' She thumped herself on the chest. 'I am respectable. And marrying you wouldn't make me more so. I don't think either of us has anything else to say to one another, do you?'

She was afraid her whole body was shaking so hard it would stop her putting one foot in front of the other. But she managed to go through the yard gate and close it behind her before she sank onto the ground.

She didn't notice the first heavy drops that splattered and darkened the flags in an uneven pattern. She didn't notice the steady downpour that drenched her in minutes. Nor was she aware of Edna rushing out of the house to lift her to her feet.

Chapter 66

The rain clattering on the panes woke Jessie. She lay still for a few moments aware that she was going to sneeze and that the skin under her nose felt hot and sore. She didn't remember much about the night before, only that Edna had helped her to get out of her wet clothes and into bed. Glancing towards the window she saw it was almost dark outside. She must have slept all day. Harry was crying. She needed to get up. What was she doing lying in bed when he needed her? The crying grew louder, her bedroom door was cautiously opened and Edna peeped in carrying him.

Struggling to untangle herself from the sheets and sit up made the throbbing pain in her head worse.

'Feeling better? You've slept the day away, pet. How do you feel?'

Jessie pushed her hair out of her eyes, aware for the first time how greasy it was, how reeking of sweat she smelled.

'You've got a bit of a cold and no wonder, sitting out in the rain all that time. You must 'ave been there ages before I spotted you.'

Edna sat Harry on the bed next to Jessie. He stopped wailing and snuggled next to her. 'And you've not been eating proper for months now, I should have done summat about that.' She tipped her head towards Harry. 'That one's missed you no end. I 'ad to bring him in here a dozen times today to show him you were still here.' She pulled the curtain to with a sweep of her hands.

'Bob...'

'Aye. Well, he's been back and forth from across the road all day, mithering the living daylights out of me.' There was a note of grudging respect in her voice. 'He's been in a right state. Said it were his fault.'

'We quarrelled.'

'So I believe.' Edna stopped at the bedroom door. 'I've got some soup made up downstairs. I'll go and get a mug of it now – leave you two to get reacquainted, like. Oh, and there's a letter for you. Came yesterday. I'll bring that up an' all.'

'Thank you.' From Clara, she hoped.

Edna met Jessie's eyes. 'I'm sorry, lass. I know it's been hard since...' She pressed her lips together. 'I know I've not been that easy to live with. I've no excuse...'

'You have. You have, Edna. You lost your son.' Jessie pulled Harry to her. 'I can't think of anything worse. I've grieved for Arthur, I will always grieve for him – for him and the life we should have had with him, Harry and me. But I still have Harry. You lost your son.'

'Aye, well, I shouldn't 'ave taken it out on you. And I shouldn't

184

'ave tried to stop you having a different life.' She turned and left the room abruptly.

Jessie heard her go down the stairs, her tread heavy. Harry had fallen asleep. She kissed the top of his head and turned to look out of the window, Edna's words echoing in her mind, '...having a different life.'

Chapter 67

My Dear Jessie,

I'm writing this quickly to catch the return of post. Now, although our lives have taken different paths and we cannot see one another as often as I'd like, you know you are my dearest, my best friend and please be assured you are always in my thoughts.

There have been many times in the past when you have helped me that I will always be grateful for. So I hope that you will take my words in the spirit in which they are written. I'm afraid I am going to say there are only two choices.

Although I know you say you have been friends with Bob Clegg for many years, I have to say that you first knew him as an employee of your parents. That is something to bear in mind for what I next say...

Jessie dropped the letter onto the bedcovers, her thoughts muddled. She felt an unusual twinge of irritation at her friend's words. After all Stanley had only been the foreman at the mill when Clara first met him; her father owned a business. Not much difference between herself and Clara then. So why say that? Edna's words came back to her: '...he's been back and forth from across the road all day, mithering the living daylights out of me.' If a man cares, what else matters? She picked up the next page of Clara's letter.

It is impossible for a man and a woman to be seen as just friends, unless they are always in a group or in a family circle. You will be becoming, I'm afraid, as Mrs Dawson say, the subject of gossip. And, believe me, I do know what Nether Brook is like. I, myself, have been gossiped about there.

So, your first choice must be to consider whether to break off this friendship.

Your second choice is obvious, Jessie. You must decide if you like the man enough to marry him. I'm not talking about love. I am well aware that you still love Arthur, and probably always will. No, your decision must be based on three things. The first, as I said, do you like Bob enough to marry him? The second will be a consideration of what kind of life you would have with him. Does he have his own home, for instance, enough money for you to live comfortably? Most importantly, I think you will agree, will he love Harry as his own? I would add a proviso of my own here. Will he give you the freedom to have your own views? I would never have married Stanley if he had tried to stop my attendance at the Suffragists' meetings.

I am afraid those are the only choices you have, Jessie, and they are based on my own life. For I have no judgement of any other. But your first priority, I think you will agree, is your son, Harry. His future, welfare and happiness.

Think carefully, my dear friend. Life as it is now for you and Harry, or, within a marriage where you can be your <u>own self and yet live respectably</u> as a wife and mother to Harry and, perhaps, other children.

I realise, too, there is Arthur's mother for you to consider.

Do write and let me know what you decide.

Always your friend,

Clara x

Jessie let the page drop from her fingers. So much to think about and her head hurt so much. Harry snuffled and wriggled, restless in her arms. She lifted him to her lips and kissed his forehead. He was her priority.

'Another letter!' Edna peered at the envelope. 'Same handwriting an' all.' She put it on the pillow and the mug of soup on the bedside table. 'Here, let me 'ave 'im.' Taking Harry from Jessie, she cuddled him. 'I'll take him down with me while you read that.' She nodded at the envelope, her head tilted, curiosity written all over her face.

Jessie smiled. 'From Clara.'

'Ah. That's nice. Two in two days, eh?' She waited, rocking Harry. Getting only a nod and another smile from Jessie, she said, 'Bob's here again. In the kitchen. Shall I tell him he can see you? When we've tidied you up a bit?'

'I'd rather not see him yet, Edna,' Jessie whispered. 'Can you tell him I've gone back to sleep, please?'

'Aye, okay. If that's what you want, pet. Right then.' Edna hovered in the doorway. 'I'll go and tell 'im downstairs you're asleep.'

Her loud whisper made Jessie wince. Hopefully, Bob wouldn't have heard.

'Right, then. Don't forget to 'ave the soup.'

'I will. And thank you, Edna, you're a godsend.'

'Give over. You know I'll do owt for my little family.'

A not so subtle reminder, Jessie bit her lip. Whatever she decided to do about Bob, it would affect Edna. 'Oh, Arthur,' she murmured. 'Why?'

She waited until she heard the stairs creaking before ripping open the envelope.

My Dear Jessie,

I needed to write again because, although you asked for my advice, I had, perhaps, taken your request too far? I do hope I haven't offended you. I've been a little concerned. And, I'm hoping you will accept my invitation to come here. Both Stanley and I would love to see you.

I know, my dear, that life has been hard for you and I hope my next words don't distress you too much, but we too miss Arthur. I am sure he would be still in our lives even though we have moved so far away.

And forty miles does seem to me a long way when you and I don't see one another. And I know I am equally at fault, I could have come to Nether Brook before now, but to be truthful, Jessie, I was not sure you would want me to call on you. And I'm not sure that Mrs Dawson actually approves of me still – so I would not want to make you uncomfortable in your own home.

So I am appealing to you to visit us for a few days. You would be most welcome. Mama and Papa employed some men to make the house into two apartments. They live on the upper level while we, of course, are on the ground floor. Stanley is well used to his wheelchair now and moves around quite easily. He even takes himself across the yard to the workshops every day. Pa trained him in his first job here and Pa said he was so skilful at it. But that did not surprise me; he was always able to mend the machinery in the mill, if you remember. Anyway, he is now in charge of some of the departments.

In that moment Jessie made up her mind; she would go to Greenbridge. She and Clara could talk properly. Maybe then she would see things clearly; see which path to take.

Her friend's next words took her by surprise, she didn't know why. Maybe it was because Clara and Stanley were moving on with their lives when she wasn't. When she still yearned for the past.

I have news for you which I didn't want to say in my last letter. I am expecting another baby. This time it will be in April. I have waited so long to tell you as I'm afraid I wasn't too well for the first few weeks. But I am fine now, and the baby is safe. Abigail is so excited, though, of course, she doesn't understand where the baby is at the moment. She is very sweet about it. As I am sure you will see if – no, not if – when you finally come to visit us.

So, back to my plea, my dear. Please do come to stay with us. I long to see you, to show you our home and our daughter. And we so want to see Arthur's son.

With much love,
Clara x

Chapter 68

December 1916

It had been a scary business, sitting for so long on her own in the train as it rattled along the lines. Sometimes she was alone in the carriage, sometimes there were so many people she was squashed into the corner, with more travellers crowded on the station platforms and flinging open the door to clamber in. The smell of the dusty seating, stale sweat and perfume, cigarettes and cigars had long turned her stomach. Jessie thought she was over her cold but everything about this carriage was making her cough. She clenched her teeth in the hope that she wasn't going to disgrace herself by vomiting in public.

She was so glad she hadn't brought Harry; she'd been right, not being sure how she would feel on the train. She'd worried that the journey would have done him great harm with the stench in the carriage and the cloying smoke and soot from the train's engine. And he loved being with Edna. She was missing him already but pushed down the anxiety. He would be fine, and it was only a few days.

By the time the train arrived at the Manchester London Road railway station, she almost tumbled down the step in her haste to get off. She scanned the platform, unable to see her friend anywhere, jostled so much by other passengers that she was sure she'd be covered in bruises by nightfall. Hugging her valise close to her chest, she started to move with the crowd towards the exit gate, her throat tight with anxiety.

And then Clara was standing in front of her, laughing and hugging her.

'Oh, Jessie, I am thrilled you could come.' She looked over Jessie's shoulders. 'No Harry? Abigail will be so disappointed.'

'No, I'm sorry, Clara, not this time. I thought it might be too much for him.'

'Oh? Oh, all right then.' If Clara was surprised, she said nothing.

She still held on to Jessie but at arm's length. 'You look pale. And you've lost weight. Are you all right?' Her eyes stretched wide open. 'You're not ill, are you?'

'No. Nothing like that.'

'Oh, I'm so glad.' Clara looked at the valise Jessie was clutching. 'Is that the only luggage you've brought, I thought you were staying for a few days?' She pretended to pout.

'I am and I don't need much.' Jessie was determined her friend wouldn't know how she and Edna struggled to get by each week, even with the help from the British Legion and the money received from the government. Clothes for Harry were more important than for her. She dipped into her mother's money for that; it was something both she and Edna had agreed.

'Right...' Her friend looked doubtful. Then she brightened. 'But Pa let me have his car because I thought you'd be loaded up. So, we'll get a ride in it anyway.'

Jessie felt slight apprehension in her stomach. 'I've not been in a car before.'

'Oh, it's fun. It's a Landaulette, which Jim, our driver, calls "the cream of the crop".' She linked arms with Jessie. 'It goes as fast as ten miles an hour on a straight road, he says. Though how he knows that with all the hills around here, I don't know.' She laughed at Jessie's raised eyebrows. 'Don't worry! I'll tell him to go really, really slow.'

All the time she was talking, she was leading them from the station. When they got out into the streets Jessie glanced upwards. It was a bright clear day, the sky almost silver in its translucence, but there was a chill wind that herded the wisps of clouds high above and caused her to shiver in her thin coat.

Clara squeezed her arm. 'Come on. Let's get you into the car. It has a built-on roof so it's quite cosy under the rugs. Look, there it is.' She pointed to a large black car parked further along the street, its engine chugging. A man sat in the driver's seat. Seeing Jessie's face lighten with relief, she laughed. 'Yes, Jim is driving us. You didn't think Pa would let me drive, did you?' She flipped her hand towards her stomach. 'Or Stanley, in my condition. Besides,' she whispered in Jessie's ear, 'I would be too scared. But I don't tell them that.'

Her secret made Jessie feel a little better. If Clara was nervous then it was all right for her to feel the same. How safe was it to be in a motor car? She had no time to speculate; in an instant she was being pushed into the back seat.

'Jim, this is my friend, Jessie.' Clara's excitement was contagious.

The stout, red-faced young man laughed. 'Afternoon, miss. Pleased to meet you.'

'Jim.' Jessie could hardly get the word out; her throat felt dry.

'Isn't it lovely?' Clara arranged the thick woollen rug around them. 'It's Pa's car but he'll only let Jim drive it. He tried once but Mama says he almost killed the two of them so she insisted he hire a driver.' She hesitated before saying brightly, 'Stanley is working on a way to drive it, but hasn't quite cracked it yet.' She smiled. 'But he will...'

'I'm sure he will.'

'In the meantime we have Jim to take us everywhere.'

'If and when your father says so, miss.' It sounded to Jessie that the man's words and firmness were well used.

Clara giggled. 'Mama and I went shopping last week without telling Pa. And we told Jim he'd agreed to us going into town in the car.'

'You'll get me sacked one of these days.' Jim grinned at her through the windscreen mirror.

Jessie felt a pang of loneliness. Clara seemed content. But why shouldn't she be? The man she loved had been returned to her. She wouldn't have cared what injuries Arthur had, either, if he'd come home.

She swallowed away the tears and concentrated on looking out at the scenery speeding by: first Manchester with its streets, shops and a few market stalls and muffled-up traders and shoppers, then narrow streets of terraced houses, their smoke tossed by the wind from the chimneys. Until, finally, grey-brown fields, devoid of crops at this time of year, and hilly countryside dotted with grey sheep and stunted wind-blown trees.

Eventually, after passing many hamlets, they entered a village: squat houses and cottages with small, square windows, and few people. A canal ran parallel to the road, its surface rippling in metallic curving lines in the wind. The car rattled along until the road widened again and Jim drove through two large, black, iron gates into an enormous yard with stone buildings at the far end.

'Here we are.' Clara pulled on the door handle of the car and pushed it wide before Jim had time to open it for them. 'Our house is just though there.' She pointed to a wide passageway between two buildings where two large mongrel dogs huddled together, long tails slowly thumping the ground. Keeping a wary eye on the animals, Jessie stepped down onto the ground. A strong smell made her nose twitch.

Clara laughed. 'I know. But you get used to it, it never goes away. It's the smell of the paint and varnish and machine oil. And sometimes,' she pulled a face, 'when the wind is in the wrong direction, we get the smell of the smoke from the foundry, even though it's way over there, away from the rest of the buildings.' She caught Jessie's puzzled frown. 'It has to be as far away as possible because of the heat of the furnaces,' she explained. 'It's dangerous for the rest of the factory. There's a separate entrance from the road to it further up.'

She waved her hand vaguely in a direction away from the rest of the buildings. 'It's not somewhere I've been since we came back. Stanley has. He says the poor men are filthy and sweating from morning 'til night, it's so hot and steamy. You'll see it pouring out of the windows tomorrow.' She grimaced. 'But, as Pa says, it's all the smell of money being made. For the family – and for the workers,' she added hastily. 'Pa looks after all his workers, knows them all by name and there are over fifty of them. And we've had very few accidents. Well, not bad ones, anyway.' She said it proudly but shivered. 'Of course, before the war we had almost a hundred workers but they went ... well, you know...'

'The army.' Jessie nodded.

'Yes.' Clara sighed. 'I often wonder how many of them will come back.'

'You must have known many of them?'

'Most of them came – come from the village. I grew up here, don't forget.' Clara smiled. 'I lived here until Stanley and I were married.' A small frown creased her forehead. 'I hadn't been back until – until just before Abigail was born, you know that.' Jessie noticed the omission of the war and Stanley's injuries. 'But we don't forget and we're happy here ... all of us, we're happy we're all together...

'Well, that's enough of all that. I'm dying for you to meet my parents – and to admire our Abigail. And to see Stanley...' She paused, silently answering Jessie's unspoken question with a slow closing of her eyelids. 'He's really thrown himself into the business. Pa says he has the best mind for figures he's ever known in anyone. And he's now in charge of the assembly room. The women in there adore him.' She chuckled, a low, proud chuckle. 'I really am quite jealous of them and all the fuss they make of him. He is quite spoiled these days.'

Jessie smiled. They exchanged a look of understanding.

'Well, it's too cold to be standing outside today. Let's get in the house quickly. Come on, this way. Don't mind the dogs, they're friendly and won't bother you.' With Jim following and carrying Jessie's valise, Clara led the way past the dogs and along a long passageway.

Jessie stopped in surprise when she saw the house. It was an imposing stone building, large, square, with solid double oak doors set back inside a porch flanked with two fancy columns at the entrance and large mullioned windows. A mansion, she thought, gazing around. Behind it, a backdrop of dramatic hills rose, dark and forbidding, the craggy line of rocks at the top silhouetted against the silvered sky.

'The house was built for some posh landowner years ago.' Clara, realising Jessie had stopped, spoke louder, even as she hurried along the short drive that led from the passageway. 'Papa decided he wanted to live as close as possible to his factory.' She laughed. 'I'm not sure Mama was so pleased when she found out how noisy and smelly it was. But she says she's had to get used to it. Sometimes she feels she's as much married to sewing machines as she is to Pa.'

She looked to the hills at the side of the house. 'Oh dear, I do hope it isn't going to snow. You could be stuck here for days.' She glanced at Jessie, mischief gleaming in her grey eyes. 'Hopefully. Oh...' She flapped her hand. 'Only joking. First flurry of snow and we'll get you back on the train and home to Harry.'

She pushed open the heavy oak front door, took the bag from Jim with a smiling nod and a word of thanks and hustled Jessie inside.

'We're home.'

Chapter 69

As soon as she met Clara's parents, Jessie understood their past reservations about Stanley. It was obvious they were fiercely proud but protective of their only daughter and, by marrying her out of their religion they must have thought he'd taken her away from them. Coming alone to Britain as a young couple of Russian immigrants all those years ago, they would have been terrified that they'd lost their only daughter. Now Clara was back in the fold, they could let themselves feel care and affection for her husband.

Jessie liked them instantly. Fussing over her, they made her welcome, ushering her to the fire in Clara's part of the house and tutting over her dishevelled state.

'Here, here, sit, drink this, it will warm you.' Clara's mother handed Jessie a cup of tea.

She saw Clara watching her closely and grinning. It was strong and very sweet and she just about managed not to grimace. 'Lovely, thank you, Mrs Askaroff.' Jessie unwound her scarf and unbuttoned her coat to let the warmth of the blazing fire warm her chilled body.

'Please, call me Rayia. And Clara's father is Igor.'

Smiling, he raised his own mug of tea to her. '*Ypa*, cheers, Jessie. I have put your valise in your room.' He pointed his finger to the door. 'Right across the hall.' His voice was a loud deep growl, but he spoke with a huge beam on his face.

'Thank you Mr ... Igor,' Jessie stammered. Although only a short man, his presence seemed to fill the room. He laughed, for no obvious reason.

His wife looked at him with pride, though she still said, 'Quietly, Igor, you are making my ornaments rattle.' She pointed to the glass case in the corner of the room.

Everybody laughed.

'Oh,' Clara exclaimed, 'Stanley will be home soon. Shall we go across to meet him? He's been in the office all morning—'

'Making sure we are not losing too much money – this war! Pah!' Clara's father scowled, waved his hands above his head.

'It has caused trouble to a lot of businesses, Igor.' Clara's mother remonstrated.

'And to families.' Clara sighed.

'*я прошу прощения*. I am sorry,' Her father shook his head, his hand on his forehead. 'I am so sorry, my daughter. I did not think.' He turned towards Jessie. 'But he is a great asset to the business is Clara's *муж*, Clara's husband.'

'I'm sure.' Jessie nodded, taking another small sip of the tea before placing it onto the small table by the side of her armchair. 'I'd love to go and meet Stanley.'

The last time she'd seen him, in the hospital, brought back distressing memories. She struggled for a moment, anxious to banish them into the past where they belonged, and meet Clara's husband thinking only of the strong, pleasant man she'd known as Arthur's friend.

'But Jessie, she has only just arrived.' Her mother glanced with concern at her.

'I'm fine – Mrs ... Rayia.' Jessie stumbled over the name.

'It's *Rayia,*' Clara's mother chuckled. 'You will get used to it. You are sure you are all right to go outside again?'

'Honestly.'

A draught blew around Jessie's ankles as the front doors opened. She heard the sound of a wheelchair being manoeuvred on the floor tiles in the hall. Stanley wheeled himself in, a small child in his lap.

'Jessie.' Stanley raised one hand in greeting. 'So glad to see you at last.'

She swallowed, hoping she hadn't shown her shock at the unfamiliar lines of pain etched on his face. 'Stanley.' She half-rose, smiling, but stopped as his daughter turned her face away from her into his coat.

'Hello, *моя крошкату*, my little one.' Clara's father caught hold of Abigail to swing her around and hold her high in the air. 'You are not so shy, surely?' He pulled her towards him, giving her a noisy kiss on the forehead before lowering her onto Jessie's lap. 'This is your Auntie Jessie. Now say *здравствуйте,* Abigail, say hello to her and give her a big cuddle.'

The little girl sat stiffly until Jessie whispered in her ear. She twisted around to look at Jessie who nodded. They smiled at one another.

'Secrets, eh?' Clara raised an eyebrow, her lips upturned.

'I said I think she's the most beautiful little girl in the whole world.'

'*конечно!*' Igor shouted. 'Of course!'

Abigail clapped her hands and jumped off Jessie's knee to throw herself, giggling, into Igor's arms.

'You have made a friend, Jessie.' Clara's mother gathered the little girl up. 'Now I think it is bedtime for someone. Say goodnight, Abigail.' She went round them so the child could kiss them all.

'Goodnight.' Abigail waved from the door.

'Come, Igor, let us leave these friends to talk.'

Stanley looked from his wife to her friend. 'If you ladies don't mind, I think I'll have a lie down before we eat.'

Clara bent to give him a full kiss on the lips. 'Thank you, darling. See you in a while.'

She waited until she closed the door behind him. 'Now Jessie, let's get what's troubling you out of the way. And then we can enjoy the rest of your stay with us.'

Chapter 70

'Stanley looks well, Clara.' Jessie held her hands out to the fire and rubbed them together.

'He is now. Mostly...' Clara hesitated. 'Sometimes he has nightmares that he won't talk about. I worry about that and it's quite frightening to see him so distressed. But those times are getting less, I think.' She clasped her hands, her fingers entwined so tightly her knuckles were white. 'It's been hard, Jessie.'

'But you've not said anything in your letters?'

'I know. It would have felt disloyal. The Stanley I loved, the man who stole my heart the first time we met, wasn't the same man who came back to me. I don't mean about his – injury.' She touched her temple. 'I mean in here. For a long time he was angry and withdrawn. I didn't seem able to reach him. In any way... We didn't...' Pressing her lips together, she stopped speaking.

Jessie watched her face flush. She touched her friend's arm. 'It must have been difficult – for the two of you, I mean.'

'It was. I'm sorry, Jessie, it's too personal...?'

'No. No, we're friends, Clara. And there are only the two of us here.'

'Thank you.' Clara straightened in her chair, the flush subsiding from her cheeks. 'We're fine now. I know he loves me as he always has. It's been so awful for him. But Papa took him under his wing,

197

got him involved in the business. It took a while for Stanley to believe in himself, to know he was still useful. I've got my husband back. Pa wouldn't be without him now. And Mama adores him.'

'I'm glad.' Jessie smiled. 'Your parents are lovely, Clara.'

Her friend laughed. 'Yes, I think so. They've been wonderful since we came here as a family.'

'And they've made me feel so welcome.' Jessie was glad to see Clara relax. She paused. 'I hope you don't think me rude, and please don't answer if you would rather not, but I was wondering what made them come to Britain. Why they left their own country?'

Clara shrugged. 'Neither Mama or Papa will say much, they never have. They came here in 1881. I believe there was some sort of unrest in Russia. They've never wanted to talk about it and, of course, I wouldn't hurt them by asking too much. They have their sad moments about leaving there. But I think Stanley and I being here helps them.'

'Oh, it must do.'

'And they are over the moon about the baby.' She touched her stomach.

'You look really well.' Jessie smiled.

'I am.' There was a slight draught from the window. Clara shivered. She stood and pulled the curtains together. 'Are you warm enough?'

'I'm fine. This is a lovely big fire.' Jessie nodded towards a portrait of Abigail above the fireplace. 'And she's gorgeous.'

'She is.' Clara followed Jessie's gaze. 'And she's so well behaved. Which is lucky because Stanley and I have had to be away from home quite a lot this year and she's stayed with my parents.'

'With the business?'

'Yes. Mama won't travel and Pa doesn't like leaving her, even with us here.'

'Has the business been badly affected by the war?'

'We lost one of our suppliers in Hull last August. Jim drove Stanley and I up there when we heard there'd been raids. The warehouse was completely demolished. But nothing like the loss we made in January when the first Zeppelins came over and destroyed our biggest agency just outside Birmingham. Most of the machines gone. Papa thought we'd go out of business then. But Stanley arranged for those we could salvage to be transported to another agent company he found in London. In the end it turned out better for us with less transport costs to the large stores there. We even managed a few days away on our own to check out the competition. Mama and Pa were thrilled to have Abigail to themselves.'

Clara sat down in the armchair next to Jessie again, pulling her blue shawl around her shoulders. 'I can't seem to keep warm, these days.' She shivered again. 'Who knows what else the Germans are planning for the future? But things might be better now that Asquith has resigned and this War Cabinet has been formed. Papa was surprised that the Coalition with the Conservatives and Labour fell through because there wasn't a general election or a vote of no confidence or any proper challenge to him being leader of the Liberal Party, but Stanley wasn't. He said Asquith's fall from power was brought on by some shenanigans between Lloyd George and some members of the Conservative Party.'

'It might mean this stupid war ends sooner?'

'Let's hope so.'

Despite Mrs Giles' insistence in bringing over the newspapers to Edna's, it was clear to Jessie she still knew much less than her friend on those matters.

'But what about you, Jessie?' Clara tilted her head.

Now it was time, Jessie didn't know where to start. She thought about the two choices that Clara, in her letter, had said she needed to make.

'You wanted to talk about Bob Clegg?'

'Yes, I do.' Jessie crossed her arms over her waist. Immediately she felt the tears brim.

Clara leant forward to take hold of her hands. 'Take your time. Stanley will leave us alone. I haven't told him about it. I only told him we had lots to catch up on.'

Jessie swallowed, wiped the palms of her hands over her eyes.

'Bob's asked me to marry him again.' Her shoulders raised and fell as she sighed. 'As I said in my letter, I've only ever looked on him as a friend, older than me, but we've always got on and he was good when Mam was ill. And since.' She held out her hands. 'I think he'd be a good husband but...' Her words trailed away.

'We both know you'll never feel the same as you did for Arthur. But do you like Bob?'

Jessie blew her nose on the handkerchief her friend handed to her. 'Like you said, he would make both Harry and me acceptable...'

'In society.' Clara prompted. 'I have to say respectability is so important these days. I didn't mean to be cruel in my letter, Jessie, but you really can't be just friends. It's not the done thing. If you're asking my opinion again now...?'

Jessie nodded. 'I've almost made up my mind. I've thought about it a lot, but I would be grateful if we could talk some more about it whilst I'm here?'

'Of course we will. And you know I will always speak truthfully. So, I think – perhaps for Harry?'

Jessie jumped up and walked to the window. 'For Harry...' She stared at the dark shadow of the hills behind the house. The day had long drawn to a close. She became conscious she was watching her own reflection, the thin outline of her figure nervously shifting from side to side. Did she care what others thought of her? She pondered. No. But she had to think of her son.

'What would you do, Clara?' Jessie spun round.

Clara crossed the room and took her hand. It felt as though she was passing on her strength, willing Jessie to be strong.

'I'm sorry, Jessie, but Arthur has gone. I know there will always be a place in your heart for him. But you have the rest of your life to live – for you and for Harry. I don't really know Bob; I only ever saw him in the shop. But I trust your judgement. If you think he is a good man, then I think he's worth taking a chance on.'

Later, in the middle of the night, Jessie lay sleepless in bed. She knew she hadn't told Clara her reservations about Bob's temper. She chose to ignore the jealous, even spiteful side to him, that came to the surface occasionally. Nor had she told her how he'd reacted when she'd refused him. Would he react in the same way with anything he didn't like, if she wanted to do something he didn't approve of?

What if she followed Clara into the Suffrage movement? She had a fleeting memory of Clara's altercation with that obnoxious man about the Suffragettes in the shop that time. Had Bob been in the bakery when they were sitting in the kitchen talking about it? She was sure she must have said something about Clara being a Suffragist when he was around at one time or another. She didn't remember him saying anything against it... It would have made her stop and think about whether she could be with a man who didn't believe in the whole thing of suffrage and equality.

But it was obvious that Clara felt the same way about respectability as he did. For some reason she couldn't quite understand, Jessie didn't like thinking her friend believed the only way she could be an acceptable part of society was to be married. What about Clara's belief that men and women were equal? Wasn't that what the Suffragette movement was all about? Anyway, she thought, turning her pillow over and thumping it into a better shape, Bob loved her. He'd do anything for her. If he did ever show any signs of going back to his old moody ways, she was sure she'd be able to change him.

Chapter 71

'I've been admiring your mother's sewing machine, Clara. She showed me how it worked last night while you were putting Abigail to bed. And it is so prettily decorated.'

Clara glanced at Stanley across the breakfast table. 'I'm sure Papa would agree to us showing you our factory. What do you think, husband dear?' She gave him and then Jessie a broad smile. 'It's a family joke,' she explained. 'Any visitors we have we get a guided tour around the place. Papa is so proud of his business. He hasn't stopped asking Stanley if we've shown you what we do yet.'

'But not the furnaces.' He wiped his mouth with his napkin, giving an extra rub at his moustache. 'Far too noisy and hot in there today with all the fires going.' He smiled at Jessie in apology. 'And to be honest I think the men would be uncomfortable having ladies in there anyway. As I said, it's very hot and they – er – are not at their best.'

Clara laughed. 'I think what Stanley is trying to say, Jessie, is that the place makes the men sweat. A lot. And they get very dirty. But I don't think they actually care who is there as long as they can get on with their work. What my lovely husband really means is that he thinks it too dangerous for us. I've not been allowed in the building when the process is fully working.' She leaned over and patted his hand. 'Am I right, dear?'

Stanley studied both of them, smiling. 'I'm afraid my wife has caught me out, Jessie. The process in there, making the basic shape of the sewing machines, is indeed dangerous. They must pour the raw pig iron into the castings.' He saw Jessie's puzzled expression. 'A process too long for me to explain now, and, I assure you, quite boring, unless you have to do it. Which, Jessie, I'm sure you never will.'

He gave a low chuckle. 'But the men need to concentrate and...' He pushed his wheelchair away from the table, 'Seeing two beautiful ladies nearby would do nothing for steady hands. I'm happy to show you the sections of the factory that will interest you once you're both wrapped up against this cold.'

They hurried across the yard, Clara's hand on her husband's shoulder as he navigated the rough flags with his wheelchair. Jessie looked over to the building that held the furnaces, steam and smoke pouring from the windows. It was almost as if the huge building was

202

breathing like a monstrous animal. She shivered, relieved they were not going anywhere near it.

Clara noticed and linked her arm. 'Quite fearsome, isn't it? Now, look through this window here.'

They cupped their hands around their eyes and peered through the hazy panes of glass into a large room. Jessie could just make out some large steel bins with men standing above them.

'What are they doing?'

'The body of the machine has been smoothed down and they're dipping them into paint—'

'It's called black japanning.' Stanley, muffled up against the cold in a black overcoat and woolly hat, wheeled himself away towards another large building nearby. 'Sometimes they have to re-dip many times to get the layers just right. Come on, ladies, it's freezing out here.'

'Sorry, darling.'

'They all have their faces wrapped up.' Jessie stepped away from the window. 'The men? They have cloths around their faces?'

'It's extremely smelly work, I'm told,' Clara whispered. 'Yet another place I'm not allowed to go when they're working.'

They waited until Stanley wheeled his chair through the doorway. Jessie noticed Stanley's wheelchair crunched on the gritty stone floor. He saw Jessie glance at them. 'My wheels need to be metal, in the heat of the foundry rubber tyres would melt.'

'Oh, I didn't think of that.'

He laughed, a little wryly. 'I'd be in a pretty pickle if that happened.'

'As you can see, my husband has thought of everything so he can go anywhere he likes in the factory—'

'As is right. I am the second in command here.' He spoke in a reproving tone even though humour crinkled his eyes.

'Oh, yes, there is one rule for me and one for him.' Clara returned his smile and bent down to kiss him. 'I often tell him he's overprotective.'

'As a husband should be. And I'm sure Jessie only wants to see how the machines are put together and finished off.' He wheeled himself further into the room. 'This, Jessie, is where machines take shape.'

She looked around the room. The workers were mainly women, sitting, some hunched over and peering at small parts, filing and smoothing something in their hands.

'What are they doing?'

'Every piece of the machine needs to be perfect.' Clara led her along the rows, stopping every now and then to have a word with the women. Most looked up, most smiled. The ones who didn't, she patted on their shoulders. 'A lot of them weren't as lucky as me,' she whispered to Jessie, 'Their sons, husbands, brothers, all our workers before the war, haven't come back. Yet. But we hope – for their sakes...' She glanced back to where Stanley was chatting to an older man. 'The foreman,' she explained, 'we brought him out of retirement, and he was glad of the job, I think.

'Now, look, this is my favourite section. I often watch from the offices where I work sometimes. I help out with the ordering occasionally.' She said, answering Jessie's enquiring expression and pointing to steps leading to wooden structures above them. 'This is where we can see the finished product. Pa's favourite corner of the building, as well.'

The sewing machines on the benches were indeed works of art. The black finish was polished to a high shine. Clara ran her hand over one. 'I love the feel of them when they've just been done. But look.' She moved quickly to another set of benches. Jessie followed. 'Look at these.' She touched sheets of decorations in rich colours of red and gold. 'These are called decals. The designs are on special paper for transfer onto the sewing machines—'

'Like you mother's.'

'Exactly. They're put on and then they're polished over. Aren't they glorious?'

'They are. I would love to own one of these sewing machines. My

204

mother had one that wasn't anywhere near as fancy. And Edna says there's nothing wrong with a needle and thread. She called Mam's machine "a new-fangled contraption". Her smile hid a twinge of sadness. 'I don't know what happened to Mam's sewing machine.' She shrugged. 'Perhaps one day I'll have one of my own.'

'I think that soon they will become a household item in *all* homes.'

'And then we'll be rich.' Stanley appeared behind them. 'Time for luncheon, I think, Clara?'

'Yes, if you've seen enough, Jessie?'

'It's been fascinating, thank you.' She was aware that Stanley looked chilled through.

'So, now you know what we're doing here, what would you like to do for the rest of the day?'

'Do you know what I'd really like to do this afternoon, Clara?' They left Stanley to go back into the house and stood watching Abigail hopping on the flags in front of the house.

'What, my dear?'

'I'd like to climb that hill.' Jessie nodded towards the fields rising above the building, 'Just a little way, just so I can look down and see the factory, the village, the countryside all around.'

'Then you will. Time to go inside, Abigail.' She studied Jessie's coat. 'But you'll need a warmer coat.'

Chapter 72

An hour later the two of them were struggling against the ever increasing breeze and holding on to one another.

'I think this is far enough.' Clara turned to look back. 'Look, we can see everything you wanted to, Jessie.' She tucked her hands into the wide sleeves of her mink coat.

Hills ranged on the horizon, a blend of greens and browns stark against the bright silvery sky. The village was a tiny cluster of dark stone cottages, a few shops, a public house in the centre and the church with its steeple at the end of the main street. The factory loomed over everything. Smoke and the shimmer of steam rose above the furnaces and the smaller buildings around them.

'The factory is certainly impressive. And yet it doesn't spoil the countryside. It's wonderful to see from up here.' Jessie pulled up the collar of the fur coat Clara had insisted she borrow. 'You can see so far.' The wind whipped the words from her mouth. She laughed. Even in the short time away she'd missed climbing fields; this reminded her of her and Arthur's hill. For a second she wondered if there was another heart stone somewhere along these walls, but quickly dismissed the idea. There was only the one. And it belonged to them.

They stayed for a few more moments before Clara shivered. 'Shall we make our way back?'

'If you like.'

It had been easier walking up the fields than down and they both needed to concentrate on where they put their feet amongst the strong tussocks of grass and loose stones.

'It was probably best your mother insisted it was too cold for Abigail to come with us.' Jessie was panted with the jolting effort of each step and holding on to Clara to make sure she didn't fall. 'And I'm sorry, this really is too much for you as well.'

'I'm fine.' Clara clung harder to Jessie's arm despite her protestations. 'You're right about Abigail. I didn't like to hear her crying, but she wouldn't have enjoyed this. I was lucky to get away with it as well. Mama thinks I should be wrapped up in cotton wool.'

Knowing how caring her parents were of Clara, a thought struck Jessie. 'What did they think of you joining the Suffragettes?'

Clara laughed. 'They didn't know. Papa would have gone to Nether Brook and dragged me home, I think.'

They stopped, panting, their breath pluming white in front of their faces.

'What will you do if ever this dreadful war finishes?'

'Oh, it will finish one day, Jessie...'

'But when...' Clara's face was pinched with the cold. 'You never know what to believe in the papers. One day it seems there are negotiations going on now America has joined us in the war and Russia doesn't want to be involved. But then we hear reports of convoys belonging to the British navy being blown up by German submarines.' Clara sighed. 'Mrs Skelton, one of the women on the production line, has a son who was on a destroyer that got blown out of the water in October. She was in a right state, she thought her son was dead until last week when she heard he was picked up in the sea and taken prisoner.' She gave a short laugh, a bitter twist to her mouth. 'This war is as hard on the women...'

Jessie took hold of her hand; she knew her friend was thinking of Stanley.

'Come on, let's get you inside.'

They didn't speak until they were standing in the hall of the house again, pulling off their hats and gloves and hanging up their coats.

Clara unbuckled her boots and stamped her feet. 'I've lost all feeling in my toes.' She laughed. 'I'll be glad of that fire.' She looked up towards the stairs. 'Abigail, we're home.'

The warmth of the parlour was welcome. Jessie held her hands out to the flames. Still curious as to what her friend would do about the Suffragist movement she was once part of, she said, 'I remember you saying Mrs Pankhurst declaring the movement only suspended to support the government in the war efforts. So what do you think will happen if women don't get the vote?'

Clara shrugged pulling her chair closer to the fire. 'It depends. Back in January there was a Speaker's Conference that discussed suffrage.' She held her hand out to her daughter who ran across the room and snuggled up to her. 'Let's see if Lloyd George keeps his word. I'll believe it when it happens.' She set her mouth. 'If it doesn't, I suppose I'll join them again. Stanley and I have talked about it. He says I must do what I believe in.'

'And your parents?'

'We will, as they say, cross that bridge when we come to it.' She kissed the top of her daughter's head. 'And you? What would you do if women don't get the vote, Jessie? Have you thought?'

'I haven't really.'

'Do you know what Bob thinks about Suffrage?'

'It's not something we've talked about. But I'm my own person, you know that.'

'I do indeed.' Clara smiled.

Jessie gave a mental shrug. If Bob wanted her, as he so obviously did, he would have to accept everything about her, including the streak of independence she'd discovered in herself over the last year or so.

Chapter 73

The last evening of her visit was a jolly one. Igor, spurred on by a few glasses of vodka, sang some Russian songs, which became more poignant and sad, the more glasses of the spirit he had. He sang his favourite, the *Song of the Volga Boatmen,* four times. Stanley, in retaliation, also fired up by vodka, decided to teach Clara's father one his own favourite songs.

'You'll like this,' he said to Igor.

'Oh Stanley, no.' Clara turned to Jessie. 'I swear he'd sing this every night if I didn't stop him.'

'There's nothing wrong with *The Sunshine Of Your Smile*,' Stanley protested.

'Except when you've heard it hundreds of times just because it's the only song your husband knows all the words of,' Clara retorted.

'Not true! Not true. That's slander, my good woman.' Still grinning he started the song.

'*Give me a smile, the love-light in your eyes...*'

Jessie thought he had a lovely baritone singing voice and, by the time he'd sung it twice Igor joined in.

They ended by both turning to their wives and, hands comically clasped on the chests, repeating the last two lines.

In the general confusion of applause and laughter, a numb feeling of isolation swept over Jessie.

'Right, Jessie.' Clara hugged her, holding her tightly. 'Just remember: do what you think is best for both you and Harry. I just want you to be happy, love, like Stanley and I are. Life's too short. We've both learned that, haven't we?'

A huge sob hurt Jessie's chest, stopping her from answering.

'So...' Clara leaned back to look at her, the effort of making her voice bright showing in her trembling smile. 'Safe journey and have a good Christmas.' Christmas! Yet another time to get through. Jessie moved her mouth into a shaky smile. 'And,' Clara gave a warning nod, 'keep in touch. Answer my letters. Let me know all your news.'

'I will. And you let me know when the baby arrives, won't you?'

'I will, you can be sure of that.'

Jessie watched Jim place her valise on the seat of the train and waited until he stepped down onto the platform before shaking his hand. 'Thank you, Jim.' She gave Clara a last hug and climbed into the compartment, breathing a sigh of relief that it was empty.

She heard the stationmaster slamming the doors of the other carriages. When he closed her door, she kept her eyes on her friend through the glass. She couldn't smile.

The train jerked to start and moved slowly until it reached the end of the platform. Clara, trotting to keep up despite the burden of her stomach, was left behind. Jessie lowered her hands to her lap. The three days with Clara and her family were over. The sadness was dispelled by the pull of returning to her son. Jessie knew what she would do. Must do.

Chapter 74

The sharp wind bit into her face, her eyes watered, her breath tight in her throat as she struggled up Wharmton Hill. When she reached the small heart stone, she held it to her breast and looked up at the dense clouds scudding across the grey, leaden sky.

Crouching by the wall, she listened to the thin cries of sheep, the whisper of the grass. When she spoke, she tried to make her voice firm.

'I love you, Arthur. I always will.' Wherever he was, whatever form he took now, she hoped he could hear her. 'But I need to move on for our son's sake. Please understand.' She brushed her lips against the rough surface of the stone. 'It's not goodbye, my love, it will never be goodbye as long as I live. And I will, one day, tell Harry about his father, his real dad, I promise.'

She placed the stone gently back on the wall in exactly the same place. 'And I won't stop coming here. Ever.' She would keep her word. She knew she had always a place to come back to, a place that would be hers alone.

But with each step down the hill, she knew she was walking away from a future that could have been so different.

Jessie waited at the top of the hill Bob toiled up each day on his way to the bakery. She'd thought long and hard about what she wanted to say, to explain her past reservations about any relationship with him other than friendship. She wanted to tell him that Arthur would always have a special place in her heart.

Every time, at that point in her rehearsal, the image of the heart stone and the note, *I LOVE YOU*, came into her mind and she faltered in her resolution. But she took a long deep breath and reminded herself what she needed to say next: her decision. She needed to know that Bob would accept Harry as his own. Without that agreement she would go no further. She would turn away; there would not even be the chance of friendship any longer. She would be truly alone.

Her mouth dried when she saw him turn from Grotton Road onto Union Street. Waves of panic washed over her, but her feet felt stuck to the pavement.

Head down, he didn't notice her until he was around ten yards away. She watched as he stopped, a half-frown, half-smile on his face.

She remembered the first line she had practiced long into the night.

'Jessie?' Bob said. 'What...?'

'Hello, Bob,' she said, 'If you still want me, I will marry you.'

Chapter 75

Six months after the wedding, when they were living with Bob's mother, he stood in the kitchen and told her she would have to work in the shop.

'I can't, Bob. Please don't make me.'

'With Eddie gone and joined up what choice 'ave we got? Damn fool didn't need to go, but he did. Now we need you in the shop.'

'But working alongside Morgan, Bob.' Jessie stopped, seeing the flicker of – something – irritation – anger in his eyes. 'I'm sorry...'

'But yer needed, there's no choice.'

'You could hire someone?'

'And pay them how? Takings are down. We're having to pull our belts in these days. Blame this bloody new Food Department if you 'ave to blame someone. Telling folk to make their own bread, writing in the paper about mixing flour with sago or potatoes and other rubbish to make it go further...'

Trying to shut off the same tirade she'd been hearing for weeks from him, Jessie thought that she knew exactly who to blame for so many things. And now her husband was telling her to work alongside him. When he knew how much she hated him. How could he?

Bob was running out of breath with his rant. 'Stupid idea. Revolting shite... War Bread, my arse...'

Jessie didn't let him see how much his aggression upset her. She knew he did it on purpose. All the promises he'd made to her, all the conditions he'd agreed to when she said she'd marry him, all faded away, all broken, in only a few months. How had she ever thought she knew him? This man wasn't the Bob she'd known as a boy, as a friend.

She caught a flicker of a grey skirt out of the corner of her eye. Bob's mother, about to come into the room, had backed away. Jessie hated that his mother had seen them arguing. She lowered her voice. Pacifying.

'It's just advice. You know what the papers are saying, Bob. About the Germans submarines sinking ships, trying to starve us into giving in—'

'What do you know, eh? Nowt. You're daft, woman.' Sarcasm clipped his words. 'Believing everything they say in the papers. It's all made up.' He stared at her, shook his head. 'And those stupid women telling folk how to make their own cakes.'

'They're called the Women's Institute, just women trying to help other women.'

'Huh! We might as well not even try to sell blasted cakes anymore. Going to put us out of business.'

'If business is so slow, why do you need me in the shop?' Jessie's throat hurt with the effort of trying not to cry.

'For God's sake, woman.' He ran his fingers through his hair in exasperation. 'Morgan kicked a bloke out last week for coming into the shop wearing one of those fuckin' badges, *"I Eat Less Bread"*. Caused a right bloody commotion in front of the other customers. The way he's acting these days, he's better off working in the bakery and keeping out of the front. You're needed in there and that's an end to it.'

He walked away from her. The following day Jessie found herself in the shop.

Jessie worked at the front serving the customers, speaking as little as possible to Amos Morgan, trying to avoid being near him. But inevitably there were times when they were in the shop at the same time and he never missed an opportunity for a quick grope, an obscene remark, a lascivious leer. How she hated him.

Enduring his sly taunts, his humiliation of her in the shop in front of those customers who were his cronies was bad enough. What she didn't understand was why Bob never intervened, never said a word to stop the man, to protect her.

It was almost two years before she understood. Bob had been biding his time.

PART THREE

July 1918

Chapter 76

Amos Morgan is dead and can no longer torment us. Jessie Clegg smiled. It was two years since her husband had insisted she work in the bakery. Alongside him and Amos Morgan, the man she'd hated for so long.

Amos Morgan is dead. The words were a constant refrain in her head since Bob had found him on the floor of the bakery a week ago. Heart attack, the doctor had said.

There'd been no baking for days. The bustle through the shop had not been customers but the doctor, the undertaker, the old woman who'd laid out her stepfather. Jessie had refused to do it, instead she'd sent for the retired midwife with the hard-calloused hands. She resented being here today, but Bob had told her she must wait for the hearse. And have Harry with her.

She stared past the scullery curtain to the backyard. Sparrows squabbled on the washing line. To the right of the lean-to, the top of the wall shone green in a slant of the afternoon sunlight. Lumps of coke had spilled over the wooden barrier of the lean-to behind the cold bakery oven. Rain had caused black liquid to leave its mark on the flags. It had streamed towards the grid in the middle of the yard, but Bob hadn't washed it away as he usually did.

Harry was sitting on the yard steps and refusing to come inside. She was angry with herself; she'd left the bakery door open and he'd seen the coffin on the trestle in the kitchen. He'd seen too much all along. Why had she thought it would be different when she married Bob? Why had she thought he would protect her and her son from her stepfather?

Picking up a plate and a mug she went out into the yard to him. 'Here, have this milk and butty but don't get jam on your clothes.' She sat alongside him, gave him a hug.

He fidgeted, pulling at the collar of his shirt, scratching his legs. 'Too tight. Trousers itch.'

'Try not to think about it, love.' She waited, glad of a quiet moment before the day that faced her.

'Finished.' Harry held out the empty plate and beaker.

'Good boy.' She gave him another hug and wiped his mouth with the dishcloth. 'Right. I won't be a moment.'

In the kitchen she shrugged on her black coat, picked up her hat and pinned it to her hair. 'We should go in and see him before the hearse comes,' she called through the back door. 'Then you will really believe he's gone to Heaven.'

'No.' His stubborn voice was muted, 'And he's not in Heaven – he's just dead.'

'Wait there then.'

The coffin was still open; the last of the chapel-goers, the neighbours, the curious, had filed past and left hours ago.

She looked down on the man who had been her persecutor. A wave of hatred rose in her.

'Bloody good riddance, you wicked old bastard.'

Deliberately she gathered saliva in her mouth, leant over and let the globule of spit drop onto Amos Morgan's face. It slid off his large nose and along his cheek. Jessie watched with satisfaction.

The way he'd stabbed his fingers into her that day.

The undertaker had combed the long strands of hair across the baldness of the skull. But a grey lock dangled over the face.

'And can stay like that.' Jessie whispered, pleased that Amos Morgan would meet his maker in a less than dapper manner that he would have wished.

Taking a deep breath, she glanced around the room. The air was stultifying, a mixture of damp and mothballs. The two candles on the sideboard were burning low. There was a triangle of light at the top of the window where the curtains didn't quite meet. Dust floated around in it. She tried to pull the material together but just made the opening longer. Intricate mote patterns were scattered in all directions.

218

The slant of sun lay diagonally across the body, shadowed the torso and emphasised the shine on his boots. Moving closer to the coffin, Jessie gripped it and looked down again at the body.

'I've hated everything about you, Amos Morgan. But there's nothing you can do to me – to us – ever again. Nothing.'

'Mrs Clegg?' The tone was professionally subdued, the knock on the front door soft. 'It's Mr Davey, the undertaker?'

'Just a moment,' she called. She looked down at her stepfather. The globule of saliva had slid to his ear. Satisfied, Jessie smiled. 'Goodbye, Amos Morgan. Rot in Hell.'

The car carrying Jessie and Harry followed the hearse taking Amos Morgan to the Methodist chapel through the narrow, terraced streets of Nether Brook.

'Why isn't Dad in this car with us?' Harry twisted around to look through the back window. 'Is there another car?'

'He's gone for Granny Clegg.' Jessie forced herself to speak calmly though she didn't know why Bob refused to wait with them for the hearse to arrive, why he needed to be with his mother rather than his family. There was a constant quiver of worry in her. Something was wrong. 'They'll be waiting for us at the chapel.'

The soft leather seat squeaked loudly under their buttocks every time they moved and Harry giggled, made nervous by the unfamiliar attention they were receiving from the people huddled on their doorsteps.

'Shush,' Jessie said, but smiled at him from under her veil and squeezed his fingers. 'Nearly there now.'

A few groups of people straggled behind them up the hill to the cemetery. At the chapel four men stood by the archway. The hearse stopped. One of the undertaker's men helped Jessie and Harry from the car. She gripped her son's hand. He was trembling.

'Soon be over.'

The men moved forward in well-practised precision. Her stepfather had been a small man and they slid the coffin easily out of the hearse and lifted it onto their shoulders as though carrying a child. Jessie and Harry followed them into the chapel and slowly along the aisle towards the altar.

She heard the whispers when she passed each row of pews.

'Not Bob Clegg's, of course...'

'Brazen with it, she was...'

'You only 'ave to look at the boy...'

'The spit of Arthur Dawson...'

'Amos Morgan was a saint to let her go back to live there...'

The last made Jessie stop. She fixed her gaze on the two women. 'You don't know the half of it,' she said quietly. 'He was a monster.'

There was a collective intake of breath, but they didn't look at her. One rummaged in her handbag, the other sniffed, adjusted her fox fur, shook her head.

'A disgrace. Speaking ill of the dead...'

Jessie lifted her chin and pressed her son closer to her side.

Bob was already sitting in the front pew, his mother alongside him. He didn't turn to Jessie when she ushered Harry along the hard seat next to him.

The organ wheezed and then, each note held just a fraction too long, rumbled out the hymn *The Day Thou Gavest, Lord, Is Ended*. Putting her arm around Harry's tense figure, she pulled him towards her. 'Okay?'

He nodded and she felt him relax.

A hand pressed on her shoulder. Jessie flinched.

'It's me.'

Jessie turned. Edna smiled at her but the corners of her mouth trembled.

'You all right, pet?'

'Edna.' The relief of seeing a friendly face coursed through Jessie. 'I will be, I think.' Jessie looked past the older woman. None of the people sitting on pews behind them acknowledged her.

Jessie shrugged, turned to face the altar again. A stab of bitterness shot through her. She wondered what they would say if they truly knew what Amos had been like.

She knew. Even when her father was alive, even when Amos Morgan was just one of the many customers who came into the shop, she knew. Knew to be afraid of him. Jessie understood that the man wasn't to be trusted.

There was movement, a clearing of throats, a rustle of clothes.

Bob nudged her in the side. Hard. 'Right,' he said. 'Let's get this next bloody bit over and done with. Then we can get off.' His voice was harsh.

Jessie looked at him surprise. He hadn't liked Amos Morgan any more than her. But he'd never spoken to her in that way before. When she looked into Bob's eyes, it was as though she was looking at a stranger, not the man she married.

Chapter 77

'We need to talk.' Bob threw the remark over his shoulder when he took his mother's arm and led her along the path from the graveyard to the hired car.

'I'll come with you now.'

'Not at Mother's, at the bakery.'

'Why?'

He didn't answer.

There had been no wake planned for Amos Morgan's funeral. It was the one thing Jessie had been adamant about. And Bob didn't seem to care one way or the other. She walked back with Edna to her house. At the door she kissed Harry.

'You stay with Granny Edna, sweetheart, and I'll be back for you in a while.' In answer to Edna's questioning raised eyebrows Jessie shrugged. 'Don't know,' she mouthed. 'Tell you later.'

She quickly crossed the road to the shop.

When she walked through the shop to the bakery, Bob was already there, sitting at the table, his legs jerking rapidly, foot tapping on the floor, a sure sign of his irritability. Jessie looked around.

221

Her stepfather's presence still pervaded the bakery. The mop and bucket stank of the smell of ammonia he always insisted they use to clean the stone floor. His white apron, draped on the hook on the wall below Bob's, reached down to his indoor plimsolls. His cotton gloves, worn shiny black, hung alongside the curved metal bars used to drag the shelves in and out of the oven. Rolling pins, arranged by size, were lined up on the shelf above the worktop. And, underneath, the pie trays were neatly stacked, just as Amos had demanded.

'What is it, Bob?'

'Sit down.'

'I'm fine.' Jessie knew from his harsh tone this was something she wasn't going to like.

'Please yourself.' Bob shrugged.

'What is it?' she repeated

'Before I tell you, I want you to know 'ow much I've 'ated working with that bastard...' He stood, began to pace around the bakery.

'As I did,' Jessie said. 'You made me work here, Bob—'

He spoke over her words. 'There have been times when I looked at 'im and you—'

'Don't. You know how humiliated I—'

'How do you think I felt, eh? What about me? But I had 'im by the short hairs.' He nodded to himself, thumping one fist into the palm of the other. 'I told him what I knew—'

'What?'

'I told 'im what you told me.'

'No!'

'Yeah, fuckin' yeah.' He mocked her, still pacing the floor. 'An' I told 'im that I'd tell all that lot at 'is chapel. All that tight-arsed, too pure to pee lot. An' I told 'im I'd tell all the customers and he'd lose takings.' He laughed, a short derisory noise. 'That frightened the shit out of 'im.'

Jessie closed her eyes against the cold crudeness of his words.

'And I told 'im you'd back me up, an' all.'

'How could you? You wouldn't have made me do that, Bob?'

'I would an' all.' Bob nodded his head vigorously. 'It worked.'

His next words shocked her. 'I got 'im to sign the shop over to me. I've had a copy of Amos Morgan's will for a long time. He left the bakery to me.'

'I don't believe you. It wouldn't be legal for him to do that. I know Mam left the bakery, the business to me. She told me she'd made a will leaving the shop to me.'

'So why didn't you claim it when she died?'

She couldn't answer at first: I was afraid of Amos Morgan, I was grieving and then it was too late; Mam died then Harry was born, I'd lost Arthur, nothing else mattered? 'I thought a solicitor would write to me...'

'But he didn't, did he? Because your mother lied. Because what was hers belonged to him once they married.'

'The bakery should come to me.'

'Well, it doesn't.' He didn't bother to hide the triumph. 'It's mine. To make sure, I made 'im find a solicitor chap in Manchester and got all the legal things tied up. I had a copy and Morgan had 'is.' He turned and pointed his forefinger at her. 'But I 'ad to be careful. I knew he could've destroyed the will I 'ad from him, make another one, like, and them papers...' He nodded his head and grinned as though in admiration. ''E was such a crafty bugger. So I kept my papers safe, along with the will, and reminded him of what I knew – just every now and then, like. Amos Morgan was a bloke who liked 'is reputation as a chapel-goer – a God-botherer – and a businessman.' His top lip curled into a sneer. 'That's what 'e called 'imself: a businessman. Huh! He left the bakery to me.'

It was as though he was talking to himself. 'I've waited long enough for it. I've been waiting since you told me he'd 'ad you before me. That little runt! You fuckin' waited to tell me that until our so-called wedding night, didn't you?'

Jessie flinched as he swung around and hit the table with his fist. That wasn't a night she wanted to remember, any more than the evening of her mother's funeral. The evening Morgan raped her. But her husband was glaring at her, demanding she relive it all.

She'd bought herself a new nightgown of fine white linen for her wedding night. The high neckline and long sleeves were hemmed with broderie anglaise. The material was cold when she slipped it over her body, and she felt uneasy with the looseness of the garment; it wasn't protection enough for what she faced. Fear wasn't something she'd expected to feel when she accepted she would marry Bob. But it would be all right. He loved her, he'd be gentle. It would be all right

Earlier she'd been self-conscious and embarrassed leaving the parlour and going upstairs to Bob's bedroom in his mother's house.

It felt such a long time before her husband came into the room and closed the door. And yet too soon. No, this was Bob, it would be all right. Jessie repeated the words over and over in her mind.

But when Bob lifted the bed covers and slid into bed with her, the surge of panic made her catch her breath. This was the moment she had been dreading. It's all right. It's all right. She clenched her teeth.

'You okay, Jess, sweetheart?' Bob turned on his side, his face next to hers. He put his hand on her breast, gently stroking her nipple with his thumb. He kissed her, his lips hot on hers. He skimmed his hand over her flat stomach, paused for a moment at the top of her thighs.

'I can feel the heat of yer.' His mouth close to her ear, the tip of his tongue flicking, his breath hot. He gave a low laugh.

Jessie squirmed. Oh god…

'You like that, huh?' Lifting himself to look at her, he laughed again.

No! She couldn't. It wasn't all right. 'I can't…' Jessie gasped the words out. 'Bob.'

'Don't worry. We can tek things as slowly as yer want.' But he'd raised himself up on his elbow and was pulling her nightdress up towards her knees, running his fingers along her thigh.

Stop it. Please stop in, she thought, tightening her legs together. 'Bob…'

'Shush, it'll be all right.' He pushed his hand between her thighs, stroked the hair there. 'So soft.' Pressed his thumb inside her.

Tell him, she told herself, you have to tell him. Jessie couldn't prevent the tears. 'I need to tell you something.'

He stopped. 'What's wrong? Jess?'

'I need to say something.'

'What?' He sounded wary. He was listening. Waiting.

She gulped, the tears salty in her throat.

'Wait a moment.' He rolled over in the bed. After a moment the soft glow of the candle was held above her. 'What is it, sweetheart?'

She forced herself to watch his face as she told him what happened to her: Morgan's violent violation of her body. Except for one moment when she thought she saw a darkening of anger in his eyes, she couldn't detect any emotion in him other than, she thought, an awakening of understanding, of compassion.

He put the candle back on to the bedside table. So she couldn't see his face when he took her in his arms, soothing her sobs.

'It's okay, it's okay.' He gently pressed his cheek against hers. 'Yer should have told me, Jess. You really should have told me.'

'I know.' Was that a warning tone in his voice?

But she relaxed, reassured when he only sighed. 'It will all be hunky dory. Let's just cuddle tonight. I love yer. I'll wait...'

'Thank you.' Relieved she pushed her nightgown down past her knees and put her arms around him. 'Thank you.'

She remembered she'd not said she loved him in return. Had she ever said she loved him? She couldn't remember. But she knew now that in the weeks before they were married she should have told him what Amos Morgan had done to her the evening of her mam's funeral. That way he would have had a choice; he could have turned away from her or he could have chosen to accept what had happened and still wed her.

He was talking again. 'So all this is now mine, lock stock and barrel.' He grinned at her; it wasn't a pleasant grin. 'Come on. I want to show yer what I've decided.'

'Where?'

'Upstairs.'

'What for? Why?' she asked, the familiar nausea curdling in her stomach at the thought of him wanting her in that way.

'Oh don't worry. I'll not be wanting that from yer.' He left the bakery. She heard him climbing the stairs, whistling that long, one note she so hated.

'We'll 'ave this bedroom,' he said, standing at the door of what had been her mother's room. And Amos Morgan's.

'What?'

'Well, we'll be moving in, of course.'

'We can't.'

'We can and we will.'

The prospect of having to live again in the house was a nightmare. But even worse would be having to sleep in Mam's room. In the room she'd shared with Amos Morgan.

Could Bob not see the revulsion she felt? Or was it spite on his part? 'I don't want to sleep in here, Bob. Please.'

'Don't be stupid. It's the largest room and it looks out onto the street so we can see what's going on out there.'

'Why would we want to know what's happening in the street when we're in bed?'

He didn't answer her question. 'The kid can 'ave the back bedroom.'

'The kid? Our son, Bob, you always said he was our son.'

'Yeah, well, I said a lot of things I didn't mean before, when I had to—'

'Why are you being so cruel? Why now?'

'Truthful. I'm being truthful. Something you should 'ave been before we were wed, don't you think?' He crossed to the window and peered out, not looking at her. 'An' we 'ave a lot to do before we open up tomorrow so we'd better get a move on.'

'Tomorrow? I need to think about this, Bob. I need to go out for a while, get some fresh air.' Everything in her life was spiralling out of control. The pulse in her neck was throbbing as though her throat was closing. 'Bob, I need—'

'You need to get on with what wants doin'. There'll be no gallivanting up those fields for you today.'

He knew! He knew where she went, the times she had to escape? Had he been spying on her? Had he watched her going each time to the same place, to the heart stone? 'I don't know what you mean. I just need some fresh air,' she repeated. She swept her arm around, taking in the room, the house. 'This has been a lot to take in. I thought we'd carry on living with your mother. She seems content for us to stay. Especially with Eddie not there now—'

'Yes, well. Fat lot you know. There'll be more changes because that daft sod decided to join up, but that can wait for now.' Bob pushed past her to go through the doorway. 'You need to start getting our traps together at mother's and on the cart I've hired. Then they'll need unpacking 'ere while I get the oven fired up again and everything ready in the bakery.'

He stopped on the landing, his eyes not quite meeting hers. 'Nothing in this life turns out as we want it to, Jess. The sooner you accept that the better.'

Chapter 78

'Where is he now?'

'Gone back to his mother's house, I think. He said I have to pack our things. We're moving back to live at the bakery.' Jessie shivered. 'I don't think I can live there, Edna. It was bad enough having to work there again since...' She wiped her eyes. 'I've not been upstairs in the house since Mam...'

'I know.' Edna's voice was grim. 'But think on, pet, you and the little 'un'll be nearer to me.' She looked out of the kitchen window. 'Harry always enjoys playing in my yard, happy as Larry 'e is out there now. You'll always be able to escape over 'ere. For good if it gets too much, yer know that.'

'I just don't understand how Mam could have left Amos Morgan the bakery. She said it would be mine – after – she'd...'

'Perhaps she thought he'd play fair in the end.' Edna snorted at her own words. 'Didn't you see 'er will?'

'No. You know what happened. I didn't even think about it, not after that...' Memories of Amos Morgan raping her still haunted her nights.

'What about the solicitor chap, that Mr Mathias? Didn't you tell me once 'e was yer dad's legal chap?'

'Yes, he was. But I saw his wife once on the High Street, just before I knew Mam had taken poorly. She told me he'd had a bad stroke and was still ill. She said she was nursing him at home but sometimes he didn't even know who she was, he was that confused. I presumed his office was closed.'

'So your mother's will was with someone else? A different solicitor, do you think?'

'Maybe. Maybe with the same one in Manchester that Bob got Morgan to make his will with, leaving everything to him.' Jessie lifted her shoulders in despair. 'Perhaps. I don't know. I bet Mam didn't even know Mr Mathias had the stroke, she didn't go out much in the weeks before she took to her bed, before we knew anything about her being so bad.'

'Perhaps Amos Morgan made her go to a different one. Happen that's why she saved all the money for you in your box upstairs? Because she knew that's all she could give you?' Edna pointed to the ceiling. 'It's still all there you know, barring what we've spent on the little'un.'

'I know.' Jessie stood. 'And if it's still all right with you, I'd rather it stayed here. And if ever you needed anything...'

'No, I'll not be touching it. But thanks, Jessie.' Edna's face softened with her smile. 'It's no bother. As long as you know it's still there.' She glanced out of the window again. 'I think Harry's coming in.'

'And we'd better get going.' Jessie straightened her back and forced a smile on her face when her son burst into the kitchen, his tie askew, his shirt hanging out of his short trousers. 'Want to get out of those clothes, Harry?'

'I do, Mam, they've itched me all day.'

'Well, give Granny Edna a kiss bye-bye and let's get off. I've something to tell you.'

'What is it?'

'I'll tell you on the way.' Jessie hugged the older woman. 'I'll see you soon.'

'Let me know if you need owt?'

'I will.'

Walking to the end of Castle Street, Jessie glanced up at the fields. It was a while since she'd been to touch the heart stone, since she'd talked to Arthur, tried to hear the sound of his voice in her head.

Holding Harry's hand, she walked slowly.

Since that first night and over the months she'd been grateful that Bob had only made love to her occasionally. Even then it was a silent hasty fumble, never spoken of afterwards. Jessie had accepted those times, it was his right as her husband. And Bob never knew she held Arthur in her thoughts even as she held him in her arms. So there was a part of her that was filled with guilt. She had to take some responsibility for the way things had turned out between them.

What she hadn't known was that he'd been biding his time. His resentment and fury had shocked her into realising how much her life was going to change. And that it was possible there would be many more bad things ahead to make her life, and her son's, worse than they already were.

Chapter 79

Lying sleepless in the bed that had, not so long ago, held Amos Morgan, Jessie stared into the darkness, tears of frustration rolling down the sides of her face. How could Bob do this to her? How could he even bear to be lying on the same mattress himself?

The resentment had festered inside her all day, building up until she thought she might explode. Bob had stolen the bakery from her, from her and Harry. Gradually it burned into her brain that it had been one retaliation after another since the night of their wedding. She wished she had kept silent, gritted her teeth and accepted Bob's lovemaking without a word that first night, without showing her fear. But she'd not been able to.

Well, she would play him at his own game. Somehow or other she would find a way to get the bakery back. She owed it to Harry. Her next thought came without warning. I owe it to you to look after your son, Arthur. I give you my word.

Chapter 80

She couldn't stand being alongside her husband any longer. She slipped out of the bed and tiptoed into Harry's room to kneel beside him.

Most of the time, working at the bakery, she'd tried to ignore Amos Morgan. Only once had she retaliated. To protect her son.

She'd left the shop to go into the kitchen to get the knife sharpener so she could slice a loaf for a customer. Harry, sitting in his usual place when she was working in the shop, on the last tread of the stairs, was cowering against the wall. Amos Morgan stood over him, his fist raised. Rage had surged through Jessie. Hatred for everything the man had put her through. Grabbing his wrist, she twisted his arm down behind his back. Taken by surprise, he yelped and struggled, twisting to try to look at her.

'Geroff!'

She didn't speak. Jerking his arm higher she jabbed her knee into the back of his leg. It unbalanced him. He yelled, seizing the bannister to stay upright.

'Harry, go into the shop. Stay in there.'

Jessie watched until her son closed the door behind him.

'Right, you bully.' She wrenched on Morgan's arm a third time, let him see the knife held beneath his chin.

'You wouldn't fucking dare.' He was breathing in short, sharp bursts. Jessie pressed the point of the blade into his skin. She saw a line of beaded red and felt, for the first time in a long while, in control.

'You wouldn't.'

She pressed again; more force produced more blood.

'Think of the kid.'

This made her pause, the knife wavering in her fingers. But Edna would look after her son, he would be safe.

'Shut up.' It didn't sound like her voice. 'Don't even speak my son's name.' She closed her eyes, willing herself to jab harder with the knife. But she couldn't do it.

She pushed him away and he fell to the floor. She bent over him, waving the knife in his face. 'Don't ever threaten my son again. Don't speak to him. Don't go near him. And don't ever come near me again.' She noticed his face had a strange grey pallor, his lips were pale blue, circled with a white line. The man was terrified. Satisfaction made her smile.

When she straightened up, she saw Bob watching her. She couldn't fathom his expression.

'I came for the knife sharpener,' she said.

He nodded, turned and opened a drawer in the large table.

'You all right?' he said.

'I'm fine.' She took the tool from him, turned, opened the door to the shop.

'Sorry to keep you waiting, Mrs Broomhead...'

That memory returned to Jessie as she stoked Harry's hair from his forehead. Nothing was said about that incident afterwards. But Morgan had kept his distance.

231

Watching her son turning restlessly in the bed she thought about how much he'd seen and heard over the last two years. And the way Bob was now, there would be more trouble ahead for both of them.

Chapter 81

That first month after they'd moved into the bakery, the weeks merged into each other for Jessie. Most days her head felt so heavy on her neck she could hardly lift it. Or the strength in her knees gave way and she was forced to sit down on the nearest chairs and endure the sour scowls from Bob. But worst of all were the silences between them.

Her only outlet was the hour she spent with Edna, late in the evening, after the shop had closed and the bakery had been cleaned and ready for the following day. An hour Bob only permitted because she had to collect Harry, who he'd insisted was not allowed in the bakery during the day.

'You look worn out, pet.' Edna rocked the sleeping boy in her arms. ''Ow much longer d'you think you can carry on like this? Why don't you gather your traps together and move in 'ere with me?'

'I can't Edna. How could I? He'd make our lives a misery if I left him.' And all the false respectability she'd gained from marrying him would be lost. She and, more importantly, Harry would be worse off than before.

'More than 'e does now? It's ridiculous.' Edna closed her eyes. 'If only Arthur was—'

'Don't, Edna. Arthur's gone. I brought all this on myself so I have to live with it. Yes...' She held up her hand to Edna who was shaking her head.. 'All we can do is to make Harry's life as good as we can. I thank God every day for you, love. You've been like a mam to me. I couldn't have carried on these last two years without you.' Jessie watched the slow tears trickle down the folds of the older woman's cheeks. She leant forward and put her arms around Edna, folding Harry into the embrace. 'As long as I've – we've – got you, I can get through this.'

There was no way to escape her future, it was a path she'd willingly taken.

Chapter 82

'I'm moving Ma in.' Bob narrowed his eyes, challenging Jessie.

'What? No. Why?'

'She can look after the kid. I don't like that old cow across the road. God only knows what she's saying to 'im.'

'What do you mean? What could she say?' Even as she spoke, Jessie knew that Edna talked about Arthur to Harry all the time, showed him photographs, desperate for him to know his real father. Had Bob heard her son say something? 'I'll talk to her.' Warn her, even though it would break her heart.

'I've made up my mind. And I'll need you to help more in the bakery and the shop. There'll be no more gadding off across the road every night.' He pulled his jacket off and threw it on the bed, tugging at his tie. 'There'll be no need, you'll have your kid 'ere.'

'I already help – I'm in there every day. And I make sure I've done everything before I go to Edna's in the evening. There's no need to bother your mother. Edna's more than happy to have him.'

'And don't I know it. No, that'll stop. I don't like that woman any more than I ever liked that son of hers.'

Heat rose in Jessie's throat. 'Edna's never done you any harm.'

'Only given birth to that sod that foisted his bastard on me.' He stretched up his chin and struggled to unfasten his collar studs.

'I didn't ask you to marry me, it was you that mithered to get wed.' Fear trickled through Jessie. She tried to soften her tone. 'Look, I know you've struggled to accept Harry and I understand why. Arthur and me—'

'Shut it!'

Memories of the humiliation of Amos throwing her out of the house and the way Edna hadn't hesitated to take her in, were at the front of Jessie's mind when she spoke.

'I understand all you've had to put up with because of Harry and me.' She tried to cajole him, though it went against all her instincts. 'Edna's always taken him to her house to...'

Jessie almost said to keep Harry out of sight, away from all the gossip, the scorn some men had no hesitation in voicing at Bob for taking her and her son on.

'To give us, you and me, some time together. She's been a good friend, Bob, to both of us—'

'Not to me, she's nowt to me.'

'And she knows, she's always known not to come in here – not even to the shop – since Mam died.'

'And she never will.' Bob lifted his braces with his thumbs and let them snap back onto his shoulders before pushing them along his arms. 'Anyhow, I've stopped the rent on Mother's house. She'll have to be out of there by next week and she will move into the back room.' He unbuttoned his trousers and let them slide down to his shoes.

Jessie took a couple of steps away from him, apprehensive. He smirked. 'Oh don't worry about that. I wouldn't touch you now with a bargepole. It's always made my skin crawl when I needed to,' his mouth curled into a sneer, 'let's say, get a bit of relief...'

Jessie flinched. 'Why are you being so nasty, Bob?' She forced herself to keep eye contact with him. 'What's happened to you? I always thought we got on all right. We were always friends, if nothing else.' Had he always, secretly, hated her since she'd had Harry? Was it really only to get his hands on the bakery that he's married her? She didn't want to believe it, but...

His answer dispelled any doubts. 'It's been a long time since I felt owt for you. I'll never come near you again, not in that way, any road.'

'I'm your wife.'

He ignored her. 'In future I'll want this room to myself. You can move into the back room with Ma.'

'No.' The anger had been slow to rise but Jessie felt it would choke her now. 'She hates me, I know she does. She's hardly acknowledged me since we were married. You let her ignore me even while we sat in her parlour. You talked over my head most of the time. I've cooked in the same kitchen, ate our meals at the same table and she's hardly spoken to me. Or to Harry.' She saw the barely concealed smirk. 'You're doing this to spite me. I won't put up with what you're suggesting—'

'You'll put up with whatever I decide.' The words spewed from his mouth. His face flushed a deep unpleasant scarlet. 'It's my turn to call the tune now. Takin' on your bastard, takin' everything Amos Morgan threw at me all these years.' His voice deepened, grew coarser. His finger prodded her hard in the chest. She stumbled backwards, as much to get away from his hatred as the blow. 'Knowing two blokes 'ad 'ad you before me. 'Ow do you think that's med me feel every time I shoved my dick in you, eh?'

'Stop it!' Jessie turned, stumbled from the room and down the stairs, her hands over her ears. But she could still hear his voice, strident in his cruelty.

'Made me want to chuck my guts up. You 'ear me? Every time. Amos Morgan was right: once a whore, always a whore.'

Chapter 83

'I don't care what yer want, Ma, it's a done deal. There's no point on me payin' rent on that place just for you to rattle around in when you could be of some use here.'

'One minute you refuse to let me anywhere near this place, the next you expect me to live here? What does your wife think? You know, the wife you've refused to let me speak to even in my own house.'

'My house. I pay the rent.'

'It's my name on the rent book.'

Jessie jumped back, startled, and felt the hard ridge of the shop doorjamb dig into her back. The tea she was bringing to Bob slopped over the rim of the cup onto her hand, but she was almost oblivious to its scalding heat.

She pushed herself upright and turned to peer through the crack of the door. The shop was empty except for Bob and her mother-in-law, who was holding on to the counter so tightly Jessie could see her sharp white knuckles.

So it had been Bob who'd stopped his mother from speaking to her, made sure the two of them didn't get on. Mrs Clegg must have been as lonely in that house as her. Jessie understood his hatred for her, but what had his mother ever done to him to make him so cruel?

She watched the woman's face crumple until she was hardly recognisable.

'What about Eddie when he comes home? Where will he go?'

'*If*, you mean. There's every chance 'e won't get back from whenever he is, the way this bloody war is goin' on.'

'Stop it!'

'An' then 'e can go in lodgings for all I care.' Bob pushed his face so close to his mother's they were almost touching. He knocked the brim of her large green hat askew.

'He's your brother—'

'He's old enough to pay 'is own way.'

The silence between them was broken by his mother's quiet sobs. Jessie tightened her lips together not to cry herself.

He was speaking again, his voice low. Jessie put the cup on the bottom stair tread and moved closer.

'I told you last week; she's a slut and I should never 'ave married 'er. I'm a soft touch and I felt sorry for 'er, wanted to protect 'er from that old sod. But no more. Things are going to alter around 'ere. And you'll do as you're told, Ma, like she will. She's 'ad me for a fool long enough.'

'I don't understand...'

Bob caught hold of his mother's shoulder. Jessie saw the way she recoiled. Saw her hat dangle by the hatpin onto her shoulder.

'I told yer, don't yer remember, you stupid woman? She says she was raped.'

Jessie covered her mouth with both hands to stop her cry. She thought she was going to be sick. He'd told his mother what Amos had done to her. How could he?

Her arm hit the door, knocking it against the frame with a soft thump.

Jessie stood, rigid. Don't let him hear, please don't let him find me here, listening.

She waited. Hearing nothing, she forced herself to touch the handle, pull the door gently open a tiny crack.

Holding her breath, she put her eye to the opening again.

Her husband was staring straight at her. When he spoke, it was directly to her.

'She says she was raped but I don't believe the old bastard raped 'er. I think she enjoyed it. I think she let 'im 'ave 'er loads of times.' The vicious words were meant for her. 'Much as she let Dawson 'ave 'er before. And 'ow many others, eh? 'Ow many others?'

He turned his attention back to his mother. Jessie dragged her eyes away from him to Mrs Clegg. She was shaking so much the hat pin gave way and her hat fell to the floor. Tears followed the lines of skin either side of her nose.

'Don't, son.' Jessie heard her pleading. 'Don't be cruel. I'm sure you're wrong, she's a decent girl—'

Jessie screwed up her eyes, forcing back the stinging.

'Decent girl, my arse.' He thumped on the counter. 'You haven't a bloody clue, you know nowt about—'

'Don't I?' His words were cut off by the fierce cry. 'Oh, don't I? What about me, Robert? Haven't you ever thought – ever wondered where your father – who your father—?'

She stopped. Jessie saw her mouth open, fear vying with panic tightening the skin across her face.

237

It was as though the shock froze the three of them into a frame of silence. Jessie backed away, conscious of the soft scrape of her footstep on the hall linoleum. She sensed what would follow, even before she heard the slap, the cry of pain. Whirling, she grabbed handfuls of her skirt, lifting the material so she could take the stairs two at a time. In the bedroom she wedged the chair under the handle and leant back on the wall closing her eyes, holding the air in her chest. Listening.

'Mam?' Through the rushing of blood in her ears she heard Harry, Forcing her eyelids lids open she saw him sitting up, his arms held out to her. 'Mam? What's wrong?'

In one stride she had her son in her arms.

She breathed in the familiar warm smell of her son. What would happen now?

Chapter 84

The hour since she'd fled upstairs had crawled by. When Harry finally drifted to sleep, Jessie could stand the silence no longer. Getting off his bed, she brushed her hand over the creases on her dress, looked into the wardrobe mirror and smoothed back her hair. Straightening her spine, she let herself out of the bedroom, and paused a moment on the landing, listening for any sound, before going down the stairs into the shop.

Bob was alone behind the counter. He crossed to the door, sliding the bars, clicking the snick on the lock. Jessie looked over her shoulder at the kitchen clock. It wasn't time to lock up, even though there were no customers. They didn't lock up until the hands were dead on six. Ever.

He swung around to face her.

'You told me Morgan forced himself on you.'

'He did. Why are you doing this, Bob? What for?'

'Because I can.'

'Why?'

'Because I want to hear you say it again.'

'I don't want to live through it all again. I can't.'

'When?'

'What?'

'I said when did 'e 'ave you? Or are you saying what I've been thinking: there was more than the one time?' He threaded his fingers together. His knuckles cracked.

'No! I told you. It was the night Mam died. That one time. It was horrible, the worst thing that ever happened to me.'

'I don't believe yer.' He pushed his face towards her, his lips curved into a sneer. 'And how many times with Dawson, eh? Bet 'e had yer loads of times. And how many others?'

He'd been drinking. He'd served in the shop stinking of ale. It was the first time she'd smelled the fumes on him.

Jessie flushed. 'Arthur and me ... I told you this even before we were married. Arthur and me – we were – together just the once...'

She thought she was going to drop to the floor. She needed to get away from him. Holding on to the door frame, she forced her legs to take her into the kitchen.

He followed.

'Together?' He gave a snort of laughter. 'You're so prim yer can't even call it what it is. Well, you're not going to get away with that. Go on, say it. Say he fucked yer.'

Jessie gaped at him, unable to think how to answer.

'Ah,' he waved his hand, dismissing her. 'I know he fucked yer plenty of times. I know yer spread your legs for 'im dozens of times. You can't tell me any different. You don't get a kid by just doing it the once.'

'It was.' Even though she knew it was pointless, still she protested.

'I. Do. Not. Believe. You.' He was brutal, pushing her shoulder with each word.

'Well, believe this, Robert.' His mother stood at her side. She hadn't left. Jessie gaped at the woman who had come into the

239

kitchen, her arms folded, her face set with determination. 'You were made – conceived – in the same way. You were born because of…' 'She took a stuttering breath, 'what happened to me…'

'I don't know what yer talking about.' Bob jumped to face her, his blustering words spraying spittle.

Beryl Clegg moved alongside Jessie and startled her by placing her hand on her shoulder.

'You wouldn't listen to me before, but you will listen now.' The lace on the front of her high-necked white blouse quivered with each long breath she took. 'I always told you that your father died…' She stopped, swallowed before speaking again. 'That man didn't die, he ran away. He ran away that very night, the night he raped me. He was never seen in the town again…'

'Bitch!'

Beryl gave a small scream and staggered back as Bob shouldered her out of the way. Jessie caught hold of her.

'Bob, wait!'

He ignored Jessie. Stumbling up the stairs he gave a loud hoarse shout to drown out her words. The bedroom door slammed shut.

Jessie led her mother-in-law to a chair. 'Sit down. I'll get a cup of water.'

'I can't believe…'

'I don't think either of us believed Bob could be like this.' Jessie set her mouth in a grim line. 'Here.' She watched the older woman sip at the water, her hand shaking.

'What now?' Beryl looked up at Jessie. 'What do you think he'll do now?'

They didn't have to wait long for the answer. Bob crashed down the stairs and, without looking at either of them, crossed the kitchen into the bakery.

Jessie cringed at the sound of tins and trays being flung across the room, the stools being upturned, the harsh shattering of glass and, finally, the crash of the back door.

'He's gone.'

'Dear Lord.' Beryl put the cup on the table and covered her face with her hands. 'Dear Lord. What's to become of us?'

Jessie sat on the chair next to her and waited. The clock on the mantelpiece marked the long minutes pass. She heard the rattle of the shop door handle once or twice, querulous voices.

Finally her mother-in-law's snuffles and sobs stopped and she blew her nose.

'What now?'

Jessie walked over to the door of the bakery and looked into the room. The place was in chaos: flour, sugar and salt from the large upturned containers covered everything. A sharp November wind blew through the broken window, whipping and swirling the mess everywhere. She sucked in her cheeks. Then she spoke without turning her head.

'What now, Mrs Clegg? It appears that we have a lot of clearing up to do. And then we carry on with the business. And, I'm guessing, without Bob.'

'But I haven't the faintest idea about how a bakery runs. I have no idea what to do.'

'You know how to wash up. So you'll know how to wash the loaf tins and the trays.' Determined to push away all the fear and panic that Bob's words had brought, Jessie made herself concentrate. 'We'll work together.'

'I don't—'

'I'll show you most of what needs doing in the bakery—'

'Bob won't pay rent on our house. He says I have to move in here.'

'Well, we'll manage.'

'I don't know what will happen to Eddie when he comes home…'

'I think I know someone who will take him in as a lodger when necessary.' Edna would be glad of the money. 'I'll ask.'

'Thank you. But the baking—'

Jessie wafted her hand. However she felt, she needed to sound calm. To sound confident that she – they, could keep the business going. For now. 'I can bake the bread and I can make the pies. It'll just be the general work I'll need you to do.' But not in those clothes, Jessie added to herself, and not in one of your fancy hats. 'And you've been in shops before.'

'Not to serve.'

'You'll be fine.' Jessie spoke with a conviction she didn't feel. Beryl wasn't easy with people at the best of times, but now, knowing her son hated her, how would she manage to pretend all was well?

She spun around. 'We'll be fine. We have to be, Mrs Clegg. If we want to keep a roof over our heads,' she said. 'Don't we?'

'Yes, I suppose so.' The woman nodded in reluctant agreement. 'Where else would I go?' There was a long pause before she sat up in the chair. 'Yes, we do, Jessie.' Her breath still faltered in her chest, but she spoke calmly. 'And, if we are going to work together, I think you should call me Beryl.'

'Right then – Beryl – I suggest we start by clearing this lot up. And then we'll sit down and work out how we're going to do it.'

Chapter 85

'Why is the shop closed?' His voice was loud and aggressive.

Jessie looked up from scrubbing the floor. Beryl turned on the stepladder where she was cleaning the shelves, her eyes widened in fear and alarm.

'It's all right, Beryl.' Jessie raised a hand, holding on to the corner of the table to help herself keep steady as she stared at her husband. 'Because we're still clearing up the mess you left.' They hadn't seen him for over a day.

He moved towards her, his fist raised.

Jessie heard the stifled cry behind her but didn't move. 'Go on, Bob, hit me. Just the once and I'll turn the tables on you. I'll stand behind that counter and I'll let all your customers see what kind of a man you are.' She tightened her jaw to stop her fear showing while, in turn, she watched him struggle to hold in his rage.

He twisted and hit the back door. It crashed against the wall and bounced back, knocking into him. Jessie saw his shoulders move as he took a long breath. When he swung round again his eyes were narrowed, the skin around his mouth white.

'And, while we're at it,' she said, 'Harry is with Edna, where he's been since you walked out and where he will stay while your mother and I are working together here.' Jessie put her palms flat on the table, keeping it between her husband and herself. 'And I've put a notice in the shop window for a general help in here.'

'I saw it.' The words were spoken through gritted teeth. 'You can take that out now.'

'No.' Jessie felt the movement behind her, Beryl's hand on her back, passing on her strength. 'No. We'll need help with the washing up, the cleaning in here. Your mother will be serving in the shop, I'll be baking. If you're going to stay—'

'This is my business.' Bob's breath was deep and heavy with threat. 'I say what happens.'

'You gave up the right to do that when you smashed the place up and walked out, Bob.' Jessie felt an unusual calmness spreading throughout her body. 'I'm not frightened of you anymore and I certainly don't love you.'

She heard Beryl's intake of air and reached her hand around her back to clasp the woman's fingers.

'I'm not sure I ever did. I liked you, I always liked you. Now I don't even have that. But if we are going to work together—'

'Like I said, it's my business.' Bob jutted his chin forward. 'Brave all of a sudden, aren't we, wife? Well, think on.' He sneered. 'I can kick you out at any time. And you.' He looked over Jessie's shoulder to his mother. 'You can both be replaced, like that.' He snapped his fingers. 'Just as easy as that.'

Jessie sensed Beryl hovering by the bakery door. She glanced up, gave her a brief smile. 'Okay?'

Beryl fingered the ruffle of Broderie Anglaise on her sleeve. She opened her mouth and then closed it again.

Jessie continued to roll out the pastry for the potato pies, waiting. She'd got to know her mother-in-law well over the last year and discovered that the aloofness she'd always associated with Beryl was actually shyness. That and Bob's determination they would not be friends.

The lump of unhappiness sitting firmly in Jessie's stomach was constant. Even the shift of sympathy from the customers towards her instead of Bob didn't help. Even the friendship of the woman standing by the door didn't get rid of the loneliness.

'Are you all right?' she asked again, cutting the rounds of pastry with the tin cutter.

'Jessie...' Beryl tugged at the cuffs of her dress. 'I've found something.' She moved closer. 'I'm not sure how to tell you, my dear.'

'What is it? You're like a cat on hot bricks.' She stopped pressing the pastry into the tins and studied the woman; she was paler then she'd ever seen her before and her eyes were bloodshot as though she's been crying.

'Is it Bob?' Had something happened to him?

'Yes. No. I haven't seen him since he left this morning.' Beryl cleared her throat. 'I was tidying Harry's toys away into that old bedding box in his room last night...'

'Last night?' Jessie rested her hands on the sides of a huge pan, puzzled.

'Yes, you know, just pottering while Harry settled down to sleep, as he likes us to.'

'Yes...' Jessie spoke slowly, wondering what was coming next.

'Well,' Beryl coughed, 'I found this at the bottom of the box.' She held out a large flat envelope. 'There were two boards there that covered the base. The edge of the top one was broken and I saw this.'

Jessie took it from her. The outside of the envelope was creased as though it had been pressed flat for a long time. The only writing on it was her mother's name 'Dorothy'. She turned it over in her hands. The flap had been ripped open.

'It was opened?'

'No. I'm sorry, I opened it.' Beryl spread out her fingers in a gesture of apology. 'When I saw what it was...'

'What? What is it?' Even as she spoke Jessie was sliding her fingers into the envelope and pulling out the document. 'It's a will.' She skimmed down the pages. 'It's Dad's will.' She pulled out another document. 'This one says "Irrevocable Trust".' She read it, excitement running through her.

Sitting down heavily on the stool next to the table, she glanced up at Beryl. 'Dad's will left everything to Mam but, from what I can make out, it was left in trust to me.' She looked down at the paper again. 'It says I'm the "Beneficiary".' She read it out, '"Dorothy Jenkins as Custodian ... to manage property...". It's here, Beryl. The bakery, this address: 5 Castle Street. The house, the business...' She dropped the documents onto the table, scattering puffs of flour. 'It says the business has been mine all along...'

'Yes, it seems so, Jessie.' Beryl smoothed her skirts underneath her and sat on the stool opposite. 'I'm sorry,' she said again. 'I should have told you last night, but then Bob came home and I didn't dare to chance it. He gets so aggressive. I wasn't able to sleep, worrying about it.'

'I know, I understand.' Jessie reached across and covered Beryl's fingers. 'But I don't understand, Mr Mathias must have had the original copy of this. Why was nothing said when Dad died? Why didn't Mam tell me?'

'I don't know, my dear. But it's obvious you need to go and see him.'

'Do you think Bob knew about this?' Jessie frowned. 'He told me Morgan had made a will leaving the bakery to him.' She thought back to that day, tried to remember what Bob had said. 'He said something about papers. I thought he meant he'd made Morgan have some sort of paper drawn up separately to make sure the Will wasn't changed. But perhaps it was these papers, these documents, he meant as well...' Her eyes burned and she blinked. 'He blackmailed the man because of what he did to me. Bob told me he threatened Amos that he'd let everyone know what he'd done to me the night of Mam's funeral...'

'Oh, dear Lord.' Beryl held her head in her hands. 'I am so ashamed of him.' Her voice was muffled when she asked, 'Did you see it? The will?'

'No. I was grieving for Mam. And then I had Harry. I suppose I just believed Bob. And I was afraid he would tell people what had happened anyway, once Morgan was dead. Well, Bob's version of what happened, Beryl, you know what he thinks of me.'

She paused. 'You know, sometimes I think I've made Bob into what he is now. We used to get along. I shouldn't have married him. It wasn't fair on him. I never really loved him, not in the way I loved Arthur. I don't think I'll ever love any man in the way I loved Arthur.' She saw Beryl wince. 'I'm sorry.'

'No, I understand. And you're wrong. I know my son,' she said. 'He's wanted this bakery for years. He thought he would get you to marry him right from the start, even when you were a young girl. I saw his rage when he found out you were having Harry. Even before that, when you were friends with Arthur. He was so jealous. Nothing you could have done would have stopped him. I'm sorry for what he's done to you.'

'It's not your fault.' Jessie picked up the two documents, blew off the flour. 'There's really only one thing to do. I need to go to see the solicitor, find out if these are legal and what it means for me. For me and Harry.'

Chapter 86

Jessie had not been in the solicitor's office before. When she knocked on the frosted glass door, even though she knew it wasn't possible, she still half-expected to hear Mr Mathias' familiar voice, but the 'Come in' wasn't a voice she recognised.

The large room was panelled in dark mahogany and crammed with large, glass-fronted bookshelves stuffed with books, and high-backed brown leather chairs studded with metal buttons, so that, despite the large window that looked out onto the busy High Street, it seemed dark. And filled with clouds of pipe smoke from the man sitting behind the long desk that dominated one side of the office. Jessie could hear muted chatter and the clunk of typewriters coming from another room.

'I'm sorry, I don't have an appointment. I was wondering if someone could spare a few minutes?' Jessie clutched her purse to her waist, hoping the five pounds she'd taken from her mother's savings was enough for the solicitor's fees.

He looked up, smiling. 'Good morning. Just me here today, I'm afraid. My partner is out on an appointment. But I'll help if I can, Miss...' He glanced at her hand. 'Sorry, Mrs...?

'Clegg. Mr Mathias used to be my father's solicitor. Mr Jenkins was my father's name...' Jessie hesitated, noticing, for the first time, the black armband around the man's jacket sleeve.

'I'm afraid my father hasn't worked here for some time. He had a severe stroke quite a long time ago.' The young man's eyes were kind behind the wire glasses. 'But please, where are my manners? I'm Adrian Mathias.' He rose quickly, 'Please sit here.' He gestured to a large red leather armchair. 'And tell me what I can do for you?'

'I'm sorry.' Jessie wasn't sure what to say. 'Mr Mathias...?'

'He passed two weeks ago. We only had the funeral yesterday so I'm afraid I'm not...' He looked down at the piles of papers on his desk, shuffled them around, turned envelopes over. 'Have you written to us?'

'No. But I've found these documents at home and I'm wondering if you could help.'

He took the will and the trust papers Jessie held out and scanned through them. 'Hmm. So your mother, er, Dorothy Jenkins, has also just ... I'm sorry for your loss.'

'My mother died in nineteen-fifteen.'

'Oh, so you are the proprietor of the bakery? The owner of Five Castle Street.' He nodded, looked up again to Jessie. 'So—?'

'No, I'm not. Well, not officially. That's why I'm here, Mr Mathias.' Suddenly the office felt too warm. Jessie took off her gloves and fumbled with the top button of her coat. 'My husband says the business is his. He says my mother left it to my stepfather and he passed it on to my husband.'

'Oh!' Adrian Mathias frowned. 'If you'd be so kind as to give me a few minutes.' He walked to the window reading the papers. In the silence Jessie heard the town hall clock strike ten, followed immediately by ten low thuds of the grandfather clock in the corner of the room. 'If you could excuse me...'

She dipped her head. 'Of course.'

He opened the door leading into the other office. The chatter stopped at once. Jessie watched him speaking to someone and then he moved out of sight. He was gone for quite a while.

There seemed to be some sort of commotion outside. Jessie shifted restlessly on the chair, stood and looked out of the window.

A cart was in the middle of the road. A tram was slowly moving towards it, small sparks flashing on the overhead line. A women conductor in a brown uniform was shouting at the man in the cart, who was sitting back, holding the reins in one hand, his pipe in the other. People stood watching, until the man, reluctantly, it seemed to Jessie, guided the horse around the tram. Once she could no longer see either the tram or the cart, she glanced both ways along the street.

Outside the butchers was a line of women, those with shawls covering their heads side by side with well-dressed women in large hats and long coats. A man in a white apron stood outside the greengrocer chatting to a newspaper seller who lolled against the door. She noticed a 'John Bull' poster pasted on to a wall opposite the office. The personification of the United Kingdom was pointing outwards, with the words *Someone's missing ... Is it you?* in lurid green letters. Jessie wondered if it had been deliberately put there.

Was it aimed at the young Mr Mathias? Did someone think he should have enlisted?

She moved back to the chair when he came into the room.

'I am so sorry, Mrs Clegg. I see that these documents were drawn up from this office, but I cannot find...' He stopped, caught his lower lip with his teeth. 'Just a moment, please.' He pulled open a desk drawer and took out a binder. Files and papers fluttered from it. 'I wonder...' He riffled through them.

Jessie settled in the chair, waited.

Adrian Mathias' hand hovered over an envelope, opened it and took out the contents. He looked across the desk at her.

'I am so sorry, Mrs Clegg, it seems as though we did indeed act on your father's behalf. I found these papers in my father's private bureau in his room at home. We hadn't realised he'd taken some of his work home before he had his stroke. I haven't had a chance to look through them.' He cleared his throat. 'It may be that he was dealing with your father's will and trust, possibly after he heard of your mother's death. It seems to me that, whatever your husband says, you are the legal owner of both the property and the business.'

Chapter 87

'So, I'm afraid, Mr Clegg, Mrs Clegg owns everything. The property and the business.' Adrian Mathias cleared his throat in the manner Jessie had become used to over the weeks since she'd met him. Just as she'd grown used to the apologetic way he greeted her each time, ushering her to the armchair and offering tea.

Jessie saw Bob's fists tighten against his twitching thighs. His chair, a wooden, upright one, had been placed at the opposite end of the desk from her. She'd taken that as yet another gesture of remorse for what the solicitor knew was an error on the firm's part.

'But...' Bob held up Amos Morgan's will and the sheet of paper. 'I 'ave this—' His face was slowly mottling red.

'Not worth the paper it is written on, I'm afraid.' There was no hint of contrition in Adrian Mathias' voice. Indeed Jessie heard satisfaction. She'd told him how Bob had gained possession of the bakery. 'Mr ... er ... Morgan deceived, might I say, fooled you in that matter.'

Jessie watched Bob half-rise in the chair, his mouth working.

The solicitor shrugged. 'The man you saw, the offices you went to, were fake. Whoever you saw was no more a solicitor than I am a...' He looked around before his eyes settled on the door of the other office. 'A typist.' He nodded, as though pleased with the analogy.

Jessie held her hand over her mouth. She didn't look at Bob.

'None o' this matters. I'm her 'usband. What's 'ers is mine – that's the law. What was 'ers before became mine the day we were wed—'

'And that, I'm afraid, is yet another point on which you are mistaken.' Adrian Mathias allowed himself a small twitch of his lips even though his tone was apologetic. 'You are right that once upon a time, not too long ago, that was the case. But no longer.'

'This is shite. I'll not put up with this – this farce.' Bob did stand now. 'I'll be lookin' into this with another – with a proper solicitor—'

'And you will get the same answers as I have given, Mr Clegg.'

Bob took three steps across the room to stand in front of Jessie. 'You've been the one to fool me. You said we 'ad papers to sign 'ere for some soddin' government thing – some way o' getting more wheat than we are allowed...' He was blustering, spittle landed on the sleeve of Jessie's coat.

She stopped her instinct to wipe it off. 'You wouldn't have come otherwise.' Staring up at him, she spoke calmly. 'You know the true situation now, Bob. The business is mine.'

'You! You – bitch. Just wait.' He crumpled the false will and threw it at her. 'Just wait until we get back home.'

'May I just say...?' Adrian Mathias rose from his chair and strode around his desk to stand between them. 'If any harm comes to Mrs

Clegg, I will immediately contact the police and demand your arrest, Mr Clegg.'

He was small and slighter than Bob and, for a moment, she thought her husband was going to hit him. Instead he spun around and walked to the door. He didn't turn when he spoke.

'I'm finished with the fuckin' business. Mark my words. You're so bloody clever. You can run the place on your own. You and that other bloody bitch. I'm finished.'

He flung open the door. Jessie listened to the sounds of the street outside grow louder and then muted again when the outside door closed behind her husband.

'I think we need a cup of tea,' Adrian Mathias said. She saw his hand trembling when he lifted the small brass bell from the desk to ring it. He opened a drawer. 'And with a spot of brandy in it.'

Chapter 88

'Well, for once my son is being true to his word.' Beryl hardly paused in washing the baking tins. The gate outside in the backyard slammed. 'He's gone again. No doubt he'll be back stinking of ale.' She turned her head slightly. 'Has he spoken to you yet?'

'Not a word in the last month.' Jessie wiped her forehead with the back of her arm and blew a wisp of hair from her face. 'Right.' She picked up the tray of warm loaves. 'That's the last. I'll take these through and open up.'

'You tidy yourself up after you've taken those into the shop.' Beryl picked up a towel and dried her hands. 'I'll open the shop and hold the fort until you come through.'

'All right. Thanks.' Hurriedly pulling the curtain across at the corner of the scullery, Jessie splashed water over her face and re-pinned her hair. Taking a deep breath, she left the bakery and walked through to the shop. There were no customers as yet and the shelves were tidy. Beryl was cutting squares of tissue paper for the bread.

'Thanks, Beryl.' Jessie gave her a hug.

Bob's mother looked surprised but pleased. 'You're very welcome, my dear. I'll get back to washing those tins.'

'Thank you. But you do know we can't carry on like this, don't you? It looks as if Bob has absolutely no intention of working here anymore. We need to get help, at least with the washing up, if you're still happy to serve?'

'I must say I quite enjoy it now, except when it gets really busy and then I panic.'

'We should find someone to wash up then? Me back there?' Jessie tipped her head towards the bakery. 'You in here? We could give it a go?'

'Are you sure you don't mind?' Jessie put the loaf of bread she'd brought from the shop on Edna's kitchen table and unbuttoned Harry's coat.

'Not at all, the rent money'll come in useful and 'aving a lodger will be company for me in the evenings besides the cat. And,' Edna smiled at Harry, 'with this one keeping me on me toes in the daytime while you're working, I'll be fine.'

'Thanks. Alice will be with us Monday, I'm glad to say.' She lowered her voice, watching her son kneel on the rug by the kitten that Edna had recently taken in. 'We badly need help now Bob has decided he's not doing anything in the bakery.'

'Bet 'e's still taking money from the till though.'

'He is. I've asked him to leave, but he won't go. He has nowhere *to* go, Edna. I should never have married him.'

'I 'ope you're not blamin' yourself for what's 'appened? You did what you thought best for Harry.'

'But I didn't love him, *you* know that. And I still went ahead and married him.' Jessie raised and dropped her shoulders in a brief gesture. 'So we'll just have to put up with things as they are.' She hung Harry's coat on the back of one of the chairs and watched him stroking the cat.

'If it were earlier in this blasted war you could have reported 'e wasn't working there – got the authorities to send 'im in the army.'

Jessie knew she wouldn't have done that, she couldn't have it on her conscience. She didn't answer the bitterness in Edna's voice, instead saying, 'Beryl's promised Alice's mother we'll look after her, with her only being fourteen and her first time away from home.'

'Good job she won't be living with you. There'd be no space in your bedroom with all those 'ats you say Mrs Clegg has.'

Jessie chuckled. 'She does have a fair few, I must admit. Quite fancy and all.' They'd shared the joke when her mother-in-law first moved in. In the end Jessie had resorted to piling the hatboxes on top of her wardrobe. 'Anyway, Beryl says Alice's family are quite poor but she's known them a long time and they're honest. And hardworking. Her father's an odd-job man and her mother does some sort of work from home.'

'It'll be fine. We'll be fine.' Edna began cutting the bread into slices. 'We'll all be fine, won't we Harry?'

He looked up at her, his hand resting on the cat, and smiled.

'You like Queenie, don't you?'

'I do.'

'Bread and dripping?'

'Please.'

'See?' Edna glanced across to Jessie. 'We'll all be fine.' Tears suddenly reddened her eyes. 'Nearly all, anyway.'

Jessie felt the smarting of her own sadness. 'I know, love.' She moved around the table to give her a quick hug.

'I'm all right.' Edna nodded, slathering the beef dripping on the bread. 'Wash your hands and come to the table, Harry, there's a good lad. Your mam has to get back to the shop so come and give her a kiss.' She brushed crumbs off her fingers.

They waited until he was settled with his breakfast.

'I'll just see your mam out.'

At the front door Edna paused, her hand on the catch. 'Seems it could all be over bar the shouting, lass. Papers have been full of how our lads are shoving back the Germans to that what's-it line?

'Hindenburg Line. It's some place the Germans took over in the spring. But I'll only believe this awful war is over when we see men coming home...'

Jessie took in a quick breath, the image of Arthur holding the heart stone, showing her his message, suddenly in her mind.

She saw the slackening of muscles in the older woman's face. She put her hand over her mouth. 'Oh, I am so sorry, Edna.'

'No, you're right. I just wish...'

'I know...' Jessie gave Edna a swift kiss on the cheek. 'I'll see you later.' She pulled open the door and ran across the street. If it was all over, she'd need to be strong for Edna. She didn't know what she would have done without her over the last few years. Now it was her turn to look after Arthur's mam.

Chapter 89

November 1918

My Dear Jessie,

Things seem to have moved so quickly these last few days. I can scarcely believe it. When we heard the news we threw open the windows and breathed in the fresh air, much like you do after a thunderstorm when the air is so heavy and seems to have been bearing down on one.

There seemed to be stillness over Greenbridge as we watched Papa raise the flag on the pole over the furnace. All the workers were out and I saw a lot of them, even some of the older men, crying. Everyone seemed so solemn. But that didn't last long. Papa got out his ukulele and sang us a song or two before declaring the day as a holiday. So we all went into the village to watch the celebrations.

The Town Hall bells have been chiming all day, I swear they are

254

still ringing in my head. The whole place was full of jubilation. Flags appeared all over the place and anyone with a big enough flag led great long processions that formed and marched through the streets. I wondered if you were watching something of the same in Nether Brook. As the day went on the sound was of tramping feet, cheering and singing echoed everywhere. I even saw some girls with their hats trimmed with red and blue and doing a really wild foxtrot. All the shops were closed, the clerical workers in the offices in the town hall stopped work and even the little school had a day's holiday. So much high spirit, Jessie!!

I was exhausted by mid-afternoon and Stanley insisted we came home for me to rest. I must admit I do get very tired. Abigail is a very lively four-year-old now (as I'm sure Harry is too) and little Bertie is eighteen months old and HUGE, much too heavy for me to carry him for very long. I cannot believe how much time has passed since you were here and that you have yet to see him. I only wish you were able to visit, especially at this wonderful time. But I know how busy you must be and I'm afraid I too am busy, both with the children and in the office. There are signs that the business will expand.

It feels odd to look out of the window and see so many street lamps lit at night, though they still have the "mufflers" over them. And even though it is now evening I can still hear bugles and drums. It's as though people can't stop celebrating.

But on a sadder note, Stanley says fighting continued on the Western Front in the final hours before the ceasefire at eleven o'clock and men would have been killed right up until then. Isn't that a dreadful thought? To be killed on the morning it would all be over?

I wanted to write to you because you have been so much on our thoughts, both today and over the last few months since you told us what has been happening. I don't remember much about Bob and then only from him working in the bakery when we lived in Nether Brook. But to have tried to cheat you in that way is despicable. In fact his treatment of you since you married has been so wrong. But

I am glad you are such good friends with his mother, and she is helping you in the shop. And that you still get on so well with Edna. I wonder if she will ever come around to liking me! And I'm glad she is looking after Harry so well.

Anyway, my dear friend, I will close this letter now so that I can post it first thing in the morning and keep fingers crossed that the Post Office people don't extend their day's holiday.

Our love to you and Harry,
Your best friend,
Clara x

Jessie folded the letter and pushed it into her coat pocket. The brisk wind tugged at her hair as she leaned on the wall, her fingers touching the heart stone. Down below, the surfaces of the canal and the river, running side by side, reflected the dull grey of the sky. The smoke from the houses was scattered in ragged wisps. The town looked different somehow, but perhaps that was her imagination. It was two weeks since the end of the war and still there were rumours that the Allies were squabbling over the terms of something the papers called the Treaty of Versailles. She worried that the ceasefire had been a sham.

She thought back to the eleventh, the day it had been announced. The streets were full of the women from the munitions factory just outside town; the procession of them in their blue overalls had reminded her of the dye that sometimes coloured the canal. There had been noisy shouting, singing and brass bands, similar to the crowds Clara had described. And many flags.

But underneath she'd sensed sadness. There were many of the boys and men of Nether Brook who'd marched off that September morning, four years ago, full of bravado and excitement, who would not be coming back.

Like Arthur.

Dark splotches formed on the heart stone and she realised she was crying. She cried so easily at the moment. She straightened, shivering, feeling the chill of the sharp November wind through the thinness of her coat. Wiping the back of her hands over her face, Jessie turned to make her way back to the shop.

PART FOUR

Chapter 90

Sunday, April 1920

'One hundred and twenty.' Jessie stopped and looked around. 'And here we are again, Harry, my love.' The air was still and heavy. In the distance she could see light-grey clouds bubbling up over the edges of the moors. 'We mustn't stay long today, it looks as if a storm is brewing.'

The words wavered with disappointment. Sunday afternoons were the only times she had alone with her son. Bob was sleeping off his lunchtime visit to the pub, giving her a break from his silent, brooding presence.

Over the last year, he'd begun to drink heavily every night and, having stumbled from his bed mid-morning, had got into the habit of sitting in the kitchen, positioning the armchair so he could watch her every movement in the bakery. At other times he would slouch against the door frame at the back of the shop, ignoring greetings from any customer and refusing to move aside if Jessie needed to go past. Often she was forced to push against him, an action that inevitably provoked a sneering, whispered insult.

Unable to help in any other way, Beryl always encouraged Jessie to escape for these two hours on Sundays. She silently thanked her mother-in-law. These precious minutes of solitude gave her the strength to carry on.

She spread the blanket on the ground.

'Can I go and play, Mam?'

'Of course.' She gave him a quick kiss on the top of his head and laughed when he immediately threw his ball into the air and chased after it through the grass and patches of cow parsley. Sure she'd be able to hear if he went too far, Jessie lay down, content to feel the heavy warmth, but still alert to the sounds of her son's play and to the imminent storm.

It felt like no time at all when she heard the soft whisper of footsteps approaching. A shadow fell across her face.

Someone was standing nearby. She could hear panting. Her muscles tightened. Had she been asleep? Harry! Jessie rose on one elbow, shielding her eyes against the sun with her hand, searching for her son and unwilling to look at the figure near her. She was sure it was Bob, angry that he'd found her there, at her and Arthur's place.

Harry was at the top of the field, still running through the grass.

She leaned back, resting on both elbows now, mouth set in defiance. His figure was dark against the sky, she couldn't see his face.

But it wasn't Bob, the man was too tall. Jessie started upright, glancing back towards her son, ready to protect him from this stranger.

'What is it? What do you want?'

The shallow breathing quickened, became erratic.

'Jessie?'

The sound of his voice brought sudden pain flooding through her. She winced, clutched at the grass on either side of her, feeling for the solidness of the earth.

'Jessie, it's me. I thought...' The words were whispered. 'I hoped you'd be here.'

His voice echoed and faded with each throb of blood rushing through her ears. She struggled to drag air into her lungs. Her skin was cold and clammy. When he knelt beside her, she recoiled.

'It's okay, love, it's – it's me.'

'Arthur?'

Trembling, she lifted icy cold fingers to touch his face. So thin. So pale, except for an angry-looking jagged scar from the corner of his left eye down to his mouth. And there it was, that aroma: that faint pleasant, musky mix of Brilliantine and tobacco that was so impossibly familiar. 'Arthur?'

His name felt strange in her mouth. She let her hand drop and he grasped it tightly, watching her as she studied his face again, his body. His arm. One arm! Jessie bit back a cry. His left sleeve was pinned to the side of his jacket.

'Oh Arthur...' She let her forehead rest against his cheek, felt the warmth of his tears, let her own fall. 'Oh, my love...'

And then they were kissing, his mouth firm on hers, her body responding to him. Kneeling up, she wrapped her arms around him, ignoring the empty sleeve. 'You're here, Arthur, you're home. You're safe.'

His hard sobs shook them both and they slid to the ground, holding on to one another. Jessie waited for him to calm, an overwhelming sadness flowing over her in waves.

Finally, Arthur sat back. 'Sorry.' He wiped his eyes with the heel of his hand.

'Don't be.' Jessie stroked his hair away from his forehead. 'It's all going to be all right.'

She stopped. How could it be all right? She was married to Bob. She was in a difficult and unhappy marriage, but it wasn't one she could escape. Her instinct was to hide her left hand beneath her skirt, hide her wedding band.

'I know,' he said, noticing her movement. 'I saw. You're wed.'

'I'm sorry.' Jessie couldn't bear the sadness in his eyes. 'I...'

'My mother...'

'Last winter. She had a fall. I'm sorry, Arthur.' She picked up his hand and held it to her face. 'It was pneumonia in the end.' Her words were no comfort to him, her despair was echoed in his eyes. 'I nursed her. She wasn't alone. We talked about you all the time.'

'I went home. There were strangers...' His voice was toneless.

'The landlord let it again.' She didn't tell him that Edna's things were cleared out of the house on the day of her funeral. She'd only just managed to retrieve the box containing her mother's money from under the floorboards in Arthur's old bedroom before the landlord had arrived with his horse and cart.

He didn't speak. He couldn't take his eyes from hers. He seemed baffled by all the changes he'd come back to.

'I'll take you to her grave sometime, shall I?'

'Please.'

Jessie saw the tears spilling over again. She stopped herself from reaching over to him and wiping them away. She had to remember he wasn't hers anymore. She wasn't his. She was married to a man she didn't love.

'What will you do now?' The question was too soon, too abrupt.

'Dunno.' Arthur lifted his shoulders and shook his head. 'Get digs, I suppose.' He stretched his lips into a thin smile.

'Mam?' Harry's voice was loud, anxious.

Jessie twisted round to see him standing halfway from the top of the field. 'It's fine, love, this man's my friend.'

'You have a boy?'

Arthur watched Harry running down the hill towards them. When he reached Jessie, he fell against her. She gathered him into her arms. He felt warm and sweaty.

'What's your name, son?'

Jessie held her breath. It hurt so much to see the two of them together. *Too late.*

'Harry.'

'You're a strong-looking chap.' Arthur smiled at him and stood up.

Already she sensed he was distancing himself from her and there was nothing she could do. With a start, she heard the low growl of thunder. When she looked past Arthur, she saw that the clouds were almost overhead.

'I need to go. I'm – it's late. I'm sorry,' she said again.

'Don't be.'

She knew that, for both of them, their words meant more than they were saying.

'I should have believed...'

'You couldn't.' Arthur shook his head. 'I know you thought...' He dipped his head towards Harry. 'I'm glad you're settled – happy.'

I'm not. Jessie wanted to shout the words. I'm not. Tears scalded her eyes.

'I'll stay here until you've gone,' Arthur said. 'Go on, go now...' his tone was gentle. 'He's tired.' He gestured towards Harry, who was leaning into Jessie, his eyelids drooping.

'We'll talk,' Jessie said. 'I promise.'

'Perhaps.' Awkwardly unbalanced, he held out his hand and helped her to her feet.

Jessie nearly wept when she felt his skin on hers.

Full drops of rain began to fall, the splashes cold on her skin. She picked up Harry, but he struggled to get down and ran down the sloping field in front of her towards the stile. She turned and began to stumble after him, but then stopped. When she looked back at him she couldn't stop herself.

'He's yours,' she said, her voice soft. 'Yours and mine, Arthur. He's our child.'

Chapter 91

Arthur

I don't answer. I don't say anything because I don't understand. I look from her to the boy, now balanced on the stile and waving to me. I lift my left hand, the only hand I have now, and I wave back, feel the space on my other side making me dip slightly forward on the uneven ground. I should be used to it by now. It's two years...

I know she's waiting for me to say something but I don't. If I open my mouth, the crying will start again.

All the way back to England I struggled to hold back from skriking. I'd hoped, imagined, everything would be the same. I'm different, but I thought nothing about here would have changed.

But it has. I've no home. There are strangers in our house. No Mam. No love. She's backing away, still watching me. I see the sadness in her face. And something else. It's pity. I don't want her pity. I want her love. She's turning away now.

Don't go. I want to shout the words. Don't go. But she's running. Running to catch up with her son. Our son, she said. Still with my hand held high I step forward. One step. Then another.

The field falls away and I'm running. Faster. Faster. The whistling in my ears is louder. I clap my hand over one ear, then try to cover the other. And I fall full length.

Lying here, my chest presses against the grass with each heaving breath.

The rumble is low at first, in the distance.

I'm glad not to be on the front line today.

But the rumble is swelling into a gigantic roar. Our guns are retaliating. The din is deafening, German shells are exploding in our lines: stinging black smoke, Black Marias. All around me men are shouting, screaming: 'Keep 'em off, boys, keep 'em off!', 'Get down!', 'My God! I'm hit.' 'Put more sandbags on the barricade.'

These damned shells! I put my fingers in my ears, press my head against the ground. Stop it. Stop it!

The earth is heaving, a dirt column rises up in the sky, higher and higher. It seems to hang for a moment in the air like the shadow of some great leafy tree. But now it's falling in a widening funnel of dust and debris. The ear-splitting rattle of the machine gun stops. And then a second mine, another airborne gun, a dark skeletal outline in the grey sky.

I'm crawling now; I need to get back to our line. Tiny shapes cut into the ground around me. Machine gun fire?

I'm muttering the Lord's Prayer, or the parts of it I can remember. 'Our Father ... our Father ... Forgive us our sins...' Can't stand this any longer.

I've found the trench. I fling myself into it, land on something soft. Bodies. Bits of bodies. I look at my hands. Just one hand? Covered in bloodied, torn flesh and splinters of bone. I reach across my chest; can't find my other arm. Arm, hand, gone. No pain.

266

There's Walter Hurst, his arm around his brother's shoulder. But Ronald has no head. There's just a bloody mess where his head should be. The heaving begins from somewhere deep inside me. I kneel and throw up.

'Arthur!'

It's a woman. Why are women in the trenches? A nurse?

'Get away. This is no place for you.' I wave my arm, try to grab her, but I fall over, unbalanced by the weightlessness of my side. No arm. No arm. I can feel my arm now. The pain. My fingers are tingling but I can't find my arm. I scrabble on the ground looking for it. But she's there again, the woman.

'Arthur.' She's shouting.

She knows me. She's holding me. She's crying. I don't like her crying.

'I'll save you,' I shout. But she won't let me move. She's lying on top of me, holding my head between her hands and she's shouting.

'Look at me, Arthur, look at me!'

And I realise it's me that's skriking. Loudly. And, for a moment I'm ashamed. But the warmth of her body on mine comforts me and I stop moving. Lie still.

I'm drenched.

'It's a storm, Arthur. Rain.'

'Rain?'

'Rain. Yes.'

'Jessie?'

'Yes.' She laughs, a strange shrill, gasping laugh. 'Just a thunderstorm. Just rain.'

The calm flows over me. As always. Always there's the calmness afterwards. After the fear has gone. When I know I'm still alive.

'I'm all right,' I say.

'You're coming home with me.'

I gaze into her eyes. So blue.

'I didn't know where I was,' I say.

Chapter 92

'I'll leave the two of you to talk.' Beryl's hand brushed Arthur's shoulder. She stuck a long pin into the small grey hat on her head, patted the crown of it and said, 'There. Ready. I won't be long.' She raised her eyes to the ceiling before she left the kitchen.

Jessie knew she was warning her that Bob was still upstairs.

'She's very kind,' Arthur said, when Beryl had closed the door behind her.

'Beryl is one of the kindest people I know. I don't know what I would have done over the last year or so.' Jessie's mind flickered to Edna. 'Her and your mam – two of a kind.'

A slight smile moved Arthur's lips. He nodded, not taking his eyes off Harry, who was playing quietly in the hall with his wooden cars and occasionally glancing up the stairs. Jessie knew her son was watching to see if Bob was coming out of his bedroom. The boy had become increasingly wary of his stepfather and his drunken moods.

She could tell that Arthur had seen through Harry's nervousness, knew there was something wrong.

'Are you sure I should be here? Your husband...?'

'It's Bob. Remember Bob? Who worked in the bakery with Dad for years?'

'I remember. So he won't mind?' Arthur rubbed erratically at his hair with the towelling that Beryl had handed to him when he'd stumbled through the back door.

Jessie shrugged. 'It doesn't matter.'

'I don't understand?'

'It's a long story, Arthur. Let's just get that wet jacket off you. I'll hang it over the pulley, it should dry there in no time.'

There was a moment's awkwardness when, after she'd unfastened the buttons, the jacket slid from his shoulder to reveal the empty shirtsleeve dangling.

Jessie gently touched it. 'What happened, Arthur?' She heard him swallow. 'But please don't say if it upsets you.'

268

In their moment of hesitation, the clamour of the bells from the Anglian church, announcing the imminent start of the evening service, ebbed and flowed, a long peal of sound.

'No, it's okay.' Arthur coughed, gave her a quivering half-smile. 'I'm used to it now, it happened a while back.' He coughed again as though giving himself time, Jessie thought. 'I was hit by machine gun fire.' He rubbed his hand over his mouth. 'It knocked me out so I don't remember much. Apparently I was thrown up into the air and landed on my stomach minus my arm.'

Jessie tried not to show the horror she was feeling.

'The blood from my shoulder ran around my ears.' He nodded, before speaking in a matter of fact way. 'The chaps round me thought the blood was coming from my ears and so they left me—'

'Why?' She couldn't prevent the outburst.

'Usually, when chaps were bleeding from the ears, they had little chance of survival.' He raised his shoulders in a gesture of acceptance. 'I don't remember much.'

'What happened?'

'Apparently I was found, soon after my unit had left. I was alone. A French farmer took me to his farm and the local doctor stitched me up and sorted out this.' He flicked his hand towards his shoulder. Jessie could tell he was making light of his injury. 'And this...' He touched his ear and the side of his face. 'The farmer and his family nursed me until I was better.'

He didn't speak for a while, just watching Harry running one of the cars along the last tread of the stairs, making low humming noises. Still, every now and then, glancing towards the landing.

'When I finally recovered I had no idea who I was or where I'd come from. They'd had to cut my uniform off. I didn't know anything about them taking me to the farm or what the doctor did.'

'How did you understand what they were saying? They must have spoken in French, surely? You must have been so confused.' Jessie could only imagine how awful it must have been for him.

'I was in a muddle most of the time, but they spoke English

269

around me. I think I just thought they had odd accents. Then after a while I picked up the language. I didn't think anything about it really, I suppose. It was a long time before I got my memory back.'

He stopped. Looked down at his hand cupped on his knee. A frown furrowed his brow. 'I didn't understand, at first, why someone from the army hadn't come looking for me. That was when I was told they had left me for dead. And when they came back the trench had been completely destroyed. The farmer, Monsieur Daquin, said that the doctor was a friend of his and he'd persuaded him not to report me being there. I don't think they expected me to live.'

'Why didn't you write to us, Arthur?' For the first time she felt bitterness creep through her. If he'd let them know he was alive things could have been so different. 'Your mother was heartbroken.' She waited for him to answer, pushing back the despair and anguish she'd gone through.

'I'm sorry. Things happened.'

'What?'

He didn't reply, rubbing his hands over his face. He avoided looking at her. 'By then I knew I would be classed as a deserter and shot. I didn't know what to do. I was afraid...'

'I know.' She spoke softly. 'I know, Arthur.' She could only think how terrified he must have been; after the war there had been rumours of men being shot for running away from the front line.

'So I stayed until the war ended. I didn't know when it would all finish. I think in a way I pretended there was no war. The fighting had moved to the west some miles away.' He pressed his lips together, blinked hard. 'I was a coward.'

'No.' Jessie made her voice firm. 'No. You weren't, Arthur. I understand.' She forced herself not to press him to say more. He would tell her in his own time. 'It's enough you're here now.'

He twisted his head to one side in denial. 'I should have found a unit – a company, reported to it. But I didn't...' Tears dripped from his jaw. 'I didn't. Then four months ago, Monsieur Daquin had a heart attack and died. His brother took over the farm. I panicked at first. But I knew I wanted to come home – to you – to Mam. I knew I needed to take a chance.' He wiped his sleeve across his face. 'I walked for miles – days – until I found an artillery unit and reported to the officer there. Everything was in chaos. He just took my details and I was sent to join other soldiers coming back home. No one seemed to know what was happening and a lot of them were injured or were very weak from the influenza that seemed to be everywhere.'

'People have died, Arthur. It's horrible. Soldiers seem to have brought it home with them, spread it through their families. It's been in all the papers for weeks and weeks. So many people...' She shook her head. 'Even here, in town. It's been frightening. And then so many so badly injured.' Jessie stopped, aware of what she'd just said in front of the man she's always loved; a man now so disfigured himself. What was wrong with her to be so thoughtless?

If Arthur had noticed he said nothing. 'Blokes coming back from the front where they'd fought so hard to stay alive. I kept to myself, I was – am – so ashamed—'

'You shouldn't be,' she said fiercely. 'Oh, you shouldn't, Arthur. The war should never have happened. So many awful things...' He leant forward and brushed the tears from her cheek.

'But I'm sorry, Jessie, I should have taken a chance earlier, when I remembered—'

'No!'

'I wanted to come home to you.' He looked from her to Harry. 'I didn't know...'

'I know.' Jessie took hold of his hand. 'We hadn't heard from you and...' She swallowed. 'Things happened,' she said again, patting his fingers in answer to the question in his eyes. 'I'll tell you sometime.' Just as she would one day tell him the things that had happened to her. 'But your mam and me, we decided we would wait. We thought – if we heard from you we would tell you about your son. We thought it would give you something to hold, to make sure you

271

knew you had to keep yourself safe – for us. But we didn't receive any more letters. And then Edna got the telegram...'

She would tell him about Stan – about what had had happened to his friend, about the letter he'd given her in that dreadful hospital – another time.

All at once Harry dropped one of his cars and ran to burrow his head in Jessie's lap. She listened to the unsteady thump of her husband's tread on the stairs.

'Who's this?' Bob held on to the bannister with one hand, his left foot held just above the floor. He narrowed his eyes.

'It's Arthur. Arthur Dawson.' Jessie tried so hard to control her voice, but it betrayed her.

'What?' He gave a huff of scorn. 'Not the all-conquering 'ero? The bloke you'd wished you'd married 'stead of me? Well. Well. What stone have you crawled from under?' Bob looked from one to the other of them. 'And what do I see 'ere? Lovers together again?'

Arthur moved his head from side to side. 'I haven't come to cause any bother.'

'I bet you 'aven't.' Bob settled his feet wide on the linoleum, scratched under his arms. 'So you can go now.' He scowled at Harry. 'Want to take yer bastard with you?'

Jessie saw Arthur's back stiffen.

She said, 'Perhaps better you go, Arthur.'

'Yes, better yer go, lover boy.' Bob attempted to swagger but bumped into Jessie's chair. He rested his hand on the back of her neck, fingers curled to grip her skin. 'And don't come back.'

'I just saw Mrs Giles in the street as she passed, Arthur.' Beryl stood in the doorway of the hall, unbuttoning her long grey coat. 'She says she has a spare room you can rent if you like? She's expecting you.'

Unpinning her hat she looked across at Harry, still huddled against Jessie. Her voice grew softer. 'Harry, it's your bedtime, my dear. Would you like to come with me?' Without even glancing at

Bob, she held out her hand to Jessie's son. 'We still have that book to finish – I think a little read is a good idea, don't you? Give your mother a goodnight kiss, then.' She smiled at him and Jessie and then turned to Arthur. 'Goodnight, Arthur. I hope you find Mrs Giles' room to your liking.'

Chapter 93

'I've been watching you all this last week.' Bob threw up his arms, pacing the floor of the empty shop. 'Fluttering yer eyelashes at that one-armed sod.'

Jessie longed to shout back. Instead she said, 'There's no need to malign a man who has been injured fighting for his country.'

'My arse!' He watched while she unbolted the door and straightened the 'Open' sign, ready for the day. The morning sun shone through the shop window leaving a slanting shape of the frame on the tiles of the floor. 'My arse,' he repeated. 'Well, I've made up me mind and yer won't be seeing him again.'

'That will be difficult, he's only living five doors down.' Jessie knew her calmness irritated him, but any respect she had for her husband had long gone and she didn't care. 'You are hardly ever here, you do nothing to help your mother or me in this place.' She began to fill the shelves with loaves of bread. 'So, as far as I'm concerned, you have no say as to who I speak to.'

He came towards her, his fist raised. Jessie didn't flinch. Looking past him as the shop door pinged, she said, 'Good morning, Mrs Robinson.'

He swung around and pushed past the woman out to the street.

'How can I help you today?' Jessie was shaking inside but kept a smile fixed, a habit she'd made herself learn.

'He's gone again, then?' Beryl waited until Mrs Robinson left the shop. She went to the door to look out on the street. 'If you want to get Harry out for some fresh air, I'll mind the shop for the rest of the morning. It's a lovely day.'

'Are you sure?'

'I am. It will do you good as well. It's beautiful out there. And once all the orders have been collected there isn't much else to do on Saturdays, with it being the half-day. I think I'll have a lie down this afternoon.' Beryl gave her a strained smile. 'If Bob comes back before teatime I'll be surprised.'

Jessie silently agreed. And when he did, he'd be too drunk to do anything but stagger up to bed himself.

'I'll call at Mrs Giles'. Take Harry up the fields.'

'Good.'

Neither of them said what was obvious. If Arthur was in his lodgings, he would go with them. When Jessie reached for her grey shawl and folded it over her arm, she gave Beryl a hug.

'Thank you.'

'Just be careful.'

'I will.' Jessie's respectability over the last year or so had been hard-earned. It wasn't only by the way she ran the bakery, with obvious approval from her mother-in-law, but also in the dignified wayway she'd managed her husband's behaviour and ignored the gossip that he frequented Park Road where the streetwalkers paraded. 'I'll be back by five o'clock at the latest.'

Arthur was nowhere to be seen at his lodgings and neither she nor Mrs Giles mentioned him. But as Jessie swung Harry's hand in hers and strode up the fields, she knew he wouldn't be far behind. At one point she stopped to gaze at the top of the hill where the stunted, wind-bent trees were dotted along the clear bright skyline. A great surge of happiness took her by surprise.

Chapter 94

'I saw you from my window.' Arthur flopped down beside her, leaning back on his elbows. Their fingers almost touched.

'I hoped you might.'

When he finally looked up at her, he said, 'Will you tell me how Mam died?'

His question hung between them for a few moments. Jessie rubbed her fingers over her forearms, her thoughts tumbling over one another. How much to tell him?

Seeing Harry content, throwing his ball and chasing after it, she turned onto her stomach to lie close to Arthur. She plucked haphazardly at blades of grass.

'She fell in her backyard last December. It was icy. She said the gate opened and she could see someone standing staring at the house—'

'Who was it?'

'Neither of us could swear to it.' She caught her lower lip between her teeth.

'Who did Mam think it was, Jessie?' Arthur twisted around to face her.

Abruptly she sat up and looked down across the field towards Nether Brook. Heat shimmered above the grass, above the water of the river and canal, making the slate roofs hazy, as though they were lifting away from their walls.

The dark memory intruded on the peaceful day. She remembered her unease that evening. She and Bob had argued. As usual he had been drunk and there was no reasoning with him. As usual it had been about her friendship with Edna. Bob had come home earlier than usual from the pub and found Edna sitting in the kitchen. Despite Beryl's cries, despite Jessie hanging on to his arm, he'd manhandled the woman through the shop and out into the road. Jessie remembered thinking that her husband was taking after Amos Morgan: he'd banned Edna from the house because he resented her friendship with her mother, Bob was doing the same thing to her.

So, instead of answering Arthur right away, she said, 'There'd been bother at home. Bob had been drinking...' She tucked her knees to her chest and wrapped her skirt around them. 'He didn't like your mam. I think it was because of who she was; *your* mother. He was always jealous of you.'

'So it was him? In our backyard, I mean?' He sat up, scowling.

'Like I said, love, neither of us could swear to it.' The endearment had slipped out unconsciously. Jessie was already back in that awful night.

'I'm going across to Edna's to see if she's all right, Beryl.'

'Yes, you should. Please tell her how sorry I am for the way my son treated her.' Beryl crossed her arms over her waist. 'I am so ashamed of him, Jessie.'

'I know. Will you put Harry to bed?'

'I will. And I'll read him a story, see if I can take his mind off things.'

'Thanks.' Jessie was furious that her son had witnessed what had happened.

They both jumped when the back door crashed open. Bob staggered through kitchen, shoving past them to get to the stairs. Beryl shook her head in despair.

'I don't recognise him anymore, Jessie. He never was a particularly loving son – not like Eddie – but what he is now...'

'Is wicked.' Jessie finished the sentence. She pushed her arms into her thick coat, Arthur's old overcoat. 'I won't be long.'

She knocked on Edna's front door. There was no usual dim glow of light from the transom window. The whole house appeared to be in darkness. Without hesitation Jessie used her key.

'Edna?' No answer. She felt her way along the hall, brushing her hands along both walls. 'Edna?' The house was cold.

When she went into the kitchen she saw why: the back door was wide open, the low flames of the range flickered erratically in the stiff breeze, casting haphazard black shadows around the room. 'Edna?' Jessie peered out into the dark yard.

'I'm 'ere. I can't move.'

'Oh my God.' Jessie groped for the taper on the mantelpiece and pushed it into the flames. Lighting the Tilley lamp, she hurried outside. Edna was lying by the back gate. It swung to and fro in the wind, banging against her legs. 'Edna! What happened?'

'Careful, pet, it's icy as 'ell.'

'What happened?'

'He was in the yard.' Edna struggled to speak. 'Staring in through the window.'

'Who?'

Edna shook her head. She began to cough, wheezy, straining breaths.

'We need to get you up.' Jessie put the lamp on the ground and studied Edna. She put her hands under the older woman's arms and tugged.

Edna screamed. 'No. Don't, Jessie.'

'I don't know what to do, love. I can't leave you like this.'

'It's my side. My hip, I think.'

'Tell me what you want me to do.'

'I don't know.'

Jessie crouched by her side, felt Edna's face with the back of her hand. 'You're freezing.' She took off her coat and wrapped it around Edna's shoulders. 'I'll go and get Beryl.' She jumped up and ran through the house and across the street into the shop.

Her mother-in-law was sitting on the edge of Harry's bed. Jessie put her finger to her lips and gestured to her. 'Can you come?' she hissed.

By the time they got back to Edna she was shaking and whimpering.

'I'm sorry, love, we have to get you into the house.' Jessie hooked her arms under Edna's. 'We'll be as gentle as we can.'

It took them a long time. Despite Edna clamping her lips together, she couldn't prevent the stifled screams escaping. All three of them were sobbing by the time they lowered her onto the kitchen floor by the hearth.

Jessie slammed the back door. 'I'll get blankets. If you can cover her up and stoke up the fire?'

Beryl nodded. She attacked the fire with the poker, throwing wood and small pieces of coal on to it until the flames crackled higher. Taking the blankets from Jessie, she urged, 'You go for the doctor.'

The cobbles in the alleyway glistened in the light of the Tilley lamp. Twice Jessie slid, almost fell, her breath clouding white in front of her face. It wasn't until she was banging on the doctor's door that she became aware that she wasn't wearing her coat. It opened.

'We need your help.'

'The doctor was so good with your mam, Arthur. But pneumonia set in. I stayed with her all the time, but after a week or so it was plain there wasn't much anyone could do. Only make her as comfortable as possible.' Jessie hastened to add. 'It was quick in the end.' She wouldn't tell the truth, wouldn't say how Edna had sweated and shivered, cried out for her son. Jessie had watched Arthur's face grow tighter with anger.

'So who was it? Looking through the window?'

She didn't answer.

'It was bloody Clegg, wasn't it?'

'Your mam never actually said, Arthur. She always said she couldn't make out who it was pushed her.'

Jessie tried to keep eye contact with him. She didn't tell him that Bob had sworn at Edna and she'd recognised his voice, even if she couldn't see him in the dark. Neither did she say she'd confronted her husband the day after the attack, threatened to pass on what she knew to the police if ever he hurt Edna or his mother again.

'Who else would it have been?'

'I don't know. And it's too late to try to prove anything. Please, Arthur, let's just try to enjoy the times we have together. It's what Edna would have wanted. And it's all we can have. Secret times like this. You, me – and our son.'

Jessie turned Arthur's face to see Harry. He was sitting quietly watching a small blue butterfly hover over a clump of large grasses. 'Our son,' she said.

Chapter 95

June 1920

Dear Jessie,

I can't tell you how thrilled we were to hear that Arthur has returned. But I also know how difficult it must make things for you now. Still, I'm glad you told him about Harry. It will have given him a great boost knowing the child is his, especially coming back to the news that his mother has died and you are married. I'm sorry, perhaps I shouldn't have said the last.

Stanley says he'd like to write to him if you can give me the address of where he's staying.

We are concerned a little about Papa at the moment, he gets very upset about his home country. He talks all the time about the troubles in Russia and how they are trying to divide it up. I must admit I don't really understand any of it, only that it's something to do with oil and the mines for coal and iron. Stanley thinks the iron problem could affect our factory. It hasn't been easy over the last few months with materials for the machines. We had plans to go to London this month to see one of the suppliers, but they told us about the riots. When I read the newspapers I couldn't believe the police were striking, even fighting with soldiers in the streets.

I thought the end of the war would bring peace but there seems to be trouble everywhere. I often think back to my days with the

Suffragettes. You once asked me if I'd join them again, if you remember. But I think I will have to be content with things as they are at the moment. Perhaps it will help now some women can vote. Maybe things will change, maybe not – all I do know is that I have my hands full at the moment with Mama and Papa, the factory and the children. Abigail and Bertie are well and growing so fast I can't keep up with them with their clothes and shoes!

Abigail is very strong-willed and needs a firm hand, but Bertie is such a placid child and we have no trouble at all from him. He is quite a daddy's boy and loves going into the factory with Papa and Stanley. I should think Harry is quite the little man by now? Will you one day tell him who Arthur is, I wonder?

Mama was very ill with the influenza. I believe she caught it from the girl who comes in to clean for us. I do know all her family went down with it. I think she lost both parents. We thought at one time we would surely lose Mama. But she gets stronger every day, though nothing like as energetic as she used to be. I fear the children are sometimes too much for her.

A lot of the workers were poorly as well and unable to come into work. Stanley and Papa insisted they should still be paid, which I thought admirable of them, especially as we need to be careful ourselves.

We have all been given new ration books, have you? It shows us how much food we're allowed to buy. When we got ours I wondered how you would manage with the bakery, especially with the flour, margarine and sugar. Are your own rations separate from the bakery?

I would so love to see you again, Jessie, and it would be lovely if you could bring Harry. Or perhaps I could come to see you? I would have to bring the children with me, I couldn't leave them with Mama, not how she is at the moment. Would that be too much for you?

Our love to you and Harry,
Your best friend, Clara. x

Chapter 96

Will you one day tell him who Arthur is, I wonder?

Clara's words went over and over in Jessie's mind. Would she ever tell her son who his father really was? If the question had been asked two years ago, she would have said no; she'd believed that Bob had accepted Harry, would be a good father to him. But that was then. So much had changed. Her husband had become someone she didn't know anymore.

She should have been honest with Bob, told him what Morgan had done to her, given Bob the chance to back out of marrying her. This twinge of guilt was always at the back of her mind. She'd married him for the wrong reasons. Respectability had turned out to be too high a price. Having Arthur back in her life told her that.

She folded Clara's letter and slipped it into her skirt pocket, glad it was Saturday and the shop was finally closed. Watching Alice give the sink a last wipe, Jessie took a deep breath; she wasn't looking forward to telling the girl her plans.

'I'll be off now, Mrs Clegg.' The young girl pulled her apron over her head. 'I'll take my pinny home for Mam to wash.'

'It is a very pretty apron, lovely material.' Jessie admired the brightly floral linen. 'But I've told you, Alice, I can wash it.' Jessie smiled. 'And how many times have I said to call me Jessie. I'm only about five years older than you.'

'I know.' Her returning smile was shy. 'But it just feels wrong, not respectful. And Mam likes to wash my clothes, including this.' She waved the apron. 'I think it makes 'er feel better to do it for me when I tip up my wages.'

'Yes, your wages!' Jessie took an envelope out of the table drawer. 'I've put a couple of extra shillings in. For the big clean you did on the oven,' she said, in answer to Alice's puzzled frown. 'And then there was the scrubbing of the yard. That wasn't part of your job.'

'I enjoyed cleaning the yard. But thank you, Mrs ... Jessie.' She took the envelope. 'I'll get off then. I need to call at Mrs Giles', tell her I'm going home until Monday.'

'Your mother will be glad to see you.'

'She will. And she'll be glad to see this, an' all.' Alice waved the envelope.

Jessie's smile hid the remorse she was feeling. 'Please tell Mrs Giles I'll be along shortly to pick up Harry, will you?'

'I will.'

Jessie waited until the back gate banged to.

'Did you tell her?' Beryl appeared in the doorway.

'No, I hadn't the heart. Perhaps we can carry on for a while yet, Beryl.' Even if it meant dipping into the money Mam had given to her.

'With the bakery on Yorkshire Street undercutting us so much? Mrs Ebsworth told me this morning their loaves and muffins are a penny cheaper. She said she's only coming to us out of loyalty to you and your mother and father but she doesn't know how long she can do it.'

'I know.' Jessie studied her. 'You look tired. Sit here.'

'Thanks.' Beryl slumped down on the chair Jessie dragged out for her from under the table.

'I really do think we should consider selling the business.'

'What would we do?' The older woman locked her fingers together in her lap. When she looked at Jessie her eyes held fear. 'I mean I don't know what I'd...'

'*We*.' Jessie nodded, emphatic. 'We, Beryl. Whatever happens we'll still be together. You'll go wherever Harry and I go – you're his grandmother, have been since you moved in here.'

'Oh.' Beryl struggled to smile as tears welled in her eyes. 'Thank you, Jessie.'

'Nothing to say thank you for, love. Since Edna...' She stood. 'Since Edna went, well, before that really, you've been like a mother to me.'

'What about Bob, though?'

'What about him? He's left us high and dry, Beryl. We wouldn't be in this mess if he'd helped us. I'm sorry, he'll have to fend for himself.'

'And Eddie?'

'Didn't his letter say he was settled where he is?'

'It did. He said he's happy in Brighton.' Beryl gave a small nod of her head. 'He's met a girl.' She smiled. 'He also said the weather was better than here. I suppose I could ask him if I could go to live with him.'

'No, I want you with us. But there'd be nothing to stop you visiting him, surely? We'll leave things as they are for now, see how we go on.' She glanced at the clock on the wall. 'It's two o'clock already. I must go and pick up Harry.' She took her shawl from the hook. 'And, if you don't mind, I'll take him for a walk?' They both knew Arthur would go with them. They had an understanding that neither spoke about it.

'No, you go, I'll have a rest.'

'Good. And lock your door. Don't give him the chance to have another go at you.'

'I'll do that.'

Jessie hesitated. 'I could just bring Harry back? Stay here?' Even though Bob had changed his habits over the last week or two and no longer sat in the kitchen watching her every move, he took every opportunity to bully his mother.

'No, truly I'll be fine. I should think the only thing on his mind when he does get out of his bed will be his next drink. I have no idea where he washes or has anything to eat.'

'I know you're his mother, Beryl, but he's made his choice. You can't keep worrying about him.' Jessie admitted to herself she no longer cared. 'Now go and rest.'

She waited until she could hear the door of the bedroom they shared close before she left.

Chapter 97

August

'Do you like living here?' Jessie glanced around the kitchen: the kitchen sink cluttered with pots, the grimy net curtains at the smeared window, the unswept floor. But there was also a delicious smell of stew bubbling up from a large saucepan on the iron plate of the range. 'Is it okay?'

'Mrs Giles is kind and she feeds me well.'

'She was a good friend to your mam.'

'I haven't asked her much about that.'

'Mrs Giles would be happy to talk about your mam anytime. You know how she loves to talk.' Jessie smiled. 'Where is she now?'

'She said she'd walk Alice to the tram stop.' Arthur rubbed his left shoulder, wincing.

'Does it hurt all the time?' Jessie was careful; he hadn't said much about his injuries.

'Not all the time. I think I was lying on it too long in the night.' It took him a while to pin the empty sleeve to the side of his shirt. She didn't offer to help, instinctively knowing he would refuse. Instead she went over to the window to watch Harry sitting with Edna's cat on ledge in the yard. 'He loves Queenie,' she said. 'Your mam would be glad Mrs Giles took her in.'

Arthur nodded, shrugging himself into his jacket. 'It's nice having the cat here. Thinking she was Mam's.'

Jessie only just managed to stop herself from reaching up and stroking his face. 'Ready to go?'

'Shall I follow in a minute?'

'No. We can walk together.' She no longer worried about what anyone thought. The way things were going with the bakery it was only a matter of months before there was no business. She wouldn't stay around Nether Brook. And, though she hadn't told Arthur yet, she was determined, one way or another, to be with him.

Chapter 98

The breeze hardly moved the grass and buttercups. Jessie stared across the land shaped by the stone walls and blackthorn hedges. The thorny branches shone luminous in the light. The August sunlight warmed her face.

Arthur lay back, his eyes closed. Jessie stared down at him, the urge to kiss him almost overwhelming.

He opened one eye, squinted at her. 'I can see you staring at me.' He touched her face, grinning. 'And I can tell you want to kiss me.'

'Big head.' Jessie laughed. She lowered her face to his.

'Mam, come and play tag. Please.' Harry was standing by the wall.

'Where's safe then?' Jessie straightened, gave Arthur a rueful smile. 'Come on, time to play.'

'When I'm touching a stone.'

'But you're by the wall, silly. You'll always be touching a stone.'

Harry clapped his hands. 'I know!' He giggled. 'But promise to run. See?' He ran towards her, waving his arms and then swerved away. 'Can't catch me for a penny cup of tea.'

Jessie sprang to her feet. 'Oh, really?' She started to run, deliberately slowly. 'Come on, Arthur, it'll take two of us to catch him, the speed of him.'

He groaned, pretended he couldn't get up.

'Come on, Uncle Arthur.' Harry stood further up the field with his hands on his knees. 'Catch me.'

Jessie stood still. Uncle Arthur? It was the first time Harry had spoken his name. She looked back at him, wondering how he would feel.

For a moment he seemed as shocked as her but then he laughed and struggled to his feet, pushing his hand against the ground to balance. 'Coming to get you.'

A sudden deafening crack ripped through the stillness of the air.

Startled, Jessie stopped chasing Harry, saw him turn to her holding his hands over his ears. Saw Arthur drop into the grass, his arm over his head. Frozen into the moment she couldn't move. Then her son barrelled into her, clutched her legs.

'Mam. Mam.'

She saw the birds scatter, heard the frantic stuttering calls as they flew over the far field.

'It's all right; it must be the farmer shooting crows. Tibbet's farm is over the hill, isn't it? I should have thought, they've been doing it all week.'

Jessie lifted Harry into her arms and ran to Arthur. He wasn't making a sound. His body curled into a foetal position. She could hear muffled sobs. 'Arthur?' She put Harry down and knelt next to the man. 'Arthur? It's okay, they're shooting crows. The farmer is shooting crows.'

'Mam?' Harry was trembling, tears floating down his cheeks. 'My fault?'

'No, Harry, not at all, I think Arth – Uncle Arthur was not expecting that bang.' She jerked her chin upwards. More gunshots, more flurries of birds. 'Made us jump as well, didn't it?'

'Yeah.' The little boy squatted next to Arthur. 'It's okay, Uncle Arthur, it's too noisy here to play. Let's go home?' He stroked Arthur's arm, curled his fingers around his hand and tugged. 'Home? Huh?'

Slowly, without a word, Arthur lifted himself up and allowed Harry to lead him down the field. Jessie followed, knowing it best not to say anything. Looking at where the sun was in the sky, she guessed it was about four o'clock. Could she chance that Bob wasn't in the house?

Watching Arthur stumble over the stile, Jessie gave an inward shrug. She couldn't take him back to his lodgings. Mrs Giles was a lovely woman but a dreadful gossip. Jessie didn't want her seeing Arthur like this. She caught up with them.

'I think we'll go to our house, Harry. Let Uncle Arthur have a rest there, eh?'

'Yeah.' His childish voice held a determination she hadn't heard before. 'We can look after him good there.'

Arthur didn't say anything, but Jessie saw his slow, heaving back

286

and the way he twisted his head to wipe his face against his shoulder. She saw when he let go of Harry's hand and, instead, put his arm around their son and hugged him closer to his side.

Slowly they made their way along the street, ignoring the curious stares. Jessie lifted her chin and moved to walk alongside Arthur. This man and this child were her world. She would protect them, whatever it took.

Chapter 99

'Sit here, Arthur.' Jessie helped him lower himself into the armchair in the kitchen. She felt him trembling. 'I'll get some brandy. Harry, stay with him a minute, love.'

'Yeah.' He stood by Arthur, anxiety etched on his face.

'What is it? Beryl came into the kitchen. 'What's happened?'

'We had a bit of a shock.' Seeing Arthur was unable to stop shaking, Jessie held the cup to his lips. 'Nothing to worry about.'

She forced herself to smile at Harry, saw his face relax. 'They're shooting crows up in the fields over by Tibbet's farm. I thought they mostly did that in the mornings. Made us all jump almost out of our skins.' She was relieved to see her son grin.

'Everything all right here?' She mouthed, 'Bob?'

Beryl nodded and mimed, 'Gone.'

Reassured, Jessie looked back to Harry. 'Could you go with Granny Beryl and help her to clean the shop window, love? Please,' she said, when he wavered, anxious, his eyes on Arthur. 'And thank you,' she said, when he nodded. 'You're a good lad.'

She waited until Beryl had filled the bucket with soapy water and cloths and left with Harry before she pulled a chair close to Arthur's.

'You better now?'

He moved his head slightly, not meeting her eyes,

'It's doesn't matter. We can sit here a while. But when, or if, you want to tell me what happened just now, I'll be here, love.'

287

Chapter 100

Arthur

I can't. I want to but I can't tell her. I don't want to talk about it.

I don't want to go back there but I do, every night when I first close my eyes. I see it all. Hear it all. The crack of the rifles. Tommy's last word: my name.

'It's hard...' I say. 'Things seem to have been hidden. In here.' I tap my forehead. 'Then they come back. You know?'

Jessie nods, takes hold of my hand as the memory returns to haunt me.

*

'I can't stand much of this, Arthur.' Tommy's voice wavers. He puts the palms of his hands over his ears. 'Have you thought any more about what the Sarge said yesterday? If we own up to being sixteen...' He plucks at my sleeve. 'He said all of us who're under nineteen would be allowed to go home to England if we wanted.'

'Well, I don't.' I wish he'd shut up about it.

'We've done our duty, Arthur. we've been in this hell for a year now. Please, Arthur.' The tears make rivulets in the dirt on Tommy's face.

'Stop it!' I kneel up to block him off from the rest of the lads further along the trench. 'Stop it, for God's sake, Tom. D'you want that lot to think you're a coward?'

'I've not felt right since that German sniper got Watson in the neck. I can't get the noise he made out of my head now. And we left him there—'

'We had no choice. They knew where we were by then, we couldn't hang around. They'd have come for us.' I sit back next to him and rub at the barrel of my rifle with my sleeve. 'We need to get these cleaned up before the Sarge comes along.'

288

'Shall we tell him we want to go back?'

'No! You go if you want. I'm staying.' I'm aching in every bone of my body, my skin is red-raw from scratching at the lice and I can't remember when I was last dry. But I'm not going back home. They'll all think I'm a coward... Well, not Jessie but—

Sergeant Mills is here, kicking the boots of the lads who were asleep and shouting. 'Come on, you lot, we're moving up.'

'Tommy, get up. We're off again.'

He doesn't speak. But he does get to his feet.

'Keep your bloody head down!' The sergeant thumps Tommy's shoulder. 'Bloody idiot. Do you want to lose it?' Now he's standing at the front of the line. 'We're moving up to our sector. Stick close to me and keep your gobs shut. We don't want the soddin' Krauts doing what they did last week, do we?'

'Oh God.'

'Buck up, Tom, and stick close.'

When I look into his eyes, it's like they're seeing nowt. He hasn't been the same since the Jerries raided us two nights ago. Buggers took us all by surprise. It were a bloodbath. Fourteen of our mates got it before we could get our own back. I know how Tommy feels. I have the same nightmares. It's the noise that gets to me most – the sound of the clubs on skulls, knives through flesh, the screams.

'Come on, shift.' The sergeant's glaring at us all fumbling into line, fastening our helmets, fixing bayonets. 'Ready?'

'Ready, Sarge.' I raise my voice above the mumbles around me, hoping Sergeant Mills hasn't seen Tommy's bewilderment.

The grenade lands feet in front of the sergeant.

The explosion blows three of the blokes in front of me off their feet. I wipe my arm across my face to clear my eyes. There's blood and tissue mixed with the mud of the trench. I swallow the bile in my throat.

Sergeant Mills seems to be propped up against the side of the trench at least ten yards in front of us, both legs missing. Slowly his body slides down the wall and falls face upwards into the mud.

Bloody parts of the three soldiers are scattered around. The head of one – Cuthbert Grimes – lies in front of my boots, the skin peppered with shrapnel.

'Our Father who art in Heaven … our Father who art in Heaven … our Father…' Tommy's voice grows higher. Others are joining in with him.

'Shut it. Shut up.' I see the cloud of the yellow gas seeping along the trench. I turn to run but the gas is tearing into my lungs, scorching my eyes. I'm choking, crawling on my hands and knees through the mud. 'Tommy, move. Quick!'

I'm blinded.

*

'It was the last thing I remembered for ages. When I came to, I was in hospital.' Jessie squeezes my hand. I'm suddenly conscious I've been talking aloud. And that I'm sobbing like a girl.

Jessie is shivering. Tears are streaming down her cheeks as well.

'Oh, Arthur. I once saw the Pathé News at the picture house, but it didn't show anything as horrible as that. And the *Nether Brook Chronicle* only said how well the Allies were fighting and articles about Kitchener and how honourable it was to join up. There were lists of the local men who were in the "Died in Action" column. Your mam and I used to read those at first, but then we stopped after you…' She leans against me. 'I had – we had – no idea it was as bad as that.'

How can I tell her there was worse stuff that happened?

*

My throat is burning. I'm vomiting a stream of vile-smelling stuff; it's pouring out of me. There's a woman's voice, soft. A hand, gentle on my back. Jessie? Not Jessie, a nurse. I can't spew anymore out but I keep retching even as I sit up away from the stench of the bowl she's holding.

'Okay, now?' she says. She looks kind. She's about Mam's age, I think.

'I think so. Where am I?'

'In the hospital at the Base Camp.'

'Tommy?' I say. 'My mate, Tommy?' I can't see him. It's a long ward, loads of beds of other blokes. For the first time I'm aware of the noise: groans, crying. It scares me. 'He here as well?'

'I'm sorry, I don't know where your friend is.'

'How long have I been here?' All the white hurts my eyes. I close them.

'A month or so. You've been gassed and you've been in shock.'

I'm skriking. Embarrassed. I lean back; the bed rail is hard on the back of my head.

'You need more iodine on those cuts on your face. I'll be back in a minute.' The nurse walks away, carrying the sick bowl.

*

Jessie's kneeling in front of me, clutching me to her.

'You were gassed?' She was still crying, her tears warm on my neck. When I nod into her shoulder she rocks me. 'Tommy as well?'

'Yes. No. I don't know.'

How can I say what happened to Tommy? The day Alf Ramsden told me that Tommy had been tried for desertion and would be executed the day after, that the chaplain was staying with him until then, was one I'll never forget. I could say he was a stupid sod for running away. But I'd done the same thing in a way, hadn't I?

What will Jessie think of me if I tell her what had happened next? My part in it?

*

The officer has stopped at the foot of my bed
  'Firing squad 0600 hours. Tomorrow. Report to—'

'I've been gassed, sir. I can't—'

'It's an order, Dawson. Are you refusing to obey an order?' The officer raises his eyebrows at me, his mouth in thin line. I know this officer; he's a nasty bastard. He's tapping his fingers on the bed rail.

'No, sir. It's just that Tommy Hampson's my mate...'

'He's a coward. He's been charged with fleeing in the face of the enemy. He's had a fair trial. The man—'

'He's a lad.'

I hear the sudden intake of breath. He stops tapping his fingers and he's fixed me with a glare.

'Sir,' I add. 'He's only just sixteen – sir.'

'He signed on as eighteen. The Army took him in good faith. But he's a coward, he deserted his post.' He turns away. '0600 hours at the cells. Tomorrow.'

*

There's a commotion outside on the road. Raised voices. Mrs Clegg and him. I haven't seen the man since Jessie told me how Mam died. I'm not sure what I'll do when we do come face to face.

I stand up. Jessie's on her knees in front of me and I nearly knock her over. 'Sorry, love.'

'No, it's all right.' She looks over her shoulder, understands. 'Do you want to go the back way?' She thinks it's because I don't want him to see the state of me. But really it's because I know I want to do him some harm.

I wipe my face with my sleeve, relieved I haven't blurted it all out. I know I never will now. It's my secret, my shame. I can't burden her with it.

I don't go back to my lodgings; I can't face Mrs Giles' noseying. That woman, kind as she is, has a talent for sniffing out good gossip. Keeping my head down, I leave Castle Street to go back up the fields. I'm hoping the shooting has stopped. Even if it hasn't, I'll be ready for it; it won't throw me back into the darkness again.

Of course, even though I'm sitting by the wall clutching our heart stone, as soon as I close my eyes, I'm back there.

*

'Eyes front!'

I'm lined up with five others on either side of me, facing the wall and the firing post. I can't stop shaking. Out of the corner of my eye I sense movement at the door leading to the cells.

I nearly cry out when Tommy is dragged, legs trailing, and tied to the post. He's got this hood over his head. I tried to blot out seeing him but he's whimpering.

He slumps even more when the captain fastens the white square to his jacket. I'm hoping he doesn't know what the man is doing but I bet he does. I see him take in a long shuddering breath. The chaplain is muttering words I can't hear.

Tommy lifts his head, tilts his chin upwards, trying to see under the hood even though it's fastened around his neck.

'Arthur?' he cries. 'Arthur? Are you there?'

He knows! I turn to the sergeant. Please don't make me do this. But he ignores me, gestures for us to pick up the Lee Enfield rifles placed on the ground in front of us.

'Arthur?'

'Fire!'

I hear him shout my name just before the volley of shots.

And that's it. We're given the order to march back into the barracks. The chap next to me gives me a shove.

'Keep going, lad,' he whispers. 'Keep it together 'til you get back to the barracks.'

I don't know how my legs are holding me up. I don't look back.

*

I haven't been to see Tommy's mam and dad yet. I'll tell 'em I was with him at the end and he was brave. It's not really a lie; I was with him.

Chapter 101

September 1920

'I won't be made to look a fuckin' idiot anymore.' Bob stood in front of the back door. 'Yer going nowhere.'

'And you'll stop me, will you?' Jessie folded her arms. She told herself she could be as determined as her husband, but knew it wasn't true. Her mouth was becoming increasingly dry. Looking into his hard, angry eyes, she was scared. All she wanted to do was to get away from the oppressive atmosphere he brought into the house whenever he came back.

'I'm sick of them buggers in the pub laughing at me.'

'So don't go there. Stay here for once. Help your mother and me in the shop. Clean the backyard, clean out the oven. Both were your jobs before—'

'Before you stole this place from me.'

'It wasn't me that stole, Bob. It wasn't me that planned and plotted from the day we were married, from even before then. And I've done nothing to break our vows.'

Not yet, she thought. She knew she wanted to, but it hadn't happened yet.

'You're the one who's cheated with that prostitute on Park Road.'

In the silence, her heart began to thud. To her relief, he turned away.

The pain exploded through her head and then her stomach. Air gushed from her lungs as she hit the hard floor. She lay there, unable to move, waiting for the agony to subside, not sure what had happened. But he wasn't finished. Grunting, he fired vicious kicks into her side. Jessie curled up to protect herself. She thought the attack would never end.

Thank God Beryl had taken Harry to the little local park to feed the ducks on the pond. They wouldn't be back for another hour. An hour when she should have been meeting Arthur.

The room swirled behind her closed eyelids. Hot tears burned. Then blackness.

At first the silence was absolute, then distant voices broke through and the throbbing started. First in her head and then throughout her body. She tried to open her eyes but something stopped her. Dragging her arm from underneath her body, she touched her face. Swollen flesh. Hot. It didn't feel like hers.

'Try not to move, my dear.'

'Wha...?'

'Stay still. Mrs Giles has gone for Doctor Tregorran.'

'Hawwy.' Why couldn't she speak properly? Why did it hurt so much?

'Harry's safe. Can you tell me what happened?'

'Bewwl?'

'Yes, dear.'

'Was Bob.'

Jessie heard the gasp — 'Oh, no'— just before the darkness overtook her again.

'She needs to stay in bed for a couple of days. She's had a nasty beating. But now I've cleaned her up, you can see it's not quite as bad as we first thought. An awful lot of bruising and she'll be sore for quite a while. Bad enough – but I don't think there are any broken bones.'

Doctor Tregorran. Jessie listened.

'Bad enough.' Beryl's voice was harsh.

Jessie lay still. If she concentrated on breathing in and out slowly, she would be all right. Their voices, the sound of their footsteps on the stairs, fading away. She was glad of the quiet.

Carefully pulling back the sheet that covered her, she inched her way to the edge of the bed and let her legs drop over the side. She winced. Every muscle, every part of her body, hurt. She struggled to see. Only one eye opened; the lid felt heavy.

Reaching under the bed for the chamber pot she lowered herself onto it, biting back the whimpers of pain. When she's finished peeing she hung on to the mattress and dragged herself up, closing her eyes with the effort. Leaning her arms on the bed, she started to slide onto it. The effort of sitting up sent a stab of agony through her whole body and brought tears.

Through blurry vision she saw her face in the dressing table mirror. The shock made her gasp. One eye was closed, the skin around it shiny and red-raw, the other heavy-lidded. One side of her mouth was swollen, out of shape, and there was a large, purple bruise down the side of her face.

'What are you doing, Jessie? Get back into bed.'

'I needed...' Jessie waved towards the chamber pot.

'Oh, Oh, right. I'll move it in a minute. But you should have shouted for me.' A pause. 'Except that you can't shout, can you, my dear. And that's the fault of my son.' Beryl gently helped Jessie to slide further up the bed and moved the pillow to the back of her head. She covered her with the sheet.

Jessie stopped her. 'How long have I been in bed? When did – this happen? '

'Yesterday.'

'So...' Jessie stopped, gathering her thoughts. 'So it's Monday.'

'Yes, I didn't open the shop, I'm sorry.'

Jessie shook her head slightly. It hurt even to do that. 'That doesn't matter. Does the rest of me look as bad?'

'I'm afraid so.'

'Let me see.'

Beryl lifted back the sheet and raised one side of Jessie's nightgown. All along her thigh was a mass of bruises and raised wheals. 'Your back and side are the same, I'm afraid. Bob has a lot to answer for.'

296

'Where is he?'

'Where he usually is.' The older woman flushed, her lips tight as she pulled at the hem of the nightdress and covered Jessie with the sheet again. 'The public house.'

Jessie slumped against the pillow. There was nothing they could do. He would get away with what he's done. 'The doctor?'

'Didn't ask. But he knew...' Beryl twisted her fingers together, her face averted.

'He'll do it again. You know that, don't you?'

'He thinks you and Arthur—'

'Well, we haven't.'

'I shouldn't have helped you to see him.'

'You couldn't – *can't* stop me, Beryl. Especially now.'

'Oh my dear, you'll make it worse for yourself. And Harry.'

'Harry!' Jessie was horrified she hadn't thought of her son the moment she came to. 'Where—'

'At Mrs Giles.'

Safe with Arthur. 'Does Arthur know?'

Beryl tilted her head.

'About what's happened? About what my husband has done to me?'

'I don't know. I haven't been there. But he might. I'm sorry. Harry did see you for a second or two...'

'Oh no!' Jessie thought she was going to be sick.

'So he might have said something.'

That didn't matter. 'I need you to go and get him, Beryl. I need him here. He'll be frightened.'

'I'm not sure that's a good idea, Jessie. You look...'

'I know how I look.' She couldn't help the sharpness in her voice. 'But it's worse if he doesn't see me, you know what an imagination he has.'

'I'm not sure he understood what was wrong. I did take him out to the front right away and, luckily Mr and Mrs Broomhead were passing on their walk, so they took him to Mrs Giles.'

'So they know as well?'

'No, I told them you'd had a fall, that you'd tripped on the carpet at the top of the stairs.'

But Harry would be upset. And whatever Arthur and Mrs Giles had tried to do to comfort him, he needed his mam. 'I've made up my mind, Beryl. I want him home with me.'

Chapter 102

Bob didn't leave the house for the whole of the following week. When he wasn't in his bedroom he lurked restlessly in the kitchen, watching but never speaking.

Neither of the two women acknowledged him. Jessie insisted the shop opened on the Wednesday, having made herself stagger downstairs to the bakery.

Harry accepted she'd fallen down the stairs and, although he clung to her when home, he seemed not to mind going to Mrs Giles – and Arthur, Jessie thought – during the daytime.

Rumours spread about Jessie's injuries. Many of the old customers returned, but Jessie had reduced her order for flour and made only bread and muffins. So when that was sold they closed the shop. Jessie was glad to be able to go back to bed; she resented being the subject of gossip.

She was often aware of Bob skulking by the door of her room. Doing that horrible high-pitched whistle, but quietly, so only she could hear it. He knew what he was doing.

By Monday he was back to going to the pub at lunchtime. When he returned home he didn't go near the kitchen or the bakery, but took to perching on the wall in the backyard and watching Jessie and Beryl from there.

Most mornings, when Jessie got up, she could hear someone in the yard and was careful not to go near the window. She knew it was Arthur and prayed Bob didn't see, for once glad his drinking kept him asleep until mid-morning. When she went into the bakery the oven had already been fired up with coke and ready for her and Beryl to start baking. Grateful though she was, she was glad he'd been thoughtful enough to keep his distance. She'd be mortified if he saw her injuries.

And she knew how angry he would be. She didn't need any more trouble.

Chapter 103

Arthur

'I saw what you did to Jessic—'

'So what? She's my wife. My wife. Belongs to me.' Clegg thumps himself on the chest. 'Mine. I can do what I want.'

So the rumours were right. God, I hate this bastard. Something in me feels ready to burst out. 'I'll...'

He cuts through my words. 'You'll what? With your one arm? And that great yellow streak down the middle of your back?'

I wait. If I speak now, I know my voice will shake with the anger boiling inside me. And I don't want him to think I'm scared of him.

'Eh, Mr fuckin' 'ero? What will you do?'

He's sitting on top of the yard wall, a bottle of beer in one hand, swinging his legs. And he's drunk as a lord.

'I'll kill you.'

He laughs. It's more of a sneer than a laugh. He has no idea what I would do for Jessie, no idea I would die for her, that I have never loved anyone as much as I love her.

Still he sits. Still he swings his legs. He begins to whistle, a long piercing note. It stabs into my brain.

'Want one?' He lifts the bottle. 'Do your nerves the power of good.'

'I'm telling you. And this is for the last time. Hit her again and I'll kill you.'

I see him raise his eyebrows at me, grinning. He starts that whistling again. Long. Loud. So loud.

The barely forgotten roaring in my ears grows. I hear the orders echoing in my head. 'Over the top. Over the top. Move it.'

I see my hands on Tommy's heels, helping him over the edge of the trench before I join him. Feel the weight of him. I push upwards. See No Man's Land, peaks and troughs of mud and posts and barbed wire, poor dead horses and corpses. See bits of bloodied and torn bodies. See the sudden anguish in Tommy's eyes.

See the sudden surprise in Bob Clegg's eyes.

And then he's gone.

And then he's gone.

Silent as the grave.

Until I hear a dull splatter followed by the bottle breaking. Not a spray of gunshots, no explosion of German shells. No stinging black smoke.

I look up at the sky: no plumes of black smoke. I listen: no pitiful cries for help. The earth is moving. No, it's me, I'm rocking. My eyelids flicker, open, shut. What have I done? Don't look.

And then I'm running, my heart is trying to burst out of my chest, pounding in my ears.

Chapter 104

'Are you okay?'

'Yes.' Jessie stopped kneading the bread dough and wiped her forehead with her arm; despite the chill outside, the bakery was almost stifling. 'But something's bothering me, Arthur, and I don't know what it is. Something...'

'Something?' He frowned, studying her. 'Something about you? Us? Him?' His frown deepened. 'Is that what's bothering you, love? Him?'

'I suppose it's having to wait for the inquest.'

'Just a formality, surely? Bob's death was an accident. The doctor said so.'

'Yes. I don't know but...' Bob's death felt all wrong. 'Oh, I don't know. Perhaps I'm just feeling guilty.'

'Tripe! He was the one who should have felt guilty.' Arthur glowered. 'I don't see why you should feel bad at all, all the stuff he's done to you.'

'I know.' Just thinking about the things that had happened over the years made Jessie shudder. She tried to concentrate on separating the dough and dropping pieces in the tins to prove. She looked at Arthur. 'I suppose I feel bad because I never really loved Bob. Not enough. And he knew it, Arthur.' Her tone was flat. 'He knew it.'

'And yet he married you.' Arthur walked around the table to put his arm around her. 'I think you should remember why that was. I don't mean to be cruel, love, but why did he push for the two of you to wed? I remember what your mother-in-law said about that.'

Jessie leaned into him. 'That he wanted the bakery? Yes, I know.'

'So, stop feeling bad.' He kissed her forehead. 'You were a good wife. At least as good as he let you be.'

Until you came home. Jessie didn't say the words. She wondered if Arthur thought the same.

Chapter 105

Arthur

Today we're in our field on Wharmton Hill. Harry is with Beryl, and Jessie and me've been talking about what we will do in the future when all the business about Clegg is over and done with. I have the money from Mam's insurance that Jessie said was mine, that she gave me. We could try building up the business again with it. I could learn to bake, 'appen. Though, to be honest, I'm not sure I want to live there. I think I'd like to buy us a little cottage in the town.

She's looking at me as though waiting for something.

'Sorry, love. Did you say something?'

She squeezes my hands. Smiles. God, how I love this woman.

'Nothing to worry about. I just said, we've been here quite a while. We must get back. Beryl might be getting a bit anxious.'

But I can tell from the look on her face she's relieved that she has no need to be frightened anymore. That Bob Clegg isn't waiting for her, his fist at the ready. Then I see the flash of self-reproach: her belief that she shouldn't be glad, that it means she's wicked, thinking that. Of course I tell her she's not, it's understandable. If anyone should feel guilty...

I dismiss the thought, wrap my arm around her back and hold her close to me, feeling her shiver.

'You cold?'

'I'm fine,' she says.

We walk. It's awkward, each of us unwilling to let go of the other. Though there is nothing to stop us, we haven't made love. I know it's something we both want. Sometimes it's almost unbearable, but I tell myself I won't force things. The decision needs to come from Jessie.

Sometimes, though, I know it's because I'm self-conscious; my body is ugly now. It's not the body she knew on that day, that one precious day, when we first discovered one another. She says it matters little to her, that all she cares about is that I'm with her again. Yet there's always a hesitation, a moment when she ... or is it really always me ... draws away.

Chapter 106

There was a lingering yeasty smell of bread in the bakery when they got back to the shop. It was mixed with smouldering coal dust from the slacked-down fire of the oven that always caught the back of Jessie's throat. The room was dim, filled with shadows.

'It's quiet,' she said. Going through the kitchen she stood in the hallway. 'Beryl?'

'Up here, my dear. Harry was tired out and fell asleep so I've put him down for a nap and I thought I would have a lie down as well.'

'It's only four o'clock?'

'I know but...'

'But you're all right?'

'Yes, just tired.'

'Well, we're home, so whenever you feel like joining us, do so.'

'I think I'll just stay here, my dear,'

Jessie dithered for a moment or two. Beryl sounded upset. Whatever Bob had done, however he had turned out, he'd still been her son. Jessie understood. It would make no difference to her what Harry was like as a man, she knew she would always love him as her child.

'I'd better start getting things ready for tomorrow.'

'I'll stoke up.' Arthur went back outside. She could hear the harsh uneven scrape of the shovel, the hesitant pouring of coke into the back of the oven, the hard clang of the iron door when he'd finished.

'Thank you, Arthur,' she said when at last he came back into the bakery, sweating with the effort it had caused him.

He grinned at her. 'Job done.'

He crossed to the scullery, pulling at the cuff of his shirt with his teeth so he could wash his hand. When he'd finished he pushed through the curtain into the kitchen, wrapping the towel around his arm and pressing it against his body to finish drying his fingers. 'How is the shop doing?' He went into the storeroom and lifted the bags of flour, salt and yeast from the shelves, carrying them easily with one hand.

Jessie took the loaf tins from the shelf and pursed her lips. 'We're ticking over – just. I'm afraid we'll definitely have to let Alice go, which I feel really bad about. We just can't afford to keep her on. Though goodness knows she's useful. Beryl gets so tired.'

'And you look washed out. These last few months haven't been easy for you and it's partly my fault.'

'No! You coming back to me has been the best thing that has ever happened in my life. Besides Harry, of course.' She smiled and moved to lean against him.

'Jessie?' He lifted her chin and they kissed, at first tentatively and then more urgently.

'Arthur.' She felt him stir against her, pulled him closer. 'Make love to me, Arthur.'

He started. Pulled back to stare at her. 'Here?' His voice hesitant.

'Not here,' she murmured. Not in this room. 'In the kitchen.'

'Beryl?'

'She won't hear.' Jessie led him from the bakery, closing the door between the kitchen and hall. 'We've waited long enough, Arthur.' She knelt on the rug in front of the range. In the dimness of the room the glow from the fire reflected on her face.

He knelt beside he, slowly, unsteadily, his face anxious. 'I'm not the same man, Jessie.' He touched the empty sleeve of his shirt.

'It's all right. We are who we are now.' She unfastened the waistband of her skirt, let it pool on the floor around her. 'Let me.' Gently she unfastened each button of his shirt and, keeping her gaze on his eyes, slowly undressed him. Then, still watching him, took off the rest of her clothes.

'God, you're beautiful.' He reached out to stroke her shoulder. 'I'm not sure I can...'

'You can.' Jessie touched the scar on his cheek, tracing her fingers from the corner of his eye to his lips where the raised welt ended. She reached out to the disfigured stump of his shoulder. He flinched away from her.

'Don't, love,' she whispered. 'It's how you are now, part of you and it makes no difference to me.'

'It's ugly.'

She placed her hand over his mouth, leaned forward and kissed his shoulder. 'It's not.' She moved her lips along his collarbone, his neck, his jawline, his mouth. 'Make love to me, Arthur. I've waited so long. Too long.'

He moved awkwardly to lie alongside her. Taking his weight on his left side, he caressed her, She shifted so she was slightly under him, took hold of his hand and guided it between her thighs.

'Touch me,' she whispered.

Hesitant, his fingers explored. Jessie raised herself to meet the gentle pressure and then slid her own hand down across his chest, his stomach, until she took hold of him, felt him swell, throb between her fingers. For a few moments they stayed still, kissing. Then Arthur moved, taking the weight of his body on his right hand and she guided him inside her.

Lying in his arms afterwards, Jessie marvelled. Not once had the memory of Amos Morgan's cruel violation of her body or Bob's hurried dry thrusts entered her mind. She sighed in relief. Arthur's gentle lovemaking had banished all that. Forever. She snuggled against him, lifted her head to study his face, so relaxed in sleep.

They could heal one another, she thought. And they would.

Chapter 107

Arthur stretched his legs out to the far corners of his bed, contentment flooding through him, amazed at the memory of the day before. It had seemed so natural, had finally torn down the last barrier that had been between them.

But then he remembered that they still had Bob Clegg's inquest and funeral to get through and his happiness faded away. He sat up, swung his legs over the side of the bed and stared out of the window at the fields in the distance. The horizon blended into a sky hazy with the heat, not with drifting gun smoke and fires.

The anger he felt towards the man before was consumed by guilt. The remorse he'd carried for those young men he'd killed in the war haunted him. They were strangers, men he'd been told to consider his enemies. But each of them had families, loved ones waiting for them back in Germany. Some of their faces, the ones he'd bayoneted, came back to him in his nightmares. Too many deaths. And he'd added one more to the number.

So, today was the day he needed to settle one death on his conscience. Tommy. It was time he lifted the lid of the box that held the memory of that day and faced his part in it. He'd waited long enough. If he was to move on with a life with Jessie, it was time to see his friend's parents.

Only Tommy's mother was in. Arthur was glad in a way. Tommy's father was well known for his volatile temper.

'Thanks, Mrs Hampson.' Arthur took a long time to wipe his feet on the rough coco matting mat at just inside the front door. Now he was facing Tommy's mother, his mouth was dry. 'I wasn't sure you'd want to see me.'

'Don't be silly, Arthur. It's lovely to see any of the twins' friends.' She ushered him through to the washhouse in the backyard. 'I'm in the middle of a wash so hope you don't mind me carrying on. I want to get this lot out on the line for a blow before it rains again. I can't make head nor tail of the weather these days.'

She was thinner than he remembered and when she glanced at him, there was an emptiness in her deep-set eyes. But she smiled and, once they were both in the small outhouse in the backyard, she said, 'Oh, sorry, where are my manners? Go back into the kitchen and put the kettle on, Arthur, will you?' She pumped the posser up and down in the hot scummy soapsuds in the dolly tub for another minute or two before poking around in the water with a pair of wooden tongs, trying to grasp whatever was in there.

'I'm not bothered about a brew, Mrs Hampson, thanks. Here, let me do that, it looks hard work.' She was red in the face.

'I'm used to it, love,' she said. 'And – your arm...'

'This one does the job of two.' He made a joke of it to dispel the discomfort in her face. Really. Here, let me.' Arthur took the tongs from her and gripped a heavy bedsheet, pulling it out of the tub and into the large Butler sink, sloshing cold rinsing water over the stone-flagged floor.

'I'll make a brew then?'

'No, honestly, I won't, thanks, Mrs Hampson.' Arthur made a show of concentrating on tussling with the laundry, not looking at her when he next spoke. 'I've been thinking I should be visiting you for a while...'

'Like I said – any friend of the twins...' Her instant fervour unnerved Arthur. It was as though she'd been waiting, desperate to know something. How much had she been told about her son's death? Did she already know what he was going to say?

'I thought you might like me to tell you about Tommy.'

He heard the low catch of breath.

'Yes! Yes!'

'Only if you'd like,' he added, turning towards her so hastily the sheets slipped, drenching his jacket with water.

She helped gather up the sheets and pushed them down into the sink.

'Yes.' Her voice low, tears reddening the whites of her eyes. 'Leave those, Arthur. Come and sit down a minute.'

She gestured towards a narrow wooden bench outside the doorway of the washhouse. 'Yes, I'd like that, love.'

Arthur perched next to her, uncomfortably aware of her eager expression.

'Tell me,' she said, 'tell me about my son.'

He clenched his fist between his knees, head down, unsure how to begin.

'Was he brave, my Tommy?' Mrs Hampson didn't wait. 'Did he do me proud? Can I be proud of him?' The pleading threaded through her words.

'You can.' He shifted on the hard bench, uncomfortable but determined to go through with this. 'He was a brave man, your son.'

'A brave man,' she repeated. 'Were you with him all the time, Arthur? Were all you lads from the town still together? Teddy won't talk about it.'

'No, not all of us, Mrs Hampson. When we got out there, we

were mostly split up...' Hearing her sharp indrawn breath, he trailed off. 'But Tommy and me, we were lucky enough to stay together nearly all the time.'

'Nearly?'

'Training,' Arthur explained swiftly. 'We were sometimes spilt up for training.'

She nodded, patting his arm. 'Of course, yes. But fighting, Arthur. You were with him then? Fighting the enemy? Our Tommy conducted himself well?'

'He conducted himself well.' Arthur coughed and swallowed, cornered by her willingness to believe, to soak up any news of her son. 'Tommy was brave to the end. It was a cruel and horrible war, Mrs Hampson. Miserable.' He rushed through the words. He wouldn't tell her about the slimy, cold mud, the rats, fleas, lice. Trench foot. Fear, the all-encompassing cloud of fear. 'But he was a brave soldier.' He stuttered. 'B-b-brave...'

Martha Hampson leaned forward, kissed him on his cheek. 'Thank you, Arthur. Thank you.' She sat back, her chin on her chest. Large tears fell onto her flowered apron, the yellow petals enlarged with each drop.

'I'd better go.' Arthur jumped up, rocked on his soles. 'I have things to do, Mrs Hampson, I'm sorry.' He touched her shoulder. 'I'll let myself out, huh?'

She moved her head without looking up. 'Thank you, Arthur.'

He was in the narrow hallway before he heard her call out. 'And I'm sorry about your mam. She was a good woman.'

'Thank you, Mrs Hampson. She was.'

Standing on the pavement in front of the dull, varnished door, Arthur squared his shoulders and took a long-needed intake of air. He'd done it. Letting go of the burden he'd carried so long weakened his legs and he stood still, gazing up to the thin clouds above the roofs of the brick terraced houses.

'Come on,' he told himself. 'Buck up.' Giving an inwards nod, he strode away from the lies.

Turning the corner onto Yorkshire Street, he collided with a solid figure, standing at the entrance to the ginnel.

'Arthur.' The man nodded, his arms folded across his broad chest, legs planted heavily on the flags.

'Teddy.'

'Well, well, well. So our Tommy was brave to the last, eh?' Teddy Hampson stuck out his lips, snorted through his nose. 'Not what I know. I was shamed to call him me brother.'

'You haven't told your mother, then?' Arthur faced his former friend. 'At least you've spared her that.'

Teddy was nothing like his brother. There was nothing soft in this man, who was built like a brick shithouse.

'Didn't do it for her.' Teddy shrugged. 'You think I want the fuckin' neighbours knowing me brother was a coward? I was home, injured with me knees buggered from shrapnel when the telegram lad came. Bloody telegram said he was dead – "killed in action". But we both know the truth, don't we? Stuff like that didn't get 'idden fer long. Enough of the bloody lads have come back to tell me the truth. Wasn't much liked, I reckon, our Tommy.'

'Not true.' Liked better than you, Arthur thought. He glared at the man. He'd always been a boastful type. And a bully.

Teddy Hampson scowled 'Though now I reckon you've made me life a bit harder. Turning our kid into a fuckin' hero, like.' Straightening his arms full out in front of him in a nonchalant manner, he laced his fingers together and stretched them till his knuckles cracked. 'Another thing I know,' he said. 'Just before I was shot in the knees and sent home, I wor sent back into the Nether Brook Pals. Told you were dead. Some chap found a body, blown to bits an' a haversack wi' your stuff.'

He took a couple of steps nearer to Arthur, who forced himself to stand still. 'An' yet here you are; large as life an' twice as ugly.'

Arthur clenched his fist. 'So? What's it to you?'

'Nowt, I suppose.'

Teddy stepped back, took a pipe from the top pocket of his jacket and tamped the tobacco down in the bowl. He looked around before bending towards Arthur. 'A couple of the lads were sent back to clear the trenches of bodies: Keith Pogson and Barry Baker? They said you were nowhere to be found. Course, if it were you blown to bits, they wouldn't 'ave found you, would they? Still, 'ere you are.' He pulled out a box of matches and slowly took out one match to strike it on the emery paper on one side.

'The trench was blown up. What do they know?' Words of bravado. Arthur watched the yellow flame be sucked in, escape, sucked in again. The whole of his body quivered with the urge to run, to run and not stop.

'So...' His pipe popped as he drew on it. 'So I'm wondering where yer went?' He tilted his head, fixed narrowed eyes on Arthur's face. 'Well, I'm not really. I know what happened. What yer did. I've heard the rumours. Lucky fer you no bugger has grassed.'

Arthur couldn't take his gaze off the glowing tobacco. His chest tightened. 'So? What are you saying?' Sweat beaded on his forehead.

'I'm saying...' Teddy took the pipe and poked Arthur's shoulder with the stem. 'I'm sayin' yer wouldn't want me spreading what I think – what I know – all around town, would yer? About that and what yer did to our Tommy. An' yer wouldn't want our Da to know about that either – what with 'is temper?'

'What do you know?' He shouldn't be confronting him. But he couldn't stop himself, he needed to hear it.

'I know yer ran away and—'

'I didn't.' Arthur was going to throw up. He ran his fingers around the collar of his shirt. 'It's a bloody lie. Do you think I cut my own arm off, too?'

'I know that yer a coward – just like our Tommy.' Teddy Hampson lifted his chin. 'Coward.'

The word drifted between them. Arthur held his arm down by his side, tightened his fist until it ached.

Teddy saw, nodded towards it. 'You'd like to thump me, wouldn't yer? But think on...' He glanced around. 'Someone might see yer, call the coppers on yer. Yer wouldn't want that, would yer?'

Desperation took Arthur's breath, turned his voice into a growl. 'Come to think on it, Hampson, I didn't see you either. Mind you, that's not surprising, is it? There were thousands of us. Just like there were thousands of the poor buggers spread out in fucking bloody bits all over No Man's Land. Screaming for some poor sod to shoot them, put them out of their misery.' He saw Teddy Hampson freeze. They stood, staring at one another, sharing the memories.

But the man quickly recovered.

'Do them in charge know yer back from the dead?' he asked, slanting his head. 'Bet they don't.'

'Yes. They do.' Icy dread spread through Arthur's veins. 'I reported in. When I was in France, I reported to the 55th West Lancashire.'

'Hmm. The 55th eh? And yer told them you'd run away? Been missing, like? Deserted?'

'Oh, I'm sick of this. What do you want?'

Teddy put his head to one side. 'Not sure yet. But I'm not happy you made our kid an 'ero to me mam. Me life'll be a misery at home now, having to listen to all that crap about him.' He moved his head slowly from side to side. 'I think I'll have a chat with me Da, 'appen. See what he says. I'll put a bet on it he'll not be happy with your part in what 'appened to our Tommy. Not one little bit.' He grinned. 'Anymore than you will be, Dawson, when he's done with you...'

Moving to one side to let Arthur pass, he knocked him with his shoulder. 'If I were you, I might want to disappear, yer know. Just like you did in France. Yep, that's just what I'd do.'

Arthur didn't move. He looked firmly at the man. He had no choice but to pretend nonchalance. He shrugged his shoulders. It clearly aggravated Teddy Hampson.

'Yeah, you allus did think yerself better than us, didn't you? So I will, I will tell Da an' he'll wipe the smirk off your gob.'

There was a moment of stillness between them.

'I have to go. I have things to do.'

A hand splayed on Arthur's chest, thick fingers dug into his skin stopping him. He saw Teddy's arm swing back, fist clenched, and ducked, bringing his own fist up under Teddy's jaw with such force the man fell to the ground. His pipe skidded across the flags in an arc of sparks.

Arthur, unbalanced, almost did the same but recovered. He put his foot on Teddy's chest.

'Stay down.' There was no rage in him now, just a dull acceptance of how his life would go from then on. But he wouldn't let Tommy's brother see the despair creeping over him. 'Don't get up.' He forced harshness into his voice. 'You'll be sorry if you do.'

'Bastard!' Still on his back, Teddy swiped around on the ground to find his pipe. 'Not as sorry as you'll be when me Da gets hold o' you,' he said. 'Oh, and summat else you'll need to worry about an' all. That slut you've been seeing. Poor bastard Clegg's missus, her you've been fuckin' right under the poor sod's nose. 'Appen she's the one Da'll have to see to... Or better still, me. Aye. Get a taste of what you've had.'

Arthur pointed his finger at Teddy Hampson, angry with himself when he couldn't stop it shaking. 'You leave her alone. D'you hear me? Go near Jessie Clegg and I will kill you.'

He took a few steps back and let his voice drop. 'Bob Clegg died, didn't he?' He nodded. 'Now, how do you think that happened, eh?

'Accident. They said it were an accident.'

'Yeah, that's what they said...'

'You pretending you had summat to do wi' it?' The man attempted a snigger that didn't quite work. His voice hesitant, he said, 'Nowt to do with you, Dawson. You 'aven't got the bottle.'

'Oh? You think not?' Arthur smiled. 'He hit Jessie. Beat her quite badly...' He squared his shoulders, ignored the instant guilt that rose in him for what he'd done to Bob. 'I couldn't let that go. I'd my pride to think about. But afterwards, you know, I did a bit of thinking. I realised Jessie Clegg wasn't worth the bother, not worth getting into that sort of trouble for...' He let his eyes roam around the empty street, the walls of the ginnel, the nearby houses with windows blinded by the net curtains, before settling back on the man on the ground in front of him. 'So I decided to move on.' He desperately needed to make the man believe him. 'Got me an eye on a little widow the other side of town. No, Jessie Clegg's nothing to me, so why should she be anything to you? Still, with all the bloody gossip that goes around about me and her, I'd still have to do something if anything bad did happen to her. I wouldn't want folk believing I don't pay back stuff – if you get what I mean?'

Arthur waited until he got a nod of understanding. 'So all I'm saying is just remember what happened to Bob Clegg. I might not be around, where you can see me – but I'll be watching. Anything happens to either her or the lad. You. Will. Be. Sorry.' With each word, he touched Teddy's foot with the toe of his boot.

Teddy Hampson glowered at him and scrambled to his feet.

Arthur gazed up towards the dark grey sky. 'Hmm, looks like rain now. You'd better get indoors before you get wet.' He unfolded his flat cap from his jacket pocket and put it on his head. Pulling the neb lower over his eyes, he stared for a long while at Teddy. 'Think on about what I've said. And keep in mind Bob Clegg.'

Walking away Arthur knew he'd made a big mistake chinning Teddy Hampson. It wasn't something Tommy's brother would forget. He hoped he'd said enough to protect Jessie, but it would be best if he kept his distance from her. He didn't know how but there had to be some way he could just disappear.

Chapter 108

The answer came to Arthur when he got back to his lodgings. The letter was pushed under his bedroom door.

Dear Arthur,

I know our dear ladies have corresponded with one another since we moved here in Greenbridge so I thought it about time we did the same, though I must confess I am not as articulate as my wife.

I am much changed from when we last met, as you can imagine. I'm thinking that Jessie will have told you? But I have accepted what happened to me during those dark days that we shared and am settled well and am quite content.

I need first to say how relieved and happy I was to learn that you had returned to Jessie.

To get to the main point of my writing, Igor, my father-in-law, wants to cut back on his involvement in the day-to-day running of Askaroff's. Each week he hands over more of the responsibility to me and Clara. So I am asking you to consider coming to work with us. Please do not dismiss the idea, Arthur. I do, of course, know about the loss of your arm and I remember the despair I felt when I was left with no legs after Verdun. But nothing is impossible. There are many areas in the manufacturing of our sewing machines where you will be able to learn skills.

There will be no problem in finding a home for you. Because of the war and so many men not coming home, there are cottages lying empty in the village, crying out for families to fill them with love and laughter again. And it is only a short walking distance to the factory.

Please think about what I have written, Arthur. It would be a fresh start for you and Jessie. And I know I am speaking on behalf of my own family as well. We would love to have our dear friends so close to us.

But perhaps first you will visit us so you and I can catch up properly?

Your old friend,
Stanley

Arthur sat back against the headboard of his bed; what Stanley was offering stunned him. This was a chance of a new life, a way out, a way forward. It could be more than just moving to Greenbridge. He could go without anyone in Nether Bridge knowing where he'd gone. Without Teddy Hampson knowing. He could disappear, leaving no trace behind. Since his confrontation with Teddy Hampson he'd accepted he'd need to do that, but had no idea how. Here was the answer.

Jessie could go with him. But would she? Would she be willing to give up everything she and Harry knew?

Chapter 109

October 1920

'Well, that's that then.' Beryl blew her nose. 'Accidental death while intoxicated.' She shook her head. 'The shame of it, Jessie.'

'It's only what we expected, love.' Pulling on her long black cotton gloves, Jessie drew her to one side to let the two policemen and the doctor pass. She waited until they'd stepped off the last stone step of the small court building and onto the leaf-strewn path. 'Doctor Tregorran said as much on the day.'

She linked arms with the older woman. 'Let's get home. We have a lot of things to sort out.' One of which was what to do about the shop. The bakery sales had gone down drastically over the last few months. She needed to talk with Arthur about that. And about so much else. After yesterday she was more sure than ever that she wanted to spend her life with him, for her and Harry to be with him. She had so many plans.

'Do you mind if we walk, my dear? It's lovely and clear for the time of year and I fancy a bit of fresh air after being in there for the last hour.' Beryl tugged at the black net of her hat lower to cover her swollen eyes. 'I don't think it will look unseemly, will it?' Her voice was hoarse.

'Who cares?' Jessie saw she was struggling to stay calm. A walk would be good for both of them. She glanced up at the line of three oak trees in the small courtyard, their branches entangled as they spread. Chirping sparrows darted from the trees to the ground, pecking at the sparse grass at the side of the path. 'Let's go, then.'

The street was surprisingly quiet for a Friday afternoon; a motor vehicle bounced past them making a great chugging noise, a pony and trap clattered on the cobbles, two men strode along the opposite pavement, talking, heads down and holding on to their trilbies as though it was windy. It wasn't, though the air was cold enough to burn in Jessie's nose when she breathed in.

They walked in silence.

The Coroner's words came back to her. *No witnesses to this unfortunate incident.* He'd adjusted the pince-nez on the bridge of his nose, surveying the people sitting on the red leather benches in front of him. 'Nevertheless, I am satisfied that this was indeed an accident and I will be instructing the Registrar to register the death of Mr Robert Clegg and to issue a Burial Order.'

An accident? The thought disturbed Jessie but she didn't know why. She knew Bob wasn't as drunk on the day of his death as he normally was. He'd been unable to steal as much money from the till as usual for two reasons: they hadn't taken much that week and she'd hidden what there was. So he hadn't been able to spend a lot at the pub.

Was she thinking too much about it?

'You hadn't given Bob any money that day, had you, Beryl?'

The words were no sooner in her mind than she spoke them. And immediately regretted it.

Beryl withdrew her arm from Jessie's.

'Indeed not. And where would I get that money from, may I ask?' Her eyes widened with resentment.

'Of course not, I'm sorry. He must have had some money hidden somewhere to get as drunk as the doctor said he was. And yet...'

'What are you saying?' Beryl stopped and turned to face Jessie.

'Nothing. Nothing. I suppose I'm finding it difficult to come to terms that he's gone after all this time. I knew Bob almost all my life. He wasn't always like – like...'

'Like – he ended up. I know.' Beryl sounded bitter. 'But perhaps he was more like his father than I knew. I never did understand him.' She tucked her hand through Jessie's arm again, seemingly excusing her. 'It's no use trying to understand some things, my dear. We only need to accept. We have a funeral to organise. And then, as you said earlier, we need to decide what we're going to do now my son has gone.'

Chapter 110

'Gone? What do you mean he's gone? We were supposed to meet tonight. It was the inquest today. I told Arthur I'd let him know what happened.' And she needed to see him, to reaffirm what yesterday had meant to both of them.

'Well, I don't know about that, love. I got up this morning and he'd left this note.' Mrs Giles flapped the piece of paper in her hand. 'I'm not that good at reading so I got Alice to read it for me. Here...' She handed it to Jessie who took it with shaking fingers.

'Dear Mrs Giles, many thanks for all your kindness. I have to leave now but here is the rent I owe and rent for one more week to tide you over until you find another tenant. Yours, Arthur.'

'I don't understand.' Jessie's heart thudded. 'Why?' She met the other woman's eyes. 'Why, Mrs Giles? Did he say anything yesterday?'

'I didn't see him much. He came in late afternoon, said he didn't want any tea. Said he'd eaten at a friend's—'

'What friend?'

'I dunno. All he said was that he wasn't hungry.' She offered a concerned frown. 'Good of 'im to leave the extra money, though. He's a good lad.'

'But I don't understand,' Jessie said again. Had she done something, said something, that would make him want to leave her? 'He didn't leave a note for me?'

'No. Nothing. Mind, I haven't cleaned his room yet. You could go and have a look round, if you like? First on the right.'

'Please. Thank you.' Jessie pushed the old grey blanket at the bottom of the stairs to one side and ran up to the room. The door caught on the torn linoleum. It was sticky underfoot but she ignored that and crossed to the bed, which had been stripped. The sheets and blankets were folded neatly into an oblong shape on top of the green shiny eiderdown. No doubt Arthur's doing. She turned around in growing bewilderment and anxiety.

There weren't many other places to search. She rummaged under the pile of bedding, yanked open each drawer in the set of drawers by the large oak wardrobe. Nothing.

Jessie sat down on the thin striped mattress, the bedsprings twanging under her, and held her fingers to her mouth. Cold shock prickled her skin and she fought against a rising sense of dread. What had happened? Where had he gone? There was no reason, no explanation. No note for her.

Chapter 111

Arthur

Through the rain-smeared glass Arthur watched the world outside the train go by. The wall-enclosed station, bricks black with smoke, gave way to lines of terraced houses, then the flat waterlogged fields, split by the canal and the river, pockmarked by the heavy rain. Until, finally, the open countryside, wind-blown trees, huddled sheep, tattered-feathered crows shunted this way and that in the air. Mile after mile.

Away from Jessie and Harry.

He hoped he'd done the right thing. He hoped she'd understand, work out what he'd done. And why.

In the fug of the pipe and cigarette smoke and against the low murmurs from the only other travellers in his carriage – three men sharing news from the papers they were reading – Arthur's chin sank lower onto his chest with each mile. A fitful night in cheap lodgings in Manchester, fleeting nightmarish scenes of being arrested, of seeing Jessie through glass but not being able to make her hear him, took its toll and, finally, he slept.

He woke with a start to find himself alone as the train squealed to a halt alongside a low platform and a faded cream and red building drenched with rain. He shivered, staring out to see the name of the station.

Greenbridge!

'Damn!' He jumped up, snatched his bag from the overhead shelf and hurried into the empty corridor. Jumping out of the open door onto the platform, he looked around. Perhaps Stanley hadn't received the telegram he'd sent from Manchester. Arthur tightened his jaw, told himself it shouldn't be difficult to locate the factory.

'Arthur? Over here.'

He twisted around, his bag swinging in a half-circle by his side. 'Stanley, mate.'

He hadn't expected the lump in his throat when he saw his friend under layers of blankets in the wheelchair. It took him three strides to reach his friend, his hand held out. Then, without any hesitation, he leant over and hugged Stanley.

'My God, it's good to see you.' Stanley leaned back in the wheelchair to study Arthur. 'Isn't it, Clara? Isn't it brilliant he's here?'

'It is, love.' She reached over him to kiss Arthur on the cheek. 'Brilliant. Now, come on, out of this rain. We'll all catch our death standing around like this. Let's get back home.'

'Typical of my wife to leave us to chat.' Stanley swirled an inch of whiskey around in a glass. 'Always sensitive to what's needed. She's a gem, Arthur, a gem. I really don't know what I'd have done without her.'

Arthur nodded. Relaxed after beef suet pudding and treacle sponge, they basked in the warmth of the fire. Arthur couldn't remember the last time he'd felt so at ease.

'How's Jessie? Have you two decided what you're going to do?'

Arthur started, his relaxation gone. Had he done the right thing, leaving without actually speaking to Jessie? Especially after their last time together? Again he hoped that she'd understand, that she'd work out what he'd done.

'I love her, Stanley. It will all work out in the end. It's best I'm away while ... until Bob Clegg's funeral is done with...'

If Stanley had noticed the way he stumbled over the words, he said nothing. After a long sigh, he huffed. 'Aye, that was a bad do – her marrying that one. The things Clara's told me... Another?' He reached for the whiskey decanter and, without waiting, stretched over and poured more liquor into Arthur's glass.

'I've never hated somebody as much as I did him, you know,' Arthur didn't meet Stanley's eyes. Could he tell his friend what he'd done to Bob Clegg? No, it was his secret to keep. Forever. 'Not even any of the poor bloody Germans we had to fight – to kill.' He saw Stanley's quick glance. 'Well, did you? Hate them? Even what they did to us?' He touched his left shoulder. 'I doubt most of them hated us, you know. They were just following orders – same as us.' He threw back a gulp of whiskey. 'Following orders from them sat safe behind desks – same as us,' he repeated, the cynicism sour in his mouth.

'I suppose.' Stanley stared into the flames, shadows flickering across his face. 'It was like us: obey or get shot.' He clutched the arm of the chair. 'We were always the poor bastards who had to follow the sodding orders. Or suffer the consequences.'

Arthur closed his eyes, the image of the white square on Tommy's chest imprinted on his lids. Was it his imagination or did the air now crackle with tension between the two of them? Had Stanley, even here miles away from Nether Brook, heard the rumours of his part in Tommy's death? But Stanley spoke again, his voice rough.

'There was one I didn't kill, Arthur. I left one young chap to live. For some reason, probably a mistake on somebody's part, a few of us volunteers had been seconded to the BEF. We shouldn't have been with them. They were experienced, well-trained soldiers and, of course, we weren't. But, after a few skirmishes there was a shortage of officers and I was made up to captain. We'd been holding a position outside Langemarck, on the forward line, east of Wipers. Anyhow, on that particular day, these Germans just appeared. And they were only boys. You could tell by their faces they were as stunned as we were. They were no match for us. They turned and fled. We were ordered to give chase. This one, this young lad, I found cowering in a ditch on his own. It was just me and him. I looked at him and he looked at me. I've never seen such abject terror in anyone's eyes, before or since. I was as shocked as him. I'd climbed over a hedge in a field and there he was. I was sickened by the whole thing. I turned to go. I remember lifting my hand to him and he raised his. I thought he was acknowledging what I was doing, giving him a chance to live, like. But he wasn't. He had a hand grenade and he threw it at me – that's how I lost these.' He patted what was left of his thighs. 'I should have shot him. But I'm not sorry. I'd seen enough killing, enough maiming of good men on both sides. I was sickened of the whole bloody mess,' he said again, tipping his head back and draining his whiskey. 'I was glad to get out of it.'

He banged his glass down on the table. 'I've often thought I would have deserted if I hadn't been injured.' He moved his head up and down slowly, as though agreeing with himself.

Arthur forced himself to stay still, hoping the shuddering inside him didn't show. Did Stanley know about his own desertion? Had Jessie told Clara – Clara, Stanley? No, surely not. There was this agony of shame inside him longing to confess his cowardice to this man, this friend he both admired and respected. But what if Stanley wasn't aware? And then despised him? What if he told the authorities? Were they still looking to find and punish those who had deserted?

'I would understand,' Stanley said. 'Wouldn't blame anyone who'd got out of that horror, believe me.' He looked at Arthur straight in the eyes. 'I'd never blame any man who'd done that. I just wish I'd had the courage to turn my back on all that massacre and say enough.' He shifted in his chair. Grimaced. 'Whatever it meant – even this...' He thumped his shortened thigh again. 'I'm glad I didn't kill that young lad. I hope he lived to see the end of it all. How about you, Arthur? Was there a time for you? When it all got too much?'

Arthur heard the creaks of floorboards above them as someone walked about, the groans and whistle of the wind outside trying to force its way through the window frames.

How the past hides, Arthur reflected, waiting to be faced. Was Stanley waiting for him to tell him about Tommy? About deserting? He forced a careless shrug. 'There was one time. I was facing the enemy, a man, who felt like me.' It was a memory he clung on to in his darkest days, when he believed all men were evil. When he woke up sweating from his nightmares.

'I'd crouched between branches in a tree all night, my rifle at the ready, just waiting for dawn so I could move. The cramp, the cold, made me think I would never be able to move again. And yet I was afraid that when the sun did come up, I would be a sitting duck. Then it was light. I looked around, making sure it was safe to climb down, get back to the trench. And there, perched in a tree a few yards away, just by the enemy trenches, was a German sniper looking straight at me. We were eye to eye. I raised my rifle to sight but then, at the same time, the bloke saluted me.' Arthur glanced at Stanley who was listening intently. 'I saluted back and the next thing we both shinned down our trees and went back to our trenches.'

He waited for Stanley's reaction, his shoulders slumping with relief when his friend gave a short grunt of appreciation. 'Good for you … and him. Just what I would have done and all.' His voice slightly slurred by his intake of whiskey. 'Ah well – to bed, I think, my friend. Tomorrow I will show you the factory.'

He heaved himself from armchair to wheelchair with practised ease. 'Goodnight, Arthur.' Passing him he patted him on the shoulder. 'It's good to have you here. I'll leave you to make your own way to your room. Sleep well, mate, sleep well.'

So much unsaid, Arthur reflected, draining the last of his drink. But so much understood? He hoped so.

Chapter 112

Arthur was a bit worse for wear when he stood with Stanley the next morning, watching the men pour out of the foundry in the same way he remembered the men streaming through the doors of Kindle Mill years before. But he'd never seen men from the mill so dirty after a day's work. The oil and grease was ingrained into these workers' fingers and faces, their clothes and overalls so filthy. Rags slung over their shoulders, some still wiping the sweat from their foreheads.

The foundry had been unbearably hot when they'd set foot in it an hour earlier. He wasn't sure if it was the amount of whiskey he'd drunk or just the feel of the place. But he could see why Stanley said they had to keep anything flammable to a minimum, how the building wouldn't take long to be an inferno. Hell's inferno, he thought, only just stopping himself saying it aloud.

Yet, each and every one of them greeted Stanley with a grin or a touch to the front of their cloth cap. He was astonished how cheerful they all appeared to be.

When he mentioned this to Stanley, his friend said, 'I suppose they think at least they're home and alive. And, don't forget, during the day, there's plenty of beer for them to quench their thirst with. Weak beer,' he added hastily, laughing at Arthur's raised eyebrows of alarm. 'Good job they don't all take until lunchtime to wake up like some.' He gave Arthur a light punch on the arm to show he was joking about him stumbling down the stairs at eleven o'clock that morning.

Arthur hadn't told him it wasn't only alcohol but worry about Jessie that had disturbed his sleep. And, as the afternoon wore on, his churning stomach convinced him he would never be able to work in the factory or go back to Nether Brook. The noise of the machinery, of the shafts and pulleys along the ceilings, gave him constant flashbacks: of the bombardment of shells, the bursts of shrapnel, the rattle of machine guns. Nether Brook brought other dangers: from the Hampsons or from the authorities.

Despite his feelings, he could see the workers' acceptance of their lot, a kind of contentment. Even in the block where the screeching grinding of the lathes sent dust and metal chips flying off the machine and steam hissed and spat from steel parts, there were smiles as well as frowns of concentration.

Would he ever find such acceptance, such contentment, in his own life?

Stanley saw the turmoil on Arthur's face when they went into the next department, not as hot but still noisy. He hurried them through.

'Let me show you the quieter places.' He spun his wheelchair around. 'Where I was thinking to ask you to work.'

To Arthur's relief the next room was quiet, subdued chatting replaced the grinding hum of the machinery in the last building. Stanley nodded his thanks when Arthur held open the door for him to go through.

'This is where our machines take shape.' Stanley looked along the rows of people, sitting on metal chairs and holding small parts close to their faces as they filed and smoothed. 'Mr Boardman, our foreman here, only came out of retirement to help us during the war. He's eager to get back to his allotment. This is where I was hoping you could take over?'

'It's certainly a lot better than the other departments. Quieter. But I know nothing about all this.' Arthur flung his arm out, taking in the rows of workers. 'How could I make sure the work is satisfactory when I haven't a clue?'

'You will be trained up, don't worry. Mr Boardman knows his job inside out. He'll make sure you do too before he leaves.'

Arthur nodded. Perhaps he could learn. Maybe this was his chance of a new life. For him. And Jessie and Harry if she agreed.

'Do you need time to think about it?'

'No. No, I don't think I do. And thanks, Stanley. You don't know how much I appreciate this.'

They grinned at one another and shook hands.

'Then I'm glad to have you on board, mate.'

Arthur looked past the factory towards the hills that rose above the roof. He would leave it a few days before he told his friend about changing his surname. Something else he hadn't discussed with Jessie.

Jessie! What she was doing? How she was feeling? What was her reaction to his decision? If she fell in with his plans, would she like living here?

He looked past the gate where the last of the workers were making their way along the road to the village. He was keen to have another look at the cottage Clara had mentioned to him when they'd driven past on their way from the station. Jessie had given him his mam's insurance money. Perhaps there was enough for him to buy a family home.

He rubbed the heel of his hand on his forehead, vowing not to try to keep up with Stanley's whiskey drinking ever again.

'The machinery that's too heavy for the men to move is carried by the horses.' Stanley pointed down the yard to a large Shire harnessed to a cart and impatiently pawing the ground, its hooves sharp rasps on the concrete. 'We used to use the canal but we still had the problem of getting the sewing machines from the factory to the canal, so we went over to using the horses for everything. That one is our latest acquisition. A fine stallion. He was shipped home from France. One we rescued from being shot unlike so many of the other poor animals.' Stanley's voice revealed his satisfaction. He wheeled his chair across to the wall opposite Arthur. 'He'll be moving away in a minute or two. You'll need to stand back.'

Arthur smiled, trying not to think of the poor animals he'd seen blown to pieces during battles. Trying not to think of the horses shot at the end of the war because it was too expensive to bring them home. He told himself afterwards that it was why he wasn't paying attention.

He saw Clara standing on the step smiling. 'Hello,' she called, being dragged towards him, an eager child in each hand.

'Hello back,' he laughed. 'And hello you two.'

'Hello!' they chorused.

'They've been nagging me to come and find you for ages.' Clara let go of their hands.

Arthur wasn't sure what spooked the horse. All he saw was it bolting towards him, ears flat against its mane, black eyes wide open and rolling wild, dragging the empty cart behind it, bucking on the flags.

He saw Bertie run and then stop, his eyes frightened, mouth open in a wail Arthur couldn't hear. He saw the child frozen in fear, the horse thundering along the yard. Looming over him.

Arthur leapt forward and, scooping Bertie up in the crook of his arm, tossed the child to Stanley, hoping he would at least stop his fall.

Twisting around, Arthur grabbed hold of the strap of the reins. It burned through the flesh on his hand. Clinging on to the bridle, he felt his bones crack as he was dragged sideways, his arm wrenched from its socket. Gritting his teeth against the pain, he held on until the horse slid to a halt.

Forcing himself up from his knees to his feet, Arthur laid his face against the horse's shivering neck awash with sweat. He breathed low words to calm the stallion down, aware of the groaning and trembling deep inside its body and loud fluttering air in its nostrils.

Then it was only men shouting, the clattering of heavy boots, the cries of children, a descending darkness. Pain.

Chapter 113

Disbelief rolled reluctantly into belief in Jessie in the week that followed Arthur's disappearance. She stumbled through the days, leaving the funeral arrangements to Bob's mother.

It was Beryl's insistence that they cremated her son. Cremation was something Jessie had vaguely heard of, before Beryl read the newspaper article to her. That gave her mother-in-law the idea. Neither of them would want to visit Bob's grave. Pulling her reading glasses to the end of her nose she glanced over them at Jessie.

'It says, "...*following the carnage of the war, the theological argument that the body of the deceased should be preserved and given a burial, so then being ready for resurrection on the Day of Judgement, is indefensible, in the light of so many young men killed whose remains were never discovered or whose bodies were totally destroyed, to declare there was no resurrection for them...*"'

Beryl drew a long breath. 'This, a cremation, would mean that, after his funeral, it would all be over and done with for both of us, my dear. There would be nowhere we would have to go, nowhere that we'd need to think about. My son, the child I once knew, would be the only memory I need to have of him.'

Jessie didn't quite follow the woman's reasoning, but she was more than content to go along with what she wanted. She felt Beryl was more his mother than she herself had ever been his true wife. In her heart she was glad to have Bob completely wiped from the earth. He would just be gone.

The thought was followed by another. Gone. Just like Arthur.

Chapter 114

Bob's funeral took place on a dreary grey November afternoon in Manchester. Jessie had allowed Beryl to decide on the clothes they should wear. It didn't matter to her, but she still felt a frisson of shock when her mother-in-law produced the two navy dresses.

'Not black?'

'Not black.'

She and Beryl followed the plain spruce coffin in a small coach along Barlow Moor Road to the crematorium. The carriage that carried them, equally small and plain, was the only one. When they arrived at the impressive building, there were only a handful of men waiting to follow them inside.

Jessie was barely aware of them. She kept the dark veil of her small hat over her face to hide the misery. Not grief at losing a husband but anguish at losing a lover.

She didn't recognise any of the men. She didn't think of them as mourners. She guessed they were mostly there out of curiosity about the process of cremation, saving the thruppence the place usually charged to visitors to see how the innovation worked. Bob hadn't been a particularly popular man even before it became known that he had beaten her. She suspected that a lot of wives had been instrumental in the absence of men at the ceremony, such as it was.

Even so, there was a stunned silence when it was understood there was to be no religious service. Jessie was aware of the gasps as Bob's cremation was set in motion by the doors of the cremation apparatus opening and the coffin slowly moving into the furnace.

'If you wait for an hour or so we will have your husband's ashes, Mrs Clegg.'

'We don't need them.' Beryl turned away from him, pulling her navy gloves further along her arms with a sharp tug.

The man's brow crinkled in a curious mix of confusion and disbelief. He looked at Jessie, who stared blankly back at him. 'Surely his widow must—'

'We don't need – or want them, Mr Atkinson.' Beryl looked over his head.

'It is usual. The proper thing to—'

'Mr Atkinson, Mrs Clegg's husband – my son – was neither a proper husband nor a loving son. Do with them as is your wish.' Jessie saw the hardness in Beryl's eyes. 'We do not wish to have anything to do with his ashes.'

Leaving the crematorium Beryl leaned her head towards Jessie and whispered, 'Well, that was ten shillings and fourpence well spent, my dear. I suggest we go for tea and cake. Come on, there's a little place I want to show you, it's just along the road.'

The "little place" turned out to be a small café selling the most delicious cakes. Beryl told her they were mostly made by Alice's mother, who worked there two days a week to supplement the family's income. They spoke about anything except the funeral and afterwards caught the one-carriage, local train back to Nether Brook in silence. Each with their own thoughts.

Jessie wondered what Beryl was really feeling, despite her earlier words. All she could feel was relief that the day was over, but the desolation of Arthur's desertion overwhelmed her again.

She'd ended up hating Bob, yet still she thought that perhaps she'd contributed to the man he became. He must have always known he could never compete with her love for Arthur, but she'd thought he'd accepted that. Now she knew she'd been naïve. His resentment had festered, grown over the years and she'd ignored it. Chosen to ignore it, she admitted.

Jessie made herself remember the old Bob, the Bob she knew as a child: the times she'd sat cross-legged on the yard steps talking to him when he was cleaning out the coke shed or polishing the cart. The young lad who had teased her, laughed at silly things with her, comforted her when she was upset. Who once mended the head of a pot doll that had broken off its body, only to find out later he'd stuck it on back to front. That was the Bob she wanted to remember.

But she knew it was too late. She would drive herself mad wondering how much of it was her fault that he turned out how he did. How much was there anyway: the jealousy, the possessiveness, the violence.

Chapter 115

December 1920

He left us. He went without a word. Arthur's unexplained disappearance hung heavily over Jessie – it felt like a betrayal, especially after that afternoon in the kitchen. She moved automatically through the days, the weeks. At first, it was a struggle, but she got out of bed each day, to bake, to open the shop. She tried hard to be normal in front of Harry, but, as time moved on, she knew she was failing. She saw the puzzled expression, the solemn look in his eyes.

Sometimes, during the night, she felt as though she could hardly breathe. By day her hands moved without thought: making the dough, kneading, cutting, shaping loaves and muffins, her arms sticky with the heat of the oven, legs and feet aching. It was an effort to even speak. She stopped going into the shop, letting Beryl, even Alice, serve the few loyal customers who still stuck by them.

A creeping cold chilled her blood, spread through her body, until one day she didn't climb laboriously out of her bed. She could no longer bear to try to fill the emptiness inside her. And so she stayed under the bedclothes, sometimes crying so deeply that, afterwards, she was too exhausted to move.

One morning, Beryl sat on the edge of her bed and took hold of her fingers, turning them over in her palm before speaking.

'What are we going to do about the shop, my dear?'

Jessie felt her spine stiffen. She turned her head away from Beryl's worried face.

'It's been days since you baked, the shelves are empty and we're turning people away.'

Jessie tried to release her hand from Beryl's, but her mother-in-law wouldn't let go. 'Do you realise that Christmas is almost upon us?'

'Go away, Beryl. Please...'

'I can't. We can't carry on like this. I miss the young woman I used to know. Harry misses the mother he used to have.'

Hearing her son's name, Jessie lay still. Eventually she said, 'He's all right, isn't he?'

'No, Jessie, he's not. He doesn't understand. Have you not heard him by the bedroom door? Waiting for you to speak to him? He always thinks you're asleep, that you're ill. He doesn't want to disturb you but...' Beryl stopped.

'I'm sorry.' Jessie forced herself to look at the woman. 'I just can't face everything.'

'And your son is suffering because of that.'

'No!'

'Yes. And I still want to know what we are going to do? With the shop? For Harry? We need to make Christmas special for him, but with no income from the shop...'

Remorse flooded through Jessie. It was the first time in days she'd thought about her son. She had taken it for granted that he'd be looked after by Beryl.

'Where is he now?'

'He's gone out for the day with Alice's mother.'

'He doesn't know her. He'll be scared—'

'He does know her. She's been looking after him quite a lot.' The words could have been accusatory, but they were spoken in a gentle tone. 'She has been very good with him.'

Beryl settled Jessie's hand back on the eiderdown and patted it. She stood, smoothing down her skirt. Glancing at the small table next to Jessie's bed, she said, 'There's a cup of tea and a slice of sponge cake there for you.'

'I'm not hungry.'

'Do try to eat it, my dear. Alice's mother made it especially for you. She makes lovely cakes. We tried them once, Jessie, do you remember? The café we went into in Manchester. After the funeral? She worked for them for years, making the cakes for their customers. She can't now, of course.'

The last sentence, the way it was spoken, cut through the shadows in Jessie mind. 'Why?'

Beryl sighed. 'Alice's father passed away with the influenza. The other children have left home and Lily was lonely. I suggested she could come to Nether Brook. She's lodging at Mrs Giles.'

She waited for Jessie to speak. When she didn't, Beryl sighed again. 'I don't know what else to say, my dear. I thought you stronger than this.' She crossed the room to hover at the door a moment. 'Try to drink the tea, eat the cake, Jessie. Please. And I've left warm water in the bowl, soap and a flannel on your dressing table. I'm sure it will make you feel better if you can have a wash.'

Jessie doubted that. When the door closed she lay back, rubbing her forehead, ashamed that she'd neglected her son. That she had let the two other women struggle to keep the bakery going over the last few weeks. Pushing back the bedclothes, she forced her shaking legs over the side of the mattress.

Her hand trembled when she held the cup of tea to her lips. She looked at the cake; it did look good. She took a bite. It was delicious, so light and sweet. Chewing slowly Jessie thought about all Beryl had said.

She pushed thoughts of Arthur away. She'd dwelled too long on him, she knew that. But what to do? The bakery was her business, had belonged to her mam and dad. She'd fought Bob for it, she couldn't let it go. And yet she had little enthusiasm for it.

She hadn't bothered to wash or dress for days. Now she pulled her grubby dressing gown tighter around her, got up from her bed, and wobbled over to the dressing table mirror. Ghostly pale with lank, greasy hair hanging around her shoulders, she was shocked by how gaunt she looked. How had she let it happen?

She wiped soap on the flannel and scrubbed at her face. Untying the belt, she let first the dressing gown, then her nightdress drop to the floor. Washing herself thoroughly, she let her thoughts drift. It was difficult but she knew the bakery was finished; she hadn't the heart for it anymore. And anyway, their customers must, by now, have gone to the bakery in Yorkshire Street. But what next?

Fierce gusts of wind rattled the door and window. Goosebumps rippled along her arms and legs as she towelled herself dry before pulling on the clean clothes that Beryl had laid out for her. Jessie smoothed the sheet; it would be so easy just to slide back into bed again.

But she couldn't, she couldn't hide away again.

She lay down, stretched out on top of the covers. She needed to think, to find the strength she had found when she and Beryl had to run the shop alone. She crossed her arms over her face. Think, she told herself, think. Closing the bakery would mean no money coming in, no money for food or clothes for Harry. No Christmas. There was her mother's money, of course. But how long would that last with no income? She had to think of other ways to use the shop.

Taking in a deep breath, she sat up; if she stayed lying down she'd go back to sleep. She picked up the cup of tea and drained it. Without thinking, she pressed her finger on the crumbs of the cake left on the plate.

All at once the haze, like the fine threads of a net curtain that had separated Jessie from everything and everyone for weeks, lifted.

Alice's mother made cakes. She could do the same for the shop. 'I could make the bread for sandwiches,' Jessie murmured to herself, a bubble of excitement beginning to rise inside her.

'A tea room?'

'A tea room.' Jessie's words tumbled out of her in her excitement. This was something they could do. 'Why not? There isn't one in Nether Brook.'

She sat at the kitchen table opposite Beryl and Alice.

333

'Your mam's cakes are gorgeous, Alice. We could have posh sandwiches cut into triangles. After all the difficult times people have had because of the war, I think a tea room would be a lovely place for anyone to sit and chat. I think it would work.'

Beryl and Alice exchanged glances. 'It's a lovely idea, Jessie, but the way—'

'The way I've been.'

'No, I didn't mean that. I meant the way things have been.' Beryl swept her arms around, encompassing the whole building. 'I'm not sure we could...' She shrugged. 'How could we afford it?'

Jessie laid her arms on top of the table, her fingers knotting and unknotting. 'I have some money I can use.' Jessie was convinced her mam would have been thrilled to know it would be used to give her a new life, to lift her out of her despair. 'Think about it. Please?'

Alice clapped. 'Mam will love it.' She stopped, her hands in mid-air, doubt clouding her face. 'You do mean her to be properly part of this, Jessie?'

'Of course. It was her cake that gave me the idea just now. We couldn't manage without her. I'll make the bread for the sandwiches and your mam will make the cakes.'

Jessie laughed when Alice leapt up to rush around the table to hug her.

Beryl hadn't spoken since she'd voiced her doubts.

'Beryl?'

'Can you give me a day or two to think about it, my dear? I feel I might be too old to be taking on such a venture. I'm sorry.'

'Of course.' Jessie tried to hide her disappointment. It was only fair. Beryl had been waiting for the best part of a week for her to rouse herself from her low mood. She would spend the two days being a better mother to Harry.

'I've thought a lot about your suggestion, Jessie, and I think it's a challenge. But I also think we could succeed if – if – we all work together.'

'We will. Won't we, Alice?'

'Oh yes. And Mam too. Mam's a hard worker.'

'I'm sure she is.' A sudden and unexpected hope filled Jessie. She took hold of Beryl's hand. 'Alice?'

The girl grabbed her other hand. They stood in a small circle. Jessie jiggled their hands up and down in rhythm to her next words.

'We will make it work, I promise you.'

She saw the worry in Beryl's eyes.

'I will make sure it works.'

The three of them stood behind the counter looking around the shop.

'We could fit in at least four tables, maybe five if we took away those shelves.' Jessie nodded to the far wall where they used to put the baskets of ordered bread. She waited for Beryl and Alice to reply, anxious for them to give their opinions on everything.

'Yes, that sounds right.' Beryl nodded.

'And Mam would make curtains for the window and the tablecloths for the tables.' Alice grinned. 'She can turn her hand to owt, our Mam. And it will cheer her up no end after losing Dad.'

Jessie nodded. 'Good.' It was something she and Alice's mother could share, a mutual 'cheering-up'. 'And she's happy to make the cakes?'

'She is.' Alice was jigging from one foot to the other, unable to contain her excitement.

'I'll do the bread.'

'And you and I, Alice, will serve.' Beryl said.

'We could have uniforms. Mam would make them...' Alice's voice trailed away, looking in doubt at Beryl. 'That's if it's all right with you, Mrs Clegg? Would you mind wearing a uniform?'

'I'll even wear a cap, if you like.' Beryl laughed. 'And it's Beryl, remember. Let's not have that nonsense about Mrs again, Alice.'

'I could order the tables and chairs from the Co-op in

Manchester.' Jessie was restless, impatient. 'Let's plan it out. We won't have to change much. And we can do it ourselves. Yes?'

'Yes,' they chorused

'That's settled then. We'll start on things tomorrow. It's going to work, I know it is.' Jessie turned to look at them. 'I think this deserves a celebration.' She put her arms around their waists. 'We need to make a toast to our new venture. Sherry, ladies?'

Chapter 116

February 1921

Months passed: grey, dismal months during which Stanley and Clara had cared for and cajoled Arthur into joining in with family life. He appreciated their efforts but, in the privacy of his own room, he was dispirited, baffled why Jessie hadn't answered his letter.

He found it odd that Clara's family hadn't celebrated Christmas but was thankful; it was the last thing he wanted to do. But he loved the day they'd cleared one of the warehouses and held a huge party, inviting all the workers, local people and their families to a nourishing meal, and given the children presents that he helped Clara's father and Stan to make in the weeks leading up to the day. Watching the children playing with the colourful spinning tops with leather whips, skipping ropes, peg dolls and paper windmills, he pushed away thoughts of Harry, knowing that his son was lost to him. The silence from Jessie had convinced him of that.

He'd been sure she would understand why he had to leave. Why he wasn't able to write to her again. His letter had explained how he needed to disappear, to make a new life.

Stanley and Clara accepted his wish to change his name. He had confided in his friend, but only about his part in Tommy's firing squad. And that Teddy Hampson knew about his part in it and was determined to get revenge. He left it to Stanley to explain something to his wife and, on the face of it, she seemed to understand that he had moved on in his life without Jessie. He knew it made her sad, but she never questioned him.

He grew more restless with the boredom, waiting for the broken bones in his fingers to heal. He took to wandering, his unhappiness following him through the days and keeping him awake at night.

Chapter 117

March 1921

It was as if Arthur had never returned to her. Jessie managed to keep the ache for him under control in the daytime. The success of the tea room gave her no time to brood. But in the sleepless nights, her anguish turned to anger, anger that Arthur had not told her that he was leaving Nether Brook, leaving her.

Jessie worked in the bakery with Alice's mother. Lily had quickly become part of the team and Jessie liked her. She was an unobtrusive woman who soon discovered that there were days when Jessie wanted to speak and days when she didn't. With Beryl and Alice in the tea room, the two women worked quietly side by side.

One day Teddy Hampson stepped into the tea shop, just as Jessie was carrying in a tray of bread muffins for Beryl. The chatter of the women sitting at the five tables, brightly covered by the checked red-and-white tablecloths, stopped. Curious stares followed him to the counter. Beryl handed two plates of small cakes to Alice.

'Jessie Dawson.'

'I think you mean Jessie Clegg, don't you?' Beryl looked swiftly from him to Jessie. 'What do you want with her?' She nodded to Alice. 'You serve these, Alice.' Not taking her eyes of the man, she murmured, 'Jessie?'

'It's all right.'

Jessie wiped her hands on her apron while thinking what to do. This was trouble, she just knew it.

'Can I help you, Teddy?'

'Outside.'

His tone gave her a chill. She heard Beryl's intake of breath, the rattle as Alice put the plates onto a table with a thump. The customers pretended to ignore the tension.

Jessie pressed her lips together. 'What do you want?'

'We need to talk.'

She reached behind her and took down her shawl. 'Outside, then?'

'Jessie?' Beryl's voice shook.

'It's fine.' She lifted the end of the counter and slipped through the opening and crossed the tea room to the door.

He followed her.

In the street, she spun round to face him, tucking her hands inside her shawl to hide her trembling. 'What's this about?' Did he know where Arthur was? She met his stare, refusing to be intimidated.

His sloping forehead narrowed; his thick eyebrows low over his eyes.

'Seen Arthur Dawson lately?'

'No. Why? Should I have?' Jessie was relieved her voice sounded stronger than she felt. 'I haven't seen him in a while.'

He moved closer. She forced herself not to retreat.

'So you don't know where soft lad is, then?'

She shook her head. She felt suddenly calm: he didn't know where Arthur was any more than she did.

'Well I don't believe yer. You just tell him I'm waiting for 'im. And I'm a patient man. When I've got unfinished business wi' someone, I'm patient.' He stressed his words with a nod. 'Very patient.'

Jessie put her hand on the shop door. 'I haven't a clue what you mean or what you want, Teddy Hampson. But Arthur Dawson is out of my life and good riddance. So, if you think you're frightening me, you're wrong.'

338

She glanced towards the window. Curious faces peered at them.

She lifted her chin. 'I'm going in. I'll thank you to stay away from here from now on.'

'I'll go where I like. And when you do see 'im next, tell 'im I'm lookin' for him.'

'I won't. Because I don't expect to see him ever again.'

Keeping her eyes fixed on his, she stepped into the tea room as calmly as she could. Ignoring the inquisitive stares, she crossed to the counter. She gave Beryl and Alice a reassuring shrug and went through to the kitchen. Once inside, she bent forward from the waist, gripping a chair, the strength draining from her.

In the past she'd always thought the Hampson twins were just two stupid lads who messed around. Looking into the eyes of Teddy Hampson, she saw the dangerous man he'd become. For the first time she decided that, one way or another, she wouldn't wait for Arthur to contact her. She would look for him.

But where? Instinct told her she couldn't contact the army. Knowing he had deserted at one point during the war, she couldn't chance bringing more trouble down on his head. Nor could she ask the police to help her, for the same reason.

The answer came to her that evening. She would write to Clara and ask her if Stanley knew anyone from his time in France who had known Arthur. He might have friends from the army who lived in a different part of the country. He could be there. It was a slim chance, but it was somewhere for her to start.

After Harry had gone to bed, she sat at her dressing table with a pen and a blank sheet of paper. It was a difficult letter to write. Lost in her misery, it was months since she last heard from Clara and she hadn't responded, hadn't told her that Arthur had gone. It would be a great shock to her friends.

Chapter 118

My Dear Jessie,

I am writing this in some haste to try to catch the return post so please excuse any brevity or mistakes in this missive of mine. We have so missed hearing from you these last few months, so it was lovely to receive your letter. But to read that you are trying to find Arthur and how worried you are has distressed me. So I must firstly tell you that he is here with us and that he has been in Greenbridge now for some time.

I had no idea you were unaware of this. I have often wondered why you haven't replied to the letter he left for you before he came here. I have almost written a few times before to ask why, but I thought it none of my business, even though you are both so dear to us.

And if you are wondering why Arthur has not contacted you again, I should tell you that there was an accident here that prevents him writing. He is fit enough now but you can imagine how that has affected him. With having only the one hand it has meant he has struggled with so much. One of the horses bolted when we were all in the yard the first week he was with us. Bertie ran in front of it. It would have killed him I'm sure. My heart just stopped beating, I was dreadfully afraid. Arthur moved so quickly. He saved little Bertie's life, there is no doubt about that, and he hung on to the horse until it calmed down. We will be forever grateful to him but unfortunately, the horse dragged him and by not letting go of the reins he broke some bones in his poor hand and fingers.

To know you still care enough for Arthur to be concerned for him has been a great relief to me and I urge you to write to him as soon as you are able. I have been so worried about him. I have never seen him so unhappy, so down in spirit, as he is these days. I believe, from what Stanley has told me, he thinks you are angry with him for moving here. But Stanley has told me there were good reasons he had to get away from Nether Brook so quickly without talking to you. Arthur has confided in Stanley and I haven't pursued the matter. But to hear you are anxious for him tells me there are problems in Nether Brook it is best he avoids.

I'm hoping he will settle here as, once his hand is better, he will be working in the factory with us. He has a good future and there is a cottage here that he is hoping to buy.

Since receiving your letter I have wondered whether I should tell him you are looking for him but have decided that it is between the two of you; whatever the future holds is in your hands, Jessie. Arthur doesn't know I am writing this. He would never ask me to do so, even though he has not heard from you. He is a proud man. But I do know he still loves you.

I must finish now if I am to catch the last post.

I am, and will always be, your loyal friend,

Clara xx

Jessie let the paper drop through her fingers. It was almost five months since he left. He'd had an accident and she'd known nothing about it. No one had told her. They hadn't told her because they thought she didn't care.

But her friend's words stung. There'd been no letter. Arthur hadn't tried talking to her. He'd just disappeared, leaving only the terse note and rent money for Mrs Giles.

Yet Clara said he'd left a letter for her. Where was it? Who had he given it to? There was nothing at Mrs Giles'. Nothing pushed through the letterbox of the shop.

A flash of bitterness shot through her. She still didn't understand why Arthur hadn't confided in her, given her a chance to decide what she wanted to do? Why hadn't Clara told her earlier that he was with her and Stanley?

Filled with resentment, she vaguely heard the new chime of the tea shop doorbell, the buzz of conversation, laughter, the jingle of crockery.

She hadn't known he wanted her with him, still loved her. But he must have told Clara he did. Her friend wouldn't lie about that. And Clara said he'd needed to leave Nether Brook. Surely it could only be because of Teddy Hampson? Had he known Hampson would seek her out? How? And why hadn't he written to her, even if only to warn her?

But he had, hadn't he? Yet again, Clara's words came to her: 'replied to the letter he left for you'. The confusion bewildered her.

Jessie looked around the room as though it held the answer. She paced the floor and stopped to stare through the window, to look over the wet, shiny tiles on the roofs opposite. The churning clouds, carrying the last of the rain, were moving swiftly away, whipped by the March wind; leaving a white haziness over Wharmton Hill.

The stile was greasy with green slime built up through wet winter months. Jessie clung tightly to the post as she climbed over it, the wind buffeting her, tearing at the shawl she'd wrapped around her head. Under her boots the grass was slippery. She clung to the wall, pulling herself up the slope of the field, stone by stone.

The heart stone was wedged between the two larger stones. The edges dug into Jessie's fingers when she grabbed it in both hands, pushing and rocking it from side to side. With one last hard tug, it lifted.

There. There it was, the edges discoloured, rippled with damp. Hand shaking, Jessie raised the side of the heart stone until she could pull out the folded square of paper with her thumb and forefinger.

It took a few minutes but gradually she was able to prise the letter apart.

How could she have not guessed? The ink had blurred most of the words but there they were...

'My darling Jessie...'

Chapter 119

Curled up on the dusty seat in the empty compartment, Harry was heavy against her side. Jessie bent to kiss the top of his head, breathing in the familiar smell of carbolic soap and warm skin in sleep. The movement of the train soothed her into a contentment she hadn't felt for a long time. The sense of betrayal she'd carried around for months had vanished the moment she found Arthur's letter.

Jessie rested her head against the train seat, looking at but not seeing the world outside the window. She was moving on to a life she didn't know. Yet even though she had moments of apprehension, she was eager to confront whatever faced her. With Arthur by her side, she knew she'd be safe.

It had been a long week. The only people she revealed her plans to were Beryl and the solicitor. Mr Mathias has drawn up the contract for Beryl to be part-owner of the tea rooms. Jessie was happy she'd been able to hand over the business to Beryl in return for a small share in the profits. The tea room was thriving; her mother-in-law and Alice and her mother would be looked after. The red carpet, bright tablecloths and matching curtains attracted more customers than she'd ever envisaged. Beryl's smile widened every day and Jessie was glad for her.

Word had quickly spread about the wonderful cakes Lily made. Each day she placed a different confection on a large plate in the window to entice customers in. Jessie was delighted that Eddie, Beryl's youngest son, had moved back to Nether Brook with his new wife and had taken up the reins as baker. Jessie felt the tea room couldn't fail; between them all they would make a success of it.

She was sad that she hadn't been able to say goodbye to any of them except Beryl, but she couldn't chance anyone, especially Teddy Hampson, knowing where she was going. Despite that, it had been easier to sweep away her life in Nether Brook than she thought it ever would be. Knowing she hadn't let them down, she was relieved to be leaving. Castle Street's memories, good and bad, were so melded together it made it difficult to separate them.

The light was draining from the day, the sky dark against the winter sunset. Before long they, she and her son, would be in Greenbridge. Harry began to stir, a snuffling, wriggling awakening.

'All right, sweetheart?'

'Mmm.'

'Nearly there.'

'Will Uncle Arthur be waiting for us?'

Uncle Arthur. Yes, that will do for now. Someday soon, she thought, we'll tell our son the truth.

'Yes, love. Yes, he will.'

Jessie put her hand into her coat pocket and closed her fingers around the small fragment of stone wrapped in the crumpled pieces of paper, her heart beating a little stronger at its touch.

Acknowledgements

I would like to express my gratitude to those who helped in the publishing of *The Heart Stone*:

To all the staff at Honno for their individual expertise, advice and help. To both Caroline Oakley and Janet Thomas for their thoughtful and empathetic editing.

And my gratitude and thanks to each of them for their support with all my writing down the years.

Special thanks to Thorne Moore, Alex Martin and Sharon Tregenza, dear friends and fellow authors, for their encouragement and enthusiasm for The Heart Stone.

To Alex Askaroff for all his considerable help with my research. Alex was born into the sewing trade, has spent a lifetime studying sewing history, and is considered a leading expert on the 19th-century sewing machine pioneers, having written many books on the subject.

Lastly, as ever, to my husband, David: always by my side, always believing in me.

ABOUT HONNO

Honno Welsh Women's Press was set up in 1986 by a group of women who felt strongly that women in Wales needed wider opportunities to see their writing in print and to become involved in the publishing process. Our aim is to develop the writing talents of women in Wales, give them new and exciting opportunities to see their work published and often to give them their first 'break' as a writer. Honno is registered as a community co-operative. Any profit that Honno makes is invested in the publishing programme. Women from Wales and around the world have expressed their support for Honno. Each supporter has a vote at the Annual General Meeting. For more information and to buy our publications, please write to Honno at the address below, or visit our website: www.honno.co.uk

Honno, D41 Hugh Owen Building, Penglais Campus,
Aberystwyth University, Aberystwyth, SY23 3DY

Honno Friends

We are very grateful for the support of all our
Honno Friends.
For more information on how you can
become a Honno Friend, see:
https://www.honno.co.uk/about/support-honno/